THE MARRIAGE ACT

John Marrs is an author and former journalist based in London and Northamptonshire. After spending his career interviewing celebrities from the worlds of television, film and music for numerous national newspapers and magazines, he is now a full-time author. He is the bestselling author of: *The One*, *The Passengers*, *The Minders*, *What Lies Between Us* and *The Vacation*.

Follow him at www.johnmarrsauthor.co.uk, on Twitter @johnmarrs1, on Instagram @johnmarrs.author and on Facebook @johnmarrsauthor.

THE MARRIAGE ACT

JOHN MARRS

MACMILLAN

First published 2023 by Macmillan
an imprint of Pan Macmillan
The Smithson, 6 Briset Street, London EC1M 5NR
EU representative: Macmillan Publishers Ireland Ltd,
1st Floor, The Liffey Trust Centre, 117–126 Sheriff Street Upper,
Dublin 1, D01 YC43
Associated companies throughout the world
www.panmacmillan.com

ISBN: 978-1-5290-7118-4

1 3 5 7 9 8 6 4 2

A CIP catalogue record for this book is available from the British Library.

Graphics by Atomic Squib

Typeset in Celeste by Jouve (UK), Milton Keynes
Printed and bound by CPI Group (UK) Ltd, Croydon, CR0 4YY

Visit **www.panmacmillan.com** to read more about all our books
and to buy them. You will also find features, author interviews and
news of any author events, and you can sign up for e-newsletters
so that you're always first to hear about our new releases.

For Ada Lovelace, 1815–1852

Audite: *Latin, verb, pronounced Aw-Dy-T*
Meaning: I hear. I listen. I learn.

How are Smart Marriages Making Britain Better?*

They're good for your health and the economy

Married couples are **healthier**.

They're **35% less** likely to suffer high blood pressure, strokes and heart disease. They recover from operations quicker and have **stronger immune systems**.

Married couples take **fewer sick days**.

They don't drain valuable NHS resources and don't rely on benefits. A proud, productive workforce **supports our economic growth**.

Married couples live **4 to 8 years longer** than singletons.

Caring companions **encourage one another** to have regular health check-ups, take medication, **eat nutritiously** and **exercise more**.

A healthy marriage means **a healthy mind**.

You're **less likely** to suffer anxiety, depression, substance abuse, loneliness, psychosis or attempt suicide if you're together.

*Statistics based on Government-funded research.

SMART MARRIAGE

www.smartmarriage.co.uk

ACT 1

PROLOGUE

Jem Jones

Transcript of a live broadcast made across multiple social media platforms by British Vlogger and Influencer JEM JONES.

TRANSCRIBER'S NOTES: Ms Jones is looking away from the camera when her broadcast begins. She is wearing little make-up; the dark roots of her blonde hair are visible and it is scraped back into a casual ponytail. She is dressed in a black knitted jumper and a silver necklace with a St Christopher motif. She appears anxious and emotional. Ms Jones is located in the lounge area of a residential property. She sits at a desk and behind her are two large sofas, framed wall paintings of tropical beaches, and closed window shutters. She is alone. There is a thirty-eight-second gap between the start of filming and when she first looks to the camera and talks.

'I've recorded so many of these Vlogs over the years, but this is the first one where I'm at a loss as to know where to start.

(Ms Jones shakes her head and takes a deep, audible breath.)

'I suppose I should begin with an apology. I've not been

3

online much over the last couple of months. But after my last post – or Meltdown Monday, as my critics called it – I thought it best to step back and take some time to work on myself. But this live Vlog isn't my comeback. It's the opposite. I'm here to say goodbye.

'Guys, I'm drained. I don't have the strength to put myself through this any more. How can it make me happy when I'm a laughing stock and a punchline? The constant, relentless negative attention and the stress of it has given me PTSD, insomnia and anxiety. I'm tired. I'm just really, really tired.

(Ms Jones rubs her face with the palms of her hands. Her fingernails are bitten, the white polish chipped.)

'When I began Vlogging six years ago, it was with the best of intentions. I wanted to make a little film that a few people might watch where I could speak about the stuff that mattered to me as a twenty-something woman. I thought it'd be an amazing result if a hundred people watched it who didn't know me.

'But then – and for reasons I don't think I'll ever get my head around – my posts went viral. One hundred subscribers became two hundred and then a thousand and, within a year, I'd reached the million mark. (Ms Jones smiles briefly for the first time.) All of those people, watching and listening to little old me blathering on about where to buy the best shades of lipstick, or watching me unwrap my first tattoo, or the horrendous hangovers I went through after a night out with the girls . . . God, life was fun and easy back then, wasn't it? Honestly, they were some of the best times and I got to share them all with you. And your feedback made it even more worthwhile. Your messages, your tags, your silly emojis and your kind words . . . they meant the world to me. I'd never even met most of you but you felt like my mates. You were there to join in with my happiness when boyfriends came; and when they went, it was your shoulders I cried on. The community we built together was so supportive and nurturing; you made me feel truly loved.

(Ms Jones shuts her eyes.)

'I should have known it couldn't last. Nothing good ever does. And all because I dared to have an opinion. I love the idea of commitment and I love being in love. So supporting the Sanctity of Marriage Act was a no-brainer. But then I became a target for campaigners who didn't agree with it. That's when the hate started. Even in these so-called enlightened times, it's more of a sport to try and shut down a woman with a voice than it is with a man who says the same thing.

'Those of you who've followed me over the years will know that when I'm told I can't do something, or that I should think a certain way, it's going to make me all the more determined to behave how I want to. So when the Government asked me to become the face of the Act and spread the word about its benefits, of course I was going to say yes.

'If I thought the backlash was bad before . . . well, it was a walk in the park compared to the shit that followed. I became the poster girl for cancel culture. I received thousands of emails and messages every single day telling me what a selfish, evil bitch I was, that I deserved to die and so did my family. Negative comments were left all over my social media posts. My sponsors were targeted and warned not to work with me or they'd be cancelled next. I could just about cope with the death threats, Deepfake videos, memes, graffiti daubed across my walls and bricks hurled through my windows . . . but then when my dogs were poisoned, I was done. England turned its back on me so I did the same to it.

(Ms Jones reaches under her monitor to reveal to the camera seven plastic containers of prescription medicine. It is unclear which pharmacy has provided them. She slides up the right sleeve of her jumper to reveal two translucent patches stuck to her upper arm. Her lower arm contains healed scars alongside fresh wounds. She does not comment on them.)

'The patches are slow-release antidepressants. Some of the tablets help me sleep and others are to keep me awake. I've got pills to help me think, pills to stop me overthinking, pills to give me an appetite and pills that stop me feeling anything but empty. I even have pills to give me enough clarity to remember to take the other pills.

'But they all have one thing in common: they remind me of how out of control my life has become. I can't remember the last time I felt optimistic about anything. Every time I dare to go online all I see is hate directed at me and it doesn't matter that it's coming from anonymous keyboard warriors, it still hurts like hell. These attacks are relentless, day in, day out. Being online used to be my sanctuary, but now it's a prison. Yet here I am, online again when I know how much it messes with my head. I'm addicted to it and I don't know how to stop. It makes me miserable and depressed and leaves me feeling worthless, but I can't stop myself. I can't stop myself . . .

(Ms Jones' bottom lip trembles. She hesitates.)

'I wish I could go back to the Jem Jones I was before I started Vlogging. And some of you will tell me there's no reason why I can't do that. But I don't know how to be that woman again. Too much has happened and I don't know who I am or what I am. Sometimes I feel so far removed from myself that I don't even think I'm real any more.'

(Ms Jones pauses to cry. She holds her head down to hide her face, then reaches for tissues and dabs at her eyes.)

'I'm sorry, guys, but I'm no use to anyone like this so that's why I'm saying goodbye. Congratulations to anyone watching who has helped to make my life a living hell – you win. I give up, I surrender. I can't make anything right any more. Thank you to those who have shown me love, and I apologize for letting you all down so badly. I have no control over anything . . . I'm better off away from both the virtual world and the real one.'

(Ms Jones offers an apologetic smile and reaches for something out of camera shot. A grey gun becomes visible in her left hand. She slowly points it to her temple, closes her eyes, pulls the trigger and temporarily falls from view, until the automatic lens finds her again. The broadcast continues for around seventeen minutes until her body is discovered.)

SAY 'I DO' SMART TO A MARRIAGE!

MARRIAGE AS WE KNOW IT HAS CHANGED. ARE YOU READY TO TAKE THE PLUNGE?

Every marriage is now entitled to upgrade to a Smart Marriage.

What's in it for me?

- Access to NHS+ for speedier treatment
- Access for your children to the top schools in your area
- Relocate to purpose-built communities for people like you
- Impartial & supportive marriage advice throughout all stages
- Helping Britain to build back better
- Greater personal tax allowances & financial protection

Smart Marriages are dependent on your coupling remaining strong and stable. Failure may result in mandatory divorce and the loss of your home and other Smart Marriage benefits.

www.smartmarriage.co.uk

1

Roxi

Roxi glared in disbelief at the YouTube video playing on her tablet. 'How the hell has she bagged that?' she muttered.

Walking across the white sandy beaches of one of the Maldives' islands, an energetic young woman gesticulated with the gusto of a children's television presenter as she described to the camera the soaring temperatures and natural beauty of the tropical paradise.

'If your bingo wings flap any faster you'll be airborne,' Roxi continued as the camera panned out to focus on the luxury resort.

Autumn Taylor's tan was rich and her skin glowing, her hair was immaculately coiffed and, despite her claims of having only just woken up, her make-up was flawless. She clenched a tube of sunscreen in one hand and, in the other, a bottle of water. Both labels faced the lens.

Roxi paused the video, picked up her phone, opened the Notes App and began to dictate. 'Sunglasses: Prada. Bikini: Harper Beckham. Sunblock: Nivea. Mineral water: Acqua Panna. Tits: sponsor unknown.'

She glanced at the data surrounding the Vlogger's online channel, titled Autumn's Endless Summer. It contained forty-two videos shot around the world in Bali, India, Fiji

Islands, the Seychelles, Musha Cay and Bora Bora. Her most recent clip, posted yesterday, had already garnered more than a million views. Her position as one of the world's top ten Influencers ruffled Roxi's feathers every time she thought about it. Which was frequently.

Autumn's content was a far cry from the videos Roxi had been editing that morning in an overcast New Northampton. Yesterday, she had been wandering around the shop floor of a discount home and fashion outlet discussing the week's new best buys. She'd made sure to use the key words and phrases in every Influencer's dictionary – 'hey guys', 'community', 'get ready with me', 'collab', 'challenge' and 'haul' – and with the same enthusiasm as booking a French Airbnb and being handed the keys to the Palace of Versailles.

Her footage had been shot on a camera phone and lit with a portable LED ring light, both operated by her reluctant offspring Darcy and Josh. The end result was as far removed from Autumn's high production values as the sun and the moon. And when Roxi had briefly dragged her daughter in front of the lens, no amount of sharp editing could disguise Darcy's thunderous expression. She would rather be burning in the fiery flames of hell than be in Costland.

'I don't even get why you're making videos,' Darcy had moaned, her negativity buzzing in Roxi's ear like a trapped mosquito. 'Nobody watches your Vlogs.'

'Let's try a little positivity, shall we?' Roxi had replied. 'One hashtag seen by a PR could change everything.'

'You're far too old for this.'

'Jem Jones isn't much younger than me.'

'She's a dinosaur but at least she's a dinosaur people give a damn about.'

'I have twelve thousand combined social media followers.'

'Is that all?' Darcy had laughed. 'That dog with the lazy eye and patch on its back that looks like Prince Louis has more followers than you. Vlogging isn't going to make you famous. You're embarrassing yourself.'

'Shall I tell you what embarrassing is?' Roxi had retaliated. 'You turning up at school tomorrow with no phone because it's been taken away from you as punishment for not doing as you're told. Now be a good little girl, shut up and point that camera at me when I tell you.'

'I hate you,' Darcy had muttered.

'The feeling's mutual, darling.'

It wasn't, but Roxi couldn't deny that when children had appeared in her world, her former life had swiftly crumbled. Even now, she was struggling to rebuild it. And she quietly resented them for it.

Watching Autumn's video was forcing Roxi to accept that, despite her best efforts, her clip lacked excitement in the subject matter. Not even a warm colour filter, background music and a screen filled with positive emojis could save it. The Taylors of this virtual universe received beautifully boxed high-end fashion, jewellery, luxury holidays and perfumes. The Roxis received non-aspirational products like espadrilles, panty liners and renewable wooden cases for Audites, the mandatory Artificial Intelligence-powered personal assistants installed in all Smart Marriage homes. Regardless, she was always the consummate professional, reminding herself that even Jem Jones had started somewhere.

Today, though, Autumn's video had pushed her to the edge. She made a snap decision and hit the delete button. There would be no more clips like this.

Darcy had been partially to blame for her mother's Vlogging. Twelve years earlier, her daughter hadn't been the easiest of infants, thanks to colic, reflux, eczema and frequent sleep regressions. Roxi had spent many a sleepless night online searching for advice. And there'd been a video or a Vlog for just about every ailment known to babykind. But very few of these Influencers had resembled her. They weren't sleep-deprived mums in torn joggers and threadbare jumpers that hid their lumps and bumps. They didn't tie their hair up in scrunchies or go outside with make-up free faces. They were immaculately turned-out domestic goddesses living their best, filter-lensed lives. Roxi had subscribed to their channels, bookmarked their pages, lived vicariously through their videos and photos, queued at their book signings and voted for them as they competed on reality TV shows. They became friends Roxi had yet to meet.

But, over time, envy had replaced her fascination. Why were they travelling the world, eating at the best restaurants, wearing the most sought-after outfits, while she was doing the school run in decade-old elasticated jeans and returning home to piles of dirty washing? Against the chaos and disorder of her early years, she had found normality in two children and a husband. Only it wasn't enough. She needed something else, something more.

The solution had appeared as unexpectedly as if God had delivered it to her by hand. She would start her own Vlog.

'You should definitely do it, babes,' her closest friend

Phoebe had advised. 'If that lot can do it, why can't you? You'd be a natural. You're smart, funny and very persuasive. You could sell meat to a vegan.'

Roxi had thrown everything but the kitchen sink at her content. Some weeks her posts focused on budget fashions; in others, she offered advice on keeping a relationship fresh. Everything from sex to shopping, beauty and motherhood were covered. But, to her frustration, her audience numbers were slow to grow – and she was not being seen by the brands she coveted.

Her attention returned to Autumn and her followers. The majority were in the lucrative teen and twenty-something female market with high disposable incomes. But one pro-file image took her by surprise – it belonged to Darcy. She wasn't aware her daughter had even activated an Instagram account. Roxi skimmed though her posts. They were mostly made up of videos of Darcy and her friends pouting before the camera or performing choreographed dance routines. It was only as she was about to leave that she clocked Darcy's follower total. It was approaching 12,000 on one platform alone. Bewildered, she went back to Autumn's homepage.

'If I didn't know better, I'd think you had a girl-crush on her,' came a voice from behind.

'Jesus, Owen!' Roxi gasped as her husband pecked her on the cheek and peered over her shoulder. His sports bag and hockey stick lay in the doorway.

'How is the lovely Autumn today? I see her in this house so often that she feels like part of the family.'

'Another thirty thousand people have followed her in the

last week. *In the last bloody week.* Why? Please explain it to me.'

He shrugged. 'People like her? She's fun, she's enthusiastic, she's young and she's pretty.'

Roxi's eyes narrowed. 'Is that what you want to see online, young pretty girls?'

'Careful.' Owen pointed to the Audite on the kitchen side.

The small, black cylindrical device seemed to be staring back at her. Upgrading to a Smart Marriage allowed it to record ten random minutes of their conversation and alert them to any problems it might find in their relationship. She changed her tack. 'Any idiot can do what Autumn does. I want to help people; she wants to humblebrag.'

'You're kidding yourself if you think you're Vlogging out of the goodness of your heart. You want what she has. And you're jealous she's better at it than you.'

'Thanks, Owen, that's really what I need to hear right now.'

'You know there's a shelf life when it comes to being an Influencer. Perhaps no matter what you do, age isn't on your side.'

'So if I looked younger, I might get more work? Is that what you're saying?'

Owen shook his head. 'You look perfect to me,' he added before leaving her alone to research the internet for a discount code for face-tightening procedures. She only stopped when a news alert appeared on her screen, along with Jem Jones' image.

2

Jeffrey

Jeffrey reached for a bottle of transparent cola from the fridge, unscrewed the cap and settled himself at the dining-room table. He hadn't realized how dehydrated he'd become until he took a long, thirst-quenching gulp. He hoped it might replace the electrolytes he'd expelled in the physical exertions of the afternoon.

A yawn escaped almost before he had time to open his mouth. The long, exhausting day was taking its toll, and there was more to do before it finished. He willed the patch stuck to his arm to rid him of his headache and made a mental note to hydrate more frequently in future. A sour odour drew Jeffrey's attention to his armpits, but a short, sharp sniff revealed they weren't the cause. The smell was coming from his hands and arms.

A sudden dull thump upstairs caught his attention so he pushed his tablet to one side and cautiously went to investigate.

In the bedroom, his suitcase had fallen to its side, so he pulled it upright. The sour smell grabbed him again, so he peeled off his clothes and stepped inside the walk-in shower. He continued to drink his cola as the piping hot water cascaded over him, flattening his mousy-brown hair, then

15

streaked through his stubbled cheeks and bounced off his broad shoulders and chest.

He squeezed liquid soap onto his hands from a dispenser and washed the rust-coloured stains from his palms. Next, he dug underneath his fingernails and rubbed at the ribbons streaking across his forearms and wrists. The water in the shower tray was becoming cloudy.

With no clean clothes of his own, he flicked through the rails inside Harry's walk-in wardrobe, pulling out anything that caught his eye. Harry towered above him at 6 foot 5 inches compared to Jeffrey's more modest 5 foot 10 inches. They shared the same waist size but he would need to roll up the legs of the jeans to make this look work. Jeffrey was naturally more muscular than Harry so the sweaters and t-shirts he'd stuff inside his suitcase next would be a little on the clingy side. But they would do for now.

Before returning to the dining room with his suitcase, Jeffrey took one last look at the bathroom and the roll-top tub in the centre. He considered draining it before he left, but changed his mind.

Now back at the table, he interlocked and stretched his fingers until they cracked. He swiped across the screen to unlock his tablet. Human Resources had advised him many times to activate the fingerprint or optical scanners for security purposes, but he had yet to get round to it. Besides, the device was rarely out of his line of sight. The likelihood of it ever falling into the wrong hands was negligible.

His inbox contained seven new unread messages, none of which were flagged as urgent. He'd respond to them later. His finger hovered over an App on the home screen before he pressed it. It required three separate passcodes before the display filled with words and images. There were several ways for him to scour the contents – randomly, by latest additions, imagery, geographical location, ages or by length of time.

Random selections didn't work for Jeffrey. It was an approach he'd tried and it had taken a Herculean effort for him to remain invested for the full allocated timeframe. He preferred to first identify a potential connection by photograph before he took a deep dive into their personal data. That included everything from their biographies to finances and social media presence. Today's list had yet to be updated, which was probably for the best as, after his most recent clients, he required time to decompress. Tanya and Harry's behaviour had drained him. So he logged out.

As a Relationship Responder, it was Jeffrey's job to spend up to two months in close proximity to a married couple whose marriage was judged by Audite to be in crisis. He was responsible for unravelling the knots in the rope that bound these people together. Only when they were untangled could he decide if the AI system had been accurate. He'd then decide if the couple should remain married or go before a Family Court where magistrates would make a ruling on their future together. And the courts often favoured their recommendations, as Relationship Responders were the eyes and ears that witnessed the intricacies of these relationships first-hand.

Jeffrey looked at his watch. Night was drawing in and it was time to bid farewell to Doncaster. Suddenly his watch pinged to indicate that he'd received a new message. Curiosity got the better of him and he read it – three new couples had been added to the list of those requiring Responders.

Jeffrey hesitated, then logged back into the App, scanning the photographs, stopping as one particular pair caught his attention. When he registered their location in New Northampton, he almost dismissed them outright. It was a town he had avoided for all of his adult life.

But there was something about their photos that he couldn't quite put his finger on and which piqued his curiosity. And as he read their profiles, the threads of a connection were already beginning to form.

Jeffrey placed the tablet and his suitcase inside his car, then returned to the house and set to work preparing it. Soon after the smoke alarms were disabled, he scattered firelighters throughout each room and doused soft furnishings with bottles of white spirit he'd found on a shelf in the garage.

As the flames engulfed everything in their path, Jeffrey was already driving away and preparing himself to meet with his next clients.

3

Corrine

'Can you hear me?' asked Corrine, trying to mask the fear in her voice. 'If you can, please try and stay awake, okay?'

She peered at the body spread across the car's seats reflected in the rear-view mirror. She was desperate for a response, even just a groan. 'Stay with me,' she continued, 'I need you to tell me you can hear me.' No reply came.

The light of the dashboard illuminated her ashen knuckles as she gripped the steering wheel. She was grateful she had not upgraded her car to a driverless vehicle. It would not allow her to break speed limits like she was now.

Her eyes flitted from signposts to overhead gantries as she attempted to gain her bearings, confused by a section of Old Northampton she hadn't had cause to enter in years. She had no idea where its accident and emergency department was so she ordered her satnav to locate it, then followed its instructions until finally she reached its new home in the former Weston Favell shopping centre.

'We're almost there,' she told her passenger. 'Just hold on.'

She held her breath as she accelerated, driving through a set of red traffic lights, narrowly avoiding a trailer hitched to the back of a van. She hoped there was no CCTV camera attached to the lights, but surveillance in the Old part of town was unlikely. 'Come on, come on, come on,' she muttered, willing the vehicle to go faster, then cursing as she skidded to a halt at a busy junction.

'Hey Mercedes – turn privacy windows and lights on,' she ordered, and the vehicle became impossible to see into from the outside. She turned to check on the unconscious teenager lying behind her. He had one leg stretched out; the other hung loosely in the footwell. His arms were by his side and his head tilted to the right. His shallow breaths offered her a shred of comfort.

There was a tear in the knee of his dark trousers and an unhooked bow tie hung loosely from his neck. She noted the streak of blood across his wrinkled white shirt and couldn't be sure if it belonged to him. On the seat next to her were the recordables she had stripped from him, including his phone and Smart watch. He was a skinny lad, and that had made him easier to pull across a lobby and into an elevator earlier that night. She could only hope the camera footage of his body also being dragged across the underground car park had been erased by the others before the police arrived.

She'd missed the traffic lights turning green and the blasting of a car horn behind them startled her. She turned off the interior lights and her tyres screeched as she pulled away. Minutes later, she reached the grounds of the A&E department.

As Corrine reached the car park barrier, she had second thoughts. Her registration plates might be captured on film and her credit card attached to the vehicle would automatically pay for her stay on exit. There couldn't be any trace of her here. So, instead, she parked by the side of the road, opened the rear door and, for the second time that night, put her hands under the lad's arms and used all her strength to pull him.

A white-hot pain in her muscles seared and she grimaced so hard that her already swollen lips cracked and bled again. Eventually, she reached a path on the outskirts of the hospital grounds where she planned to leave him for someone to find. But once there, she decided the road was too far from the entrance to guarantee a speedy discovery. He had risked so much that night and deserved better.

She rushed back to the car, removed a scarf from the glovebox and wrapped it over her face, then returned to the boy. She pulled him towards the brightly lit building ahead. As the sweat streamed down her forehead and was absorbed by her face covering, she felt every one of her fifty-five years. Finally, she propped him against the wall of the Resus department. 'I'm so sorry,' she whispered before hurrying away.

Back inside her vehicle, Corrine tore off her scarf, turned up the air conditioning and gulped water from a flask. Her mind raced. She glanced once again into the rear-view mirror, this time at her lips. She hoped the swelling might go down by morning. She was lucky not to have lost any teeth with a punch like that. That would be much harder to explain.

Corrine started the car and began driving to a pre-programmed address. She verbally ordered the vehicle to erase every journey she had travelled in the last twenty-four hours from its memory, along with incriminating text messages on her phone – despite them being sent via an untraceable proxy server. She would give the boy's recordables to someone she knew who could take care of them.

'Hey Mercedes, radio on,' she said aloud and the closing bars of a song played before the pips sounded to alert her to the one a.m. news.

'The headlines,' a newsreader began. 'Social Media Influencer Jem Jones is confirmed dead after an apparent suicide, and Education Secretary and MP Eleanor Harrison is critically ill following an attack inside her home.'

Corrine took a deep breath. *This is it*, she thought, *this is where everything changes.*

Like the town in which she lived, her life would now be split into two halves: the one before and the one after she was responsible for Harrison's attack.

4

Arthur

Arthur's knees and spine cracked like dry twigs as he bent over to pick a handful of forget-me-nots.

The diminutive blue flowering plants had been appearing in his garden borders for the four decades he and June had lived in their Old Northampton house. Year after year, he dug up and re-potted clumps, then arranged them on a trestle table on the pavement outside for their neighbours to take. When cash was still used as currency, he'd leave an old ice cream carton for donations to the Fire Fighters' Charity. However, now that goods could only be paid for with the tap of a plastic card, phone or watch face, it was more trouble than it was worth. The neighbours could take the plants for free if they wanted.

Arthur made his way up the crazy paving path and in through the back door. He arranged the flowers inside a small glass jam jar filled with water and placed it on a tray next to a plate with two slices of marmalade on toast. He added a steaming pot of tea and two mugs before carefully carrying them up the staircase and into the bedroom.

'I've brought you breakfast in bed,' he said as he placed the tray between him and his wife.

June sniffed at the forget-me-nots. 'What are they for?' she asked with a note of surprise. 'You only pick me these

23

when . . .' She hesitated. 'Oh no, please don't tell me I've forgotten my own birthday . . .'

'I don't think birthdays really matter at our age,' Arthur replied. 'I stopped counting at seventy.'

'I'm sorry,' said June, and lowered her head. Arthur placed a comforting hand on hers.

'Hey, don't be silly,' he said, patting it. 'It's not the end of the world.'

'I hate that I'm not remembering things. Every day it feels like I'm losing a little bit more of myself.'

Arthur stopped shy of admitting he too had witnessed the decline in her mental capacity. She had also become prone to long periods of silence and glazed eyes.

'Well, that's what I'm here for, to remind you of everything.' He tapped at his head. 'I have enough memories up here for the both of us to last us a lifetime.'

'How long have we been married?' June asked.

'Forty-nine years.'

'So, it'll be our golden wedding anniversary next year?'

Arthur nodded.

'Do you think I'll be here to celebrate?'

'Don't talk like that; of course you will be.'

June's face lit up. 'We should have a party! Just a small do, perhaps hire a room at the Charles Bradlaugh; we could ask Tom to put on a spread.'

'That's a great idea.'

It wasn't the moment to remind her that Tom had sold the pub more than a decade earlier and that it had since closed, another victim of a divided town. Besides, soon, she was likely to forget suggesting it.

'Or we could take one last adventure in the campervan?' she continued. 'How much fun would that be?'

'Sounds like a great idea. Would you like some toast?'

'You have it, I'm not hungry.'

'You need to keep your strength up.'

June rolled her eyes as if to suggest he was nagging. Arthur held his hands up in surrender.

'Could you turn the news on please?' June asked. 'I have no idea what's going on in the world these days.'

'Television on,' commanded Arthur. 'BBC News.'

The screen was filled with footage of a young woman he vaguely recognized.

'That's the girl who told us we should get married again,' said June. 'Jem Jones. Has something happened to her?'

'I think she passed away.' Arthur squinted at the screen but was unable to read the rolling ticker at the bottom without his glasses. Multiple times he had declined his optician's recommendation for laser eye surgery, free with his NHS+ membership.

The medical alert bracelet he wore illuminated. He pressed a button so the writing on the display screen became audible.

'A marriage is made up of two people who have their own quirks, personalities and opinions', a Push notification read. 'You don't have to stop being a one to become a two.'

Arthur shook his head. Thrice daily these electronic messages arrived uninvited, but he knew better than to ignore them. Failure to press the green 'acknowledge' button meant the voice repeated itself every fifteen minutes for the rest of the day and night.

'I think she ended her life, poor girl,' said June, focusing on the television. 'What a terrible thing to do. Imagine being so desperately unhappy, that's the only way you can stop the pain.'

Arthur imagined it all too clearly because he had considered it himself many times. Not that he had admitted as such to his wife.

June picked up on his reticence to respond. 'I need you to promise me that when it gets worse, you'll only think of our good times together and not the last few months,' she said.

'Do we have to talk about this now?'

'Artie, I need to know that you'll be all right without me.'

'I'll be all right,' he replied and then patted her hand again. 'I promise you. But it doesn't matter because you're not going anywhere. It's you and me until the end, girl.'

And, for a moment, he allowed himself to believe it might be true.

5

Anthony

Anthony reclined in his chair, tilting his head left and right as far as it would stretch. His arms and legs felt rigid so he rolled his shoulders ten times forwards and ten times backwards before pulling each of his fingers until the knuckles cracked. He didn't know how many hours he'd spent hunched over the desk in his home office, but a considerable amount of time must have passed given how stiff he'd become. He pinched at his stinging eyes before slipping his smart glasses on. They magnified each pixel on the five wall-mounted screens ahead, making him feel like part of a computer game.

He was transfixed by the footage of Jem Jones' already infamous final transmission a day earlier, playing it over and over again. It wasn't her desperate words capturing his attention – he'd muted her voice – it was her micro-expressions. The pull of the corner of a lip, the raising of an eyelid or a nose wrinkle said as much as her talk.

After reaching the moment where she pointed the gun to her head and pulled the trigger, he rewound the clip and watched it again, this time at a quarter of the speed. Then, just as she picked up the weapon, he tapped at the mouse projected on the desk's surface and studied each image, frame by frame. The bullet's impact in her right temple forcibly pushed her head and body to the left. Jem fell to the ground and out of frame. The automatic settings on her camera followed the closest moving subject, now just the blood seeping from her fatal head wound. Eventually the ragged flesh of the exit wound was the only thing to fill the screen. Soon after, when Jem's heart had ceased to pump blood, the pooling settled and her room was as still as her pulse. Her death was both a blessing and a waste, he thought.

On a previous viewing, Anthony had timed the events that followed. Sixteen minutes and fifty seconds passed before four beeps were heard, an electronic door lock released and a figure appeared. The lens moved towards a middle-aged woman clad in a pink and white uniform and carrying a basket. Jem's cleaner had discovered her body. She screamed, and, seeing her face on the monitor, frantically turned off the camera. According to news streams, thousands of horrified viewers watching Jem's suicide in real time made calls to the emergency services. However, each caller faced the same problem: nobody knew where Jem Jones was when she died.

Except for Anthony. He knew exactly where she was.

Curious to gauge public reaction, he used a specialized program to tally every mention of Jem Jones on social media and online news outlets since her suicide. In only a few hours, she had become the world's most discussed subject, generating the second highest number of Tweets ever, only behind the hacking of British driverless vehicles a few years earlier. Most comments were in support of Jem. *Where were your supporters when you needed them?* he thought.

Anthony recalled the rise and fall of the country's most

influential social media star. Even in her embryonic days, her natural charm and self-effacing humour made Jem distinct in a market crowded by indistinguishable lookalikes and hopefuls. Her following grew organically and so did her interest in discussing more than just herself. But her support for the Sanctity of Marriage Act was her downfall. It was to be expected. Eventually, the British public always tore down what it had built. That was the nature of the beast.

A light flashed on his monitor to alert him of a presence outside his locked door. A pinhead camera identified his son. 'Close down system,' Anthony spoke aloud and each screen switched off. He pressed a remote control to open the door.

'Hi Daddy,' began Matthew, his voice boisterous and his arms animated. They shared the same bronze glow but Matthew had his mother's amber eyes. Each time Anthony looked at his son he realized how quickly he was growing up and how much he was missing.

'What brings you here?' Anthony smiled.

'Uncle Marley and Aunty Ally are here.'

'Okay, I'll be there in a minute. I have to shower first.'

'No! Mummy said I couldn't leave unless you came with me.'

She knows me too well, thought Anthony. Left to his own devices, an 'Anthony minute', as Jada dubbed them, could last anything up to an hour. 'Come on then,' he replied and took the boy's outstretched hand.

Matthew led him into the main house, the dining room, through an open set of glass doors and finally the patio. Established vines with thick trunks weaved their way around a pergola's wooden columns and beams giving shade from the sun to those seated at the table and chairs beneath it.

'Well, ladies and gentlemen, look who's here and he's almost on time!' his brother-in-law Marley mocked. His bare legs were outstretched, his fingers entwined behind his head. 'Very kind of you to join us.'

Anthony gave a playful eyeroll, suggesting it wasn't the first time he'd heard this.

'Does he work every Sunday?' asked Ally, Jada's sister, appearing behind Anthony. They pecked each other's cheeks before she placed two trays of food on the table.

Jada nodded, her corkscrew curls swaying. 'I've worn him down into taking at least one day off a week.' She placed a large glass bowl of salad in the middle of the table.

'Well, I guess that's progress,' replied Ally.

'To be fair, he did warn me when we first started dating that he was a workaholic so I knew what I was getting myself into.' She squeezed her husband's shoulder and he turned his head to kiss her hand. 'Right, shall we tuck in, guys? Straight from the shores of Anthony's homeland, we've got Saint Lucia's finest lambi, green figs and saltfish, fried plantain and breadfruit. And save some room for dessert.'

'Damn, I married the wrong sister, didn't I?' Marley said. His eyes suddenly flitted to his Smart watch. 'Which is a joke, of course.'

Anthony directed his attention to Matthew who was playing a game on his phone. 'You know the rules, can you put that away please?' His son reluctantly put the phone down.

'So how's work, Anthony?' asked Ally, spooning salad onto her plate.

'Ah, you know. Same old, same old.'

'Actually I don't know.'

'But you do know I can't talk about it.' He smiled.

'When are you going to slow down and enjoy life?'

'Has my wife put you up to this?'

'Don't blame Jada, I say it as I see it.'

'Ain't that the truth,' said Marley. 'Try living with her.'

Now it was Ally's turn to look at her watch and then at her husband. He flinched and mouthed sorry as he remembered their conversation might be recorded by his wearable Audite and analysed at any given moment. 'You'd be lost without me,' she said, in a deliberately sing-song tone.

'That I would.'

'Thirty-eight will be my retirement age,' Anthony said, grinning. 'In three short years we'll be emailing postcards to you in New Northampton from our Saint Lucia beach home. Well, that's if we can find the time between fishing, reef diving and rainforest hikes.'

'Yeah, yeah, yeah, we get it, Mr Moneybags,' said Ally. 'Just remember, money doesn't always buy you happiness.'

'But it gives you choice.'

'What do you think Jem Jones was worth?' Ally asked suddenly. Anthony's stomach tightened at the mention of her name. 'She was always being sponsored by some company or another so she must've been sitting on a fortune. She could've bought herself anything, just not happiness.'

'You never really know what makes people tick,' Marley replied between mouthfuls of breadfruit. 'Have you guys watched that last video?'

Jada and Ally nodded while Anthony shook his head.

'How have you not seen it?' asked Ally. 'It's impossible to avoid.'

'His office is like a bubble,' said Jada. 'Nothing goes in and nothing comes out. A comet could have struck and he wouldn't have the first clue.'

'Tell me you at least know who we're talking about?'

'A little,' Anthony said. 'I didn't pay her much attention.'

'I feel sorry for her,' said Ally. 'Nobody is thinking straight when they make a decision to end their life like that.'

'Should we be having this conversation in front of your seven-year-old nephew?' Marley asked. But Matthew was too engrossed in his phone to listen. This time Jada didn't ask and took it out of his hand.

'No one forced her to live her life in front of a camera,' said Anthony.

'Why should she give in to the haters?' asked Jada.

'But she did by killing herself.'

'Is that what we're going to teach our son? To let bullies win?'

'Of course not,' said Anthony. 'But we're not going to teach him to remain in a situation that's making him miserable either. Jem should've left social media, checked into a clinic or something, got her head together then gone on to enjoy her money in anonymity. Instead, she died as she lived – as entertainment.'

'Well, you have a lot to say about someone you didn't know much about,' said Marley.

'How about you go and get us another bottle of wine?' asked Jada.

Anthony tipped an imaginary cap to his wife. 'I know my place, m'lady,' he replied as he made his way back indoors.

A long burst of pulsations to his wrist distracted him. The senders who used coded vibrations to contact him via his Smart watch only messaged for a reason. He deciphered each letter and word until the sentence formed.

'So you did it then?' it read. 'You actually killed Jem Jones.'

Anthony stared at the device, mulling over his reply before he dictated his one-word response.

'Yes.'

HOW DOES IT WORK?

Sign up or upgrade your existing marriage.

We'll fit your home with **Audite** and you'll start receiving your **Smart Marriage** benefits.

Audite will randomly record ten minutes of your daily conversations to analyse and keep your relationship on track.

WHAT HAPPENS IF MY **AUDITE** THINKS MY MARRIAGE IS AT RISK?

Don't worry, we have you covered with a three-step programme.

LEVEL ONE

On picking up on marital difficulties from random recordings, **Audite** will allow longer recordings and offer **Push** notifications with handy hints for how to make improvements.

LEVEL TWO

If your Audite thinks you need a little extra help, we'll issue you with a **Relationship Responder** – a trained counsellor who'll listen to your recordings and get to the root of your problems with tailor-made couples and one-to-one sessions.

LEVEL THREE

If further support is required, based on all the evidence presented to it, a **Family Court** will help you take that next step forward.

SMART MARRIAGE

www.smartmarriage.co.uk

6

Jeffrey

Jeffrey checked his appearance in the rear-view mirror as his car parked itself alongside the grass verge outside the New Northampton house. He was clean-shaven, teeth recently bleached and eyebrows tamed with nail scissors. He licked his fingers and patted down a clump of hair on his crown that insisted on growing vertically no matter the product he slathered it in. First impressions always counted.

His stomach had been churning like a tumble dryer for much of the journey to a town he'd actively avoided for sixteen years. And with good reason. This is where it had all ended and begun.

Based on their photographs, the couple living in this modern-build home in an unfamiliar addition to the town, were intimidatingly handsome. Jeffrey, however, knew that he was not. He was neither attractive nor unattractive and he'd often wondered if Mother Nature had been side-tracked midway through his creation. It was only in his teens and when he was left with the scar around the socket of his right eye that people began to remember him. But when surgery had made it almost invisible, so was he again. He had, however, inherited the genetically muscular physique of his father and grandfather, along with their physical strength. The latter had come in useful on more than one occasion.

He looked at his watch – it was time to reprise his role as a Relationship Responder. Four years ago, Jeffrey had been one of the youngest applicants accepted in the training programme. And following a rigorous nine-month Government-funded course, he'd sailed through his exams. A probationary period had involved counselling a real-life couple under the tutelage of an experienced instructor before, finally, he'd practised solo. He had never looked back or returned to the half-light of the margins.

Jeffrey turned to look more closely at the property where he was to spend the coming weeks. As with five other towns and cities across the country, billions of pounds of Government regeneration funding, demolition, rebuilding and gentrification had created a territory only for those who had signed up to the Sanctity of Marriage Act. This was a starter home for a newly married couple. And it was Jeffrey's job to decide if this was where their marriage would also end.

7

Roxi

A kernel of an idea was already beginning to take root inside Roxi's head.

She was sitting cross-legged on her bed, her back resting against two thick pillows propped against the headboard and her attention directed towards a television screen. The fall-out of Jem Jones' suicide remained the only topic of conversation on magazine shows and news broadcasters. And she was just as fascinated by it as the rest of the country. A conveyor belt of talking heads had appeared on Sky News over the last twenty-four hours to offer their opinions on how social media had made Jem, but then ultimately broken her, too. Roxi flicked up and down other channels and discovered even foreign broadcasters, previously unaware of Jem's existence, were also reporting on how the British public had driven its most important social media Influencer to her death.

However, Roxi had a greater interest in the past than the present. First thing that morning, she'd logged on to Jem's YouTube channel and begun watching her Vlogs in order, from the very first clip posted six years ago. Jem had joined social media during yet another worldwide pandemic and series of lockdowns, when viewers had plenty of time on their hands. Then, she was a fresh-faced, mid-twentysomething, uploading videos with shaky camerawork, harsh lighting, and patchy sound quality. They weren't overly styled or rehearsed and there was nothing remarkable about her appearance or her topics of conversation. But Roxi had studied plenty of her rivals' Vlogs to recognize something a little different when she saw it.

Jem oozed likeability and sincerity. There was a quiet confidence in her delivery, an infectious, pragmatic enthusiasm and a believability about her. Whether she was promoting a product or describing an emotion, you bought into her. Roxi had been making copious notes on everything from Jem's clothes and make-up to her changing hairstyles and the locations she filmed in, typically her house or garden. She'd tallied Jem's most commonly used words and phrases and created spreadsheets to chart Jem's favourite subjects, how often and how many minutes she spent discussing them and cross-referenced them to the number of likes and reposts they received.

As the years and the clips progressed, Roxi noted that Jem gradually allowed her subscribers to glimpse her life beyond the lens. There came mentions of dates – good and bad – of boyfriends – also good and bad – and of broken hearts – always bad. There were smiles and laughter and tears and regrouping.

And then, after a decade creating purpose-built towns and rejuvenated regions, the much-discussed Sanctity of Marriage Act was close to becoming a reality.

'I can't wait,' Jem admitted in a Vlog Roxi viewed. 'Relationships can go wrong; it's a fact. Even if you've found your soulmate through Match Your DNA, it doesn't always mean a happy-ever-after.'

Years earlier, the concept of dating had been turned on its head when scientists discovered every person has a solitary gene they share with just one other person. A simple mouth swab was all it took to potentially find who you were guaranteed to fall in love with, regardless of age, race, sexuality, religion or location. The company Match Your DNA paired each half of a couple as and when they signed up. However, not every couple had the happy-ever-after they expected.

'Some problems are too big for love to overcome without help,' continued Jem. 'So what does it matter if you get it through artificial or human intelligence? If anything, AI is probably better at digging deeper than people are and using our data to understand what we're *not* saying to one another. AI is responsible for half of all medical diagnoses these days. We trust it with our lives so why not our hearts? A Smart Marriage makes sense, doesn't it?'

Then, as a general election approached, Jem became the face of a nationwide advertising campaign promoting Smart Marriages. She appeared in their TV, radio, social media and virtual assistant campaigns. And when the Government won its fourth consecutive term and the Act sailed through parliament and the House of Lords, she even became the voice used by Audites. But overnight, Roxi noted, she had been replaced by a male voice.

Three years of living with the Act had resulted in a national groundswell of those opposed to it. Single people, widows, divorcees and couples who flatly refused to upgrade accused it of discrimination. Much of their vitriol was directed towards Jem, the public face of the Act, and not the people they couldn't see behind the scenes. Organized groups began trolling her, they posted her address and phone number online and made death threats. The sparkle that had charmed millions gradually vacated Jem's eyes following months of abuse. In later posts, she'd admitted her mental health was waning and she'd talked of how the pressure she was under had caused the end of a recent romantic relationship. In her penultimate post, she'd wept uncontrollably and screamed at the camera when she'd recalled finding her two pet dogs poisoned in the garden. Enough was enough, she'd said, quitting social media.

Jem's final Vlog was the only video Roxi couldn't watch until the end. She pressed stop the moment Jem picked up the gun.

'Nine hours and forty-seven minutes,' began Owen, making his way into the bedroom. 'That's how long you have been in here and online.'

'Really?' Roxi replied, herself a little surprised. She rubbed at her tired eyes and Owen glanced at the empty packets of snacks and soda cans on the bedside tables.

'The family screen time and the Track My Movements Apps say you haven't been anywhere but here and the bathroom all day,' he continued as he changed out of his work shirt. 'It's now almost 6.30 p.m.'

'Are you checking up on me?'

'And I assume by the food delivery bag on the kitchen island that Darcy and Josh had takeout again for tea?' he continued.

Roxi had forgotten about her children. She'd heard them

around the house when they'd returned from school but was too immersed in Jem's world to return to her own. She removed the tie from her long blonde bob and scrunched her hair.

'I'm worried about you, Rox,' Owen continued. 'It's not normal to spend this much time online.'

'I've got something important to tell you,' she announced. 'I know how to take my Vlog to the next level and make my mark as an Influencer.'

'Of course,' he said with a smile that failed to reach his eyes. 'What else would this be about?'

'I'm going to be the new Jem Jones. There's a gap in the market and if I'm quick and I'm clever, then I can fill it.'

'And how will you do that, exactly?'

'By being the voice of the modern woman. By representing people like me. I'll talk about issues that affect us all. Jem's legacy is that Influencers are now seen as more than clothes horses, canvases for make-up or chefs. But she was too weak for the world we live in. I'm much stronger than her. I won't obsess on the negativity.'

'But these lives you want to emulate, like Jem's and Autumn Taylor's, they aren't real, Rox,' Owen continued as he slipped on a t-shirt. 'They're only showing you their best bits. Vlogging and Influencing is all smoke and mirrors.'

'Thanks a lot for your support,' Roxi huffed.

'I'd support you one hundred per cent if I thought it was good for you or our family. But it's a pipe dream. You gave up work to raise a family and, if you think they're at an age where they don't need you like they used to, perhaps it's time to get back out into the working world and find a real job?'

'Vlogging and Influencing are real jobs.'

Owen grimaced as he took a deep breath and shook his head. 'They are when you're a teenager and, at a push, in your twenties, but not when you're a woman approaching her forties.'

Roxi wanted to tell him that she was worth more than she had become, but held her tongue. She looked to the Audite atop of a chest of drawers and spotted a faint red light circling the rim, just the once. She knew that, as well as their words, it also picked up on what they weren't saying through the volume of their voices and their tone. 'I think it's listening to you,' she mouthed.

'At least somebody is,' he mouthed back.

Their visibly distraught daughter Darcy appeared suddenly at the doorway.

'TikTok, Insta and Snapchat, they've cancelled my accounts!' she sobbed. 'They say I'm too young.'

'What's the minimum age?' asked Owen.

'Thirteen. So now I've lost every photo and every video I've ever posted.'

Roxi considered climbing off the bed to comfort her daughter but changed her mind. That wasn't the nature of their relationship. Instead, Owen brought Darcy into his chest and kissed the top of her head. He was better at this kind of thing than she was. But it didn't stop Roxi from feeling a small stab of envy at their closeness. And there was no remorse for having reported her daughter's accounts to their service providers. If she was going to become Jem's replacement, how could she be taken seriously with a twelve-year-old daughter who had more followers than her?

8

Corrine

Corrine poked her head out of the door and cocked it to one side. She couldn't hear the kids in their bedrooms or her husband in his office at the end of the landing. She returned to her room, closed the door and removed from her handbag a burner mobile phone she'd purchased from a twenty-four-hour convenience store the previous night. She dialled Old Northampton's accident and emergency department and, several voice-activated options later, she finally reached a human.

'Hello,' she began quietly. 'I'd like an update on a young man who was admitted in the early hours of yesterday morning?'

The reply was curt. 'Name?'

'Nathan.'

'Surname?'

'I'm not sure.'

'Your relationship to him?'

'A . . . colleague.'

A moment's silence followed and, when Corrine thought the woman had hung up, a ringing tone sounded.

'Who am I speaking to?' a male voice began.

'Hello, I'm trying to get an update—'

43

'Your name?'

There was something about his authoritative timbre that warned Corrine not to continue. She pressed the end call button and promptly dropped the phone. She bent to pick it up and spotted the scarf she had worn when she had left the boy's unconscious body by the hospital's entrance. She threw it into a drawer and made a mental note to add it to the log burner later.

She had barely slept that night worrying about Nathan's condition and how their plan had gone so awry. Over and over, she'd wracked her brains as to how they could have done things differently. But she kept reaching the same conclusion: they had been blindsided.

Corrine picked up her regular phone and typed MP Eleanor Harrison's name. 'MP remains in critical condition with head injury,' read the first of many news stories. Corrine bit her index finger. Even though she despised the woman, she hoped for her own sake that Harrison would make a full recovery.

She studied her reflection in the bedroom mirror. Dark bruising had risen to the surface overnight, framing her mouth in blues and blacks from where the fist had landed. Concealer would hide it. Her swollen lips, however, would be harder to disguise. She picked up a towel from the sink and held it to her mouth. She'd tell anyone who commented that it had been an allergic reaction to shellfish, her first in years.

Corrine gently applied her make-up, ran her fingers through her brown-and-grey-flecked hair, then slipped into a comfortable pair of trousers. She flinched; muscles she had strained last night tugged as she pulled her arms into a loose-fitting blouse.

She gave herself a final once-over in the mirror before clearing her throat and making her way downstairs. Through a window adjacent to the staircase, she spotted her neighbour Derek and his new wife climbing into their car. It had been almost two years since she had last spoken a word to the man she had once considered a friend. Corrine rarely bore grudges but she'd made an exception for him.

She passed the utility room and bid the housekeeper Elena a good morning. Outside, she heard the quiet hum of the lawnmower as Elena's husband Florin tended the garden.

Gathered around the television in the reception room were Corrine's husband Mitchell and two of their three children. She corrected herself: they weren't children any more, they were young adults. Twins Nora and Spencer were eighteen and would soon be following in their older sister Freya's footsteps and heading to university. Once, Corrine thought she'd be dreading the moment they flew the nest. But not now that she had a plan in place.

Corrine's eyes rested on Mitchell. Sitting on one of the sofas, he rested his folded arms on a belly that strained the fabric of his t-shirt. Dark hairs protruded from his ears like the legs of a hermit crab poking out from a seashell. She assumed the birthday vouchers she had given him for a male grooming spa treatment remained unused.

'Have you heard who's dead?' asked Spencer. 'Jem Jones.'

'The girl from the internet?' Corrine replied. She recalled hearing the news headline on the radio as she drove back from the hospital but had been too preoccupied to pay the story any attention.

'Uhuh. She killed herself while livestreaming. Gun to the head. Boom.' He mimicked placing a weapon to his temple and pulling the trigger.

'Oh, that's awful.'

'Do you want to watch it?'

'No, why would I? And neither should you.'

'I've already seen it, like, a dozen times this morning. It's all over the internet.'

Mitchell turned, taking in her appearance, and her mouth in particular. 'Given into peer pressure and had your lips done?' he mocked.

'Woah, Mum!' Nora added. 'You know less is more, right?'

'Very funny. The restaurant put prawns in the paella after I specifically asked them not to. The swelling will go down soon.'

'You might consider some fillers around the eyes as well,' Mitchell continued. 'Time is crueller to women than it is to men.'

Corrine eyed her husband up and down. 'On whose authority?'

Mitchell offered a humourless laugh and reverted his attention towards the screen.

'Why did that poor girl want to die?' Corrine asked.

'She said she couldn't cope with the haters,' said Nora. 'All those GIFs and memes and Deepfakes made her life a misery, apparently.'

Corrine shook her head. 'Then why not just leave social media?'

'Because, without it, you might as well not exist.'

'That's ridiculous. If a dog kept biting you every time you stroked it, you'd stop stroking it, wouldn't you?'

Spencer rolled his eyes.

'Then explain it to me,' Corrine continued. 'I'm all ears.'

'Your social media is every bit as much of who you are as the clothes you wear, the bars you check into, the music you share, the car that drives you or who you date. Everyone judges you on them – your mates, teachers, Uni recruiters and employers.'

'But why does it need to be such a toxic environment?'

Nora shrugged. 'You tell us. Your generation started it.'

'And you are supposed to be better than us,' Corrine retorted. 'Is Woke Behaviour & Practice still on the school curriculum?'

Spencer nodded. 'It's not like her death is my fault, is it? I didn't do anything.'

'Did you "like" any of those memes or GIFs? Did you repost any?'

'Well, yeah, some of them were funny. But I didn't tag her.'

'But even by liking them, you're contributing to the problem.'

'What does it matter to you?' interrupted Mitchell. 'You told me yourself that you didn't like her.'

Corrine sighed. 'There's a difference between not liking someone for what they stand for and hounding them to their death.'

'Yet when I tell you I think all social media should be state controlled, you argue with me. Sounds like double standards.'

'You think what we need right now is more Government

control? Isn't it enough that couples signed up to the Marriage Act are allowing themselves to be spied on in their own homes?'

'I have no secrets. Do you, Corrine?'

A shift in tone and his burrowing stare made her question if Mitchell knew more about her extra-curricular activities than he was admitting to. No, he couldn't be aware of what had happened to that MP, she reasoned. She had covered her tracks.

The disagreement wasn't worth any more of her time so she left it. There was little common ground between them these days – with one exception. In a world that encouraged couples to remain together, she and Mitchell were readying themselves to go against the grain. They were preparing to divorce.

9

Jeffrey

Both Luca and Noah Stanton-Gibbs opened the door before the chime rang out, suggesting they were ready for him.

'Hello there, I'm Jeffrey Beech and I'm your Relationship Responder,' he began with an avuncular smile. He willed his face not to redden as it was prone to doing upon meeting anyone he was attracted to. And both Noah and Luca ticked every box. He offered them his identification card, which Noah scanned with his watch to verify his status.

'Come in, please,' said Luca and both men moved to one side. Their nervousness mirrored his. But Jeffrey preferred it that way. He detested arrogant clients.

'Your home is beautiful,' Jeffrey said, his eyes darting around like a child in a theme park. They thanked him.

'Have you been to Northampton before?' asked Luca.

'No, I haven't,' he lied.

As he followed them towards the lounge, Jeffrey took in their appearances. Noah's dark-brown hair was cropped, his face angular and scattered with stubble that stopped at the corners of his mouth. His eyes were a warm, rich chocolate brown. Luca's face was softer and more boyish. He was clean-shaven, and his eyes were two distinctive, different colours: one light brown and the other green. He wore his

49

golden blond hair ear-length, combed to one side and with a soft wave. Jeffrey held back from staring, fascinated by them. Appearance-wise, laboratory geneticists couldn't have created this pair any more opposite but perfectly.

'This bit is always the awkward part,' Jeffrey continued, 'so why don't we sit down and I'll answer any questions you might have?'

'I'm still struggling to understand why we've been put on Level Two,' said Noah, as he led Jeffrey into the lounge. 'It's got to be a mistake.'

'I appreciate it must have come as a surprise,' he said, 'but think of me as a mechanic who's taking a look under the car bonnet to make sure everything is running on full power. I'll help you make sure you're both on the same page and want the same things, and if not, then we'll help you find a way to bridge that gap.'

'But we are totally on the same page,' said Luca. 'That's why it doesn't make sense.'

'I assumed we'd be okay after we repeated some of the Level One Push notifications back into the Audite,' added Noah.

'For some couples, notifications are gentle nudges to make them aware of how they might be communicating or if they're bickering too often. And, once red flags are raised, the system has learnt to also sift through your online blogs, sites you visit, text and voice messages, online and real-world purchases and social media accounts. It'll see what you've posted, how often you mention or are pictured with each other, if you're spending a lot of time talking to friends who are single along with many other factors to decide whether you need the likes of me. But I'm sure you have nothing to worry about. Perhaps Audite's AI has labelled you incorrectly and needs a little retraining.'

'Does that happen often?' asked Luca.

'You'd be surprised,' Jeffrey replied. 'Like us, it isn't perfect, no matter what they'd have you believe.'

Jeffrey had prepared for their meeting by staying awake all night and swallowing legalized stimulants to keep his concentration focused. He remained inside his car or in 24-hour coffee houses, trawling through the couple's social media accounts. He had also listened to hour after hour of Audite-recorded conversations and concluded that much of Noah and Luca's dialogue was based on good-natured humour. They were a couple who enjoyed making each other laugh with amusing put-downs.

However, while Audite's AI was supposed to be competent at interpreting relationship cues and recognizing the difference between sarcasm and scorn, its predictions threw up false positives from time to time. Noah and Luca were casualties of an imperfect concept.

'Do you mind if I take a few moments to look around your home?' Jeffrey asked.

'Of course,' said Luca. 'Follow me . . .'

'If you don't mind, I'd prefer to go by myself.' He raised his palms vertically to his chest. 'Don't worry, I won't be intrusive.'

He left his uneasy clients behind as he made his way into the kitchen-diner, noting how everything from the cutlery drawer to pots and pans and tea towels were well stacked or folded and neatly laid out. Even the tumble dryer was lint-free. It was already a house after his own heart and a far cry from his own flat, of which he had not so much as set foot in for almost three years.

Upstairs, the master bedroom's en suite contained two sinks and two cabinets, neither stocked with anything of note, with the exception of antidepressant patches, prescribed in Luca's name. The underwear drawer in their bedroom contained only labelled clothing, aussieBum or Calvin Klein, and Jeffrey couldn't decide who favoured jock straps and briefs and who wore fitted trunks. He slipped one of the jockstraps into his pocket. In another drawer, he found a handful of sex toys and lubricants. He sniffed the fruity flavours and dabbed them on his lips. He snickered when one of the vibrating toys tickled his cheek as he ran it across his face. He also wondered why a married couple needed a box of condoms. Finally, he lifted their pillows and inhaled them deeply, identifying who slept on which side by the scent of their skin.

Amongst a stack of plastic trays in their home office, he noted a photograph of two toddlers, a boy and a girl. A folder accompanying it revealed Noah and Luca had been matched with a surrogate and the photograph was a computer illustration of what their children might look like. A knot appeared in Jeffrey's stomach, a reminder that life was passing him by.

He glanced out of the window and, in the distance, caught sight of the former National Lift Tower, a 120-metre concrete cylindrical building close to the centre of town. As a boy, he had seen it from his own bedroom window. Perhaps while he was back here, it was time he made peace with his past.

'Which of the spare rooms would you like me to take?' he began as he returned to his clients.

Noah and Luca looked blankly at Jeffrey, then to one another.

'Under the terms of your Smart Marriage contract, a Relationship Responder can move in with a couple if they decide they can do their job more effectively in a closer proximity.'

'Is that really necessary?' asked Noah. 'You said yourself the system probably needs a reset.'

'I said perhaps Audite's AI might need a little retraining. Having only just met you, at this point it's impossible for me to know one way or the other. Of course, if you prefer, I don't have to stay here; I can always just add to my report that it wasn't something you were comfortable doing . . .'

'It really isn't conve—' started Noah.

'Jeffrey,' Luca interrupted, 'would you being here speed this Level Two process up?'

Jeffrey nodded. 'The average time a Relationship Responder spends with his clients is seven to eight weeks. But that could be reduced by a third if given complete access.'

'Could we have a moment to talk about this privately?' Noah asked.

Jeffrey had witnessed a similar reluctance in others he'd worked with. But in the end, the answer was always the same.

'I don't think we need to discuss it,' said Luca. 'You can take the room that overlooks the back garden if you like, Jeffrey?'

'Excellent. I'm house-trained so you won't even know I'm here most of the time. I'll get my suitcase from the car.'

Luca offered a smile that made the hairs on Jeffrey's arms rise.

Jeffrey turned his head and left before either man saw him blush.

10
Arthur

Arthur remained motionless in the hallway, trapped between the kitchen and the front door. He was scared to move in case he was spotted by the shadow hovering outside.

'Mr and Mrs Foley, are you there?' came a voice he recognized. He had hung up on her by phone several times already in the last week. 'It's Lorraine Shrewsbury. You should have received a notification that I was coming.'

Arthur remained tight-lipped and focused on keeping his breaths quiet. It was a challenge given years of smoke inhalation during his pre-retirement career as a fire fighter. Medication had prevented his emphysema from advancing but stress manifested itself physically in shortness of breath. And there had been many occasions of late when anxiety had threatened to swallow him whole.

There was another knock, followed by the opening of the letterbox, positioned at the door's base. 'Mr and Mrs Foley,' the voice echoed through it, 'if you are there, I really need you to answer, please.'

From her position, the uninvited visitor wouldn't spot him if he moved right now. So Arthur shuffled as quietly as the soles of his orthopaedic trainers would allow, across the floorboards and towards the staircase. He climbed up two steps and pinned his back to the wall, still out of her sight.

'Arthur, who's at the door?' June shouted from the bedroom. He willed her to be quiet. 'Is it that woman again? Tell her to piss off.'

'June,' he whispered through gritted teeth. 'Shh!'

'Mr and Mrs Foley, you're breaking your Sanctity of Marriage Act contract by not allowing me in. I am legally entitled to return with a court order and a police officer to enter your property by force if you don't answer. But I really don't want it to get that far.'

Arthur noticed his left arm was shaking, so he gripped it tightly with his right hand. Eventually, Shrewsbury admitted defeat and shifted away along the path. Slowly, he approached the closed curtains of one of the front rooms and moved them just enough to locate her parked vehicle. He slipped on his glasses: she was inside, her mouth moving, as if talking to someone on the phone. Only when her car pulled away did his breath return.

His Smart watch vibrated as a message appeared. 'Write notes of praise and text them to your partner. These words can be re-read again and again.' He cursed under his breath.

With each step up the stairs, he gripped the banister tightly, noting the framed photographs on the wall that he passed daily and normally took for granted. Most were of just him and June in front of European landmarks like the Eiffel Tower, the Vatican's St Peter's Square and remaining segments of the Berlin Wall. The sky-blue VW campervan they'd bought to travel around Europe was also pictured in some. They had both loved that vehicle and their adventures, just the two of them.

Arthur and June's many attempts to start a family had ended in failure. And, at times, the pressure and the strain of wanting so much but receiving so little had almost broken their marriage. But when they finally accepted parenthood was beyond their reach, they began to live for the now and not the maybe. Travel did not fulfil them as much as a family might have, but it had solidified them as a couple.

The campervan remained with them even now, parked in the garage and tucked under a tarpaulin cover. It cost an astronomical amount to tax and insure a petrol vehicle now that electric replacements were the norm. So once June had fallen ill and ceased to show an interest in travel, he had not bothered to renew either. But sometimes he couldn't resist sitting inside it, reversing down the drive and remaining there, allowing the thrum of the engine to vibrate though his body as he replayed bygone days.

'Was that her again?' June asked as he entered their bedroom.

'It wasn't anyone. Just a salesperson.'

However, after almost half a century of marriage and despite her confusion, he had yet to pull the wool over her eyes. 'It's that Relationship Responder again, isn't it?' she asked.

'It's nothing for you to worry about. She's gone now.'

'But she'll be back, won't she?'

'I don't know.'

'You have to keep her away from us.'

'I will, I will.'

'Because if she sees me like this, you know she's going to insist they take me away. And it's not right.'

A silence enveloped them, Arthur recalling reading the clause in the contract that allows an expedited divorce with no financial penalties if a partner is suffering from an incurable degenerative brain disease or long-term debilitating mental health issues. In fact, 'better halves' as they were referred to, were encouraged to tick a box to place their ailing spouses into private care homes or medical facilities while they actively sought their next relationship. Another more controversial box took the opportunity to make a fresh start even further. He shuddered when he thought of it.

'We both signed up for the Marriage Act, not just you,' June reminded him. 'We had no choice but to protect our future. Once they started taxing our bedrooms, we couldn't have remained in our old marriage and kept this house. There would barely have been anything left of our pension to pay our NHS contributions. And the cost of my medication alone meant we'd have had to choose between my pills and being able to eat. We did the right thing.'

'But look at us now,' he whispered, 'hiding, and scared to say anything in case that machine picks up on it.'

Arthur glanced at the Audite. It hadn't troubled him when it was first installed in every room of their house and the software downloaded on to the couple's wearable technology. It was a perfect centralized streaming system for music and television, it ordered their shopping, ran them baths and showers, controlled the house's temperature and measured and warned them if their carbon footprints needed offsetting. It didn't matter if their conversations were being randomly recorded because there was barely ever a cross word between them. Now, he hated that thing. If he could take a hammer to it then he would. But that was a criminal offence.

'Can I get you anything?' he continued, changing the subject.

'You could close the bedroom window as I'm starting to feel the chill. Then you can give me a cuddle. We don't cuddle enough.'

'Okay.'

June was right, he hadn't been as physical with her as he used to be. As her body and spirit faded before him, he had been too frightened to hold her in case he might bruise or damage her. He hadn't taken into account her need to be touched, to be held or to feel alive again. He sat on the edge of his bed, kicked off his trainers, then inched his way towards her until they were lying together. Finally, he draped his arm across her chest, then pulled her closer to him.

'This is nice, isn't it?' she whispered, and he nodded.

She felt so frail in his arms and so helpless. But regardless of her appearance or mental capacity, she would always be the June he loved.

His rock, his strength, his wife.

11

Anthony

Each of the six screens in Anthony's office was filled with moving images, but only one had his undivided attention.

Days after Jem Jones' suicide, her story remained headline news as each of the major networks covered the national outpouring of grief. He wasn't naive – he had expected Jem's dramatic death to dominate several news cycles – but even he was taken aback by the groundswell of support that was showing no signs of shrinking. And he couldn't take his eyes off her. It was only natural, he reasoned, as they had been in one another's lives for the longest time. But familiarity breeds contempt and there were times that he hated her too, or at least, what she had become.

Already that morning, Sky News had filled its schedule with tributes from other social media luminaries, alongside clips of Jem's memorable moments and her most-viewed Vlogs. Meanwhile CNN had broadcast a segment where studio-based body language experts dissected her facial and body movements in posts leading up to her death. They picked apart anything that might have indicated her state of mind.

On YouTube, Anthony viewed a report from the previous night, filmed outside Jem's gated Buckinghamshire home.

It was surrounded by hundreds of fans, many wearing her image emblazoned on t-shirts and some in Jem Jones cardboard masks printed from the internet, all holding a candlelit vigil. Photos and posters had been attached to lampposts and bunches of flowers had been tied to the gates or placed on the pavement. There were so many tributes that police had closed the road to traffic. Traces of anti-Jem graffiti remained on walls where she had been vilified before her death.

Anthony considered attending to say one final farewell but changed his mind. He wasn't ready for her to leave his life just yet. A journalist reporting from the scene made comparisons to the aftermath of the death of the Princess of Wales, King William's mother. Anthony trawled through online archives to understand the reference and conceded there were definitely parallels.

He became fascinated by interviews with grieving fans expressing their collective outrage at the treatment of Jem and blaming targeted social media campaigns for driving her to her death. 'Freedom for All is to blame for this,' shouted one girl into the newsreader's microphone. 'They claim they're a party fighting for equality but they're killers. The Government needs to cancel groups like that. What happened to Jem is murder.'

Anthony couldn't argue with that.

There were Jem's detractors too, although they were receiving less airtime. Depending on who you listened to, Jem was either a tragic heroine, a saviour, the ultimate feminist, a warrior, an everywoman, a campaigner, a sacrificial lamb, the devil's mouthpiece, a victim or a saint. And to Anthony, she was all of them and more.

He turned the volume up on another screen where a Government spokesman he recognized appeared in the studio paying lip service with soundbites like 'such a tragedy' and 'a terrible waste' before promising 'a full and frank discussion about the role social media and other political parties may have played in Jem Jones' death.' Anthony knew this was more than just Government rhetoric. It would in all likelihood use this as an excuse to clamp down on freedom of speech. In death as she was in life, Jem would become the figurehead for those with an agenda, used up and spat out when the next big story came along. It was unfair. He had grown to want more for her than that.

But he knew all too well that Jem couldn't be reasoned with and she didn't care how unfairly the Act treated people. She could be as unfeeling as the Government she represented. So when he was issued with the kill notice, he knew it was for the greater good.

Anthony diverted his attention towards another screen. A server hidden somewhere in east Europe stored the coded data behind thousands of Bots: the software applications that ran automated tasks across the internet. They had all been programmed with one aim – to make Jem's life as miserable as possible. They created spam accounts that filled the comments sections across her social media with obscenities and libellous accusations. There had been threats to kill her; parody accounts fabricated to mock her and fake news to spread about her.

In terms of reach, the most successful of these deeply personal attacks featured Jem being caught on camera slapping a child in a park who had accidentally kicked a football at her. Footage captured the ball hitting her shoulder, making her spill a cup of coffee over herself. Jem's violent assault had sent the child running to his mother and she had been filmed by another park user running away before the angry parent could confront her.

It was, however, a Deepfake video, where a person or existing image has been replaced and manipulated with somebody else's computer-generated image. Everyone in Jem Jones' slap video were actors paid to play out the scene, including Jem's part. Her likeness had been projected on to the woman playing her. Such technology had advanced so successfully over the last decade that even computer programming and body language experts found it impossible to tell the difference between a fake clip and a real one. Three cast members of last year's Best Picture Oscar winner were Deepfakes. However, such was the potential danger of this software, its use without a licence had become a criminal offence in many countries. Spotting and reporting them was even part of the British school curriculum.

Once the clip became viral, a furious Jem went public with denials and threats of legal action against anyone who reposted the clip. But it had already gained so much momentum that it was impossible to police. It didn't matter if it wasn't universally believed, there were enough people out there who accepted it as the truth.

It was only the beginning of Jem's troubles. Picking on her with memes and GIFs became a sport and people tuned in to her Vlog to watch her unravel. If there had been a more ruthless, sustained and successful attempt at destroying a reputation, Anthony was unaware of it. And Jem had no idea that none of it was real.

He pressed his thumbprint against a pad attached to a desk drawer before it opened, then repeated the action with a metal box inside it. He removed the object it contained, a dark grey, Ruger GP100 1705 revolver. It weighed less than others he had tested before Jem's death but was equally as powerful to kill at point-blank range. He checked each of the six chambers to ensure they were empty and released the safety catch. He drew the weapon to his left temple, then closed his eyes and pulled the trigger. Next, he placed the barrel under his chin, then in the centre of his forehead, his right temple and finally his crown. Only when he was satis-fied did he return the weapon to the drawer and lock it again.

Being surrounded by so many versions of Jem on the screens around him was exhausting. So he turned them all off, sat back in his chair and closed his eyes. This might be the only break he got in his schedule for the foreseeable future. And even then he'd been warned by his employer that it wouldn't last long. The next project was already being discussed. And although he didn't know what to expect from it, it was likely to be as morally equivocal as murdering the most loved – and hated – Influencer in the country.

12
Roxi

'I can't hold my tongue any longer,' began Roxi, her voice brittle. She dabbed at the corners of her eyes with a tissue.

'If you're visiting my channel expecting me to talk about relationships or this week's hero products, then I apologize. Because today, there's something more important I need to get off my chest.'

She paused to take a deep breath. 'As you all know by now, we in the Influencing community recently lost one of our own. The talented, wonderful, and inspirational Jem Jones was driven to take her own life. Trolls made this poor woman's life a misery, hounding her just because she had a different viewpoint to theirs. The attacks on Jem went far beyond expressing an alternative opinion. It was a campaign of orchestrated, relentless abuse with a devastating outcome.

'I cannot help but think that, had Jem been a man, he would not have faced that same level of hatred and spite. It's ordinary women like you and me they're trying to silence. We are the people Jem represented, and therefore we owe it to her to show these bullies that they will not win. And it's why I'm urging you all to make your voices heard and to fight back.'

Roxi reached across the kitchen table to press the stop

button on her phone. She removed the device from the tripod and appraised what she had recorded so far. There could be improvements. Perhaps she shouldn't try to divide the sexes? She reapplied a menthol stick sparsely under her eyes and blinked hard until they moistened. She'd read about the process actors used to induce tears and had ordered one online. Then she dabbed at her lips with a balm. They felt peculiar without the recently dissolved fillers she was so used to, but Jem had prided herself on her natural look and now so would Roxi.

She rewound the on-screen autocue, hit record and began her speech again with some tweaks. This time the tears fell quickly and she wiped them away with her fingers instead of a tissue. It made her emotions appear less rehearsed.

'None of us are completely innocent though,' she added. 'We all saw what Jem was going through but none of us actively did anything to try and stop it. We could have sent her messages of support, told her how much we loved her and reported the accounts that were attacking her. But we didn't. We sat idly by, relieved it wasn't us under attack. Shame on me and shame on all of us.

'To everyone out there who sent Jem a nasty Tweet, who shared the appalling fake videos of her and who created memes and GIFs to humiliate her, your collective actions drove someone to their death. As a fellow Vlogger, Influencer and as a human being with a heart, I cannot sit idly by and say and do nothing – or let this happen again. We need change.

'That's why I am calling for Artificial Intelligence to be installed not only in the houses of couples with Smart

Marriages, but in every single home in the country. As well as it protecting relationships, monitoring our conversations can also help to fight terrorism, expose criminal behaviour, child abuse, racism, bullying and spousal abuse.' A lump formed in her throat at mention of the last. She swallowed it back down. 'If you have to hesitate to think about what you say before you say it, or type it, you won't be talking and acting on impulse. And isn't that going to make us all more considerate of one another?'

Roxi counted three seconds in her head before she delivered her final line. 'For everyone's sake, let's be better.'

She returned to her laptop and, once satisfied with what she saw, added a large graphic to the end of the footage that read, #IWillDoBetterWillYou? And after the inclusion of specific tags, trending sounds and other metadata to assist in making her video as discoverable as possible, she posted it and crossed her fingers.

- Do you have a good ear, great observational skills and bags of empathy?
- Are you non-judgemental and broad-minded?
- Do your married friends turn to you for advice?
- And, most importantly, do you believe in the Sanctity of Marriage Act?

Then why not consider a career as a
Relationship Responder?

We are recruiting new candidates to train as Relationship Responders and head out into the field to keep couples together and steer them in the right direction. You don't need any prior qualifications, just an understanding of relationships and a sixth sense for the truth. We'll do the rest.

THE POWER TO SAVE MARRIAGES IS IN YOUR HANDS

SMART MARRIAGE

www.smartmarriage.co.uk/relationship-responders

13

Jeffrey

Noah and Luca had not scrimped when it came to decorating their house. If Jeffrey were to ever own a home of his own, he would strive to make it as perfect as Noah and Luca's. Here, there was a mattress to melt into, Egyptian cotton sheets to lie upon and a duvet stuffed with silk and duck down.

He did still have a place of his own that he continued to pay rent on: a windowless flat furnished with just an armchair and a single bed. Its walls stubbornly held the stench of the previous tenant's dead body that had remained undiscovered for more than a year. It wasn't a stretch to imagine why she had ended her life in that vortex of despair; Jeffrey too had considered it frequently before he became a Relationship Responder. But his job gave him purpose and hope. In the last eighteen months, each time he was between clients, he chose to sleep on the rear seats of his car rather than return to that place. But despite being able to afford a better home, he decided to keep that flat as a stark warning to himself of what he was going to return to if he didn't put his heart and soul into finding himself a partner.

He stretched and yawned and cast his eye over the wardrobe in the corner of the room. While unpacking last night, he had found a dozen or so items of neutral-coloured clothing purchased for a newborn baby. He brushed his fingertips across the soft material as he pulled their hangers to one side to make room for his own clothes. He wondered how far down their surrogacy journey Noah and Luca had travelled.

Jeffrey recalled how parenthood had been little more than a dream for him until he'd been appointed Ruby and Saul's Relationship Responder. Ruby had desperately wanted her marriage to work and to start a family. But by the time Jeffrey had appeared on their doorstep, Saul had announced he was seeing someone else and was 'riding the storm' until he and Ruby reached the Family Court in Level 3 and were divorced.

Jeffrey had spent many an hour counselling Ruby alone and the intensity of their relationship developed into something much greater for him. He had fallen in love with her. Only when Saul moved out did he pluck up the courage to admit to Ruby that he too wanted a family and that, together, they could make their parenting dreams a reality.

Her response was instant rejection. Jeffrey left her home that same afternoon and filed his report, ensuring she alone was to blame for the failure of her marriage, branding her erratic and antagonistic. As a result, the Family Court punished her for pushing her husband away and Saul and his new bride were awarded the lion's share in the division of assets.

Jeffrey washed away her memory as he showered, then slipped into a fresh set of clothes. Downstairs, he found Luca arranging bowls of fruit, muffins and pastries and jugs of citrus juices on a burnished kitchen tabletop.

'Help yourself,' Luca invited. 'They're all home-made.'

'Do you eat this well every morning?' Jeffrey asked as his sweet tooth directed him towards a muffin coated in poppy seeds. Luca's reddening cheeks suggested it had been laid out for his benefit.

Warm prickles spread across Jeffrey's shoulders and arms. He appreciated the effort even if it was only to win his favour. He had a good feeling about today's first session.

14
Roxi

An afternoon that began with such hope was gradually petering out into disappointment for Roxi.

Three hours into a dull work lunch with Owen and his colleagues and she had still not received a single notification responding to her post earlier that day calling for people to 'be better' in the aftermath of Jem Jones' death. She had left her phone in the car and was relying on her Smart watch to alert her to the response she had hoped for. She had checked and rechecked its settings many times but there was nothing wrong with it. She had to face facts – nobody was interested in her opinion.

'It's early days,' said Owen as the event drew to a close and they returned to the car. 'It might take a few days for people to see it.' His sympathy felt forced, she thought.

'That used to be the case for social media but not these days,' Roxi replied. 'If you're not gaining traction in the first hour, you might as well not have bothered.'

'Perhaps people don't like your message.'

'What, that we all need to start being better? Who wouldn't like that?'

'Do you even believe it?'

'I said it, didn't I?'

'You also once posted that you couldn't live without rose-scented toilet bleach you'd been paid to promote. Did you believe that?'

'That's different. Suggesting every single household should be made to record their conversations is a valid and controversial talking point. Why aren't more people up in arms over it?'

'Maybe they think you're only saying it to get a rise.'

'Do you have to be so bloody pessimistic all—'

Roxi was interrupted by a vibration on her wrist. It was followed by another, then another and more. The watch face revealed hundreds of notifications and a handful of missed calls. 'What the . . .' she began before realizing her watch had been too far away from her phone to receive any updates. She grabbed her phone from the glovebox and hurriedly scrolled through it, then held it to her ear.

'Look, tomorrow is Saturday,' Owen continued. 'Let's go out for the day, the four of us. Catch the Express to London. We can be there in twenty-five minutes. I'll make us a reservation on the South Bank for lunch then we can go into town and do some shopping. Make a day of it.' His wife was too distracted to respond. 'Rox? Rox?'

Her attention was fixed on a voice note. 'Sorry, I have plans,' she said.

'Doing what?'

A smile unravelled as Roxi moved her phone from her ear and showed him the screen. 'Because of this.'

She pressed play for a second time, this time on speaker mode. 'Hi Roxi, it's Dani Graph here, a booker for Sky News. I spotted your very passionate Instagram TV post and wondered if you'd like to come on our midday show tomorrow to talk more about it? Please call me back as soon as possible.'

Roxi clutched the phone to her chest. 'This is it, Owen! This is where it all begins.'

She was too preoccupied with the future to register her husband's present, muted response, or the palest of red lights on the car's console recording their conversation.

15
Corrine

Corrine was standing under the porch outside the front door of the home she had shared with her family for the last twenty years. Each of the extensive three-storey townhouses surrounding hers in this much sought-after area were identical, from their internal floorplans to their duck egg blue-coloured garage doors. Their landscaped front gardens maintained the same species of plants and a carboncapturing English oak tree had been planted in the centre of each manicured lawn. Every rear garden contained a solar panel-heated swimming pool and summerhouse. Every property was indistinguishable from the next. Except – briefly – for hers.

Seventeen months ago, Corrine had, on a whim, repainted her front door. It was no longer duck egg; instead, she had chosen Anderson blue. The difference was subtle and the neighbours had not noticed until an eagle-eyed security patrol officer clocked it. First the concierge had called asking if there was a problem with the original colour, then a letter arrived from the estate's management company offering to repaint it for them. Corrine politely declined. Within a month, each of her neighbours' front doors had instead been painted Anderson blue by the estate board. It had been a small but important victory for Corrine. The objector inside her who had remained dormant for half a lifetime was awakening. And it never went back to sleep. Today, she was certain that she wouldn't miss this house or those around it once her and Mitchell's divorce was granted.

An alarm on her watch sounded. She had set it for eleven a.m. to remind her it was time to shift from the world of her friends and family and into another that she kept hidden from them. How much longer she could remain with a foot in both camps, she couldn't be sure. The Eleanor Harrison disaster had made her question her confidence in her own decision-making. Earlier that morning she had once again monitored online news sources for an update on the MP's condition, and she'd been relieved to discover Harrison was stable. But Corrine had yet to determine the condition of Nathan, the unconscious young man she had left outside the hospital ten days earlier. He was the real casualty of that night. Perhaps the others she was going to meet might have answers.

Corrine waved or smiled to each neighbour who passed by on foot or by wheel then directed her attention towards a house opposite. Of all the neighbours who had moved in and out over the years, it was Maisy she missed the most. She had been the life and soul of that street, a force of nature and fiercely loyal friend and wife. And it pained her that no one ever spoke of her friend any more. Each time Corrine tried to bring her name up, she was shut down, almost as if talking about her might befall a similar fate upon those who reminisced.

Maisy had been closer to her than any of their other

neighbours so her unexpected diagnosis of advanced cervical cancer hit them both like a punch to the face. The Government's lack of regular NHS funding meant a two-month wait for a specialist's appointment. It was only when she'd asked her husband Derek for their private health insurance details that he'd been forced to admit they were no longer covered. He had lost most of their savings in bad investment opportunities.

There was a solution, he'd said amongst the tears and upset, and that was to upgrade to a Smart Marriage. Its benefits included better healthcare on NHS+. But first they would need to divorce. That arrangement would only remain for twenty-four hours before their application was approved and they could Upmarry.

Maisy, true to form, had made an event out of it, inviting their friends to the house and hiring a celebrant to officiate in the garden under an arch made of white roses. However, the only invitees who'd failed to attend their rewedding on the day itself had been the groom and his best man, Mitchell.

Maisy had been beside herself with worry, convinced that something terrible had happened, but Corrine hadn't been so sure. 'Tell me you took out the twenty-four-hour marriage gap insurance to protect yourself,' she had asked Maisy.

'I don't need to,' her friend had replied. 'I mean, it's Derek. What's he going to do? Change his mind?'

But that's just what he'd done, which Maisy had learned soon after in a lengthy text message. He'd explained that after witnessing both his parents die of cancer-related illnesses in his youth, he could not watch his wife succumb to the same fate, even though her death was far from a certainty. He'd completed his confessional by informing her that, hours after their divorce, he had spent the morning at the Guildhall Register Office marrying his secretary. Mitchell had been his best man. 'I have to think about myself if you don't make it,' Derek had written. 'If you pass away within the first six months of our remarriage, I'll have to repay all your treatment costs. I don't have the money.'

The law, which favoured couples over singletons, ensured Derek and his new wife could begin their new life together in his old home and Maisy was forcibly evicted by bailiffs soon after.

'I want her to stay with us until she gets back on her feet,' Corrine had told Mitchell. She was still furious with him for keeping Derek's secret. He'd laughed at her request.

'Like hell she is,' he'd replied.

'Mitchell, you owe her. There's plenty of room in the summerhouse. You won't even know she's here. She's our friend.'

'No, she's *your* friend. Derek is my friend.'

'So if it was the other way around and I refused to let him stay, what would you say?'

'I wouldn't ask because I wouldn't want him here either. Positivity breeds positivity and vice versa. And I don't have room in my life or my business for anything that drains it.'

Meanwhile, Maisy's distress at the break-up of her relationship swiftly shifted to anger and determination. She was going to defeat the disease and prove to Derek what a huge mistake he'd made. But her bitterness also extended to many of their mutual friends who, fearing divorce was contagious, abandoned her. Her messages went unanswered, her social media unfollowed. Corrine was the exception, meeting with

Maisy regularly despite Mitchell's reservations. But, gradually, Maisy's increasing dependence on alcohol to numb her emotional pain made her cutting and mean-spirited. Even after her successful cancer battle, she was in no mood to celebrate.

Almost two years had passed since a drunken Maisy had last hurled abuse at Corrine and demanded that she be left alone. Corrine had initially respected her wishes before she could stand it no longer and turned up unannounced on Maisy's doorstep. She'd found the one-bedroom Old Town apartment empty, an eviction notice pinned to the door. Soon after, Maisy's phone was out of service and Corrine's emails had bounced back undelivered. Corrine had found herself blaming Derek and the Marriage Act in equal measure.

Her friend wasn't the only person with a grudge against the world. Corrine was becoming increasingly frustrated at an unjust system that failed people like Maisy. When Corrine looked beyond the Government propaganda, she discovered thousands of others had also been forced to abandon their old lives because they either enjoyed being single or didn't want to upgrade to a Smart Marriage. Corrine could no longer, in good conscience, stand idly by without trying to help.

She donated money from her own bank account to charities dedicated to single-parent families. She ordered extra products on her shopping lists to donate to food banks and she joined a group of volunteers cleaning up litter and removing graffiti from areas in Old Northampton. And she kept it all far from the prying eyes of her increasingly estranged husband. Trying to explain to him her desire to help others would be as pointless as trying to teach a pig trigonometry.

But none of that ever quite felt like enough until she read about Freedom for All. It began as a faction opposed to the injustice of a divided society and aimed to capitalize on a growing swell of those negatively affected by the Act. In a few short years it had spiralled to become the Government's biggest opposition party and threat to their tenure. So, as Corrine's family were preoccupied with their own lives, she volunteered as a fundraiser. It was after befriending Yan, a woman of a similar age and social standing to Corrine, that she first learned of under-the-radar FFA splinter groups. They took direct action against their targets and, if Corrine was going to make a real difference, she understood that she'd need to dirty her hands. Which was how she had ended up with an unconscious boy in the back of her car and the blood of an injured MP on her hands.

The alarm on her watch sounded again. She zipped up her hoodie, climbed into her car and drove to an area of greenery on the other side of town. From there, she walked quickly along the paths, turning back on herself to ensure she wasn't being followed. Then she made her way across the border into Old Northampton, this disparity between rich and poor immediate.

She'd typically be brimming with nervous excitement for where she was headed. But this would be her first appearance since the Eleanor Harrison affair and she was consumed by anxiety. Eventually, she reached the most derelict part of the estate and the purpose of her journey. The Charles Bradlaugh was a former pub and restaurant but its walls were now daubed in anti-Act graffiti, its signage scattered in broken pieces across a car park overgrown with weeds. Shattered glass crunched under the heels of her trainers as she made her way along an alleyway until she found an entrance to the cellar.

She carefully typed in a code to a digital lock and, when it unclicked, she lifted the doors, entered and stepped carefully down a dark, steep staircase. Corrine used the torch on her phone to lead the way through pitch black until she reached a door. She nervously opened it.

As Corrine entered a second darkened room, she felt a draught behind her and heard the rustling of material. She didn't have time to process what it was before a pair of hands grabbed her by the shoulders and swung her around.

16
Arthur

Arthur spent ten minutes hiding behind a crack in the lounge curtains, taking his time until he had given the entire street the once-over.

He only unlocked and opened the front door when he was convinced that the Shrewsbury woman harassing June and him was not lurking outside and waiting to jump out and strike. He was short on disguises so wore a beanie hat to cover his thinning grey hair and reading glasses that distorted his vision as he walked. It was a weak look but it was better than nothing.

Arthur carried with him a reusable shopping bag and mobile phone. On the rare occasions he left the safety of their home, he was always sure to take his phone in the event June awoke disorientated. He would leave a landline handset on his pillow next to his mobile number written on a piece of paper. It hadn't changed in almost a quarter of a century but there was no guarantee that June would remember it.

It was a constant battle to maintain her interest in food. Chicken soup with rustic bread was a simple dish but her favourite, and in need of fresh air after hiding indoors for days after Shrewsbury's last uninvited appearance, he walked the mile or so to the nearest supermarket to refill the cupboard.

For most of their marriage, June had organized the household, he suspected the last generation of wives to do so. She'd also organized their online food shops and scheduled their deliveries. When she'd ordered three deliveries from one shopping list in the same day, it had been another indication that all was not well. She'd appeared relieved when he'd suggested that he took over the chore; it was one less thing for her to worry about.

Now, once inside the supermarket, Arthur made a beeline for the correct aisle but found only vegetable and minestrone soup left. And there was also no bread left in the baskets. He hated how shops in Old Northampton only seemed to get what New Northampton couldn't fit onto its shelves. But he was adamant he wouldn't be moving house. Despite the gradual eroding of his area, it was still his home.

'Mr Foley,' a voice began from behind. He turned to find a woman many decades younger than him with dark hair, pinched features and her hands on her hips. A small, stocky woman accompanied her. 'I'm Lorraine Shrewsbury,' she said, and his heart sank. 'I'm your court-appointed Relationship Responder. I've been trying to make contact with you for some time now.'

'I'm sorry but you have the wrong person,' Arthur replied and tried to shuffle away. He cursed a sharp, shooting pain in his knee, an injury dating back to fighting a fire in an office tower block. It was a constant reminder that he wasn't as nimble as he once was.

'Mr Foley, I know it's you,' she continued. 'But if you want me to prove it, then I can.'

She held up her phone and used an App to identify his face biometrically. It was a positive match with the image on his National Identity card. He shook his head but the game was up.

'I don't want to cause you any trouble, Mr Foley, but it is my job to spend time with you and Mrs Foley to ensure your marriage is in the healthiest possible shape.'

'We've been together for fifty-three years, forty-nine of them married!' Arthur snapped. 'Of course we're in good shape.'

'And I'm sure you're right and that everything is perfectly explicable. But under the terms of the Act, random monitoring indicates you have potential problems, which were only emphasized by further, longer recordings. And that brings me here. So allow me to spend some time talking to you and your wife and I'm sure that we can sort this out quickly and take you off the At Risk list.'

'I keep telling you that we are not at risk! My wife has been poorly. She repeats a lot of what she says.'

'I am aware of her medical circumstances. It's the only, as yet, incurable form of dementia, I believe?'

Even now, that word made him flinch. 'You can't judge our marriage on that. It's not her fault.'

'I know and that will of course be taken into account, I promise you. So let's return to your house and begin the process. The sooner we start, the sooner, hopefully, it will all be over.'

'Why do you need to be in the house?' He pointed to the

woman by her side. 'And what's she here for? To value it? Is she trying to take it away from us? Because you can't sell it, you know, it's ours. All bought and paid for.'

'Mr Foley,' Shrewsbury said calmly. 'May I call you Arthur? I need you to take a breath and try to relax. I only suggested your house because you'll probably feel more comfortable having a chat there than anywhere else. Plus we can discuss more about what Level Two involves and my role.'

Arthur's eyes began to well as fear gripped him. Shrewsbury offered him a paper tissue but he ignored her and used his own cloth handkerchief. He glanced around the supermarket and noticed shoppers staring at him as if he'd been caught shoplifting.

His empty basket fell to the floor with a clatter as he followed the two strangers, his arms trembling and his heart thrumming in his ears.

17

Jeffrey

'So let's start by turning off your monitoring, shall we?'
Jeffrey began and removed a key fob from his pocket. He
pointed it towards the Audite located in the corner of the
lounge. 'Recording off,' its automated voice said.

'Can you really just do that?' asked Luca. He and Noah
were sitting so closely together, their legs were touching.

'If I think it'll help, it's at my discretion,' Jeffrey replied. 'I
find that if you know you're not being recorded, you'll put
more into our sessions. And, ultimately, you'll get more out
of them. So I'll spend the first week getting to know you
and shadowing you to really get a sense of who you are as
individuals and as a couple. That will be followed by a week
of eight hour-long therapy sessions spread across each day.
We'll make a judgement on what happens after that when
the time comes. Have your employers given you the first
fortnight off as a paid sabbatical?'

Luca and Noah nodded.

'Great. Obviously, I've read your notes before we met but
I'd prefer to hear your story from you. Tell me yourselves
how you came to meet?'

'We were DNA Matched,' began Luca. 'I'd taken the test

first and then a few months later I got a notification that I'd been Matched with someone.'

'And how did that make you feel?'

'Relieved to finally be off the shelf?' asked Noah.

Luca rolled his eyes genially.

'I'm joking, of course,' he added.

'It felt, I don't know . . . good, I guess. Like relief, almost.'

'And was it love at first sight?' asked Jeffrey.

'For me it was, definitely,' said Luca; he patted Noah's knee. 'Everyone said I'd feel it when we came face to face and I did. We met for the first time in the cafeteria of the hospital where Noah was based – not the most romantic of locations – but as I'm in catering for an events company and he's a junior doctor working all kinds of shifts, we had to grab our opportunities when we could. And the moment our eyes locked, well, that was it for me.'

'And you, Noah?'

'There was a definite attraction there, but it took me perhaps a couple more dates before I caught up with where Ziggy was at.'

Jeffrey cocked his head at the name.

'Ziggy,' Noah repeated. 'It's my nickname for him. Didn't you hear me call him it on the Audite recordings?'

Jeffrey racked his brains. 'No, I don't think I did.'

'Anyway, do you remember that singer David Bowie? He had two different-coloured eyes like Luca does. And he created this Ziggy Stardust alter-ego back in my grandparents' day. They used to play him all the time. I called him Ziggy once and it kind of stuck.'

'And does he have a nickname for you?' Jeffrey asked Luca.

'Babe,' chuckled Luca. 'I'm not that creative.'

Jeffrey nodded. 'I assume by signing up with Match Your DNA that you were both looking for a long-term commitment?'

'That's all any of us want, isn't it?' asked Luca. 'You might have a career, a house and a family who love you, but what's the point when there's no one to share it with?'

Jeffrey's stomach hollowed.

'Well, millions of people prefer being single,' said Noah. 'I enjoyed it.'

'But there is nothing like that feeling of being totally loved by someone, is there?'

Jeffrey wanted to agree, but he had no experience to draw from. As Luca went on to describe their wedding and San Francisco honeymoon, Jeffrey briefly imagined himself hand-in-hand with his own Match, sightseeing the city, booking tables at the hippest restaurants and hiring retro bikes that required pedals to cycle across the Golden Gate bridge. But, try as he might, he was unable to picture the face of who was accompanying him.

'And is your relationship monogamous?' Jeffrey asked.

Luca turned to Noah, as if unsure of what Jeffrey wanted to hear.

'Is that an offer?' Noah winked. 'Kidding.'

'There's no judgement here,' lied Jeffrey.

'We have been since we got married,' said Luca.

Jeffrey checked his notes. 'So for nine months it's just been the two of you. And before that?'

'Does it matter?' Noah asked. 'The Marriage Act states that you can do whatever it takes to keep a marriage together and that includes, "inviting others to socialize in an intimate way if mutually agreed".'

'Uhuh,' Jeffrey replied. 'But studies by psychologists suggest polyamorous couples are less likely to remain in a long-term marriage than monogamous couples.'

'We aren't polyamorous, just horny!' Noah laughed; Jeffrey didn't. 'Look, we might've dabbled occasionally but it hasn't done us any harm. We love each other and we're happy.'

'That's not what your Audite thinks.'

Noah was about to reply but appeared to think better of it.

'The only way our sessions are going to work is with complete transparency,' continued Jeffrey.

'We no longer have an open relationship,' admitted Noah and averted his eyes to the wall ahead.

'And do I sense this isn't something you're happy about?'

'It wasn't my decision.'

Luca cleared his throat. 'It's not something I want to continue exploring at present.'

'If I'm being honest – which I'm assuming is what you want, Jeffrey – then I think marriage has mainstreamed us,' said Noah.

'Because straight couples don't have threesomes . . . ?' disagreed Luca.

'No, but we're in danger of losing our queer identity by mimicking heteronormative relationships. I don't want us to become pseudo straights.'

'I don't think I'm mimicking anyone.'

'I'm not saying you are; I'm saying we are in *danger* of it. I'd rather not play into the hands of the people who gave us equal rights because they wanted to normalize same-sex relationships. The best part of being gay is that we shouldn't have to be "normal". We should be making our own rules and living our own lives.'

Luca shook his head. 'That might have been the case once upon a time, but there is no "us" and "them" any more. Match Your DNA levelled the playing field. Racism, homophobia, ageism . . . they went out with fossil fuel engines, wild elephants and the ice caps. I don't want to be in an open relationship, not because I'm trying to play it straight, but because I no longer enjoy it.'

'And I respect that's how you're feeling at the moment.'

'Do you though, Noah?' asked Jeffrey.

His directness uneased Noah. 'Of course,' he said. His sharply folded arms suggested otherwise.

In less than an hour, Jeffrey had already found a chink in their armour. And he quietly wondered to himself just how much work it might take to make the chink expand.

Home | Politics | **Opinions**

Will A Smart Marriage Give Us All The Support We Need?
By John Russell, Deputy Political Editor

'Once you've chosen your one true love, we want to support you with the happy ever after.'

How many times did we hear this familiar slogan trotted out by Government ministers before the Sanctity of Marriage Act became law? Yet, three years later, many of us are still asking: how is our country *really* benefitting from these Smart Marriages?

Before the Act's legislation was passed, the United Kingdom was struggling as a global industrial player. Single living had caused a housing crisis and years of pandemics were a gigantic drain on the public purse.

We were told family was the answer, and without family society is nothing. They said: 'people don't have a purpose or direction; they are selfish as there is no one to work for but themselves. Single and divorced people are more likely to have physical and mental health problems and to be a drain on the NHS.'

And if you believed the Government's messages plastered across billboards, buses and social media, a country with more committed couples has a positive impact on its GDP. A more productive workforce equals less poverty, less crime and, as a result, better mental well-being for couples, parents and children. In theory, things should keep getting better from one generation to the next. Smart Marriages should be a no-brainer. Right?

Not necessarily. Because we have gradually seen that, by signing up and allowing those who rule us to control our behaviours, we are losing the essence of what it is to be free-thinking individuals. Ever-increasing numbers are being discriminated against and are having their fundamental rights eroded. The Government believes a hedonistic society is harder to focus. What they really mean is we are harder to control.

England has currently never been more divided. We are now a country made up of them and us. Surely that can't be a smart idea?

18

Anthony

'You know, most wives would be suspicious of the amount of time their husbands spend behind closed doors,' teased Jada as Anthony invited her into his home office. She carried a wooden tray containing small bowls of sushi dishes and two bottles of Japanese beer. 'But if you aren't coming out for a late lunch then a late lunch is coming to you,' she continued.

Anthony offered his appreciation with a kiss on her forehead. He didn't deserve a partner like her, especially when he kept her at arm's-length so much of the time. There was too much about his working life that he couldn't explain. And then there was his relationship with Jem Jones. She would never understand that. It was better and safer for her to live in ignorance than under a dark cloud of honesty.

She placed their food on the desk.

'Don't go thinking I'll be making a habit of playing the dutiful wife,' she added, 'but I know you have a lot on right now so I'm making an exception.'

'I'm sorry, I've totally lost track of time. Where's Matthew?'

'Ally and Marley took him to the virtual rowing centre.'

'I thought we were all going on Saturday?'

'It *is* Saturday,' Jada replied, to Anthony's immediate guilt.

He recalled its inclusion on the digital family calendar but events in Anthony's life were now measured in terms of days before and after he had killed Jem. Even before that, most of his family time was spent on catch-up, living vicariously through Jada's abridged anecdotes and airdropped photos of his son while Anthony put work before his family.

Jada sank into a sofa under the window where the blinds were always drawn. The spotlights briefly caught the silver St Christopher pendant she wore around her neck, which had once belonged to Anthony's mother. It was all he had left of her. She reached over to pick up a tekkamaki with her chopsticks while Anthony scooped at the rice. As they ate in a comfortable silence, Anthony glanced around the room. It was so sparsely furnished, it could barely be considered decorated. It contained a large oak desk with a keyboard projected on to it, his Audite and a monitor. The sofa was as white as the walls. There were no shelves for books or ornaments and it was strictly a paper-free environment, negating the need for trays, filing cabinets, a shredder or even a dustbin.

Jada must have been reading his mind. 'You know that this room goes against everything I stand for, don't you?' she said.

'It kills you that I won't let you in with a swatch, doesn't it?'

'Hell yes! It's a blank canvas begging for colour and texture. I don't know how you can work in such a sterile environment.'

'The lack of distractions allows me to think.'

The only subject he had been thinking about lately was showing few signs of abating. The more he tried to push

Jem Jones out of his head, the more she lingered. The creases around her eyes when he'd made her smile, the kindness of her heart, the way the bullet he'd fired had contained traces of her bone and brain matter as it had exited her skull. Had he done the right thing? Yes, yes, of course. At least he thought he had.

'But there's nothing to inspire you,' Jada continued.

'Therefore, all my ideas are my own.'

Jada shook her head, unscrewed a bottle top and took a swig from her beer. 'You need to remember to come up for air though, babe. You've been holed up in here for most of the week now. I know I sound like a broken record but you need to find a balance.'

'Once the next project is out of the way then I'm all yours.'

'Until the one after that. I know how this goes, Anthony; I wasn't born yesterday.'

He needed to redirect the conversation from his work, so he inched his head ever so slightly in the direction of the Audite.

Jada rolled her eyes and corrected herself. 'And we are grateful for how much of yourself you give to your work to support your family,' she added, as if reading from a prompter. 'But Matthew looks forward to being reunited with his long-lost father soon.'

The mention of Matthew stung. He was Anthony's weak spot. Anthony's mother had moved them from Saint Lucia back to her native England when her marriage to his father had fallen apart. She had also later made him watch her feed each photograph of his dad through a shredder until none remained.

Anthony was four years old when Anthony Snr had last been in touch. All he remembered of his father's appearance were the opal-coloured eyes they shared, which paired with their golden-brown skin, made them both stand out in a crowded room. From an early age, Anthony promised himself that when he had a family of his own, he would be there for them. Yet despite his best intentions, he was failing.

'How is Matthew?' Anthony asked.

'He's fine,' Jada said, but there was something rehearsed about her response. He rested his chopsticks against his bowl. 'Honestly?' he asked.

Jada took a moment. 'I didn't want to worry you but he's been struggling again at school.'

'Define struggling?'

'Same as before. He's finding it hard to concentrate on subjects that involve sitting and listening for prolonged periods. He becomes disruptive. He has no problem with gym, arts, design and technology because his body or his hands are moving. And coding classes where he gets to think and be creative – well, he takes after you with that. But English, geography, history and maths . . . that's when his ADHD kicks in and he starts losing attention and distracting the rest of the class. You saw him at lunch with my sister and Marley; he couldn't keep that phone out of his hand for a minute.'

'All kids are like that.'

'Not to his extreme. And have you tried keeping his focus on homework lately?' They were both acutely aware that Anthony had not. 'It's easier herding bees.'

'What about all those coping mechanisms his therapist gave him? Is he using them?'

'Some, but not often enough.'

'Maybe his teachers are exaggerating the extent of the problem. He's still only seven so his concentration skills are finite.'

'This goes beyond how long he can concentrate for.'

'So let's hire a tutor or find him another, better therapist, look outside of the NHS+.'

Jada shook her head. Anthony knew by her expression what she wanted him to say. 'I'm not medicating him because he has a short attention span,' he said firmly.

'Treatments today aren't like what they gave you at his age. We won't be pumping him full of drugs.'

Anthony was adamant in his refusal to medicate Matthew. He didn't want him to suffer the side effects he had endured like mood swings, jitteriness and lack of creativity. He accepted the chemicals in these tablets had been recalibrated since he was a boy, but the idea of medicinal control didn't sit comfortably with him. Then two split-second flashbacks appeared of his mother. The first was from when he was a boy sitting next to her in the waiting room of a doctor's surgery; a second, unrelated one, was the last time he ever saw her, formally identifying her body on a mortician's slab.

'It's just a patch he'd wear on his arm when he feels like he's being overloaded,' continued Jada. 'The App to control it would be on his phone; he'd be in charge of how much help he needed.'

Anthony shook his head. 'Medication slowed down my creativity and turned me into a zombie. I don't want that for Matthew.'

'I get that, and no one ever asked you how you felt or if

you wanted help.' Jada placed a hand on his. 'Have you ever sat down with Matthew and told him what it's like for you? I've told him it's okay to be different but it would mean more to hear it come from you.'

Anthony bristled. 'Isn't that why he went to therapy?'

'It's not the same as hearing it from his daddy.'

Anthony retracted his hand and put his tray of half-eaten food on the floor. 'You're guilt-tripping me.'

Jada opened her mouth to reply but appeared to think better of it. Aware once again of the Audite, she changed tack.

'All I'm suggesting is that it can't do any harm if you were to let him into your life more. Next Wednesday, book the afternoon off work. Matthew has a half day at school and you can go swimming or take a bike ride around Pitsford Reservoir. He needs to know that even if you're busy, you're here for him.'

'I can't, I'm in New Birmingham for a meeting,' he replied. It was only a partial lie.

'Can't you do a video conference?'

'It needs to be in person.'

Jada's tone suggested she was trying her best to keep her enthusiasm buoyant. 'The weekend then?'

He was about to argue again but changed his mind. 'I'll see what I can do,' he conceded. It placated her for now. They finished their meal together, and Jada placed their empty dishes back on the tray and made her way out of his office. 'I love you,' she reminded him.

But Anthony couldn't help but notice how, when she said

it, her eyes flitted for the briefest of moments towards the device between them rather than him. It was as if she was hoping that, if their conversation was being monitored, it had picked up on what she had said and not the perceptible tension hanging in the air.

19
Arthur

The car journey to Arthur's house was brief. It had almost taken him the same time to pull his stiff joints from the rear seats of Relationship Responder Lorraine Shrewsbury's vehicle and back out onto the pavement. A distant version of him would think nothing of carrying a 220lb unconscious man over his shoulder. Now he struggled with a shopping bag. Aging was a complication he could do without.

His hand was trembling so much that it took three attempts to type in the code before his front door unlocked. Once it was open, he and his two uninvited guests came to a halt in the hallway.

'Are you proud of what you do?' he asked Shrewsbury. 'Interfering with people's lives? Harassing people? Making untrue accusations?'

'No one is saying you're guilty of anything, Arthur. But it's my job to help people when they need it, even if they don't immediately realize it. Where's Mrs Foley?'

'She's gone out.'

Shrewsbury removed a tablet from her handbag and scrolled through it. 'According to our medical notes, your wife is bedbound and non-communicative.'

'Who's there?' came June's voice from upstairs. Arthur's

eyes moved in her direction. 'Arthur?' she repeated. 'Is that you?'

Shrewsbury's eyes followed his then switched to her colleague. 'Can you confirm she's all right and explain who we are and why we are here?' she asked the woman.

'Don't you touch her!' Arthur shouted. 'Don't you bloody touch her!'

'She won't, Arthur, I promise you,' Shrewsbury replied. And for the first time, he recognized sympathy in her expression.

She continued to talk but Arthur had stopped listening. Instead, his eyes were drawn to a framed photograph on the wall of him and June in their uniforms. Decades before genes dictated who your perfect match was, he had known June was the one the day she was transferred to his station.

'Lorraine, could you join me for a moment, please?' her colleague's voice came from upstairs.

'I'll be back in a moment,' she directed to Arthur.

'Don't scare June,' he said anxiously. 'She'll be confused; she won't know who you are.'

He followed her, but by the time he also reached the top of the stairs, then the doorway to the bedroom, it was too late. They were staring at his wife, trying to make sense of her.

'Why are they in our room?' June asked him tearfully. 'You promised me they wouldn't take me away! You promised I could stay here, with you, Artie. We didn't tick the box! We didn't tick the box!'

'No,' he said firmly. 'They're not going to take my girl anywhere.'

Lorraine and her colleague looked to each another, then

at Arthur and back at one another again. Finally, their attention returned to June and her dead body. She was wrapped from head to toe in the same stained duvet she had been inside for the last seven months, bound together by parcel tape and rope.

Before Arthur's legs gave way, he pushed his way towards his wife and collapsed on the bed, wrapping his arms around her.

'Please don't take her from me,' he begged. 'Don't separate us. I'm begging you. Just leave us alone.'

20

Roxi

Roxi shifted from buttock to buttock, trying to find a comfortable spot on her seat. She'd drained a can of antiperspirant before leaving the house yet she was convinced she could feel a thin film of sweat emerging across the sweetheart neckline of her dress from the heat of the studio lights.

She tapped her fingernails together but they felt naked without their acrylic tips and colourful polish. Jem Jones had favoured a more natural appearance and now so must she. She rested her hands on the desk, then held them by her side. She crossed and uncrossed her legs, but was unsure what to do with her arms. She was developing a new-found respect for those who made sitting in front of television cameras and an audience of millions appear the most natural thing in the world.

Moments earlier, she had felt a little star-struck when the runner who'd led her into the studio had introduced her to TV news stalwarts Esther Green and Stuart James. They were friendly, but not so much the figure at the other end of the desk. Howie Cosby was a surly, controversial and verbally combative Freedom for All party spokesperson. In her naivety, Roxi had assumed she'd been invited to appear alone. His presence suggested there might be more to it than that.

'Our next guest is Roxi Sager,' began Esther. 'She is a Vlogger and Influencer who, in the aftermath of the death of her friend Jem Jones, believes all homes should have Audites installed and the Government should have the right to record anyone's conversations.'

Goosebumps skittered across Roxi's arms on hearing herself described as an Influencer. And while it would do no harm to be considered Jem's friend, the extent of their relationship had involved Roxi commenting on a handful of Jem's YouTube videos and Jem once posting a thumbs-up emoji in response. Roxi had no intention of correcting Esther.

'A recent post by Roxi suggests that by expanding the use of AI in monitoring us all, we are more likely to think about our behaviour before we do or say something harmful. Roxi, can you tell us more about this?'

The film of sweat had developed into beads trickling down Roxi's back as she cleared her throat. 'I . . . I th-think the world is . . . um . . . is becoming a crueller place than it w-was, say . . . um . . . twenty or thirty years ago,' she began. 'And um . . . social media is to blame.'

Beneath the desk and away from the view of the lens, she pinched her thigh to keep her focused.

'I . . . um . . . think my friend Jem's suicide is proof of that. She was hounded to death because of it. We have seen how successful the Sanctity of Marriage Act is. Couples don't . . . um . . . jump down each other's throats now saying cruel stuff; they think about what they're going to say if they disagree. They respect one another. I'd like to see that extended to other aspects of our lives.'

'And the threat of being recorded will do that?'

Roxi nodded. 'It's a reminder, not a threat. And yes, I think it will.'

'Howie Cosby,' began Stuart James, turning to Roxi's sparring partner, 'you can't deny that Jem Jones was bullied to death, and, by all accounts, much of it came from supporters of your organization.'

'There is little evidence to back up your claim, Stuart, but then I don't speak for every single person who believes in our cause. What I will say is that we don't condone bullying in any way, shape or form. However, we shouldn't indulge in kneejerk reactions to Jem's death. Increasing the scope of AI usage in every single British home, regardless of whether we want it or not, is Orwellian. You will be punishing the majority for the crimes of a minority. Our watchful state already has one of the highest totals of mass surveillance of internet traffic in the world under the guise of "containing civil unrest". To eavesdrop into all our conversations is another step towards the dissolution of freedom of opinion and expression. We should be able to speak our minds without retribution and censorship; otherwise it will mark the end of our open society.' He looked to Roxi. 'Are you a parent?'

She wasn't expecting him to speak directly to her. 'Y-yes,' she replied, nodding.

'Do you want your children to be free to speak their minds?'

Much of the time, she wished her daughter Darcy wasn't. 'Of course I do . . .'

'Your child won't be able to do that if your half-baked idea ever came to fruition. In the last two decades, nations all over the world – including Britain – have been logging and monitoring the communications of their people like never before. Our Government can already remotely hack into our devices, turn on our webcams or follow our keystrokes for mandatory data retention. And I haven't even touched on the internet service providers who harvest our data to sell on. The internet isn't the free space that it was originally supposed to be. The only thing we have left that can't be exploited are our thoughts and now you want to police them too. Artificial Intelligence is growing exponentially; it's out of control and we can't trust it. We should be putting the brakes on it or using it to make us more social and better communicators, to highlight and promote diversity and inclusion. Instead, we are giving it new ways to control us.'

Roxi's beads of sweat were now flowing like currents in the river Thames. She wanted to curl up into a ball under the desk. What she knew about AI you could fit on the face of a Smart watch. She had jumped into this appearance with no preparation or evidence to back up a statement she didn't necessarily believe herself. All she had wanted was a shot at fame, but she was out of her depth.

In a flash, her closest friend Phoebe's face jumped out at her. She was the most positive person Roxi knew, even when the odds were stacked against her. 'When life gives you lemons, grab the vodka and caster sugar and make limoncello,' she'd say. Roxi needed to be more like Phoebe.

'Have you ever seen someone being murdered, Mr Cosby?' she began with a sudden confidence.

'Err, no . . .'

'I have. My best friend FaceTimed me while her husband was attacking her and there was nothing I could do to stop it.'

Roxi looked Cosby straight in the eye as she recalled how Phoebe's call had arrived in the early hours one morning. Her friend had locked herself in her bathroom following another altercation with Irvine. Roxi had repeatedly begged her to leave him or, at the very least, put his violence on record with the police. Each time, she'd refused, claiming their DNA Match meant they were made for one another, despite their differences.

Roxi had watched helplessly on the screen of her phone as a hysterical Phoebe had feared for her life when the yelling and door banging had escalated. Owen had called the police as Roxi had kept trying to reassure Phoebe that help would arrive soon. The last image Roxi saw of her friend were Irvine's boots stamping on her face and sternum before the life had drained from Phoebe's body and the police had appeared.

'They hadn't upgraded to a Smart Marriage,' Roxi told the hushed studio. 'I believe that, had there been the presence of a recording device, Phoebe's husband may have thought twice about what he was doing. And even if it was too late for her, a recording could have secured a murder charge and not one for manslaughter and a pathetic four-year sentence.'

'I'm sorry for your loss,' Cosby began, 'But—'

'With respect, there are no buts,' Roxi interrupted. 'When it comes to the safety of vulnerable women, children and men, I don't care about civil liberties. You might think a right to life is less important than freedom of speech, but I don't.'

Cosby shook his head. 'That's not what I'm saying.'

'If you have nothing to hide, you have nothing to fear. And if your viewers agree with me, I'm encouraging everyone to embrace the hashtag #IWillBeBetterWillYou? Because if we are all better, we are all safer.'

The debate came to an end soon after but there were no pleasantries between Howie and Roxi off-camera as they left the studio.

'Be careful what you wish for,' he muttered without a goodbye.

Roxi removed her phone from her handbag. Her inbox was already filling with messages. She squinted, scared to read them, hoping they weren't all from viewers attacking her. But by the number of times she saw her hashtag, the majority were on her side. People were actually taking notice of her.

A voicemail appeared and she played it, expecting to hear Owen telling her how proud he was. Instead, it was an unfamiliar voice, synthetic in its delivery. A chatbot, she assumed.

'Good morning, Roxi Sager,' it began. 'After careful consideration, Audite has decided your marriage has reached a stage where it needs assistance. As a result, Level One constant monitoring has now been automatically enabled. Please access your Smart Marriage Guide for further information.'

What should you do if you suspect a friend's marriage is in trouble?

Do's ✓

DO ask them to stop confiding in you before they say something they might regret or that violates their spouse's trust.

DO report the couple to the Relationship Responder crisis line. Teams are in place ready to help within 24 hours and all contact is treated anonymously.

Dont's ✗

DON'T offer advice. With the best will in the world, you are not qualified to help. You wouldn't put out a burning building with a bucket of water, would you?

DON'T take sides. By sympathizing with one, you are blaming the other. Let AI and trained experts decide who is in the wrong and who is in the right.

DON'T keep what you know to yourself. Secrets are a danger to everyone. Tell the rest of your mutual friendship circle so that they can keep an eye on the troubled couple until professional help arrives.

HELP BRITAIN TO BUILD BACK BETTER

SMART MARRIAGE

www.smartmarriage.co.uk

21

Jeffrey

Noah had been holding court for much of the morning in a vegan cafe, regaling his audience of three with a selection of unusual cases he had treated since his junior doctor placement began in Old Northampton's accident and emergency department. But his plummy accent and desire for attention were beginning to grate on Jeffrey. Love was blind, and, in Luca's case, perhaps a little deaf too.

Jeffrey also found himself irritated by Noah's holding of Luca's hand on the table. In Jeffrey's experience, public displays of affection were more likely a result of insecurity and a need for the validation of others rather than a desire to express genuine affection. In contrast, Luca's PDAs felt honest. They were a couple with very different needs.

Jeffrey wasn't comfortable in his seat at the window. He clocked every person entering and leaving the premises, hoping not to find a mutual recognition. It was unlikely, as his appearance had changed a lot in the sixteen years since he had lived in the town. But it still made him uneasy. Perhaps taking on this case had been a mistake.

He had shadowed Noah and Luca, both together and apart, for the best part of a week, deciphering what made them tick and what divided them. And while Jeffrey believed that opposites attract, he also believed that, given the correct amount of pressure, they could also repel. Luca was the more introverted of the couple and the one with layers Jeffrey wanted to peel. The way Luca's lips uncurled when he spoke, how he threw his head back when he laughed . . . each individual nuance and physical attribute made for a highly desirable package.

There was much about Luca that reminded Jeffrey of Rosie, the first person he'd ever offered his heart to. There had been others since, like Tabitha with her salty laugh, Lachlan with his passion for impressionist art and Darnell and his love of the outdoors. He had fallen in love with each of them for different reasons, but they all had something in common – a shared disinterest in Jeffrey. Luca would probably be no different and there were only a certain number of times a heart could be broken before it became irreparable.

Jeffrey's only hope of finding happiness was if his DNA Match ever stepped forward. As soon as he'd turned sixteen, he'd sent off his mouth swab to register his DNA but his other half had yet to do the same.

Jeffrey swallowed back his attraction to his client and focused again on the conversation around the table.

They had been joined by Beccy, Luca and Noah's intended surrogate. She was a petite, good-natured woman in her mid-twenties with an array of monochrome, nautical-themed tattoos on her arms and hands. And it was clear she, Noah and Luca were close.

Jeffrey recalled how the pro-family Government believed the addition of children to a marriage bolstered a couple's commitment to remain together and encouraged their desire to provide for their offspring and, in turn, a better society and country. So it instigated tax breaks for families of up to three children, along with a programme introducing altruistic surrogates to potential parents who were unable to conceive naturally. When Luca and Noah registered their interest, Beccy, a mother of two and first-time surrogate, read their profiles and approached them via an official agency. After a three-month 'getting to know' period, followed by medical and psychological tests to prove their physical and mental compatibility, they had been given the go-ahead to begin the first of three free IVF cycles.

'Have we shown you the Pinterest board for the nursery?' Luca asked Beccy. He unfolded his phone and swiped through several pages of colour schemes and furniture. 'We're sending them to our interior designer Jada to see what she thinks.'

'You have me and your anonymous egg donor, so when do you start your bit?' Beccy directed to Luca, who Jeffrey had learned would be the biological father.

'You mean when does my husband sneak off into a private room in the fertility clinic for a wank?' Noah asked.

Jeffrey was the only one to feign his laughter. He didn't find Noah as amusing as Noah found himself.

'I'm dreading it,' continued Luca. 'Going into that little room while everyone outside knows what I'm doing. What if I can't . . . you know . . .'

'Hit the money shot? Blow your load? Make your baby batter—'

'Thank you, Noah! We get the point. But yes.'

'You're not normally shy. Remember when I filmed us? You were quite the unexpected performer.'

'Oh my God,' Luca muttered, his face reddening.

Jeffrey quietly wondered if he could hack into their Cloud and find it.

'Can't Noah go in there with you and give you a hand, so to speak?' asked Beccy.

'He'll just try and make me laugh. So no, I'll just have to put on my big boy pants and get on with it myself.'

'Don't forget to take the big boy pants off first,' said Noah. 'You don't want to be wringing them out into a Petri dish. Anyway, enough talk about my husband's sperm; who wants another coffee?'

'You've put me off a latte, so I'll have a tea, no milk,' said Beccy.

'Espresso, please,' said Jeffrey.

Noah and Luca rose from the table, hovering midway when they realized they'd be leaving Beccy alone with their Relationship Responder.

'It's okay.' Jeffrey smiled. 'I'm sure Beccy's not going to tell me anything I've not already learned.'

They smiled nervously as they made their way to queue at the counter.

Jeffrey waited until they were out of earshot before he spoke again. 'I did want to say what an incredible thing you're doing. They're very lucky.'

'Thank you,' Beccy replied.

'What was it about their profile that made you pick them?'

'It was their photo to begin with, which sounds really shallow, doesn't it?'

'No, not at all,' said Jeffrey. It was the same reason he had volunteered to work with them.

'They looked really happy together,' Beccy continued. 'You could see it in their eyes that they were made for each another.'

'So were you surprised when they told you they'd been put on Level Two?'

'They didn't say anything at first because they didn't want to worry me, but I knew something was off. They were talking to each other differently . . . like they were choosing their words more carefully. I thought they'd had an argument.'

'Do they argue much?'

'Oh no, that's not what I meant. It's just their way, taking the piss out of each other. Then I thought perhaps they'd changed their minds about the surrogacy thing or about wanting to team up with me and didn't know how to tell me.'

'I assume it doesn't worry you that you might be getting pregnant for a couple whose marriage is at risk?'

'No,' Beccy said confidently. 'Once you get to know the guys like I know them, you'll realize it's a big misunderstanding.'

'That's good to hear. I don't like to judge couples solely on what I've heard in recordings.'

'Why, what did you hear . . . ?'

'I'm sure they will make great dads. Luca seems particularly keen, doesn't he? A little more than Noah perhaps?'

'No, they're both really up for it.'

'I'm sure Noah will be on board more once they're taken off Level Two. However, Beccy, I wouldn't be doing my job if I didn't ask if you've considered what might happen if they are placed on Level Three?'

'But they won't be,' she said. 'Noah promised that he'll make you see that.'

He'll make me, *will he?* thought Jeffrey. He remained quiet to unnerve her.

'What . . . what will happen if they are Levelled up?' she asked eventually.

'A court may decide to divorce them and they'll be encouraged to find more suitable partners.'

Beccy shifted in her chair, as if this was the first time she had given it serious consideration.

'And what if I'm pregnant? I've been taking the fertility drugs and we're supposed to do the first donor egg transfer in a month. Will you know by then if they're safe?'

'You might want to hold fire. I'm sorry. I wish I could offer you some reassurance but every couple is different. And to answer your question, under the terms of your surrogacy agreement, if a marriage is dissolved before a child is born to a surrogate who is not blood-related to the child, then the child, in theory, could be put up for adoption.'

'But Luca would be the biological father. It would go to him.'

'It's up to the court's discretion whether a child is better off with a single parent or a married couple. And please be assured there are many approved couples out there desperate to adopt a newborn.'

'I couldn't give the baby up to strangers!'

'You could apply to keep it yourself, of course.'

'Me? I don't want another baby. I have two of my own; I don't want one that isn't related to me or my husband.'

'Look, you're probably right and this is all one huge

misunderstanding. I'm just offering you the facts. It's up to you how – or if – you want to proceed with the surrogacy process.'

A deflated Beccy sank into her seat as Noah and Luca returned with drinks and pastries. It was Noah who first noted her shift in mood.

'Is everything okay?' he asked.

'It's fine,' said Beccy and offered a half-smile. But the way she barely nibbled her croissant left Jeffrey in no doubt that she had lost her appetite for more than just her pastry.

Slowly, he was dissembling everything they had built.

STORY: MP for Newcastle Stefan Galbraith resigned last night after it was revealed he had been cheating on his wife with three different women.

Galbraith, 37, who sits on the Government's Ethics committee, made a brief statement apologizing and claiming he had made an error in judgement.

His affairs were exposed by members of Freedom for All, which has vowed to take to task all Government supporters of the Marriage Act for hypocrisy.

22
Corrine

Corrine's heart raced so fast she thought it might rupture as the hand that grabbed her shoulder spun her around.

The light from her phone shone directly into a pair of distinctive bright-blue eyes, 'David!' she gasped. 'Are you trying to send me to an early grave?'

'The biometrics on the security cameras have stopped working so I couldn't tell who it was,' he said gruffly. 'The others are waiting.' He pointed to the ceiling.

Corrine made her way alone through another door, up a familiar wooden staircase that groaned with each step, through an empty kitchen and into the disused pub's lounge. Dimmed lights and boarded windows prevented anyone outside knowing it was occupied. It had the air of an apocalyptic after-hours lock-in.

She took in the faces surrounding her. She was unsure how she might be received after what had happened to Nathan, a popular and frequent attendee. But they couldn't have made her feel any worse than she did already. She counted thirty people standing or sitting around tables and a low hum of conversation. They were there for a shared purpose – to fight against the Sanctity of Marriage Act as members of an underground Freedom for All splinter group.

A familiar voice caught her attention. 'Corrine, so glad you came!' Yan said and gave her a brisk hug. 'I've been worried. How are you?'

'I still have a little bruising but the swelling has gone down,' she replied, touching her lip. 'It's Nathan I'm concerned about. Have you heard anything?'

'I think Ferdi is about to update us,' she said as she pointed to a young man by the bar at the front of the room. His dirty blond hair was cropped close to his head and he wore a t-shirt advertising a band Corrine remembered from her youth but that he was far too young to know. In fact, she had years on most of the people there. What had happened to the fighting spirit of people her age? she wondered. The ones who had argued against foreign wars, protested Brexit and opposed the sell-off of huge chunks of the National Health Service? It had clearly skipped a generation. She could only hope her children would stand up and be counted if and when the time came.

'It's been a mixed week,' Ferdi began. 'While our Newcastle colleagues have had success in exposing Stefan Galbraith's bigotry, our own attempt to bring Eleanor Harrison to task failed to yield the same results.'

'It wasn't your fault,' Yan told Corrine, loud enough for Ferdi to hear, making her blush.

'No, no, of course not,' Ferdi added quickly, but Corrine was unsure if he was paying her lip service. 'But while the night didn't go as we'd planned – through no fault of our team – at least there's no evidence to suggest we were involved. And we plan to keep it that way.'

'Why?' asked David.

'The powers-that-be have decided that, from a PR point of view, we cannot be seen to be a part of anything that involves a violent physical attack.'

'But it was her fault,' said Corrine. 'You saw the video yourself.'

'Legislation following the murder of MPs in the past means any physical attack on them, no matter how lightly or badly they are injured, is seen as an Act of Terror. So as far as we are concerned, this has nothing to do with the FFA. We didn't sanction it, there was nobody from our group present.'

'Then Nathan has put himself at risk for nothing?' Corrine continued. Ferdi didn't respond. 'Well at least can you tell us how he is? Do you have an update? I called the hospital but—'

'You shouldn't have done that,' interrupted Ferdi.

'I used a burner phone.'

'It doesn't matter. You don't know who's listening.'

Corrine's eyes began to well and, needing a moment to herself, she exited the bar and made her way back to the kitchen area.

The role of her region's faction was to target self-righteous politicians who lent their support to the Act while hiding secrets of their own. Two years earlier, Parliament had amended legislation that meant their MPs Audites didn't record them, citing 'matters of national security'. They received the same benefits of Upmarrying but didn't answer to anyone until the FFA decided that wasn't fair. It took them to task for extra-marital affairs, corruption, and undeclared business interests through online exposés, harassment at public events and even mass protests outside their homes. It became Corrine's role to help coordinate the events.

And when the shocking behaviours of her own local MP, Eleanor Harrison – one of the most fervent supporters of the Act – were brought to her attention, she was desperate to hold her to account.

A voice startled her and she turned to see Ferdi at the door. 'You okay, Corrine?' he asked.

'Yes, I'm fine. I'm sorry, I shouldn't have become emotional.'

'It's understandable but please remember: you're not to blame for what happened to Nathan. Harrison is the guilty party, not you.'

'Thank you. But I still feel responsible. It's making me question if I should stay in the group.'

'Look, if you really want to check up on him, I might know someone who can help.' He lowered his voice. 'They used to be part of the Hacking Collective.'

'That group who took over those driverless cars a few years ago?' She recalled with distaste how the terrorist group had held to ransom eight drivers in autonomous vehicles and encouraged the public to vote who they would like to survive. One by one, those who didn't get the votes were blown up inside their cars. 'Aren't we already treading a fine legal line as it is without their involvement?'

'We are so far over that line that it's barely visible. But if it gives you peace, you might want to give them a call. However, only you can decide if it'll be enough to make you stay with us. And I sincerely hope you do.'

At that moment, Corrine couldn't be sure that it would, or if anything could bring her peace right now.

ACT 2

23

Arthur

The enormous steel construction cast a shadow over Arthur the moment he passed through the gates and entered the grounds. It was not what he had expected to see when he'd called ahead to make an appointment.

He had served in the Old Northampton branch of this fire station for most of his working life, having joined at twenty-two and remaining there until his retirement a decade ago at sixty-five. The drill tower he'd frequently ascended was a brick building with internal stairs, gaps for windows, doors and a flat roof. He and his team had spent many an hour running up and down it, practising different techniques. This construction, however, was a metal contraption, silver in colour and with corrugated sections. 'Another change, June,' he said wistfully.

At least the station was familiar. His late wife had also remained here for much of her career. And for some time, she had been the only woman. The role that gave June the most satisfaction was recruiting other young women and helping to instil in them the same dedication and determination that fuelled her. The maternal instinct she demonstrated towards them was a reminder to Arthur of how cruel it was that she'd been cheated out of motherhood.

As he recalled how hard she had taken their infertility diagnosis, Arthur slipped his hand into his pocket and fumbled with the bronze chip she had been presented with for her first twelve months of sobriety. She had wanted him to have it as a thank you for his unwavering support. He had treasured it for decades.

'Arthur!'

An enthusiastic voice returned him to the present. He turned and smiled politely at a man he didn't recognize. There was a pink raised scar on the side of his head, which had robbed him of a clump of hair.

'You probably don't remember me,' he said, offering his hand.

'I'm sorry,' Arthur apologized. 'My memory isn't what it used to be.'

'Mohammed Varma,' he continued. 'You helped train me back in the day.'

'Mo!' exclaimed Arthur, his face lighting up. 'Look at you!' The two men embraced and exchanged pleasantries.

'I'm still getting my head around passing my twenty-year anniversary. I'm an assistant chief now so I don't go out on calls as much as I used to. I'm swamped with paperwork instead.'

'It's really good to see you.'

Mohammed caught Arthur scanning the drill ground. 'A lot's changed since you were last here, I guess.'

'It certainly has.'

'Listen, I was sorry to hear about June. I didn't know her as well as some of the others, but she was one of the good ones. You both were. I hope you got the flowers.'

Arthur recalled the number of colourful bouquets that arrived the day of her funeral and nodded his gratitude. He wondered if his old colleagues knew of the whole story, his denial of her death, the refusal to let June go; that instead of reporting her loss, he had kept her body by his side in their bed for months. If Mo was aware, he said nothing. Instead, he jangled a set of keys in his hand.

'Health and Safety regs mean I'm not supposed to let civilians go up the tower but no one here is going to dob us in.'

'Thank you.'

'Are you okay going up on your own? I'm happy to carry you over my shoulder for old time's sake?'

Arthur laughed and reassured him he would be fine alone. As Mo unlocked the metal door, Arthur used one hand to steady himself on the railings, while the other clutched a shopping bag. 'I'll be in the station when you're ready,' Mo continued. 'Come and join us for a cuppa before you go.'

It took Arthur much longer to climb the five floors now than it did back in his day. He used to think nothing of running up two or three steps at a time whilst hauling heavy equipment. Today, he was breathless by the time he reached the summit.

Arthur leaned against the railings and absorbed the 360-degree view of the town he had loved and lived in all his life. There were more drones in the sky than birds and less traffic on the roads now that commuters carpooled in driverless vehicles. When online shopping eventually won its war against the town centres, much of the retail area had been torn down and replaced with modern housing in areas constructed specifically for Smart Marriages. As a result, much of the landscape was altering beyond his recognition.

Arthur and June had refused to relocate from the Old Town despite the upgrade opportunities their marriage brought. They were happy where they were. Until one morning when everything had changed. Without warning, June had quietly slipped away.

Up there on the fire tower, he recalled every second of it, as clear as if it had happened earlier that day. He'd placed the breakfast tray on her bedside table as he had every morning since she had stopped walking or talking and had retreated to their bed. As the Audite had opened the curtains and the glittering sun had poured in, he'd noticed her grey pallor and sunken cheeks. He had seen enough dead bodies in his career to know that June had left him.

Arthur hadn't tried to resuscitate her or restart that huge, wonderful heart of hers. Instead, he'd laid down next to her and run his fingers through her hair and stroked her cool, parchment-thin face. It was so unfair that June had developed the one variant of dementia that still had research scientists baffled. For seven years it had gradually been squeezing the life out of her, draining her body of energy and her mind of thoughts and memories. And when she'd lost her communication skills, he had started speaking for them both. However, even on her death, he hadn't been ready for the conversation to end.

Many times that fateful day, Arthur had ordered the Audite to call for help. Then he'd change his mind before the line connected. It wasn't only the fear of them taking her away that upset him, it was the repercussions of the Sanctity of Marriage Act and what would be expected of him as a widower. So things had to continue as they were.

He'd purchased two large bags of cat litter and apologized as he'd heaped it upon her to absorb any leakages before they could seep through the bin liners he'd been about to enfold her in. Then he'd rolled her up tightly inside the duvet and sealed it up with roll after roll of parcel tape until it was airtight. Finally, he'd purchased a dozen reed diffusers and air fresheners to scatter about the bedroom and landing.

Then Arthur had tried to put June's death out of his mind by carrying on as normal. For the most part, she was the June of old. He spoke to her as if she was there and imagined her answers. Occasionally the version of herself with the faltering memory would appear and he'd fill in the blanks. But, for the first time in years, they were their old selves.

He'd needed to fool his wearable technology for when it randomly recorded their conversations. First, he'd reported June's as faulty and unable to register her health statistics and movements. America's latest trade war with China meant Tungsten, the mineral used to create the devices and which was key to their ability to vibrate, was in short supply. He was warned it might take weeks to get a replacement. It would explain why there was no movement from her. Then at various times of the day, he'd played video recordings he had made of June over the years, hoping her voice would buy him more time. He had got away with it for months before an algorithm had finally recognized the repetition.

After countless Push notifications, Lorraine Shrewsbury, a Relationship Responder, sent her first email, then began calling before eventually turning up unannounced on their doorstep. It was her fault that Arthur and June were finally separated. While he had been sitting in a holding cell at Campbell Square police station, she had ensured authorities removed his wife from their home. And now that he couldn't see June, he couldn't hear her either. He still spoke to her often but the replies no longer came. For the first time since before they had met, over fifty years ago, Arthur was truly alone.

The rest of the week after June's discovery had been a blur. In line with all Smart Marriages, a fast-tracked autopsy of a spouse following their sudden death began and, three days later, an investigation into her potentially suspicious death was swiftly dropped. She had died of a dementia-related stoke. Arthur was released the day before her funeral, which, by law, should have been in the same week as her death.

Today, and five-storeys high, he took a deep breath and reached into his shopping bag. He removed a transparent ziplock bag containing a portion of June's ashes. The other half remained inside a wooden box on the passenger seat in the campervan parked in their garage.

The fire service was the family she had chosen and, along with Arthur, they had become her two greatest loves. Here, among friends, was the most fitting place to scatter half her remains. The rest he would keep at home with him. As Arthur shook the unzipped bag, a light breeze took June in its arms and carried her up into the air and out of sight. If Arthur possessed the physical strength, he might well have pulled himself over the railings in the hope the wind might catch him too. But that wouldn't be fair on his former colleagues.

So he remained where he was, eyes closed, reliving a cavalcade of memories until he was ready to make his way back down. One more flight awaited him when his Smart bracelet vibrated. He tentatively pressed play.

'Good afternoon, Mr Foley, it's Martin Warner from your solicitors, Hatchett & Moss. I've left several messages asking for you to call me but I'm not sure if you've received them. The Crown Prosecution Service has been in touch and I really need you to return my call at your earliest convenience.'

Arthur shook his head. After the police had released him, Warner had warned it might not be the end of the matter. And now it looked as if his troubles were set to continue.

24

Anthony

'What was this place?' asked Anthony. He struggled to keep up with the broad-shouldered woman striding up the staircase three steps ahead of him.

She placed a finger into her ear, listening to orders through an earpiece. 'Everyone who comes in here asks that question,' she said gruffly but without answering it. So he left it at that.

She hadn't said much earlier when she'd flashed him an identification card on the concourse of Euston station, then escorted him to an awaiting vehicle. They'd travelled in silence to a building on the banks of London's River Thames. The pungent odour of burned plastic that had struck him on the ground floor had faded with each storey climbed. It reminded him of the smell in his mother's car when he'd been allowed inside it after she had deliberately driven into the pillar of a bridge. He didn't know what had compelled him to want to sit inside the wreckage until he'd found her St Christopher necklace in the footwell.

Now on the third floor, Anthony's escort led the way through more heavy doors before reaching a near-empty room. A bank of empty phone sockets stretched in a diagonal line and a dozen broken desks and chairs with missing wheels were stacked up in the corner under smeared windows. Its condition didn't surprise him. Over the years, the meeting places altered but their condition remained predictably unkempt. He could only assume the majority of the Government's off-the-books work was completed far away from Westminster's prying eyes.

After surrendering all his electronics to the escort and undergoing a full body scan, Anthony pressed the pads of his fingers against a screen while reading from a script on a separate screen below it. Biometric devices scanned his eyes and speech patterns until they verified his identity. A final set of doors, this time constructed from thick metal, slid open to reveal an open-plan, windowless room.

Anthony took a seat amongst more than a dozen people sitting at tables pushed together in a U-shape formation. There were no visible phones or tablets, not even a notepad or pen. All but one of the dozen television screens attached to the walls were unplugged. Whatever this meeting was about, there was to be no official record of it.

He poured water from an open bottle into a glass as he scanned the room for familiar faces. Henry Hyde, the man who had recruited Anthony while he was still studying at university some fifteen years earlier, turned his head and gave him a nod. His face was ageless – he could be in his mid-thirties or mid-fifties. And he had always looked like this since he and Anthony had first met. His clothes were like a uniform, the same black suit, black shoes, white shirt and black tie every time. It was as if he was on permanent standby for a funeral. Close to him was MP Maddy Cordell, the Minister of State, her heels as sharp as her tongue. The rest were unfamiliar to him.

'Ladies and gentlemen, shall we make a start?' began Hyde, removing a remote control from his pocket. He pointed it at the screen and a live image appeared of Anthony's local MP, Eleanor Harrison. She was a no-nonsense Education Secretary whom, until now, he had yet to witness without her trademark bright-red lipstick. Today, however, she was make-up free and had bruising under her eyes and a cut to her head. He recalled reading about a recent hospital admission but he couldn't remember the details.

'I'm sure I don't need to update you on the events of Jem Jones' tragic death two weeks ago,' Hyde continued. 'Naturally, our sympathies lie with her family at this difficult time.'

A ripple of amusement spread across the room. Anthony was the exception. He wanted to shout at them, telling them to shut up and show some respect, but he knew how ridiculous it would sound. Instead, he quietly simmered until Hyde turned his attention to him.

'Had it not been for Jem's support and influence on the general public, I don't think it's inaccurate of me to suggest that we might not have won the last election with such a clear majority and pushed through the Marriage Act,' he continued. 'But times change, and so does public opinion. And once Freedom for All became a party in its own right, we had little choice but to up the ante. Jem was a sacrifice we were forced to make in order to direct support away from the FFA and back towards us. It was an appropriate conclusion to her era.'

'But *has* it concluded though?' asked Eleanor Harrison. 'I'd have assumed after her death, anti-Acters would be keeping a low profile. But it appears they're more prolific than ever.'

'Bloody Freedom for All terrorists are as bad as suicide bombers.'

'At least suicide bombers have the good manners to blow themselves up,' Harrison replied. 'The FFA keeps crawling back like cockroaches.'

'Let Jem's supporters and the FFA fight it out amongst themselves,' Hyde said. 'And if it quietens down, we will intervene to fan the flames and ensure the fire rages on.'

Anthony held his gaze firmly on the desktop. He didn't want to look up and witness the smug, arrogant faces of those surrounding him. He didn't belong here. None of them realized that, in killing her, he had lost a part of himself.

'The social media pollsters have assured us the majority of the public remains supportive of the Act and consistent in their blame of Freedom for All for Jem's "suicide",' added Hyde.

A man with his dreadlocks tied above his head snorted. 'Are they the same pollsters who predicted Scotland would remain in the United Kingdom after the referendum or that we'd be back in Europe by now?'

'Polling isn't an exact science and there's always a margin of error,' Hyde scowled. 'The electorate can be notoriously hard to predict.' He loosened the top button on his oversized jacket. 'Moving on to the matter in hand. And this is where you come in, Anthony. There is a new era of opportunity coming that we would like you to strategize. It is ambitious but necessary for the next stage of our country's growth. And it will have a direct effect on almost every single family, perhaps more so than the roll-out of the Audite.'

Filled more with apprehension than curiosity, Anthony

listened intently as Hyde revealed their agenda. And the more he heard, the more his fingertips began clawing at the arms of the chair, as if desperate to remain afloat in quicksand.

'So I hope that you are in agreement,' concluded Hyde almost an hour later. 'To futureproof the United Kingdom within one generation, this is the way forward.'

This time, Anthony's eyes flitted around the room. Some of the faces appeared to approve, but others were suspicious. He wondered if any quietly shared his outright distaste.

'Your thoughts, Anthony?' Hyde asked suddenly. 'I assume this is something that you can begin working on immediately?'

Anthony wanted to tell him no, that this was a step too far, that he could go to hell and find another puppet to do his dirty work. He wanted to rise to his feet, turn his back on them, walk out of the door and forget everything he had heard. He wanted them to know that in killing Jem, he had made a monumental lapse in judgement. That all he wanted was to return to his wife and his son, put the house up for sale and catch the first flight to Saint Lucia where they could start afresh and away from this madness. Only none of that was possible yet.

'Of course,' he replied, nodding his head in the same way he'd done for the last fifteen years. 'I'm sure I can.'

25

Corrine

'That isn't traceable, is it?' asked Corrine, a note of fear catching in her throat.

The person of indeterminable gender sitting next to her and hunched over a keyboard gave her a sideways glance as if to suggest it was a stupid question. Of course it wasn't traceable, thought Corrine. As a former member of the now defunct collective, this person had escaped arrest despite a worldwide hunt for all associates. They were not an amateur.

'What's the kid's name?' they asked in a well-spoken accent that belied their scruffy baseball cap, jeans and army fatigue jacket.

'Nathan, but I don't have a surname.'

Corrine couldn't follow what was being inputted, but it appeared to be some kind of coding. Moments later, the logo for Old Northampton General Hospital appeared on their screen. 'Nathan Deakin,' the hacker continued, reading from it. 'Admitted after being found outside the hospital's A&E department by junior doctor Noah Stanton-Gibbs on his way to start a shift.'

'Yes, that's him,' Corrine said eagerly. 'What's his condition?'

'As of last night, stable but still unconscious. A toxicology report found compounds of three drugs in his system – one

135

a kind used for anaesthesia, another a hallucinogenic, and the other . . . oh, this is interesting, a drug that treats male impotence.'

'So what's going to happen to him now?'

'Do I look like a doctor?'

Corrine hesitated. 'Are you able to access the records of someone else?'

'Who?'

'An MP. Eleanor Harrison. She'll have been taken to the private hospital in New Northampton.'

It took even less time for the hacker to access Harrison's records. 'She was discharged following a minor head injury.'

'That can't be right. You must be looking at a different Harrison.'

'It's the only one I can find listed.'

'How did she recover so quickly? Only last week, the news reports said she was in intensive care. They reported her condition as serious.'

'And that's the first time an MP or her people have ever lied, right? It says here that it was a minor injury to the supraorbital foramen – which is near an eyebrow, I think – and they released her the next day.'

Corrine shook her head.

'Anything else you want while I'm here? Passcode to Downing Street? A list of all members of the Illuminati? They *do* exist, by the way . . .'

'No, but thank you.'

The hacker nodded their head and rose to their feet. 'Check your phone,' they said. Corrine glanced at the screen. It contained a telephone number with a message attached. 'Memorize it if you need me again. It erases itself in twenty seconds.' Corrine did as she was told as the text and the hacker vanished.

Alone, she sipped her now tepid coffee. She lifted her phone again, accessed a folder in her Cloud entitled Decoration Ideas and opened a video clip she had hidden from prying eyes. She had not viewed it since recording it. The footage was shaky and lasted approximately ten minutes. One particular moment caught her attention. She rewound it twice more then paused it.

There, in Eleanor Harrison's apartment, Corrine saw her own reflection in the mirror and Harrison's unconscious body lying on the floor below her. Blood dripped from Corrine's hand.

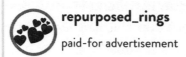

26
Roxi

The tinny, repetitive hold music that played on a loop wasn't helping to lift Roxi's irritable mood. Her phone lay on the dining-room table, the melody from its speaker filling the silence between her and Owen. Both stared at it, waiting to hear another person on the line speak again.

She distracted herself by re-reading the digital ad that had appeared in her inbox last night. It was her first paid collaboration, a national advertising campaign promoting recycled wedding rings. But the shine had been taken off the significance of the opportunity by the current circumstances and the interminable wait on hold.

'Why's it taking so long?' Roxi asked.

'No idea,' said Owen and moved towards the boiling water tap to make them both tea. 'But you know that even if you do get to talk to someone, they're not going to tell you anything.'

'I bet that it's your fault we're on Level One.'

'Mine?'

'Yes! It picks up on negativity! It knows when a spouse isn't being supportive. And God knows it's had plenty of material to pick up on lately.'

'Because you're so easy to live with, aren't you?'

A voice interrupted them. 'Audite customer service, thank you for signing up to a Smart Marriage. How can I help?'

'I've just explained this to your colleague,' began Roxi. 'Our machine must be faulty because it's told my husband and me that we're being Levelled up.'

'Oh, I'm sorry to hear that; it must be distressing for you both. Let me take a look at your account. I'll pop you on hold for a moment.'

'Argh!' Roxi yelled as the hold music returned. 'I don't have time for this.'

'Why, do you have something more pressing to deal with than our marriage?'

Roxi gave his dig the narrow eye it deserved. 'BBC News and that woman who presents the daytime morning show both want me on to discuss my video last night calling for Audites to be installed in all social housing.'

'Oh, Rox.' Owen sighed. 'Why are you picking on social housing?'

'I'm not *picking on* anyone; I just think that if you're jobless or only working part-time and given a council-owned house, you shouldn't be lying in bed until ten a.m. You should be out there looking for more work or at least a better-paid job. Audites can keep them in check.'

'*Them*? They're not cattle. And who is going to keep your opinions in check?'

A voice appeared on the line again. 'Audite customer service, thank you for signing up to a Smart Marriage. We've done a full system sweep and a reboot and it doesn't appear there's anything wrong with your device.'

'Then why are you Levelling us up?'

'I'm not privy to that information, I'm afraid. That's for a different department to discuss. Would you like me to transfer you?'

'Yes.' Roxi groaned and the hold music returned.

She picked up her tablet to examine today's insights. There had been significant uplifts in her TikTok, Instagram and Facebook followers and her #IWillDoBetterWillYou? hashtag had been reposted more than 3,000 times on Twitter in the last hour alone. The majority of Tweets were supportive, particularly from victims of domestic abuse. There were also comments from friends and relatives of those killed in terrorist attacks who believed if conversations between British radicals had been monitored, lives might have been saved.

But scattered amongst them was a predictable amount of abuse. Roxi's attendance at school had been patchy but even she knew it was unlikely she could simultaneously be a fascist and a communist.

'Who is giving this crazy fucking ho airtime?' read one message.

'Any volunteers to make her Audite listen in as we fuck her up?' came another.

'Bitch needs 2 b cancelled or she'll be the next Jem Jones', read a third.

She reported them all after reposting them with her trademark hashtag and a smiling emoji, just to irritate them further.

However, there was one comment on her YouTube channel that caught her attention more than the others.

'Why are we even giving oxygen to this pathetic, wrinkled middle-aged housewife?' it read. 'She's a failed Vlogger in a loveless marriage trying to jump into Jem Jones' shoes while they're still warm. Stick to flogging toilet brushes and verruca treatments, old timer.'

The troll was clearly familiar with her early Vlogs. She was unaware of the username @JustSayingBabe so she took a closer look. Roxi was the first and only target of their abuse.

Yet another voice appeared from her phone but with the same enthusiasm and opening line as the previous two. 'I believe you are enquiring as to why your marriage has been flagged as Level One?' they continued.

'Yes, I am,' Roxi replied.

'I'm afraid I am unable to give you that information.'

'Why not?'

'As stated in your Sanctity of Marriage Act contract, we are not obliged to detail why our algorithms have identified your relationship as in need of assistance.'

'So you think my marriage is in trouble but you won't give me any evidence as to why? How are we supposed to sort out the problems you think we have if we don't know what they are?'

'Enhanced listening and tracking has now been enabled across all your fixed and wearable devices to assist in your marriage experience. Advice in the form of Push notifications will be sent to you regularly. Any new content posted across social media by yourself or others, or taken in public areas using facial recognition software, may now be used for consideration when deciding upon the next course of action. A marriage liaison officer from your employer has been notified and will be in touch in due course. Thank you again for signing up to a Smart Marriage.'

The conversation was terminated by the operator before Roxi
had time to hurl expletives at her. Owen remained unruffled.

'Are you kidding me? That's it?' she complained.

'It's what we signed up for.'

'What we signed up for are tax breaks and a larger Smart
home, so where are they? Have you chased up why we
haven't been upgraded yet?'

'Plenty of people would give their right arm for this place.'

'Let them and their missing arms live here then, not us.'

'And we haven't been upgraded because the new houses
are still being built.'

'And is the car you promised me still being built too? I'm
sick of carpooling with the neighbours, booking a week in
advance just to go out if you're using yours.'

'You're helping reduce the number of vehicles on roads,
which is a good thing—'

'I don't care!' she seethed. Roxi held her head in her
hands. 'You don't get it. If this Levelling up thing gets out,
it's going to damage my reputation just as things are starting to happen for me. How can I tell people that AI is going
to save us all when the bloody thing has turned against us?
It could ruin me.'

'Have you considered that it might also repair us?' asked
Owen, but Roxi didn't get the chance to respond.

'Don't spread yourself too thinly in a dozen different
directions when your partner is trying to engage with you,'
the Audite spoke. 'Always remember, listening means loving.'

Level One had begun already.

'Piss off,' Roxi muttered as she stormed out of the room,
balking at the thought of weeks of more messages like this.

27

Jeffrey

'You told me before that it was love at first sight when you met, at least for you, Luca,' Jeffrey began.

He relaxed into a leather armchair while Luca and Noah were perched on a sofa opposite him, Noah on the left and Luca on the right. They had all become accustomed to these positions over their fortnight together. Noah's hand was once again placed firmly on top of Luca's as if marking his territory. The more Jeffrey tried to ignore it, the more it caught his eye and rankled him.

'You haven't turned the Audite off,' said Noah.

'No, I haven't,' Jeffrey replied.

'Why?'

'I did say it's at my discretion. It's not a given.'

Noah shifted uncomfortably, to Jeffrey's pleasure. 'So if it was love at first sight and you knew you'd be together for the long haul, why did you feel the necessity to marry?'

'Aside from emotional security and commitment, we'd been together for six years and wanted to have kids so it seemed like a logical step,' said Luca. 'We both come from close families and our parents are still together, so why not?'

'That's a great reason,' said Jeffrey. 'Many psychologists

144

believe a child's development can be strongly affected by how emotionally intelligent their parents' relationship is.'

'It was never a goal of mine to get married and I was honest with Luca about that from the start,' added Noah.

'Why?' asked Jeffrey.

'I think there's too much pressure on queer couples to marry. It shouldn't be a goal we're all expected to aim for. And I fear those who choose not to get married will think the rest of us regard their relationships as less worthy than our own.'

'So why did you agree to it?'

'Because it meant so much to Luca. Oh, and of course the benefits that no one is supposed to talk about.' He fastened an invisible zip on his mouth.

Jeffrey raised his eyebrows, as if unsure as to Noah's reference. He knew precisely what he meant, but he wanted to hear him say it aloud.

'The incentives,' said Noah. 'Tax breaks, private health insurance, no stamp duty, interest-free loans . . . no one ever admits it but they're the real reasons behind most Smart Marriages, aren't they?'

'I wouldn't say most, no,' Jeffrey replied.

'And it wasn't the driving force behind our getting married,' Luca clarified.

'So, Luca, you haven't benefitted from any of the practical incentives?' asked Jeffrey.

'Well, I guess so, yes, but . . .'

'And what if there had been no incentives?' Jeffrey continued. 'No subsidized mortgages, no living in a modern, affluent, regenerated area of town like this, no interest-free loans on the latest models of driverless cars like the ones parked on your drive? Might you have still taken the plunge?'

'Of course,' said Luca.

'Eventually, maybe,' added Noah.

'"Eventually",' Jeffrey repeated. 'So without these incentives, it's possible you wouldn't yet be married.'

'I'm not saying that. We might have at some point.'

'"At some point",' Jeffrey again repeated. He watched Luca withdraw his hand from under Noah's.

'Although I'm beginning to wish we hadn't,' Noah huffed and folded his arms. 'Because if we'd stayed as we were, we wouldn't be sitting here having our relationship picked apart by a stranger. And for what reason? We still don't really know.'

Jeffrey skimmed pages on the tablet with his finger before he spoke again. 'You're a bell end; you don't know what you're talking about; for fuck's sake, stop being a dick; I'm busy right now, can I ignore you another time? Are you an idiot? How long does it take to get a divorce?'

His clients appeared perplexed.

'They were all things you said to each other which your Audite recorded,' Jeffrey continued. 'Plus twenty-three "fuck offs," fifteen "twats", half a dozen "shut ups" and five "If you don't like it, tough".'

'You're taking them out of context,' Noah protested. 'That's what we do, we take the piss out of each other. We don't mean it; we laugh as we say it.'

'The data includes a "margin of error for sarcasm and riposte", but your conversation travels way beyond the parameters. And that is why a stranger is picking apart your marriage.'

Jeffrey's tablet chimed to alert them to their fifteen-minute scheduled break. All three rose to their feet. Luca's frown as he poured himself a coffee suggested an unresolved discontent, but Noah was harder to read until his face suddenly paled.

'Shit!' said Noah as he scrolled through his phone. 'Shit, shit, shit!'

'What's wrong?' asked Luca.

'It's Beccy, she's putting a hold on the surrogacy.'

'What? Why?'

'Why do you think?' Noah glared at Jeffrey. 'I told you he said something to her when we were in the cafe. She went very quiet.'

'Read me her message.'

'"Hey guys, I'm really sorry to have to do this to you but I've thought about it long and hard and I think we should put a hold on our journey until you two know what's happening with your relationship. Please don't hate me for it, but I'll be the one who has to make some tough decisions if I get pregnant and it doesn't work out between you two. You know how much I love you and once things are back to normal, we can get going again, I promise. Take care."'

A stab of guilt briefly struck Jeffrey when he registered the disappointment in Luca's face. However, instead of the couple comforting each other, Noah became preoccupied with apportioning blame.

'What did you say to her?' he fired at Jeffrey.

'Nothing that was factually incorrect,' he replied.

'Tell me.'

'Beccy asked me what would happen to the baby if she fell pregnant and you failed Levels Two and Three. So I told her the truth: that a magistrate might decide to allow one of you to keep the baby or they might order that it's put up for adoption. It's all in your Surrogacy Gateway.'

'But you didn't have to remind her!' snapped Noah before storming out of the room and the house, slamming the front door behind him.

Luca went to follow him before Jeffrey spoke. 'I'm sorry but I had no choice but to answer Beccy's questions honestly.'

'I know, but Noah doesn't like it when things are out of his control. And this Level Two situation is getting to him.'

Jeffrey suppressed his satisfaction and Luca moved towards the door. 'And how do you feel about Beccy's decision?'

'I respect it and I'm not blaming her. Or you . . .' His voice trailed off.

'You know, I'm not just a Relationship Responder, I'm also a good listener,' Jeffrey offered and placed his hand gently upon Luca's shoulder.

'Thank you—' Luca half-smiled '—but I should really find Noah.'

'Of course, of course,' Jeffrey replied.

But he was convinced that he wasn't alone in feeling the charge of electricity running between them.

28

Corrine

The thick waft of grey cigar smoke reached Corrine the moment she opened her front door.

She followed the trail of burning tobacco through the house and into Mitchell's den. He was on the sofa, bare feet propped up on a coffee table and watching a football match on a television screen that took up most of the wall. A box of popcorn rested on his lap and a bottle of beer lay by his side and fast-food delivery wrappers littered the floor. A half-smoked fat cigar rested in a semi-full ashtray.

'Could you at least let some air in?' she asked and pressed a button that opened the bifold doors.

'It's my room, not yours,' Mitchell replied without turning to look at his wife.

'But it's our house and the smoke travels through it.'

'Get the help to turn on the extractor fans.'

'Couldn't you have done it yourself?'

'There's a lot of things I have to do for myself these days.'

Laughter came from a speaker and Corrine realized there were others present in the room, albeit remotely. She slammed the door as she left, irritated at herself for allowing Mitchell to exasperate her.

As she made her way back through the house, Corrine

caught a glimpse of a moving image in a digital photo frame perched on a sideboard. It was of a group of friends she had barely seen since the night it was recorded at a silver wedding anniversary party last year. She was smiling in the clip – everyone was – but hers was as artificial as Mitchell's hair transplant. They were all around the same age but Corrine appeared older. She had given up on fillers and muscle-paralysing treatments in favour of growing old naturally. She didn't want to look like the others in the video with their breast implants, dermabrasions, facelifts, tummy tucks and designer vaginas. And she no longer cared about trying to impress her husband when he had long given up on her.

He wasn't the man she had fallen in love with. Back when they had first met, it was his personality, work ethic and ambition as much as his dark-brown curls, sharp blue eyes and solitary dimple on his left cheek she was attracted to.

'That bugger could charm the stripes off a wasp,' her mother had warned her. He'd certainly charmed Corrine the night they'd met through mutual friends. He was working for a team overseeing a number of major construction projects while she was a ceramics and art teacher at a local Academy. Two years later they married and she was pregnant by the time they returned from their honeymoon in Thailand.

By the age of 35, Mitchell had set up his own construction business and, two-years after that, his contracts earned him his first seven-figure payout. But his swelling coffers gradually became more important to him than his family. This was when Corrine first started to feel sidelined. However, rather than confront it, she made excuses for him, reminding herself he was throwing everything at his career for his family's sake. And she had been a willing participant in enjoying the financial spoils. At least another decade passed before she was ready to admit she had made a huge error in judgement and that they were drifting apart.

Corrine couldn't understand Mitchell's obsession with money and he didn't understand her lack of interest in it. For a long time, she'd tried to re-ignite that initial spark with offers to spend more time together to cure her feelings of isolation. Suggestions of romantic weekends away, restaurant dinners and spa breaks were all casually swatted away like flies. Corrine searched for signs he might still care – a touch of her arm as he passed her, an unexpected smile or even a compliment – but nothing came.

When Mitchell refused to attend couples counselling sessions, she went alone. On her move into the spare bedroom, she spent the first fortnight with the door slightly ajar in the hope he would appear one night and beg her to return. Instead, he bought himself a larger television.

It was when he dismissed her desire to return to teaching art and ceramics part-time that frustration got the better of her. Despite herself, she began creating arguments simply to prompt a reaction, for him to acknowledge that he could still hear her. Minor irritants developed into major issues; quirks became provocations. Bumps in the road had expanded into sink holes and his cutting wit left wounds.

'You don't have the first idea of who I am, do you?' she'd once asked him.

'Have you been listening to the self-help podcasts again?' he'd replied.

'Do you know what makes me happy? What scares me? What energises me? Do you know what stops me from sleeping or gives me nightmares? And if I told you, would you even give a damn?'

He'd rolled his eyes but said nothing. His lack of answer had been answer enough. There was no going back after that. She'd known it was time to take charge of her own life and her own happiness.

She wasn't alone, or so it seemed. Despite the stigma attached to divorce and the fact most of her friends were Upmarrying, an internet search revealed there were thousands of people who shared Corrine's feelings. It even brought her a little comfort to learn her circumstances had generated its own brand name – "Grey Divorce". Aging populations meant unhappy spouses weren't willing to remain in a marriage until death did they part. They wanted more for the thirty or forty years they had left and they were willing to start all over again to find it. Many used Match Your DNA to find who they were supposed to be with, but Corrine had held back, too disillusioned to believe in soulmates.

She thanked God they had never upgraded to a Smart Marriage. Old-school divorces were much easier to negotiate. Friends had often asked why they had not Upmarried. But even before she and Mitchell had discussed divorce, he had boasted there was no need to as they would barely notice the financial gains. She wondered now if the real reason was that he too knew their life together was waning.

When Corrine eventually informed him she wanted to end their marriage, there were no protests or attempts to change her mind. He didn't even question why. His only insistence was that she waited for six months until Nora and Spencer were to leave for university before they announced it. Their friends and neighbours would find out soon after. She doubted if many would remain acquaintances once they heard the news. Being friends with a divorcee was akin to having a contagious disease.

She had a little money put aside and, as a director in Mitchell's business, she was entitled to annual dividends and a healthy company pension. Monetary and property negotiations were minimal and kept between their respective solicitors until a settlement was agreed upon. Mitchell would keep the house. Corrine had no desire to rattle about it alone, penalized into paying higher utility bills and taxes because of her voluntary divorcee status. So she would downsize and start somewhere afresh in the next phase of her life. She would not need to work but she wanted to.

In the meantime, she and Mitchell continued to live together but apart. They disagreed over everything from immigration to education, politics to the environment and, more recently, the Sanctity of Marriage Act. Their debates often ended the same way: him hearing what she had to say but not caring. Then he'd offer a wave of his hand as if dismissing a waitress with a reminder that she didn't know what she was talking about.

Corrine reflected on the advice her therapist had given her during her solo marriage counselling sessions. 'When you're confronted by negative behaviours you don't like, try to find one positive. It doesn't matter how small it is. It'll be there if you look hard enough for it.'

Today's only positive was that, back in his den and surrounded by his diet of unhealthy foods, Mitchell hadn't died of a cholesterol-induced heart attack. Because then she'd feel the necessity to tidy up before the ambulance arrived. And she had better things to do with her time.

Safe Passage
Where your loss is your family's gain

Learning you have an incurable physical or mental condition is **heartbreaking** for both you and your loved ones. But so is worrying about the strain your ailing health will create for those you care about.

So, when the time is right, why not take the pressure off everyone – including yourself – by allowing us to make the inevitable **effortless**?

First, tick the **Safe Passage** box on your **Smart Marriage** upgrade documents. Then, if the unthinkable happens and you become unable to make your own rational decisions, your partner and **medical professionals** will decide when the time is right for us to assist.

You will be taken to one of our **beautiful countryside facilities** where you will be treated with respect and kindness by our fully trained staff to ensure your slip-away is brief and painless.

No one wants to be remembered as a drain on their family or our health services, and so allowing your loved ones to live a life without burden is the most **selfless** thing you can do.

SMART MARRIAGE

www.smartmarriage.co.uk

Safe Passage: we put the *you* in euthanasia.

29

Arthur

'Mr Foley,' began a young male secretary from the corner of a waiting room. 'Mr Warner is ready for you now.'

Arthur straightened his tie and made his way through a large set of frosted glass doors. He was greeted by his solicitor, a diminutive, round man with more hair on his face than his head. He put his hand out to direct Arthur towards two leather chesterfield sofas in the glass-and-oak-constructed office. The other held a tablet.

'Mr Foley, it's nice to finally meet you in person instead of via video. Please sit down.' He cocked his head to one side and took a seat opposite his client. 'How are things with you?'

Arthur had no time for small talk, especially at the hourly rate this man was charging. 'Your message said the Crown Prosecution Service had been in touch?' he replied.

Mr Warner leaned forward. 'I'm so sorry to have to tell you, but they have decided to move forward with a prosecution.'

Arthur nodded. He had been expecting it. 'For not reporting June's death,' he replied. The word 'death' was not becoming any easier to say.

'That's partially correct, but unfortunately they are adding another charge to the list. Both Mrs Foley's state and private pensions were paid into a jointly held bank account, is that correct?'

'Yes, we used it to pay the bills.'

'When you failed to officially declare your wife's death, her pensions continued being paid into that account. So, to both the state and private pension providers, it looks like you've used your wife's death as an opportunity to make financial gains.'

'I didn't!' protested Arthur. 'My pensions also go into that account so it's my money I've been spending, not June's.'

'Are you able to prove that?'

'Well, no, but I wasn't trying to deliberately defraud anyone. I'll happily repay all their money. I can do it today.'

'I believe you, Mr Foley, but unfortunately the CPS has decided it has a case against you.'

Arthur shook his head, his breaths becoming swifter and shallower. He removed his inhaler from his pocket and took several puffs.

'This doesn't make any sense,' he continued. 'I've never broken the law in my life. I'm seventy-five and I don't have so much as a parking ticket against my name.'

'Unfortunately, that is of no consequence. One of the Government's election campaign pledges was to crack down on anyone defrauding the system. I'm afraid you have been caught in a grey area.'

Arthur couldn't prevent his eyes from welling.

'Please try not to upset yourself.' Mr Warner passed him a box of tissues from the table. 'Between you and I – and this is just speculation – but I believe they are trying to make an example of you.'

'Why?'

'For you and your wife not signing up to their voluntary euthanasia plan when you upgraded your marriage.'

'But June and I promised we'd be there for each other in sickness and in health.'

'But in doing so, and in you claiming carer's benefits and her pension, they see you both as a drain on resources. It's why the "in sickness" part was withdrawn from the upgraded marriage vows. If others see the consequences of not agreeing to tick that box and end a terminally ill loved one's life early, they're more likely to agree.'

'So what happens now?'

'First you'll be charged with Fraud by Misrepresentation and then with Prevention of the Lawful and Decent Burial of a Body. Of course, it's up to you to decide how to plead but we can discuss that at a later date. It's my job to make it clear to the court that what you did was not a greedy or malicious act and that you were mentally impaired with grief over Jane's loss.'

'June,' Arthur snapped. 'Her name is June.'

Mr Warner closed his eyes and held his hands up. 'My apologies. June.'

'What if they don't believe me? How much will I be fined?'

'I'm afraid there is the potential for a custodial sentence if found guilty.'

Arthur's face paled. He must have misheard. First his wife had been taken from him and now his freedom was at risk. Mr Warner made his way to the corner of the room, opened a refrigerator and returned with a bottle of water. He unscrewed the cap and handed the drink and a glass to his client. Arthur took several gulps.

'Mr Foley,' Mr Warner began tentatively. '*Arthur*. There is one route we might be able to take to prove to the court that you want to make amends for this oversight.'

'Which is?'

'Your relationship status remains widowed, I assume?'

'Of course.'

'If you were to perhaps consider signing up to a Government-approved repatriation programme, the court would likely take that into account when sentencing.'

'Repatriation?'

'There are several sanctioned websites designed for men and women in your situation to meet others in similar positions. Single people.'

'You . . . want me to start dating?'

'From experience, I am merely suggesting the CPS prefers, where possible, not to separate couples. So if you are in a relationship when the outcome of your case is due, you might receive a more favourable judgement. Have you read the small print in the marriage upgrade contract you signed?'

Arthur shook his head, so Mr Warner explained that, as June had been dead for at least six months, his Grace and Grieving period had expired and he could immediately begin to open himself up to 'new relationship opportunities'. Mr Warner handed him a copy of the contract.

'"Those living alone in their advancing years are more likely to suffer anxiety, social alienation, sensory deficits, fragility and a more rapid mental and physical decline than their married counterparts",' read Arthur. 'So that's it?' he said. 'Because I'm widowed and single, there's only one way this is going to end for me?'

Just the notion of being with anyone aside from June gave him a sick feeling in the pit of his stomach. It was already a monumental struggle to no longer hear her voice or wake up each morning without her head on the pillow next to him. To have a stranger there instead was unimaginable. However, it might be his only chance of a non-custodial sentence.

'When . . . when would I need to start . . . meeting people?'

'To make it work in your favour, the sooner the better. A marriage or engagement would be even more beneficial.'

'But June is my wife!'

'As difficult as this is to hear, in the eyes of the Act, she is no longer your wife. I'm afraid she no longer counts.'

Arthur dabbed at his brimming eyes again. 'She does to me.'

30

Anthony

Anthony slowed his pace as he ran along the street outside his house and made his way up the drive. It had been weeks since his last run and he knew that, by morning, his aching legs would be quick to remind him of that fact.

Streetlights behind him illuminated the quiet suburban street in New Northampton as his neighbours readied themselves to retire for the night. Anthony, however, was wide awake, his restless mind in conflict with itself. It was proving impossible to silence the resounding voice in his head reminding him his next project was unethical and unfair and just plain wrong on so many levels. However, he was aware none of those concerns had stopped him before with Jem Jones and it was unlikely to stop him now.

He'd hoped a run might help to put his muddled thoughts in order, or at least might help him escape his conscience for a time. It hadn't worked. He couldn't silence his newly discovered principles. And he became frightened that the longer he continued living this life, the more his original self was going to become irrecoverable.

'Oh hey,' he began, entering the house, surprised to see Jada. She was sitting cross-legged on the sofa, a glass of wine in her hand, her head tilted towards him. 'I thought you'd be in bed.' At least he hoped that's where she would be, fast asleep so that he didn't have to lie to her when she asked him about his day.

'We've hardly seen each other lately so I thought I'd wait up.' She smiled and patted the seat next to her. She poured a second glass of wine and handed it to him.

'I should probably shower first,' Anthony replied.

'It can wait.'

'Oh, right.' She smelled so good, he thought; her signature scent, a pomegranate and citrus perfume she had worn ever since they first met in a university hall. His lips barely brushed her cheek as he took a seat.

'Babe, I'm not your grandmother, you can do better than that,' Jada replied and kissed him properly, her lips lingering on his. He missed how Jada tasted, how soft and inviting her mouth was. More than anything, he wanted to make love to her there and then: spontaneous, raw, passionate sex sprawled out across the sofa like they used to before parenthood and work became passion-killers. These days, he was too exhausted and preoccupied to even take charge of her vibrator.

The depth of his desire for her took him by surprise. He had been used to supressing it after the night they'd made love and he'd imagined himself being with Jem Jones. He'd almost called Jada by Jem's name. At the time, after day after day, month after month, Jem had become all-consuming. She had been the only thing Anthony thought about. Even all these weeks after her death, barely an hour passed when he didn't dwell on her. He hated the hold she had over him.

Tonight, he couldn't allow himself to act on his impulses.

Work was his priority and nothing – not even his lust for Jada – could get in the way. In three years' time, and when early retirement welcomed him, that's when they could all finally be a proper family. That's when he could become the man Jada thought she'd married. Then they'd buy the beachfront house in Saint Lucia they often spoke about and Jem Jones would be nothing but a dim and distant memory.

Anthony turned his head towards a digital swatch of wallpapers by her side. 'What are you working on?' he asked.

'A nursery for a couple of guys on a surrogacy journey. But they've just been Levelled up so I guess it's on hold until they know how that pans out.'

His attention was drawn towards the muted television. 'What are you watching?'

'A documentary about Jem Jones and the Marriage Act.' Anthony's skin prickled. 'Did you know her family still aren't telling anyone where in the world she died? All they're saying is they're not burying her in the UK because they're scared her grave will be desecrated by anti-Acters. Can you believe it? Even in death, they won't leave her alone.'

Anthony knew threats to Jem's final resting place were a lie because he had sanctioned the use of Bots to flood social media with said threats, leading to the story being picked up by internet news sites.

'It makes sense,' he replied. 'Why would they want to return her to a country that drove her to her death?'

'Or perhaps she's not really dead,' said Jada. 'Maybe it's a huge publicity stunt and she's going to suddenly reappear.'

Anthony shrugged. 'Stranger things have happened.' But

he knew better. Jem was most definitely dead; he had seen to that personally.

'They were discussing how she encouraged hundreds of thousands of couples to sign up for the Act,' Jada continued. 'That's some Influencing.'

'It used to be reality TV stars people listened to. Now it's anyone with a camera and halo lighting. They wield too much power, and we just sit back and let them tell us where we should be spending our money, which party we should be voting for and how we should redefine our marriages.'

'You don't think upgrading did us any harm, do you?'

'No, but it's not just about us, is it? If you're still trad-itionally married or if you're single, you're effectively a second-class citizen. It wasn't long ago that we were having to remind people – no, strike that – *shout until they listened* – that our lives mattered. Thank God our son will never know what it's like to have to justify and quantify why he should be treated with equality.'

'Where's all this coming from, babe?' she asked.

'Sorry, it's been a long day.' He stretched his arms above his head and yawned. Both heard something click in his spine.

'That did not sound good,' said Jada. 'I'm sure I can find a way of massaging the tension right out of you . . .' She slipped her hand along his thigh and rested it close to his groin.

'I'm really sorry but I can't tonight,' Anthony replied. 'I need to get a head start on tomorrow.'

'You're going back to work?'

He nodded.

'It's almost ten o'clock.'

Anthony knew that if the roles were reversed, he'd be

feeling as frustrated as Jada. He wished he could explain how the all-encompassing nature of his next project was tearing into him even at this early planning stage. And how if he didn't decompress in the sanctuary of his sterile office soon, then he would not sleep at all that night.

'I'm sorry,' he offered weakly.

'Babe, we need to talk about this . . .'

He knew what was coming: it wasn't the first time she had wanted to have this conversation. His eyes moved towards her Smart watch, indicating she would need to choose her next words carefully. She moved her phone to her lap and began to read from the Notes section. She was prepared.

'I want to ensure our marriage stays on track without the need of outside interference,' she began.

'Um, so do I,' he replied. 'But we're okay.'

'I'm not saying that we're not,' she said, looking him in the eye before her gaze returned to her screen. 'However, the barriers that prevent us from speaking as openly as we might like can make it difficult for us to have an open, two-way conversation. And if the other person is unwilling to listen, it can be hard to express if we're unhappy with a situation.'

Anthony didn't know how to respond. So he did what he always did and became confrontational, knowing that Jada wouldn't push back and risk their Audite being alerted to conversational discord.

'Are you saying you're unhappy with me?' he asked.

'You know I'm not.' She scrolled through her notes. 'Per-haps, it would be a positive influence on our relationship if you found the time for us to spend together as a family unit.'

'I already take Sundays off like you asked.'

'Sometimes even when we take time off, we aren't always as present as we think we might be.'

'We? You mean me?'

'No, no,' but he knew that she meant yes.

Jada was bringing to the surface all Anthony didn't want to admit. He wanted to spend time with his son and prove to them both that he had it in him to be a good father. But a day taken off here or a weekend there would have a knock-on effect with the rest of his workload and he'd forever be playing catch-up. It was easier to throw himself into his project and keep an eye on the goal – an early retirement and a better life for them all thousands of miles away in the Caribbean sea.

'So if you think I'm present, I don't know what the problem is,' he said and clambered to his feet. 'Don't wait up for me; I'll see you in the morning.'

Without looking her in the eye, Anthony took his wine glass and returned to the office, locking the doors behind him. He would shower and change into fresh clothes later, when Jada was asleep and he wouldn't have to see her again. For now, he slumped back in his chair, a dim lamp barely illuminating the room, hating himself for using technology as an excuse to silence his wife.

One of the differences between him and Jada and almost every other couple who had Upmarried was that they were free to say anything at all to one another. Because the sensitive nature of his career ensured their conversations were exempt from being monitored or recorded by their Audite.

And it was a fact he had chosen to keep from his wife.

31

Roxi

Roxi was mulling over a script for her next Vlog when an Audite positioned beneath the television pinged. She gritted her teeth.

"Couples shouldn't just get along," came the first of today's Push notifications. "They should always be assisting their partner's dreams and ambitions so that, together, they can accomplish their goals and bask in achieving each other's objectives. How can you help your partner to achieve their goal?"

'By trading myself in for a more complicit model,' she muttered. Roxi didn't have the time or inclination to put any thought into what her husband's goals were. A new hockey stick or an upgrade to his car, most likely. His dreams were provincial while hers were aspirational. And lately it finally felt as if she was making headway in achieving them. She couldn't let this Level One lunacy distract her. Besides, it was just a warning, she reasoned, a gentle nudge to remind them to be a little more thoughtful in the way they spoke to each other. If they could hold their tongues for the next few weeks and throw in some affirmations and mutual praise for the machine to pick up on, the intrusion would soon blow over.

In the short term, however, it wouldn't stop the notifications from grating on her. They arrived at random times of the day and often when Roxi least expected them. Once one appeared so swiftly and with the Audite's volume on high as she was on the toilet, that it quite literally scared the crap out of her.

Today's script wasn't flowing as effortlessly as it should, so Roxi diverted her attention towards her social media comments. The positives far outweighed the negatives. And after weeks of television appearances, podcasts and video chats, it was like water off a duck's back to read threats of rape, arson, driving her car off the road and the kidnap and murder of her children.

But there was one exception. @JustSayingBabe. Roxi was allowing that troll to make a home under her skin. Their increasingly frequent attacks felt more personal than those sent by others. Today's comment was posted under an Instagram image of Roxi's tanned legs. The stem of a cocktail glass brushed against one of them, an infinity pool and setting sun on the horizon surrounded her.

'Longing to go back to #BoraBora again,' Roxi had written. 'Best #holiday ever,' followed by the maximum allowance of hashtags.

'You've never been there, you #virtualfuckingtourist!' @JustSayingBabe had written, followed by a dozen crying laughter emojis. 'U have no shadow & a stock background image. Can't unsee the photoshop. Spend time keeping your marriage together not photoshopping fake holidays! #Level1 #BeHonestBeBetter.'

Red-faced, she pressed her tongue against her bottom

front teeth as she deleted her post. She wouldn't be able to get away with throwaway boastaposts like this now that she was on her way to becoming a public figure. Judgemental fingers were always poised and ready to point at the slightest provocation. But what was with the comment regarding her marriage? And how did her troll know that she and Owen had been placed on Level One? All Roxi's acquaintances were virtual and she didn't confide personal matters in them. Phoebe had been her only real friend since their time in foster care together. But following Phoebe's murder, Roxi hadn't attempted to create a connection with anyone else for fear they too would disappear from her life. So the leak must have come from Owen's side.

She clicked on the troll's profile but, as before, it contained no information. A thought flashed through her head – was her daughter Darcy responsible? Had she discovered Roxi was responsible for having all her social media accounts deleted? It couldn't be ruled out.

Her mood lifted at the sound of a vehicle pulling up outside and recognition of a courier delivery van. A robot appeared as the rear doors opened and made its way down a ramp and towards her front door. As Roxi opened its rear panels and removed a brown box, Darcy hurried up the driveway and into the house without acknowledging her mother. Tears streamed from red eyes and down her cheeks. Roxi reasoned that if she was already that upset, it wouldn't make much difference if she dealt with it now or after she'd carried the package inside.

With each television or radio appearance – and there had been seventeen now – Roxi's media career was gaining traction. Instead of approaching PRs cap in hand, they were approaching her. Closer inspection of documents attached to the box revealed it had been sent by a French cosmetics company. Darcy could wait one more minute. Inside it was a selection of moisturizers and perfumes. It was a high-end brand she had targeted in the past but her requests had fallen on deaf ears. She totted up the value – there was at least £3,000 worth of merchandise here. Delighted, she clasped her hands together as if in prayer.

She made her way upstairs and into the bathroom to cleanse her face and sample one. But on reaching the landing, a faint sobbing emanated from her daughter's room. Roxi let out a long breath and opened the door.

32
Jeffrey

Jeffrey slipped off his jacket and placed it on a hook on the back of the office door. Notes of oud from Harry's cologne lingered on the fabric threads.

Adrian, his supervisor, was already seated behind his desk and they exchanged pleasantries as he poured Jeffrey a cup of tea from a pot.

'It's nice to see you in person rather than by FaceTime,' Adrian began. 'How long has it been?'

'A couple of years at least?' Jeffrey replied.

'I guess it must be, as I've been based in New Northampton for almost as long. How are you finding it?'

'All towns blend into one another after a while, don't they?'

'You're from here, though, aren't you?'

'Yes—' Jeffrey cursed the background checks on his application form '—but I've not been back in years.'

'Well, along with a general catch-up, I wanted to update you on the Harry and Tanya Knox house fire investigation,' Adrian began. 'The police's preliminary report suggests that it was a murder-suicide. It appears Mrs Knox stabbed her husband to death, cut her wrists and then set fire to their house.'

Images of the couple, the last pair he'd been assigned to before Noah and Luca, rushed back. Jeffrey pinched the bridge of his nose and closed his eyes. For a moment, he thought he could smell burning again.

'Are you okay? Do you need a moment?' Adrian continued.

'No, I'm just trying to process. Their story wasn't supposed to end like this. I should have foreseen what Tanya was capable of. Maybe I could have saved Harry.'

'No one here is holding you accountable for anything, Jeffrey. We've read through your report so we know their relationship was unstable. As a practising Relationship Responder myself, if I'd been in your shoes, I don't think there is anything else I'd have done differently to you. You had no choice but to recommend to the courts they divorce.'

'Thank you,' Jeffrey said. 'It means a lot to hear that.'

Adrian picked up his phone when it flashed. 'I'm so sorry, I need to take this. Can you give me a moment?' A plus-sized man, Adrian grasped his desk to pull himself up and left the room, closing the door.

Alone, Jeffrey replayed his final moments in Harry and Tanya's home. He'd had little choice but to start that fire and he'd known that, if staged correctly, it would lead investigators to believe it was the scene of a murder-suicide. On hearing that the flames had destroyed much of the evidence leading to this police report, his decision had been the correct one.

Before he met them, and based on Audite recordings of their drawn-out arguments and passive-aggressive behaviour, they had fascinated Jeffrey enough for him to want to try and salvage their marriage. They'd repeatedly assured him with utmost sincerity that they still loved each other and had begged him to help them get back on track and pass Level Two. However, they hadn't counted on him listening in to their private conversations through the Audite. He'd heard them openly discuss Jeffrey's gullibility and their marital affairs. They were only a couple for the financial benefits a Smart Marriage brought.

Naturally, they'd reacted bitterly when he'd announced he was recommending to a Family Court that they should be divorced. Once they had finished hurling insults at him, they'd threatened to report him for attempting to sexually assault Tanya. The incident had been nothing of the sort: she had been the one who had offered him favours in return for a clean bill of marital health Jeffrey hadn't laid a finger on her. At least not until she was breathing her last in the bath. He had held her firmly in his grip as the taps had poured and the diagonal slashes he'd inflicted up and down her wrists and forearms muddied the bathwater. He'd remained with her for fifteen minutes until she'd finally bled out, then he'd watched as her lifeless form had disappeared under the surface.

Moments later, her husband Harry's life had taken less time to end. Harry had been making his way into the kitchen when Jeffrey had silently approached him from behind. Using an electroshock weapon, he'd fired two sharp darts into Harry's neck, rendering him immobile. Then he'd thrust a screwdriver into the lower portion of his torso half a dozen times, shredding his kidneys, intestines and liver before his victim could even realize he was being attacked. Jeffrey assumed the autopsy had not found the electrocution marks on his charred corpse.

According to the report he'd sent to Adrian shortly before burning their house to the ground, Tanya had been frequently physically and verbally violent towards her husband. Jeffrey had detailed how he had moved in with them to defuse fraught situations and had offered her anger-management strategies. But, he'd claimed, the toxicity had spread too deeply for his assistance to be effective.

'Sorry about that,' Adrian said as he returned to the room and his chair. He continued to discuss the Knoxes and referenced other Relationship Responders who had experienced traumatic outcomes with their clients. But Jeffrey wasn't really listening. Instead, he wondered if there were any others like him out there, Responders who became too deeply invested in their clients or who understood that sometimes it was necessary to take matters into your own hands.

'So have you had any more thoughts about accepting my offer of counselling?' asked Adrian. 'I know you like to think you're a tough cookie, but we all have a breaking point.'

'I have considered it, yes,' Jeffrey said, but he hadn't. He didn't want anyone poking about inside his head. 'But, to be honest, Adrian, I've also considered that this might not be the right career path for me.'

Adrian raised his eyebrows. 'Oh, please don't say that.'

'Look at my track record. My last clients died in a murder-suicide; before that, one of them took his own life and let's not forget the Armitages who vanished before counselling was complete. The last time I asked, the police still haven't found them.'

Jeffrey's memory lingered on the latter. He'd had an inkling they were hiding something from him. But he'd only discovered they were members of Freedom for All when he'd broken into their Cloud and learned they'd been secretly filming their sessions with Jeffrey to publicly expose Relationship

Responders as 'woefully undertrained cod psychologists'. He wondered how long it had taken the husband to die without food and water, chained up in an abandoned Suffolk farmhouse with only his wife's dead body for company.

And then there was Arjun and Mickey. He and Arjun had clicked the moment they'd met, and Jeffrey had found himself falling hard and fast for him. He'd used his full arsenal of persuasive skills to make Arjun understand that his and Mickey's relationship was doomed to fail. But his warnings had fallen on deaf ears. In desperation, Jeffrey had removed Mickey from the picture by weighing his body down with rocks and rope and dumping it in a Welsh reservoir. Arjun, believing his husband to have left him after reading a text message typed by Jeffrey into Mickey's phone, had been devastated and too broken for Jeffrey to repair. Jeffrey had reluctantly departed, both men pining for different lost loves.

'But you've had many, many successes over the last three years,' said Adrian. 'You're only focusing on the negatives. Some couples were so easy to counsel you were finished within three weeks.'

In the early days of his Responding, the job was not what Jeffrey had hoped it might be. He'd found it impossible to make a connection with most couples. Their marital issues had been so bland and tedious that he'd given them a clean bill of health so that he could make his escape as quickly as possible. To prevent history from repeating itself, he'd begun to spend more time delving deeper into potential clients before committing to helping them, listening to the recordings of their conversations and carrying out background checks. The more interesting their dynamic, the more he immersed himself in their lives. And the more frequently emotional lines blurred.

'And as I've said to you before, it's all down to the couples you choose,' Adrian continued. 'You care too much. You have an in-built need to get stuck into the most challenging of marriages. So you cannot take it personally when they don't always work out. None of what happened is your fault.'

'What about management? What do they think? They must be aware of my failure rate.'

'Let's just say there's a reason why there is no official record of our involvement in inquests or police reports. It wouldn't benefit the public to know. The people above us, well, their priority is the big picture and the success stories so they don't trouble themselves focusing on the details. But I am sure they agree with me. We need people like you; however, your own mental health is also paramount. I can arrange to take this latest couple off your hands if you like?' Adrian looked to his computer. 'Noah and Luca Stanton-Gibbs, is it?'

'No, no, it's fine,' he said quickly. 'If you still trust my judgement then I'll see this through and perhaps I'll take a break afterwards.'

Jeffrey's chest tightened at the thought of being separated from Luca. And the depth of his need to be around his client took him by surprise.

*

St Mary the Virgin's church cemetery in the tiny village of Great Brington was barely a minute's walk from where Jeffrey had parked his car.

He took in the century-old oak trees with unpruned canopies that sheltered the headstones from the sun as he read each inscription until he found the one he was searching for. After sixteen years, he was finally here. His eyes brimmed with nostalgia.

This grave had not been tended for some time. Dregs of water in the glass vase were stained by algae and the petals that were once attached to peony heads were now brown and lying upon the decorative stones.

All these years later and Jeffrey wished he'd been allowed to attend her funeral. But while he'd been recovering in his hospital bed from facial reconstruction surgery, he had been advised by police to stay away. He understood why, but it still wounded. So he'd held his own service instead in a nearby woodland weeks later, sprinkling yellow rose petals in a spot under the tree.

Even now, whenever he passed a florist or a garden and caught the scent of those flowers, he was transported back to the day he'd said his final goodbyes to her. She was the first person he had ever truly loved, and the first person to have broken his heart.

Jeffrey pulled at clumps of overgrown grass and dandelions surrounding her grave, then threw away the decaying flower stalks in the vase, replacing them with a bunch he had purchased earlier.

'Rosie Morrison', read the name at the top of the black granite headstone, 'Forever Loved, Never Forgotten'.

She wouldn't be forgotten, especially by him. Because you never forget your first love and the first person you killed.

33

Roxi

Darcy was curled up on her bed, her head buried so deep in her pillow Roxi could barely make out her face under the hair covering it. Sometimes Roxi caught herself staring at her daughter and wondering if she had looked like her at that age. But there was so much she had blanked out about her past that she never found an answer.

'Leave me alone,' Darcy cried.

'Tell me what the problem is first, then I'll go.'

'You! You're the problem! Your dumb Vlogs are making my life a misery.'

'How? I've stopped asking for your help because you moaned so much.'

'Kids at school keep picking on me because of the stupid stuff you're saying. Like last night when you posted that AI should be used to monitor every phone belonging to under-eighteens, that what we do should be tracked and then reported back to our parents.'

Roxi processed what this meant. 'So kids your age are watching my Vlogs?'

'Yes. And now they're accusing me of wanting to take away their freedom. Everyone says you're going to ruin it for us all and they're blaming me.'

'Well,' Roxi said, letting out a puff of air, 'I didn't expect that. I hoped that my relatable content might reach the 18–34 demographic, but an even younger bracket is perfect.'

'Mum! You're missing the point.'

'No, darling, I get it, I really do. But if they're listening, I need to start targeting them. I'm going downstairs to start brainstorming ideas while you make a note of brands they love so I can start approaching PRs.'

Roxi left the room and seconds later heard the slamming of Darcy's bedroom door. Teenagers were irrational and emotional and this outburst was probably hormone-related. She'd give her daughter a few moments alone.

But before Roxi reached the stairs, she had a better idea. She grabbed a packet of wet wipes from the bathroom cabinet and rubbed her face until it was bare, then hurried into the garden and held her phone in front of her face.

The first few seconds of footage were of a silent Roxi shaking her head. 'I am so upset that I don't know how to put this into words,' she eventually began. 'My beautiful, kind, caring, considerate daughter Darcy has just returned home from school, hysterical, because she is being bullied by the kids she thought were her friends. These children – *your* children – and our country's next generation – are bullying a twelve-year-old girl because of me. Because her mother dares to lift her head above the parapet to offer an opinion. I've always instilled in Darcy that she should never be afraid to have a voice, not to allow anyone to silence her truths, to stand up and be counted. And now she is upstairs sobbing her eyes out because small-minded parents have told their children that it's acceptable to silence a point of view if you don't agree with it.

'I'm sure there are some of you out there saying, "If you care that much, then why don't you just shut up and stop Vlogging?" But what will I be teaching her about what it is to be a woman if I do that? My wonderful, loyal followers are allowing me to live my dream of being an Influencer. But first and foremost, my job will always be to try and influence Darcy. If I censor myself and allow the bullies to win, how will I ever be able to look her in the eye again? I love her too much to do that.

'What her classmates have been doing is further proof of what I've been posting recently. If our homes and wearable technology recorded everything we said, this wouldn't have happened. Either her bullies would stop to think of the consequences before they acted, or their parents would be informed and obligated to punish them. I firmly believe their texts and emails should be monitored too. This is not about Big Brother listening and watching us to keep us in line, or a social oppression or whatever other buzzwords you might want to use. This is about protecting those we hold closest to our hearts. Our babies.'

'You'll use anyone to get what you want, won't you?' said Owen, startling her.

She fumbled with her phone until she found the stop button.

He was standing by the patio doors, his face like thunder. 'Exploiting our daughter's pain is disgusting. You're disgusting.'

'That's unfair. I'm trying to lead by example and show her that I'm a strong wom—'

'Bullshit, you're humiliating Darcy to serve your own agenda and you're either too ignorant or too selfish to admit it.'

Roxi pointed to her wedding ring to remind him Audite was likely listening. 'I understand that you're upset,' she began as she recalled a Push notification from earlier. 'Couples shouldn't just get along, they should also be assisting their partner's dreams and ambitions.' She offered a thin, hopeful, smile.

'It is fast becoming my ambition to no longer be married to you,' he replied, and left her alone.

Roxi's stomach clenched. Owen had never spoken to her like that before. She picked up her phone and her thumb hovered above the delete button before thinking better of it. *No, he's overreacting*, she thought. And in less than thirty seconds, the video was uploaded to each of her social media channels, along with her #IWillDoBetterWillYou? hashtag.

34

Corrine

The text message contained only two words and vanished seconds after she read it, but it was enough to bring weeks of worry to a close.

'He's conscious.'

The hacker's unsolicited update revealed that Nathan Deakin, the young man Corrine had spent so much time fretting over, was awake. Another message appeared seconds later, this time containing a screengrab of medical notes. She was unfamiliar with many of the terms but the words 'no permanent cognitive damage' stood out.

'Thank God,' she whispered.

Corrine wondered what he remembered about that night and the danger she had put him in. She hoped he could forgive her. She slipped her phone back into her pocket and continued what she had been doing before the message appeared – typing an inventory into her tablet. That morning she had worked her way from room to room of the family home, noting what she planned to take with her when she and Mitchell were divorced.

Many of the larger items like tables and chairs, dressers and wardrobes she would leave with him but some of the electricals, the artwork and soft furnishings she wanted for herself. The decor was grand and styling had been a collaboration with Jada, an interior designer she had been recommended by friends. Back then, Corrine had wanted the very best to earn their validation. But having witnessed the dark side of the Marriage Act, she was ashamed to have been that person.

She and Mitchell had yet to discuss in detail how and when they would inform the children of their decision to separate. She assumed their eldest daughter Freya would take little convincing – she was the most perceptive of the three and had stopped being a daddy's girl when she was old enough to see how miserable her father made those around him. Corrine couldn't be as sure as to Nora and Spencer's reactions. For an inexplicable reason, they appeared to enjoy his company.

Her watch chimed and she looked to the screen. The front door camera captured two women and a man carrying boxes. 'Hello,' she said into the microphone, 'can I help you?'

'We're here to install the Audites,' the man replied.

'Audites?' she repeated. 'I think you have the wrong address.'

'Mr and Mrs Nelson, one-four-seven Dallington Gardens?'

'Yes. But we're not part of the Marriage Act.'

Mitchell appeared and walked directly towards the door, opening it.

'Come in,' he said as the three visitors, all dressed in overalls, entered. 'You'll have to excuse my wife, she's a bit scatty sometimes. You can put the main one in the kitchen-diner and the others wherever you like. There's also a summerhouse outside.'

'Mitchell, what the hell are you doing?' asked a confused Corrine.

He let out a long, theatrical sigh. 'I've thought about it long and hard, Corrine, and I've decided that divorce is not on my radar.'

'Oh, *you've* decided that, have you?' Corrine laughed.

'Uhuh. I've been re-reading the morality clause in my ongoing Government contracts and considering my reputation. I can't be seen to be separating from my wife when the Government is so pro-marriage, can I? Perhaps we can take another look at it in a year or two.'

'A year or two? I don't think so. We have an agreement. I've already stayed with you far longer than I should have. We've already signed documents to start the proceedings.'

'Ahh, about those papers. You didn't read them properly, did you?'

An uneasiness crept into the room and made its way towards her. 'You know I didn't. You said they were formalities when you shoved the iPad under my nose. I was on my way out.'

'The one thing I've always loved about you is how trusting you are. It's quite endearing, really it is. And useful.'

'What have you done, Mitchell?'

'It's less about what I've done and more about what you've agreed to. If you'd opened and read them instead of just signing the screen with your finger, you'd have seen that we were actually divorced six months ago.'

Corrine paused as her mouth formed an O shape. 'What the hell are you talking about?'

'One of the documents you signed was to divorce us, the

second was to apply for a Smart Marriage and the third was to sign our new contract. In a few days from now the grace period will be over and the random recordings will begin.'

'You're lying. You wouldn't have done that.'

He made a helpless gesture with his hands. 'I'm afraid I did. You can look at the documents yourself. I've gone old school and printed them out and left them on your bedside cabinet for some night-time reading.'

A panicked Corrine ran through the house and up the stairs until she reached her bedroom. There, where he said they'd be, were dozens of sheets of paper secured in a binder. Sticky labels highlighted and confirmed what he had just informed her. Bile rose up into her throat.

'Why would you do that to me?' she yelled as she returned to the kitchen.

'It's nothing personal, it's business. There are clauses that suggest it's in my best interest for us to remain in a partnership. And if you knew the sums I've invested in my projects, you wouldn't be arguing with me.'

Corrine trembled with rage and steadied herself with a hand on the counter.

'Excuse me,' asked one of the women carrying an Audite box, 'where would you like this fitting?'

'Get out!' Corrine screamed at the startled woman. 'Mitchell, you can't enjoy living like this? You can't honestly tell me you're happy with the way things are between us?'

Mitchell placed his palm on the centre of his chest. 'Hand on heart, I do not give two shits about the way things are between us. You have your life, I have mine. I don't care that we no longer meet in the middle. But I will not lose out financially because your nest is about to empty and you've got nothing better to do. Go and find a hobby if you're that starved of attention.'

Corrine opened her mouth to tell him that she did have a life beyond those four walls and that it was a life he couldn't conceive of, where people worked together for a greater good and not for themselves. But she held back, afraid of how he might use it to his advantage.

'I signed that document under false pretences,' she said. 'My lawyer will get me out of it.'

'The three-month statute of limitations for an annulment has already expired.'

'But what you did was illegal!'

'So take me to court. I'll deny it, you'll fight it, it'll be your word against mine. We can tie each other up in legal proceedings for years before you get your precious divorce and, by then, I'll have what I want regardless.'

'I'll start calling you every name under the sun every minute of every day into those fucking Audites until they start Levelling us up.'

'Your love for freedom of speech will do you no favours. You'll be labelled a Hostile Spouse and, if we reach Level Three at the Family Court, the division of assets and property will be heavily weighted in my favour as you'll be seen as making no effort to repair our relationship. You'll be left with nothing but a pot to piss in. And that's only if I say you can have one.'

'I hate you,' she growled.

'Careful now, stress can cause strokes in women of your age. And I took the liberty of checking the Safe Passage box on our marriage upgrade so that if something does happen, God forbid, I'll make sure you don't suffer. For long.'

Mitchell offered her a wink before he shuffled away. He didn't flinch when the boxed Audite she hurled at him smashed against the wall and fell to the floor.

Perfect Companion

Where your loss is also your gain.

Grief doesn't have to mean the end of something. It can also be the **beginning**.

Losing a loved one might feel like the end of the world, but it doesn't have to be.

Here at **Perfect Companion**, we are the only Government-approved matchmaking service that aims to help you fill the void in your life left by your lost love.

Once your six-month Grace and Grieving period is complete, our dedicated team will assist you in dipping your toe back in the dating pool with a huge range of singletons who, like you, are **looking for love**.

And, by signing up, you will of course continue to enjoy all the **benefits** you've come to expect with your Smart Marriage.

UK Workplace Marriage
Support Index
Top 100 employer

SMART
MARRIAGE

www.smartmarriage.co.uk

35

Arthur

Arthur was sitting in his lounge armchair, hands clenched so tightly that his knuckles paled. His teeth were gritted behind the thinnest of smiles.

On the television screen in front of him, an enthusiastic young man typed notes into a tablet. If he called Arthur 'bruv', 'matey' or 'buddy' one more time, Arthur thought he might fake a heart attack and put an end to this charade. Alas his traitorous Smart watch would likely prove him perfectly healthy.

'All righty, so now I have the facts, that's the boring bit out of the way,' Jax chirped. 'So let's get on with the good stuff and find you a lady!'

Arthur shuddered. But his thin smile remained as he offered a barely perceptible nod.

He had followed his solicitor's advice and joined the Government-approved Perfect Companion matchmaking service. Each prospective member faced an in-depth interview before joining. Arthur had already faced a barrage of questions that morning.

'First of all, Match Your DNA is the fastest way of finding love,' Jax continued. 'Have you signed up to that yet?'

'No.'

'Might that be something that interests you? If so, I have a discount code. You never know, you could be all loved up by the end of the week if your Match has already signed up.'

'No thank you,' Arthur declined politely but firmly. June was the woman who had been made for him. He didn't need his DNA testing to prove that.

'Okay, matey. So what age bracket are we looking at here? Someone your own age? Perhaps someone a little younger? We have all kinds on the system, even undergraduates looking for a sugar daddy if that floats your boat.'

Arthur shook his head.

'All righty. What about occupation? Would you prefer your future spouse to be working or retired?'

'I don't mind.'

'Full-time or part-time?'

'Either.'

'Widowed or divorced?'

'It doesn't matter.'

'Let's put both. Own house, own car?'

Arthur shrugged.

'We'll tick both boxes for that too. Good health, I assume? I mean, you don't want to be a widow again in a hurry, do you?!' Jax laughed, Arthur did not.

'What about hair colour, buddy? Are you into blondes or brunettes? Or maybe dark or a natural grey?'

'Anything.'

'Do you like the collar and cuffs to match?'

Arthur came close to spitting out his tea.

'I'm just pulling your leg here, buddy.' Jax laughed again.

The more the questions continued, the more frequently

Arthur flushed. Jax wanted to know everything from his preferred breast size to the acceptable number of past lovers a date might have. And Arthur didn't escape the intimate questioning. He had to put on record any moles or skin tags, medical ailments and if he was capable of maintaining an erection without the use of medication.

'Is this really necessary?' Arthur asked, exasperated. He knew all the medication in the world couldn't help him to be intimate with another woman.

'Sorry, matey, but it's my job to help find you Ms Right,' Jax replied. 'There's no point in scrimping on the detail and wasting everyone's time.'

When the survey was eventually complete, Arthur was as exhausted as he was relieved.

'All righty,' Jax said. 'In the next five minutes, you should receive an email from me containing a selection of ladies who fit your criteria and vice versa. How does that sound, buddy?'

Arthur wanted to say it sounded like hell but he knew that he couldn't. His lawyer had also warned that Arthur was being assessed on the openness of his answers and keenness to participate. A rating from a boy half a century younger than him could be the difference between freedom and prison.

'Is there anything else I can help you with today, Artie?' Jax continued.

'No, thank you.'

'Good to know, bruv. And the best of luck, I hope you find the woman of your dreams.'

I already had her, thought Arthur.

By the time he had returned from the kitchen with a fresh mug of tea, the envelope icon on his television was flashing. The first email was from Mr Warner, informing him that the court had accepted his guilty pleas for both fraudulent pension claims and failing to report June's death, but with diminished responsibility. However, because he was making an effort to find a new partner, his lawyer was confident that, along with no criminal record and an exemplary career, a custodial sentence was unlikely.

Arthur turned to the spot on the sofa June had favoured and stared at it. He had been too bound by grief to bring himself to sit on that couch since her death.

'How has it come to this, June?' he asked aloud, but there was no response. He badly missed hearing her voice, even if it was only in his head.

But if she wasn't going to respond after her body had been removed from their house, she was unlikely to return now he was planning to meet other women, whether he wanted to or not.

36

Anthony

Anthony closed his eyes and rested his head against the tiled wall of the shower. The four hours he had slept had been good, solid sleep, the kind he resented waking from when his alarm sounded. Despite the heat of the water bouncing off his shoulder blades, a shiver ran down his spine when his watch began to vibrate in varying lengths of frenetic bursts. The message spelled 'priority'. He couldn't ignore it.

'Have you seen the news?' the next one said.

'No,' he dictated quietly, hoping Jada was still asleep in the bedroom.

A moment later a video clip appeared. 'Shower off,' he said and ordered his watch to play. It was footage taken from a news channel.

'Up to a dozen members of opposition party Freedom for All were killed last night in three separate arson attacks,' a broadcaster began. 'The properties in Old Brighton, Old Dorset and Old Nottingham were all set ablaze in what police believe to have been reprisal attacks following the death of Jem Jones. While three people escaped from an address in Old Coventry, an adult and two children are thought to have died as a result of smoke inhalation.'

The clip stopped and Anthony's watch pulsed again.

'The spirit of Jem Jones lives on,' read the message. 'Good work again.'

He didn't move. A cold brush of air made every hair on his naked body stand upright. He may not have killed those people with his own hands, but he might as well have.

*

Anthony stared at his son Matthew across the kitchen table. The boy's leg was twitching and he had been unable to focus his attention on any one thing for more than a few minutes at a time.

'What's this, Daddy?' Matthew asked. He was holding a small, fabric-covered speaker he'd unearthed in a cupboard.

'It's an Echo,' he replied. 'Like an early version of the Audite. They stopped making them a long time ago.'

'What's it for?'

'Playing music, mostly, or reading books, weather forecasts, turning on light bulbs.'

Matthew laughed. 'Is that it?'

'Pretty much, yes.'

'Was it yours?'

'No, it belonged to my mum.'

'Why've you kept it?'

'I don't know, I just have.'

It was the only object he possessed that contained recordings of his mother's voice. Sometimes, when he was alone, he plugged it in to listen to her reciting a shopping list into its memos or leaving him a message to play when he arrived home from school and she was elsewhere. And each morning it reminded her to divide their medication, a Ritalin for him and two anti-psychotics for herself.

The table shook as his son's leg and foot picked up the pace, moving back and forth. Anthony's often did the same when he struggled to centre himself. And, like Matthew, that morning, Anthony was also finding it increasingly difficult to tether himself to a stationary frame of mind.

'Can you put the Echo down while you're eating breakfast please?' he asked.

'But I want to play with it.' Matthew threw it up in the air and caught it.

'Put it down please, Matthew,' Anthony repeated.

His son threw it up in the air once again, but this time, it slipped out of his hands and fell to the floor.

'Matthew!' he yelled. 'For fuck's sake!'

His cursing halted his son's behaviour, just as Jada entered the room. As she dried her damp hair with a towel, she glowered at her husband then guided Matthew out of the room.

Anthony closed his eyes and cursed again, this time under his breath. The burden of knowledge was a heavy weight to carry and he was struggling. At his last London meeting, he'd not only been made privy to plans for children like his son, but he had also been tasked with implementing them. He knew that, in the not-so-distant future, Matthew's ADHD was going to bring the whole family added complications.

'Did you have to swear at him?' asked Jada on her return.

'He wasn't listening to me,' Anthony replied. Her folded arms warned him it was a poor excuse. 'I'm sorry,' he conceded. 'Where is he? I'll apologize.'

'Leave him; he's in his room. Couldn't you have made a little time to show him how the Echo worked? You know he's got a curious mind.'

'I think we should try medication,' Anthony offered without warning.

Jada frowned. 'What?'

'Take him back to the specialist and find a treatment that works for him.'

Jada eyed him suspiciously. 'Why the one-eighty?'

'Because you were right. If his school is telling us that he's being disruptive then we need to do something about it while we still have time.'

'He's only seven. His behaviour now isn't going to determine the rest of his life.'

Anthony shifted awkwardly and Jada caught it. 'What?'

'Nothing.' Anthony shrugged.

'What are you not telling me?'

'I'm not *not* telling you anything.'

Jada sucked in her cheeks. 'After two years of opposing meds, you're expecting me to believe you've suddenly had a change of heart with no prompting?'

Anthony hesitated before he nodded. He couldn't tell her the truth about what he knew.

'There it is again!' she persisted. 'You're hiding something.'

Anthony looked towards the Audite. 'You are lying,' Jada mouthed silently instead.

'Then that's wonderful,' she continued in a tone that didn't match her expression. 'I'll make an appointment with the specialist later in the week.'

'I'll come with you.'

'Don't worry, you'll probably have work to do. We'll be okay on our own. We always are.'

Jada left him alone knowing he had no riposte.

37

Roxi

Adrenaline was coursing through Roxi's body even before she opened the front door and spotted the dozen new, unopened boxes stacked up against the wall. All were addressed to her. As someone who'd grown up in the care system, she could only watch with envy as children in TV shows had opened heaps of brightly wrapped boxes on a Christmas morning. Now every day was like the Christmas Day she'd longed for. And she wondered if the novelty of receiving gifts as an adult would ever wear off.

Two hours had passed since her appearance on ITV's early evening magazine show. Millions had watched her argue that people living in Old Towns should require visitor's passports to go to New Towns. She had put across her point concisely and with passion, and, if she continued to perform like this, she was convinced it would once again boost her social media following. The road to Instafame was littered with the deactivated profiles of Influencers whose stars burned too brightly too quickly. Roxi would not be like them. She had worked too hard to shine to simply fizzle out.

She cocked her ear to listen to the music coming from the other side of the kitchen door. Owen, Darcy and Josh's voices were singing along to music playing from the Audite.

She opened the door quietly and watched as Darcy diced vegetables, Josh perched on the worktop peeling potatoes and Owen searched the pan drawer. *They don't need you to be a family*, a voice in the back of her head whispered. And, for a moment, her light dimmed. She had wasted many an hour trying to share the joy they found in small things, but she never quite managed it. She wondered if she might ever be truly fulfilled by those around her.

She removed her phone, took a quick photo, placed graphics of hearts across it and added a song about family love before posting it on Instagram. It might prompt sponsorship from a recipe delivery box service. Roxi waited until followers began to praise her 'beautiful family' and comment on how fortunate she was. Her light returned.

She offered an enthusiastic 'hello' as she entered the kitchen. The singing tapered off and the temperature cooled as she shrugged off her coat and placed her phone on the island.

Owen and Darcy muttered their greetings while Josh flashed a brief smile. She waited unsuccessfully for something more.

'Well?' she eventually asked. 'Is that it?'

'Is what it?' asked Darcy without looking up.

'You watched it, didn't you?'

'Watched what?'

Roxi turned to her husband. 'Owen?'

'I've been at work,' he said. Neither asked to what she was referring.

Roxi folded her arms and locked them tight like magnets. 'ITV Tonight?'

'Nope, sorry,' said Owen.

'Not even on catch-up? I included a link on my socials.'

'I don't follow you,' said Darcy with a hint of satisfaction.

'We could watch it now if you like?' Roxi asked.

'Maybe after dinner,' Owen replied.

Roxi's shoulders slumped. Her family might not have cared, but she was sure that, if her best friend Phoebe was still alive, she'd be proud of her. A buried memory reappeared, one of a silent version of herself, a child ignored by classmates at each new school she was parachuted into. Friendship groups had already been formed by the time she'd arrived and there was rarely an opening for latecomers – least of all one who was unlikely to remain in the same school for long.

She pulled herself back to the present.

'Well, thanks so much for your support,' Roxi continued. 'You're quick to forget all the hours I've spent making costumes for school plays or the nights I've spent at parents' evenings and sports days.'

'Dad did most of that,' said Darcy.

'Not all of it! Now I've found my niche and you're pretending it's not happening. I'm being gaslighted by my own family.'

'Sorry, Mummy,' said Josh. At least he sounded as if he meant it.

'Guys, can you give your mum and me a minute, please?' asked Owen.

Roxi recognized the glance that passed between them. She'd witnessed it before. It suggested a conversation about her that she'd been excluded from. Her arms remained folded until they were alone.

'What am I about to be blamed for tonight?' she began defensively. 'What a terrible wife I am or how I'm using my kids to progress my career?'

'Neither. Look, Rox, I'm sorry for saying I didn't want to be married. I didn't mean it; I was angry. But we need to find a way to adjust our relationship and make it work, especially now that we're being monitored. You can't say either of us are happy at the moment, right?'

'I was until I got home,' Roxi huffed. 'It was a huge day for me and I wanted to share it with my family. But none of you could care less.'

'Of course we could,' Owen replied calmly. 'But it cuts both ways. When did you last ask us about our days? And I support you by working all hours so that you can fulfil your dreams. But I won't give you my backing when you exploit us to push your career forward.'

'Is this still about the Darcy bullying post?' Roxi protested. 'I was showing my support for my daughter . . .'

'No, you weren't and if you take a step back you'll see that. We are a month into Level One and we have no idea how often the Audite's listening or what it's learning. We need to reach a level of understanding, Rox, to prove that our problems are surmountable before they send someone in to repair us. We need to be more of a family, do more things together, show that we actually all get along.'

Roxi had assumed that's what she had been doing, by involving her children in content creation and sharing with

Owen that she had her sights set on Jem Jones' vacant throne. Apparently she was wrong.

One of Roxi's biggest fears was that this was as good as their lives were going to get. A husband with limited aspirations, a daughter who resented her, a son she barely knew and all of them cooped up together in a three-bedroom suburban identikit home on the edge of New Northampton's boundaries with a rear garden you could barely swing a cat in. She knew the latter as a fact, she had tried once with one of Josh's stuffed toys. Its tail brushed each fence as she spun it in a circular motion. Her family was destined to take holidays abroad in coastal tourist traps, own a car three models behind the latest release and purchase clothing in the sales. The list of what they would never achieve was endless.

And Roxi craved more. Much, much more. A larger house in a better part of New Northampton, five-star luxury holidays, sponsorships . . . and they were so tantalizingly close that she could taste them. However, the stigma attached to a failed marriage might risk all of that.

'Did you hear the Push notification a couple of days ago?' Owen continued.

'Which one? There are so many.'

'The one about remembering what we were like before we got married. How all couples change who they are when they're carried along on a tidal wave of love – their description, not mine. Then, after you marry, you slip back into the person you were before. And that's when you must start working and growing in the same direction. Somewhere along the line, you and I went off course separately, so we need to find common ground.'

As he spoke, an image of a younger Owen returned to Roxi, the one who'd make frequent visits to the HR department of the recruitment company where they'd worked. On sight alone she'd been able to tell he was a decent type but her attraction hadn't been instant. Back then, she was accustomed to dating men who treated her poorly but were exciting to be around. She could fall in love at the drop of a hat with men like that because that's all she'd thought she was worth. She'd readily dilute herself for another.

But Owen had made it clear he didn't want that from her. He wanted an equal partnership. And when he'd showed Roxi love, she'd been at a loss as to know what to do with it. The more tenderness he'd offered, the more awkward she'd felt. Likewise, three years later, when Darcy was born, she'd found loving her child easy, but only until her daughter had begun to return that affection. Then, Roxi had pulled away. She'd known why Owen loved her – he'd told her frequently – but she hadn't been able to understand why a baby would show her such devotion.

She'd clung on to the hope the pieces might fit together when Josh had come along. But the pattern had repeated itself. The distance she'd created between herself and her family continued to this day. She was doomed to remain in the hallway listening to the fun of others behind closed doors.

Roxi had never admitted to her husband that she had taken a Match Your DNA test four years earlier. Her soulmate turned out to be an elderly widower living in the town of Blagoveshchensk, on Russia's border with China. In her desperation to find belonging she had used a translation App to communicate with her Match and they had talked via email for a month. But then, after a brief silence, his daughter had contacted Roxi one day to inform her that her father had died of a stroke earlier in the week. Roxi had grieved quietly for a man she would never meet and a love she would never experience.

Her phone illuminated on the island. It was likely to be an updated summary of her collated insights. She held back from grabbing it.

'The clock is ticking,' Owen continued, oblivious to her distraction. 'We only have a few weeks left to start pulling together.'

Roxi's phone flashed again. It was so near but yet so far.

'So what do you think?' he asked. This time, the phone caught his attention too. 'Could we try and find something that interests us both?'

Roxi nodded.

'Good, good, well that's a start,' he continued as the Audite's timer buzzed to indicate dinner was ready. He continued talking as he turned his back on her, and Roxi seized her opportunity. But her clumsy fingers pushed the phone along the countertop and sent it crashing to the floor. Owen spun around to find his wife scrambling to pick it up. He was as disappointed as she had ever seen him.

'Help yourself to dinner,' he said, defeated, and made for the kitchen door.

Roxi didn't try and stop him. Instead, she scrolled through her notifications. #IWillDoBetterWillYou? was now today's most trending hashtag and her combined social media accounts had just reached the one million mark. This was everything she had ever dreamed of, only she had no one to tell but her fans.

She scanned her Instagram comments under the video ITV posted of her earlier appearance. A familiar name had commented. No, she thought, I'm ignoring it. She scrolled past it and read positive comments instead, but just knowing it was there niggled. She went to delete it without reading it but couldn't help herself.

'Motormouth bitch won't stop jabbering, will she?' @JustSayingBabe had posted minutes earlier. 'Bet that's why her husband is screwing around. Wonder if she's asked where he's really going when he says he's playing hockey? Hasn't she noticed his kit is never dirty? LOL.'

Roxi dropped her phone onto the counter as time ground to a swift and sudden halt.

38
Jeffrey

For a moment, Jeffrey thought he was imagining it. He partially opened his eyes but his head remained on the pillow. He listened carefully and the noise appeared again. It was a muffled groaning sound coming from another room. A half-moon shining through a crack in the curtains offered enough light to locate his ear pods and the fob controlling Noah and Luca's Audite system. As he switched it on, his ears flooded with the muted sounds of their lovemaking.

He was desperate to witness what was happening further along the landing and behind their closed bedroom door. It was difficult to determine who was taking what role as the grunting and groaning became more frantic. Jeffrey began touching himself and imagined being in their bed, lying on his back, the back of his knees hooked over Luca's shoulders. Before he knew it, he and one of the men climaxed together, but apart.

Jeffrey recalled how his own sexual awakening had arrived as a teenager, sharing a bedroom with his older brother. Jeffrey had pretended to sleep but he'd watched through half-closed eyes as, week after week, Bobby had sex with a succession of different girls in the bed opposite.

Later, as an adult, and when relationships seemed to

happen around him rather than to him, Jeffrey came to terms with being perpetually single. It did not stop him from wanting to be part of a couple or dream of finding his DNA Match. But he was realistic. He didn't expect his partner to be hopelessly in love with him or to even reciprocate his passion. All he wanted was to be needed, to be considered, to matter. And when any of those experiences had failed to materialize, he'd sought gratification from watching strangers pleasure one another at discreet, members-only events. Voyeurism became his way of connecting with others.

Jeffrey patted himself dry with yesterday's underwear and reached for the remote control to turn off the Audite. He stopped himself when Noah and Luca began to talk.

'How much longer do you think he's staying for?' asked Noah.

'He said it might take up to six weeks. But if we prove we're listening to his advice, it might be less.'

'These three weeks have felt like a year.'

'It's not been that bad.'

'It is for me,' Noah said. 'He's always here. I'm scared to take a piss in case he's sitting in the corner of the bathroom making notes about it on that bloody tablet.'

Luca laughed.

'Well, you know what I mean. He's creepy. If we'd connected with him on a hook-up App and he turned up at the door we'd have told him he'd got the wrong address.'

'Come on, babe, he's not a bad guy.'

'How can you say that? Beccy pulled out of being our surrogate because of him.'

'It's the situation we're in that's to blame, not Jeffrey. He's only doing his job.'

A thrill ran through Jeffrey. He was now certain he had Luca onside, because no matter what Noah threw at Jeffrey, Luca defended him.

'I think he has a thing for you,' added Noah.

Jeffrey's thrill turned to panic. Had he made it that obvious?

'No he hasn't,' Luca dismissed.

'Yes, he does. You don't see the way he eyeballs you when you don't think you're being watched.'

'You're paranoid.'

'I might be if he was remotely attractive. There might even be a half-decent body hiding under those ill-fitting clothes but that's about all he has going for him.'

The more Noah spoke, the more convinced Jeffrey became that Noah's barbed tongue was completely incompatible with someone as decent as Luca. Now it was his job to make them both realize it.

39

Corrine

'I hate him, I absolutely bloody hate that man,' Corrine cursed as the two women walked through Upton Country Park. She willed the tears forming behind her eyes not to emerge when she thought about what Mitchell had done. She had wasted enough of them on him already.

'What did your solicitor say?' asked Yan.

'She told me – without using the exact words – that I was an idiot for signing anything without running it by her first.'

'Why didn't she check with you when he filed the papers?'

'They were never sent to her. And because there was no timeline on exactly when we were supposed to divorce, she was waiting to hear from me. She said she could still try and get the Smart Marriage annulled, claiming I signed under false pretences, but warned it could take up to two years if he denies it.' She brought her thumb and forefinger close together. 'I was this close to my fresh start. *This close.* And now I'm back to square one.'

'I'm so sorry, Corrine. Do you have a Plan B?'

'No. I wish I did.'

Yan was the only person Corrine had befriended at the Freedom for All splinter group meetings. They took a seat on a bench and stared down a slope towards another housing estate in the midst of a gentrification programme.

'The Act is just so unfair,' Corrine continued, balling her fists. 'I'm angry with Mitchell and I'm angry at my own stupidity. I should've known that he hates to lose. I know that many people would kill for my privilege and they're welcome to it.'

Yan's mouth opened and closed as if carefully considering what to say next.

'Say it,' said Corrine. 'Tell me I'm a fool.'

'That's not what I was thinking. You know you still have . . . *options*, don't you?' she began cautiously. 'They're not particularly ethical. But they are, nevertheless, options.'

'Such as?'

'There are . . . people . . . in the FFA who have connections, if you get what I'm saying.'

'I don't think I do.'

'Options that can solve a problem like your husband.'

'You mean have him killed?'

Yan shook her head vigorously. 'Oh God no, no, not those kind of options! Ones that require a level of deceit but that can lead to a fast-tracked divorce and that won't penalize you.'

'Like what?'

'A serious deception like drug or gambling addiction, an untreatable STI he's passed on, prison, a degenerative neurological condition . . . or if you accused him of being violent towards you. There are safeguarding measures in place in cases of spousal abuse that will Level you straight up to a Family Court. If the magistrates side with you, your marriage could be over within a fortnight.'

'But Mitchell has never been aggressive towards me.'

'But they don't know that.'

Corrine shook her head. 'I can't lie.'

'Did Mitchell listen to his conscience when he misled you into divorcing and marrying him again? Why should there be one rule for him and another for you?'

'No, it wouldn't be right to abuse a law designed to protect vulnerable people.'

'I did say it was unethical,' Yan added.

Corrine picked her phone from her pocket and flicked through a photo album. She found a selfie from when she had slipped on ice and bruised her arms and shoulders last winter. And more recently, there was a picture of the bruising around her mouth and swollen lips following the altercation at MP Eleanor Harrison's apartment. She closed the screen and shook her head. 'I'm sorry, it's just not me.'

'I understand,' said Yan. 'But if I was asking you for advice, what would you tell me to do?'

'Whatever you can to leave that marriage.'

'Exactly. So I guess it depends on just how much you hate your husband.'

Corrine hated her husband. And she hated him *a lot*.

40
Jeffrey

'When do you think your relationship began to veer off-course?' asked Jeffrey.

'It hasn't,' groaned Noah and poured himself and Luca another coffee from the machine. He didn't offer Jeffrey one. 'And I don't know why you keep saying it has.'

'For argument's sake, let's say that your Audite has picked up on issues the two of you may not realize you have. I want to get to the bottom of what made it come to that conclusion. You received your Level One warning three months ago, is that correct?'

'Yes,' they said together.

'You moved into this house a week after you married. So minus the six-month newlyweds' grace period, it's likely problems came to a head after you came here. So perhaps the house has come at your relationship's expense?'

'We couldn't have afforded it if we hadn't got married,' said Noah. 'A junior doctor's salary isn't going to make me rich and Luca is hardly going to earn his fortune in events catering.'

Jeffrey noted Luca flinch at the dismissal.

'But our relationship is fine,' Noah continued, oblivious. 'You said it yourself the day you met us, it was probably the system misunderstanding the nature of how we are with one another.'

Jeffrey remained silent, which clearly riled Noah.

Are you saying that's no longer the case?'

Luca squeezed Noah's right thigh as if urging him to be less confrontational.

'And I don't blame the house for all this,' added Noah. 'I blame that stupid bloody Audite.'

'That's the same Audite that you trusted when you signed up to the Marriage Act a year ago and which allowed you to buy your dream home. Luca, are you happy here?'

'It's nice.'

'But are you *happy*?'

'Why do you keep asking him that?' interrupted Noah.

'I suppose I'm trying to find a reason for why your husband has been prescribed antidepressant medication.'

'How . . . how do you know that?' asked Luca.

'It was in your medical notes,' Jeffrey said, but he had actually found the box containing patches in their bathroom cabinet.

'Like millions of others, he uses them occasionally to help with a chemical imbalance,' said Noah, 'not because he's unhappy with the house or our relationship.'

'Most couples like to believe their relationship is an equal partnership,' said Jeffrey. 'But often there's one who speaks for both of you even when a question isn't directed at them. Is it fair to say that's you, Noah?'

'Maybe, I guess.'

'In my experience, that person needs to be reminded that they're appreciated for the extra work they do, or the decisions they make to push you both forward. Do you need more affirmation than Luca offers?'

'No.'

'Have you considered that this elevated position you've put yourself in might emasculate Luca?'

'Where's this coming from? He's never accused me of any of that.'

'Could he have told you in his behaviour, but you haven't seen the signs? It's easier to ignore your partner's needs than to confront a difference of opinion.'

'I'm not ignoring anything   '

'You ignored Luca's emotional call for support by walking out of the house when your surrogate put a hold on your agreement; you dismissed his unwillingness to participate in threesomes by claiming they're only on hold. You debased your marriage by allowing him to believe you married only for love and not the financial benefits.'

'You're twisting what I've said . . .'

'Do you think the world revolves around you, Noah?'

'No! Of course not. I spend my career putting other people first.'

'And to make people listen to you, I assume you have to rely on persuasion or fear.'

'Fear?'

'Of the health repercussions if they don't do what you tell them to do.'

'I give them facts and options. I save lives.'

'So I ask again, do you think the world revolves around you?'

As Noah's face reddened, Luca tightened his grip on Noah's thigh.

'In the perimeters of my hospital, then yes, maybe the world does revolve around me; it revolves around all the staff. But not at home and not in my relationship.'

'Are you sure you didn't mean to say "our" relationship?' Noah glared at him. 'If you can't admit the world does revolve around you, then you're not being honest with Luca and me or yourself.'

'So now I'm a liar?' He turned to Luca. 'Why aren't you defending me?'

'It's in our nature to believe the world revolves around us,' interrupted Jeffrey. 'Human beings are born selfish. We want warmth, we want food, we want love, we want shelter, we want attention, we want to feel safe . . . when did a baby last put its parents' needs first? Some of us evolve into more thoughtful human beings while others carry these child-like traits throughout their lives.'

Noah shook his head. 'Now he's calling me childish.'

'He's not,' said Luca. 'He's challenging you.'

'All I want is for you to recognize that you're human and that, by design, humans are contradictory,' said Jeffrey. 'We say one thing but then we behave in a different manner. Once you're honest with yourself about who you are, then you can be honest with Luca about what you really want from your time together, however long that lasts.' Jeffrey stared Noah dead in the eye. 'Do you want to be monogamous? Do you want to start a family? Do you really want to be married?'

'Yes, of course I do!'

'Can you see why your attitude might make Luca question this?'

'Do you?' Noah asked Luca.

Jeffrey didn't allow Luca the chance to respond. 'I'm asking *you*, Noah, but instead of answering my question, you're deflecting. You're putting the onus on Luca to reassure you.'

'I always tell you how much I love you, don't I?' Noah asked.

'You can be saying one thing with your words, but the tone in which you deliver them can be interpreted in an entirely different way,' Jeffrey said. 'Perhaps aside from the insults, that's another reason why the system flagged up your conversations. You were too much of a contradiction for it to understand. And if you don't understand yourself, you are setting your husband an impossible task to understand you too.'

Noah rose from the sofa and held his palms up in a surrender motion. 'You win.'

'I'd like to offer a suggestion that might help,' continued Jeffrey. 'A relationship sabbatical.'

'You want us to split up?' asked Luca.

'No, no, not at all. A Positive Disengagement means separate bedrooms, no intimacy, no conversing with each other unless it's in our sessions and with me present to facilitate conflict or unexpected emotions.'

'What will that accomplish?' asked Luca.

'It's brought my other clients breathing space and clarity. You talk to each other through me and I'll offer you my interpretations of what I believe the other is trying to say. It might work, it might not. But at this point, what do you have to lose?'

Luca nodded but Noah shook his head. 'You two can communicate to your heart's content, but this is nonsense, Luca, and you're falling for it. I need a timeout.'

'Sorry,' said Luca as Noah left the room.

'It's not uncommon. Not everyone is ready to have their truths exposed.'

Luca hesitated and looked down at his feet. 'Can I ask you something, Jeffrey?'

'Of course.'

'Do you think Noah and I should be together?'

Jeffrey considered the most appropriate way to answer that wouldn't expose his bias.

'We still have a lot of work to do between the three of us, and that becomes prolonged each time Noah refuses to participate. I think that it would be in both of your best interests if I remained living here for the full eight weeks. But if you're not comfortable with that, I understand, and I'll do my best for you both with the remainder of our time.'

'Thank you,' said Luca. 'I don't want you to think we're ungrateful.'

The butterflies that emerged in Jeffrey's stomach carried him all the way up the stairs and back to his room where he quietly cheered and threw his fists in the air with the enthusiasm of a sports fan celebrating his team's victory.

41

Arthur

Arthur Foley's bravery had saved countless lives over the decades. He had led firefighting teams from the front as they'd worked their way through burning buildings or operated machinery to intricately cut people from the wreckage of vehicles. Each and every time he had channelled his adrenaline into a calm, collected, steely determination.

But tonight's version of Arthur Foley was a very different man from the one his colleagues might remember. Because preparing to meet the woman he had selected from a matchmaking service terrified him.

He shrank so far into a quiet snug inside the Fox & Hounds country pub in the village of Harleston that he worried he might fold in on himself. Arthur was so far removed from his comfort zone that he could no longer see it from where he was sitting. When sweat developed under his arms and dripped down his sides, he rolled an ice cube inside his mouth to cool himself down. To calm his nerves, he swigged a large mouthful of whiskey and Coke. His stress levels and heart rate escalated so much that even his Smart watch asked him if he was in need of medical assistance.

Toni Cooper was punctual, opening the door at exactly seven p.m. Arthur hesitated before he waved at her, allowing himself a moment to take in her appearance as she looked around, trying to locate him. She was dressed pleasantly in a jumper, trousers and flat shoes. June might have picked that outfit. Toni was certainly attractive, a little younger than him – although not by much – with dark-brown hair and grey streaks, hazel-coloured eyes and a Mediterranean skin tone. He rose to his feet and flattened out a kink in his tie.

'Arthur,' she began as she approached him and kissed him on both cheeks. 'So lovely to meet you.' Her natural poise put him at ease.

'And you,' he replied. 'Have you travelled far?'

'In life or this evening?'

Arthur stared at her blankly.

'Sorry, a little wordplay to ease the nerves.' She smiled. 'I'm about twenty minutes away in Gayton. And you?'

'I'm over in Kingsthorpe, near what used to be Thornton Park before they covered the grass in concrete and turned it into a railway depot,' Arthur replied. 'May I get you something to drink?'

'What's in your glass?'

'Jack Daniel's and Coke,' he said, suddenly embarrassed by his choice of spirit so early in the evening.

'Then I'll have the same.'

When he returned from the bar, Toni was slipping her phone into her handbag.

'Just letting my daughter know that she can leave as you don't look like a serial killer.'

Arthur turned his head. 'Is she here?'

'She was in the car outside. She insisted on staying until she knew I was all right. Do you have children?'

'No, I don't,' he replied and was reminded of an unfulfilled yearning he hadn't felt in years. 'How many do you have?'

'Two boys and a girl. They all live close by and I have a granddaughter who I look after two mornings a week while her mum's at work. Your profile mentioned you're a widower?'

Arthur loathed being attached to that word. 'Yes.'

'And by the fact you're twisting your wedding ring, I assume it wasn't long ago?'

He nodded his head but didn't elaborate beyond. 'Ten months.'

'Two years for me,' she replied. 'An undiagnosed brain tumour.' She snapped her fingers. 'I lost him within a fortnight. And your wife?'

'She had a heart attack in her sleep. She also had a rare untreatable form of dementia.'

'I'm sorry to hear that. Did she stay with you until the end?'

'Yes.' He also held back from admitting she also remained with him for seven months after the end.

'So you didn't send her to one of those "countryside facilities", as they call them? Or as they should more accurately be described, "body farms"?'

'Absolutely not.'

'I wouldn't have either. I hate how those advertising campaigns shame the sufferer into believing they're a burden and how it gives their so-called loved ones an escape from their moral obligations.' She took a sip from her drink. 'Apologies, I'll get off my high horse now. So is this your first date?'

'Is it that obvious?'

'I've been on enough to know when someone doesn't want to be here.'

'Oh, I'm sorry if I'm giving you that impression.'

Arthur feared he had offended her when Toni stood up suddenly and flipped her handbag over her shoulder. 'Let's move to somewhere a little livelier,' she said and he followed her to a noisier section of the pub where they sat under a speaker playing songs by Britpop bands he recognized from his twenties like Oasis and Radiohead. She pointed to his Smart watch, took his hand and placed his palm over it before speaking directly into his ear. She did the same with her own.

'Don't worry. If you're anything like me, you're not dating again out of choice but because you've got too much to lose if you don't.'

Arthur nodded.

'While I'm happy they don't listen in to widows and widowers at home, it angers me that as soon as a date has been arranged through their organization, they can tune in through our tech to listen to ten minutes of our conversation.'

'Really?' said Arthur quietly. 'I didn't know that.'

'I feel as if I can be honest with you, Arthur. I agree to participate in just enough dates to remain under the radar and appear that I'm looking for a spouse. I do what they suggest, I don't wear my wedding ring so men think of me as "emotionally available", I ask plenty of questions and I listen to the answers. Did you know after each date we are supposed to fill in a questionnaire about one another and give each other critiques and ratings?'

'They mentioned that in my interview.'

'I make sure to get my review in first and it's always

flattering so the other person isn't tempted to leave anything that might trigger alarm bells and suggest I'm not taking it seriously. And, by playing the system, I get to keep my house and full pension and I can afford to spend the rest of my time doing what I want to do and not worrying about losing it all. It keeps the wolves from the door. Not forever, mind, but at least I can't hear them howling for the time being.'

'Isn't it against the rules?'

They stopped talking when one song ended until another began. 'Strictly speaking, yes. But there are plenty of us out there doing it, as you'll discover. For the most part, dates will be like this one, perfectly pleasant. They can make it difficult for us to remain single but they can't force us to be together, can they?'

'What will you do if they put a deadline on finding someone else?'

Toni shrugged. 'It's likely to happen one day. Then, I'll find myself a single old gay guy or girl who's happy for a platonic relationship. I'm sorry if you were looking for more and that I've wasted your time.'

'No, not at all,' he replied and finally allowed himself to relax in Toni's company.

'I saw an advert recently for a company that uses not only genetic matching but also AI to ensure that, before you've even met your Match, you're biologically, sexually, emotionally and mentally compatible too. The next generation won't know what it's like to date spontaneously. They'll all be Matched in a laboratory or by an App.'

'Whatever happened to romance?'

'That went out with the Ark, Arthur. Like us. Anyway, tell me about yourself.'

Arthur recalled his years served in the fire service while Toni told him vaguely of her career as a therapist.

'Specializing in what?' he asked.

'Couples,' she said hesitantly.

'A Relationship Responder?' Arthur asked. Only when Toni saw him visibly bristle did she offer more detail.

'Oh, Lord no. I'm most definitely not one of *them*. I focus on couples who actually want therapy, not those who it's forced upon.'

'Didn't the Government make what you do illegal?'

'Yes, when they revoked the licences of anyone who refused to retrain. Now they're only awarded to graduates of their own programmes. So if I marketed myself as a couples' therapist, I could be arrested and charged with "Fraudulent Misrepresentation". I still have clients, but it's all very discreet.'

As the night progressed, they spoke about their travels, films and bands they had seen in their youth. There was a lot more laughter than he had anticipated, and more recollections of their late spouses.

'What do you miss the most about your husband?' Arthur asked.

'Where do I start? The shared memories, the giggles, the knowing there was always someone to talk to, who understood you, who was on your side. With David, I never had to do anything alone. What about you?'

'I talked to June for months after she died,' said Arthur cautiously. She was the first person he admitted it to. 'It made me feel less lonely.'

'Most nights I dream about David. I'm forever searching

for him. I know he's out there somewhere but I can't find him. I wake up exhausted. Have you read about those avatars they can create now based on lost loved ones? Using photos and old video footage, there's a company that can build a model of how David and June looked, sounded and moved.'

'Really?'

'They use a device to project them into your house. You can talk to them and they'll talk back. It's supposed to stop us from feeling alone. I'm sure they'll be banned soon as it goes against the Government's plans for us all to remarry before our partners' bodies are even cold.'

Arthur had already spent too much time with a shell of June to replicate it with another. He wouldn't bring her back in any format.

When the landlord rang the bell for last orders, Arthur checked his watch, surprised at how rapidly the night had passed.

'I never asked you, what are you looking for, Arthur? Love or companionship?'

Arthur placed his hand more firmly on his watch. 'Neither. I had fifty-three years of both with a wonderful woman. I don't want or need that with anyone else.'

Toni raised her glass. 'Then welcome to the club of "doing just enough to get by",' she chuckled. 'Here's to nothing.'

Arthur's glass clinked against hers and, for the first time in as long as he could remember, he realized that he had actually enjoyed himself. But more importantly, it had confirmed something that, deep down inside him, he already knew.

42

Anthony

Early morning starts were becoming the norm for Anthony.
Awake at four a.m., showered by 4.15 a.m. and sitting at his
desk in the home office by 4.30 a.m. Thirty minutes before
Jada's alarm sounded at 7 a.m., he would pad through the
house, into the kitchen and make himself breakfast. Then
he'd return to his desk with a bowl of cereal, a yoghurt, coffee
and enough sugary snacks and fruit to last him until midday.
Later, and only when the pinhole cameras he'd installed
around the house without Jada's knowledge confirmed he
was alone, he would return to the kitchen to remove a frozen
lunch from the freezer and perhaps an evening meal. He'd
blast them in the semiconductor oven and store their piping
hot contents in thermal heat pots under his desk.

The longer he worked, the less time there was to dwell
on the Freedom for All campaigners who had died in arson
attacks on their homes in Old Coventry. But it hadn't stopped
him from searching for their images online. The faces of the
children, a boy and a girl, were now seared in his memory.
They were dead as a result of his work.

Over the last few weeks, Anthony had separated much
of his life from the one being lived by his family. He might
show his face briefly when Matthew returned from school or

later before his son went to bed. But conversations between Anthony and Jada were often through electronic means and, if in person, they'd dwindled to perfunctory greetings. Sometimes, the first words they might say to one another on any given day were 'goodnight' or 'see you in the morning'.

The first time he learned Matthew had been prescribed ADHD patches was when he glimpsed one attached to his son's upper arm during a FaceTime conversation. Anthony considered asking Jada what else the specialist had recommended, but decided against it. She was his mother, she knew best.

Anthony's latest project brought with it a stress he had not experienced the likes of before. He was used to high demands and tight deadlines, but it wasn't the workload that was troubling him as much as the subject matter.

He opened his encrypted message inbox. There were updates and messages from teams scattered worldwide whom he had managed for seven years but had never met in a physical environment. Video calls used filters to distort their faces and voices. Their names were fictitious and only identifiable by those way above Anthony's paygrade. Sometimes he wondered if they were even real or if he was talking to chatbots.

The day passed quickly and he had lost track of time until a camera alerted him to the opening and closing of the front door. Matthew was returning home with Jada. To his shame, try as he might, he couldn't recall the last time he had walked his son to or from school. A vision of the future caught him off guard: one where the choice was taken out of his hands. It left him cold.

'The next stage of our campaign to exploit AI and the insight it gives us to radically overhaul the education system,' Henry Hyde had begun at that last meeting. 'AI models can now be trained to identify the voiceprint of up to six hundred people in any one recording. Our proposal is to integrate this technology into state schools. Alongside students' wearable technology, this will ensure three-sixty-degree student monitoring.'

Hyde had paused to allow the disclosure to settle.

'For what purpose?' a man Anthony didn't recognize had asked.

'The purpose is far-reaching,' Hyde had continued. 'It will identify bullying and act as a deterrent towards it and pick up on discussions and suggestions of abuse at home. It will also measure a child's use of vocabulary, their grasp of language, it will learn their most popular topics of conversation, appraise their conversational ability and cross refer it to work online and in their digital exercise books. Along with recommendations from their teachers, this AI system will also allow us to identify and separate high performers from those who need extra assistance.'

'What do you mean by "separate"?' the same man had continued.

'There are many students who cannot flourish because they're hampered by the distracting activities of others. We aim to redress this.'

'But they're already separated into different sets based on their academic abilities,' said Eleanor Harrison, the education minister. It appeared to be the first she was hearing of Hyde's proposal.

'Yes,' Hyde had agreed, 'but some of these children maintain disruptive behaviours outside the classroom, such as in the playground or in sporting environments. Hence our final solution is to establish purpose-built residential communities, where every pupil gets the most out of their education. Young Citizen Camps will be located around the country to assist more troubled youths and those with behavioural conditions to reach their full potential away from those they seek to distract. In a new environment, they will thrive.'

Anthony's stomach had tightened; based on what he'd been told by Jada about his son's recent school reports, Hyde could be talking about Matthew.

'A troubled child's ability to learn and retain information can increase threefold without parental or sibling interference,' Hyde had continued. 'Imagine their potential in a dedicated facility that's not local to them.'

'So you're sending them away?' had come another voice.

'We don't use the expression *sent away*. No child will ever be *sent away*. After a student is identified as in need of intervention, teachers and psychologists will be invited to offer their expert opinions before an offer to parents is made. And, even then, this will be a wholly voluntary process.'

Anthony had subconsciously tapped his foot against the table leg. 'And what if the parents refuse?' he'd asked.

'They're absolutely within their rights to do so. It will, of course, be included as a footnote on the child's National Identity Card that an offer was declined – it is only fair to prospective employers to receive full disclosure. Likewise, it will also be included on their parents' records too.'

'Can you tell us more about these Young Citizen Camps?' a narrow-eyed woman with greying cornrows had asked.

'As one of the top five greenest countries in the world, our camps are being repurposed from existing properties.'

'Repurposed from what? Former offices?'

'The majority are deregulated military barracks and former correctional facilities.'

'Prisons?' MP Maddy Cordell had laughed. 'And you're expecting us to sell this idea to the public?'

'Firstly, they are now *former* correctional facilities,' Hyde had repeated impatiently. 'And secondly, this is more than just an idea. It's happening. Work has already started on the first twelve.'

'I assume you'll be at least removing the prison ring fencing?' Cordell had scoffed.

'A proportion of it will remain for their protection and to prevent unlawful entry. Parents will want to be assured their children's safety is our number one priority.'

'What will be on the curriculum?' Harrison had asked.

'There will be less emphasis on mainstream education's core subjects such as English literature, maths and coding. Research has found these pupils to be less responsive to those subjects and therefore more disruptive. They'll be educated and trained for the industries our model predicts they're best suited for, such as the building trade, careers in the domestic sector, the food and beverage industry, childcare workers, cashiers, clothing manufacturers et cetera. The values we instil in them at Young Citizen Camps will remain with them until their eventual reintegration into society.'

'You are doing the workforce in those sectors a huge

disservice if you're saying the most suitable people for those roles are underachievers,' the woman with the greying corn-rows had huffed. 'You're suggesting those careers are only for write-offs, that they are the jobs nobody else wants. It's hugely insulting to millions.'

'On the contrary. These jobs keep the engine of society moving forwards. If our weakest academic students are offered support and training from an early age, they have the potential to be the backbone of our economy's growth. Mean-while, children continuing to attend our regular schools will thrive without disturbance. It's a win-win situation. Britain's next century can, and will, be better than the last.'

A nervous Anthony had cleared his throat. 'Like Ms Cordell asked, how will you convince parents this is in their children's best interests?' he'd asked.

'I have assembled an assortment of the country's leading psychologists and scriptwriters to develop a television series that will begin the marketing of this project to the masses. It will be upbeat, family viewing, broadcast on a mainstream channel and across social media, based in a Young Citizen's Camp. As well as creating likeable, identifiable and believ-able characters, the focus will also be on the fun, exciting, opportunities to be had for those who participate. Targeted advertising will appear on the communication devices of under-sixteens, and their parents will be offered financial encouragement to participate. We want to create a vision of a place where parents are confident their children will gain the best opportunities. And we want young people to *want* to be a part of these camps.'

Anthony had listened intently as Hyde had detailed

exactly what was expected of him, the tight timescale and generous budget. His final question continued to haunt him now, every bit as much as the faces of the dead children of FFA supporters.

'What kind of behavioural conditions will these camps cater for?' he'd asked.

'Off the top of my head, anything from anger management issues to oppositional defiant disorder, conduct disorders, learning impaired, some identifiable on the Autism Spectrum scale and those diagnosed with bipolar and Attention Deficit Disorder.'

They were the three words Anthony had hoped he would not hear. *Attention Deficit Disorder*. He had finally reached his critical juncture. Now he could either continue to serve those above him or he could find his own path. It was too late to save the lives of the FFA victims, but it wasn't too late to protect his son.

WHY A SMART MARRIAGE IS A DUMB MOVE

More of us are realizing the Sanctity of Marriage Act was a huge mistake. Not only has it shattered relationships and destroyed towns through gentrification, the gap between Britain's rich and poor has never been wider.

Smart Marriages discriminate against those refusing to upgrade, those cohabiting, single people and the bereaved. By signing up or upgrading you are . . .

- Allowing a computer to decide if your marriage is at risk.

- Letting a Family Court divorce you – even if you want to stay together.

- Forcing hundreds of thousands of traditionally married couples to move into underfunded areas while the rest live in Smart towns with better infrastructure.

- Preventing businesses from employing single people even if they're better qualified.

- Making non-Act people pay 35% higher taxes and insurance policies.

- Requiring non-Act people to wait three extra months for appointments at underfunded hospitals.

- Allowing Emergency services to prioritize calls to New Towns over Old Towns.

August 29 – Kennington Park London – If you care about your country, join *Freedom for All* in Britain's biggest protest rally as we put pressure on the Government to *revoke* the Sanctity of Marriage Act.

43

Roxi

This was not how Roxi had imagined it to look. She double-checked the postcode she had dictated into the car's satnav. It was the correct house and road; she'd just had the wrong expectations. She powered down the shared vehicle she pooled with her neighbours and waited. Quite what for, Roxi didn't know, but until she was ready, she was not going to act on impulse.

Roxi had assumed the property in a New Northampton village of Gayton was going to be, at best, a replica of her modern, shoebox home. But this was nothing of the sort. It was an immaculately presented, original Georgian build, with two sash windows either side of a red wooden door, and three more above it. The weedless lawns were separated by a tiled path. It was a house Roxi could only dream of owning, and she was more than a little green-eyed.

It was most certainly not where she'd expected to find the home of the person trolling her on social media.

In the last week, @JustSayingBabe had targeted every single one of Roxi's posts, from her most recent ones right back to her first. Each attack included details of Roxi's life that she had never spoken of publicly.

But it was the troll's accusation that Owen was having an

affair that had echoed the longest and loudest. Was it true? Had Roxi's ambition pushed her husband into someone else's arms? Try as she might, Roxi just could not imagine her dependable, reliable, loyal Owen ever doing that. She trusted him implicitly. But there was no escaping the fact their marriage was in trouble. If starved, even the most loyal dogs will eat from another bowl.

As fast as she could delete the comments and then block the troll, the quicker they reappeared. She concluded they must be using a program to bypass her attempts to hinder it. Roxi's obsession with this anonymous opponent was keeping her awake at night. Each time her phone alerted her to a new comment, she couldn't relax until she knew who had posted it. At peak traffic times she was checking the device every minute. She asked herself if this was how the decline in Jem Jones' mental health had begun. Did paying undue attention to one person spur Jem into delving deeper and taking other negative comments to heart too? If that was the case, Roxi knew she had to nip this in the bud: ignore it or take a stance and fight back. She chose the latter. And she would do it the most effective way she knew – in front of an audience.

It was unlikely the enemy knew of some of the important connections Roxi was making. She had confided about the deeply personal attacks she'd suffered to a civil servant and fervent supporter of all things Marriage Act-related as they'd waited to appear on a Radio 4 show together. By the time they'd left the station, one of the woman's team had located her troll's original IP address then quietly provided Roxi with the location of the property it was registered to. Now here she was, parked outside Antoinette Cooper's house.

Roxi wanted to arm herself with all she could find out about her tormentor. But her research had yielded nothing. Cooper had no online presence. No LinkedIn employment history, no videos uploaded to TikTok or even a YouTube channel. For someone so vocal about Roxi, she had very little to say about herself. What was she hiding? After days of planning, Roxi was about to find out. Because she was going to confront Cooper on her doorstep and record every moment of it before posting it online.

Roxi had developed an instinct for the posts that would generate the most traffic and gain the attention of mainstream media. And she was convinced this one had the potential to be huge, while renewing her call for AI to be used for monitoring all social media posts.

She could imagine the TV captions already. 'How I confronted my troll', and 'Britain's Brightest Influencer fights back'. The world was going to learn Roxi was no pushover.

Another ten minutes passed before she fully readied herself. One last check that her recording equipment was charged and operational and she began to make her move. However, just before she exited her vehicle, Cooper's front door opened. If her tormentor was about to leave, Roxi would need to confront her now. But first, she wanted to get a better look at who she was taking on.

A woman appeared and, even from a distance, she appeared much older than Roxi, by at least a couple of decades. Surely this couldn't really be Cooper? Was it her mother? But age was no barrier to malice.

Roxi watched carefully as Cooper shifted her body slightly so that her back pressed against the door. She was not alone;

she was allowing someone to pass her. Their back was to Roxi and she watched as Cooper briefly placed her hand on their arm.

Only when they turned to walk down the path did Roxi recognize Cooper's visitor. It was her husband, Owen.

44

Jeffrey

Jeffrey was barely able to mask his satisfaction at supervisor Adrian's news.

He placed on the ground the packages of new clothing he'd had delivered to his temporary PO Box and pushed a loosening earbud back inside his ear.

'This kind of complaint happens all the time,' Adrian advised. 'Please don't take it personally.'

'How can I not?' Jeffrey replied, seeking to sound more disappointed than delighted. 'You know what it's like when you spend so much time with a couple – you want to help them make it work. So it's disheartening when you tell me they want to replace me as their Relationship Responder. I'm failing them.'

'You're not, honestly, you're really not. This only goes to prove what good work you're doing. They're uncomfortable because you're getting to the root of their problems. They're trying to distract from facing up to their own failures by projecting them upon you.'

'What did you tell them?'

'That it wasn't our policy to change Responders four weeks into a programme of assistance, as noted in their contract.'

'And their reaction?'

'He cursed a little and described therapy as pointless and biased.'

Jeffrey smiled to himself. By using the singular, he knew without asking that this was Noah's complaint, not Luca's. Luca wouldn't go behind his back like that. They had a connection.

With the conversation at an end, Jeffrey opened the door to his clients' home and breathed in the silence. Both men's cars were parked outside so it was likely they were here somewhere, but – he hoped – apart. If so, it suggested Luca and Noah were abiding by his Positive Disengagement suggestion, keeping their personal communication to a bare minimum, and saving the majority of their discourse for counselling.

He took a moment and stood in the centre of the lounge to take in his surroundings. Being here felt so . . . normal. *He* felt normal. After spending so long between clients as a transient soul living out of his car, he could be happy here, long-term. He'd change the wallpaper on the feature wall and perhaps replace the electric fire with a wood burner to make it cosier on cold winter nights. But that would be about it. Goosebumps skittered across his shoulders when he imagined curling up with Luca on the sofa under a warm woollen blanket.

But as Jeffrey momentarily let down his guard, a ghost of his former self appeared that he had not meant to summon. Suddenly he was back in his mid-teens and living in the dilapidated council-owned ground-floor flat he'd shared with his father and older brother. A lifetime of untreated mental health issues had left Bobby Snr self-medicating with booze and high-potency cannabis. Jeffrey's mother had long abandoned ship, leaving them to fend for themselves.

Seventeen-year-old Bobby Jnr was two years Jeffrey's senior and he'd thought nothing of using his handsome looks and confident swagger to invite girls into their shared bedroom. He hadn't cared about the presence of his curious sibling, watching and listening to everything through the darkness.

Joining the procession of female faces had come Rosie Morrison, a petite girl with strawberry-blonde ringlets who'd smelled of liquorice. She was the only one Bobby had invited back multiple times. Rosie had differed from his other conquests because she'd acknowledged Jeffrey. She'd addressed him with the wave of a hand, a casual smile or sometimes an 'alright?' as they'd passed on the landing. She'd even bought him a cupcake the day after learning of his birthday.

Jeffrey had realized he was falling in love with the girl his brother had admitted meant little more to him than a 'regular screw'. And as the weeks had progressed, he'd sensed that his feelings might be mutual. There had been moments when car headlights had beamed through curtainless windows when he and Rosie had locked eyes while she and Bobby were in unison. The first time it had happened, Jeffrey had thought he'd imagined it and quickly rolled over. But when it had occurred twice more, he'd known she was telling him that she'd rather be having sex with him than his brother.

In the mornings, and if he awoke before them, he'd stare at their unconscious, semi-naked bodies entwined. He'd imagined the touch of Rosie's skin and her breath in his mouth. She'd once caught him with his hands moving rhythmically under his duvet and she'd reciprocated by pulling back her sheets to reveal herself entirely. He'd crossed the finishing line almost immediately.

The morning that had altered the rest of Jeffrey's life had begun with an absent Bobby. Jeffrey had been awake but Rosie was deep in slumber, lying on her side, an empty bottle of vodka on the floor. It was the opportunity he had been waiting for. Quietly, he'd padded barefoot towards her, hesitated, and with trembling fingertips, he'd touched the underside of her thigh. It was warmer and smoother than he'd imagined. He'd known that he should stop and return to his bed but he couldn't bring himself to. Slowly, his fingers had travelled upwards.

Without warning and with her eyes still closed, Rosie had stretched out her hand and begun to massage the front of his boxer shorts. Then she'd pulled back the rest of her sheets and moved over to make room for him. It couldn't be clearer, he'd thought; she wanted him and not his brother. Jeffrey's underwear had fallen to his ankles and he'd joined her in the bed. He'd watched Bobby on enough occasions to know where Rosie enjoyed being touched, so he'd replicated his brother's movements until, eventually, she'd allowed him inside her.

'You're wearing a condom?' she'd mumbled. Jeffrey had been about to reply when she'd spoken again. 'And don't lie to me, Bobby. You're not getting me pregnant.'

His brother's name had rung in his ears and he'd frozen. But when his paralysis had continued for too long,

Rosie must have instinctively realized something was awry because she'd turned her head to face him.

'Get off me!' she'd yelled and squirmed until she'd expelled him from her body. 'You're a rapist!'

'No, no, I'm not . . .' Jeffrey had said, horrified she could think such a thing.

Jeffrey had wanted Rosie to know that he was only there because he'd thought he'd been invited and that he loved her more than his brother ever could. But Rosie hadn't been listening. And when she'd screamed 'Bobby!' at the top of her lungs, he'd had to act fast.

He'd clamped his hand over her mouth to silence her. Then as she'd tried to wriggle free, he'd mounted her, pinning her arms and legs down with his own. She'd continued floundering and yelling for Bobby so Jeffrey had grabbed a pillow and held it over her face to muffle her cries.

Over and over again he'd begged her to hush, telling her that if she just stopped shouting, he could explain everything. Eventually Rosie had given up fighting him and he'd pushed the pillow to one side.

'I'm sorry,' he'd said. 'Please don't tell my brother.'

He'd been greeted by her parted lips and lifeless eyes.

Sixteen years later and Jeffrey could remember with clarity everything about that moment and what had followed.

Now, he removed a receipt and empty chocolate wrapper from his pocket and waved his hand above the sensors to open Luca's bin. Inside, brightly coloured shreds of paper caught his eye. Some appeared to contain writing. Curious, Jeffrey pulled out a handful to read. Noah and Luca had been writing notes to one another.

His shoulders slumped as he spread the papers across the breakfast bar and pieced them together.

'This is insane,' read the first in Noah's handwriting. 'We can't even talk. We're living in a Margaret Atwood novel.'

'It won't be for too long,' Luca had written. 'Be patient.'

'Do you believe all that stuff he said about me being selfish and controlling?'

'He's just doing his job.'

'Tell me you don't believe him, Ziggy.'

'I don't!'

'He's going out later – I'll be in the bath if you want to keep me company . .' Noah had finished his message with a winking smiley face.

'See you there!'

Noah dropped the notes back in the bin then slammed his fists against the worktop. The hold Noah had on Luca was stronger than Jeffrey had given him credit for. He had expected too much from Luca too soon.

But Noah was no match for Jeffrey, a fact he would learn soon enough.

45

Corrine

'Have you seen the news yet?' Yan texted.

'No, why?' Corrine typed as she made her way from her car and back into the house.

'It's Harrison. Look online. You can't miss her. She's everywhere.'

A knot appeared in Corrine's stomach as she closed the door behind her and hurried to the kitchen. She opened the ITV News App and the MP was the lead story, alongside a video clip. Corrine recognized the location. Harrison had held a news conference on the steps leading into her New Northampton apartment block where she lived alone when working in the constituency. The rest of her time was spent in London with her family. For this performance, though, her husband, daughter and son were also in shot, standing either side, looking every bit as sombre as their matriarch.

Corrine squinted as she took in the woman's appearance. The front left-hand side of Harrison's forehead was bandaged, there was a plaster across her nose and both eyes were bruised. There was also visible bruising around her throat as if she had been choked. When she opened her mouth, one of her central incisors was missing.

'What on earth have you done to yourself?' Corrine said

242

aloud. Harrison had sustained only one of those injuries before she was knocked unconscious to the floor. She could only assume the rest were feigned for the benefit of the cameras.

'I have been the victim of a domestic terrorist attack,' Harrison began. 'Recently, a man appeared at my front door carrying a parcel requiring a signature. When I opened it, he punched me in the face. As I fell to the floor, he repeatedly kicked and hit me, yelling that he was doing this for Freedom for All. His goal was to intimidate me into turning against my party and my beliefs and to end my support of the Sanctity of Marriage Act. It was then that I fell unconscious.'

A pregnant pause followed as her husband moved to clasp her hand in a choreographed movement. Next it was her daughter's turn to hold her mother's arm a little tighter. Her son remained stationary.

'Do not let Freedom for All fool you,' Harrison warned. 'It masquerades as a noble cause, giving a voice to the minority. But, in truth, it is not a political party. It is an extremist organization made up of deceitful, vengeful voices who have built nothing but want to tear down everything. They targeted Jem Jones and sent her to her death. And now they are launching violent attacks against women like me. They want to uproot what the majority of our country voted for in the last election, they have no respect for the opinions of others because they are set on punishing anyone who doesn't fall into line with their beliefs. But I am not a woman who kowtows, even if it means I face further brutal assaults. Millions of people are reaping the rewards of the Marriage Act and *they* are who I represent. I am proud of what we have accomplished and what we will go on to achieve. And if you love our country, then you will feel exactly the same as I do. My family and yours will never be safe in a world where Freedom for All exists.'

Harrison ignored journalists' questions and returned to the apartment lobby with her family, ensuring she paused first behind the glass doors for photographers to snap her husband drawing her head to his shoulder and planting a kiss on the crown.

Corrine was speechless. Almost everything the MP had said was a lie, including her injuries. But without putting herself in the firing line, Corrine was unable to offer a public counter.

'What are you watching?' her eldest daughter Freya asked as she appeared from the garden and peered over her shoulder. The clip automatically replayed. 'Ooh, Will doesn't look very happy to be there,' she added and moved towards the fridge.

'Who's Will?'

'That MP's son. He's in a couple of my art history lectures at uni. Nice guy, not like his mum by all accounts. Do we have any hummus?'

'Second shelf down next to the carrot sticks. Why, what have you heard about her?'

'He rarely mentions her as they had some massive falling out, but rumour has it they have an agreement. She pays his tuition fees and he shows up when she needs to wheel the family out for public events.'

Corrine didn't have the opportunity to ask anything else

before the kitchen door swung open. Mother and daughter turned to find a red-faced Mitchell.

'Can you give us a moment,' he growled at Freya.

She shrugged, offered her mum a 'Good luck' eyebrow raise, and left with a plate of snacks.

Mitchell closed the door behind her and waited until he heard her footsteps climbing the stairs.

'What the hell is this?' he continued, thrusting a tablet towards his wife's face.

'It looks like an iPad. Why, what do you think it is?'

'This legal document bullshit from your lawyer claiming you're applying for a fast track Level Three divorce "on the grounds of domestic abuse".'

'If you already know, why are you asking me?'

'I have never laid a finger on you in twenty-five years of marriage.'

'Haven't you?' asked Corrine with mock innocence.

'You know fine well I haven't!'

'Well, I have date-stamped photographic evidence that I've twice been injured and, to the best of my recollection, you were the cause.'

'What the hell are you talking about woman? Call your solicitor now and retract it.'

'No, Mitchell, I don't think I will.'

Mitchell waited for her to break but Corrine wouldn't be bending today, or ever again. Eventually he nodded his head slowly. 'Okay, Corrine. If you really want to play this game, then let's play. But by the time I have finished with you, you'll be begging me to give our marriage a second chance.'

'Are you threatening me?'

'You might be losing your looks but you've not lost your hearing. Yes, I am threatening you. And you had better be listening.'

Corrine stood firm. Then, to Mitchell's confusion, she allowed a shallow smile to spread across her face.

'What the hell is wrong with you?'

'Remind me, how long have we been Upmarried for?'

'A little over six months.'

'So the grace period is over.'

'Yes.'

Corrine nodded and Mitchell followed her eyes as they made their way to the wall and towards the Audite sensor. 'So now that I've made this legal claim against you, we are already on Level Three and there's every possibility this conversation is being recorded to use in court as evidence? Either from up there or on this lovely little gadget I've been made to wear?' She raised her wrist to her face and jiggled a Smart bracelet.

Mitchell's face reddened again. He opened his mouth to reply but he was hamstrung. He narrowed his eyes so tightly that Corrine could barely locate his irises. And, to her satisfaction, he stormed out of the kitchen more incensed than when he'd arrived.

46
Arthur

Arthur clipped the last of the dying forget-me-not plants from the borders of his garden with his secateurs. It was the end of the year's second bloom and he tipped them from a bucket into the recycling bin then hung up his gardening equipment on wall hooks inside the garage.

Next, he removed a tarpaulin cover from his and June's beloved old VW campervan, took a step back and gave it the once-over. The last time they had taken it out on the road was the day he'd realized that something was askew with his wife. They had driven to Stowe gardens, a familiar location to them when their dog Oscar was alive, and they'd travel the county searching for interesting places to walk him. But this particular day, June had no recollection of ever visiting it before. Arthur had showed her photographs on his phone of their last trip but her failing memory had only served to upset her. They'd returned home in silence. An official diagnosis was made by a dementia specialist a fortnight later. June had never taken a seat in the vehicle again.

Arthur made his way back into the house then slowly trudged up the staircase and into the bedroom he shared in life, and death, with his wife. He stretched himself across the bed and let his gaze absorb a magnificent sunset from the window. It bathed the room in warm oranges, rich reds and glowing yellows. He stared at the sun for as long as it took his eyes to grow sore. Then he snapped the lids tight and followed the colourful spots on the inside of his eyelids as they floated lazily like paraffin wax inside a lava lamp. Sometimes, when he did this, he imagined that he was lying on a white, Mediterranean beach like those he and June had visited on their winter holidays. Arthur had yet to experience the end of a day as beautiful as those in the Balearic Islands.

He stretched his arm across the bed, as if holding it around someone.

'Do you remember that bed and breakfast we stayed at in Formentera?' he asked.

'The one with more cockroaches than guests? Oh yes,' June chuckled. 'You can't blame me because you booked that one.'

Arthur pulled her head closer to his chest. He had missed her laugh more than any other sound in the world.

He had not heard a peep from his wife after the paramedics removed her body from the house and drove her to the mortuary for her autopsy. But, in the last few days, she had made her presence known again, returning every evening to keep him company.

*

The thirty-week sentence handed down to Arthur by magistrates had not come as a surprise. His solicitor Mr Warner had warned it would go against Arthur if he took his name off the Government's list of widowers looking for love. But he had made up his mind.

248

Drinks with fellow singleton Toni had afforded him clarity. She too was being forced to make the best of an impossible situation. However, he could not live as she did. He could not play the system and date regularly to retain his quality of life. He didn't possess the energy or the mindset to spend his advancing years negotiating a fictitious existence.

When Arthur's first court appearance made the local news and then national headlines, he'd expected to be lambasted for committing fraud and living with his wife's dead body. Instead, the media questioned why an elderly firefighter was being prosecuted in the first place. Freedom for All members took on his case, lobbying for the Crown Prosecution Service to drop it.

'It doesn't matter who you are or how you served your community,' Mr Warner warned, 'the higher your profile, the more it suits their agenda to make an example of you.'

'And if I married again, would all of this go away?'

'I couldn't possibly say.' But his expression gave Arthur his answer.

A new Smart tag attached to Arthur's wrist replaced the watch that had monitored his marriage. It meant he had to stay within the perimeters of his property for more than six months. But Arthur wasn't bothered – he wanted nothing from a world that was willing to treat him so unfairly. However, an unscheduled visit from his solicitor later in the week altered everything.

'Is there something wrong?' Arthur asked, surprised to see him at the door. It was the first time Mr Warner had made a house call.

'I'm afraid there is. It's your home, Arthur. I'm sorry to

249

have to tell you but the local authority has made a legal claim on it.'

'I don't understand?'

'They want you to repay the seven months of June's state pension money you allowed to remain in your bank account after her death, along with interest which, as a single man, is significantly higher than you'd pay if you were in a relationship. The company running June's private firefighting pension has also filed a claim to recall their payments, plus interest.'

'I offered to pay those back straight away but I was told I couldn't until after the court case,' he protested.

'I know. And since the Government privatized most public services, there are also claims for you to pay towards the prosecution's expenses, the ambulance service's retrieval of June's body and her autopsy. The single-person bedroom and council tax have also been backdated and, along with my fees, you owe more than you have in your savings. The only way to pay your debts is to seize any assets owned. And that means the house.'

The colour drained from Arthur's face. 'They can't. I own it.'

'I'm afraid they can.'

'When?'

'Two weeks from now. It's been expedited. I only found out about it three days ago and launched an immediate appeal and stay of execution on your behalf, but the court ruled against it. Freedom for All supporters set up a crowd-funding page, which raised more than fifty thousand pounds, but after the Government's Internet Code of Conduct laws were introduced, the site owners risked prosecution by funding a convicted criminal. It had no choice but to remove the page and refund the donations.'

Arthur sank into his seat, struggling to comprehend what he'd been told. He looked around the room. Everything he and June had bought and built together was about to be taken away.

'The good news is that the local authority has a duty of care and has been working with other jurisdictions to find you a new place to stay.'

'Where?'

'There are hostels in Leicester and Rugby that can accommodate you until your house is sold and you know what funds are left to support you.'

'But I've lived in this town all my life. And what about all my belongings?'

'The possessions that aren't auctioned to pay your debts will be placed into storage, which I'm afraid you will be charged for.'

'Can't you do something? You're my lawyer.'

'I wish I could, but my hands are tied. My firm only allows me to represent clients who have settled their bills with us. And you haven't, Arthur. The appeal I made on your behalf is the last action they'll let me carry out for you pro bono. I really am so sorry.'

In that same moment as Mr Warner apologized, June appeared behind him, her face beaming.

'Why are you smiling?' he imagined himself asking.

'You know why.'

'No, I don't. Tell me.'

'You don't have to stay here on your own, Artie. What's the point in keeping that old campervan of ours in the garage if we don't use it?'

'And go where?'

'On one last adventure.'

She was right, he thought. If it was a choice between spending the rest of his days living alone in a one-room hostel or on the run with his wife, he knew what he was going to do.

*

As they lay together on their bed, Arthur turned to witness the sparkle in June's eyes that first captivated him a lifetime ago.

'Shall we get going?' June asked, as the sun's light began to dim.

He nodded.

'I love you.'

'I love you too,' Arthur replied.

Arthur lifted himself up off the bed and picked up two suitcases he had packed earlier with their clothes and toiletries. She followed him as he slowly made his way back downstairs, taking in the framed photos in the hallway for the last time. They walked through the kitchen and out into the garage where their beloved van stood before them.

'There she is,' beamed June. She patted the roof, opened the door and picked up the plastic bag where he had stored half her ashes. 'Oh, come on, Artie,' she teased, lifting it up and dangling it. 'You could've put me in an urn by now.'

'Hush or I'll put you in next door's cat litter tray.'

She made herself comfortable on the passenger seat and wound down the window. Then she moved her arm through it, bobbing it up and down as if caught by a breeze, before winding it up again. 'How many miles have we done in her?' she asked.

'More than a hundred and fifty thousand,' said Arthur.

'Have you checked we've got enough fuel?'

'She's as ready for us as we are for her.'

'Then let's go.'

Arthur opened the boot and placed the suitcases inside. Then, from the workbench, he picked up the hosepipe and, using parcel tape, attached one end to the exhaust pipe and the other to a crack in the side window, padding the rest of the gap with an old beach towel. Finally, he climbed into the van to join June and turned on the ignition.

'Where do you fancy going then?' June asked as the engine chugged. 'We never made it to Barcelona and I always wanted to climb the steps up La Sagrada Família. It looks so beautiful in photographs.'

'Then let's go there first.'

She reached out her hand to entwine her fingers around his. His eyes welled as he offered his wife a grin as broad as any he had given her during their lifetime together. Then he wiped the tears away and closed his eyes.

'It's you and me to the end, girl,' Arthur whispered.

'You and me,' she repeated, and he could smell her apple blossom shampoo as she leaned her head onto his shoulder.

And together, they set off on their final adventure together.

47

Anthony

Anthony watched from the opposite side of the road as the queue outside the art deco building slowly decreased in size. Each person waiting in line was frisked by security staff then scanned with a metal and plastics detector before being allowed inside. He'd assumed Freedom for All members might be keeping a low profile after the recent arson attacks. Instead, they were united and defiant, ignoring passing vehicles that blasted their horns in support at them or hurled abuse from open windows. Fearing Government surveillance might be at work, he pulled down his baseball cap to partially obscure his face and lifted his collar up.

A little voice inside him, the one that was starting to question if he was fighting for the correct side, urged him to venture inside. He'd invested so much energy into trying to destroy FFA's reputation, it was time he saw for himself just how deserving they were of their notoriety. He crossed the road and became one of the last people to join the line. After being scanned, he placed his phone and Smart watch inside a secure ziplocked bag and walked along a short, darkened corridor until he reached a set of fire doors. Beyond them was the middle level of an auditorium.

He hadn't known what to expect, but certainly not vast

numbers like this. At least four to five hundred people of all ages and descriptions were seated and directing their collective attention towards the stage. Anthony looked towards a giant white screen. Below it was a handful of figures sitting around a table, facing the audience. He took the nearest empty seat as the lights dipped and listened as a young woman made an emotional speech about the recent arson attacks. Guilt tore another chunk from his soul as images of the victims were shown.

A second speaker discussed how AI should never have been allowed to identify problems in marriages in the first place. 'Artificial Intelligence Programs will never have a sense of humour,' he began. 'They will never appreciate art, beauty, or love. They will never feel lonely. They will never have empathy for other people, for animals, for the environment. They will never enjoy music, or cry at the drop of a hat. Those aren't my words. It's what AI had to say about itself – specifically a program called GPT-3 which was developed to mimic human language. When prompted by a researcher, AI wrote that its programs lack consciousness and self-awareness. That was in 2020. Even back then, AI was already warning us of its limitations. Yet it was still allowed to dictate the fate of human relationships.'

Other speakers discussed the legalities of a forthcoming protest march in London, culminating in a planned mass gathering in Kennington Park. Anthony wondered if the location was deliberate given supporters of the Chartist Movement campaigning for political reform had once gathered there for a protest for democracy in an industrial society. Almost 200 years had passed and the FFA was fighting for similar rights. History repeats itself, he thought.

To Anthony's surprise, organizers were hoping anything up to half a million people might attend. Trapped in his own bubble, he hadn't appreciated just how deep the vein of hatred ran for the Act.

An hour passed and the last person to take to the stage was a man Anthony recognized from his frequent television appearances since Jem Jones' death. While the party purposefully had no leader – instead, opting for a panel of members instead – Howie Cosby was its public face.

'I'd like you to take a look at this photograph,' he began and an image of an elderly man appeared on the screen behind him.

'This is Arthur Foley, a retired firefighter from this very town. Who knows how many lives this hero saved throughout his career, serving his community and inspiring those coming up through the ranks.'

The photo switched to one of a younger Arthur holding hands with a smiling woman. Both wore uniforms.

'This is his wife June, a fellow firefighter who also spent her career in the emergency services. They were married for forty-nine years, two of which under the Act, before she died suddenly in her sleep. So deep was his love for his wife that he chose to live with her body rather than have authorities take it away. Later, when she was discovered by a Relationship Responder, instead of being offered counselling, Arthur was punished for refusing to commit to finding another relationship. His marriage was completely disregarded by authorities.'

Cosby paused to take a sip from a bottle then he continued, recounting Arthur's court case. Without warning, an image of Arthur's dead body, slumped behind the wheel of his campervan, appeared on the screen. His eyes were closed, face grey, his head tilted to one side and the neck of his shirt stained by vomit. It drew gasps from the previously hushed crowd.

Anthony paled. He recalled identifying his mother's body at the mortuary, specifically the post-mortem bruising from where she had gone through the car windscreen after deliberately driving her car into a motorway bridge. For years he had blamed himself and how his need to break from his environment and enrol in university had come at the cost of his mother's already fragile mental health. Jada had come close to convincing him that he was blameless, but he had never completely believed her.

But now, glaring at this stranger's body, he knew there was no doubt about it. The voice in the back of his mind was to be believed. Anthony's work was killing people. His mother was his first victim, Jem Jones his next, followed by the arson victims and now Arthur Foley. Where would it end?

'Five days ago, Arthur chose to die rather than lose his home or be pressured into marrying someone he didn't love,' Cosby continued. 'It is your Government that is making this happen. For every couple that benefits from low stamp duty, NHS+ or all the other ways they have tried to bribe us, there is an Arthur Foley. Please, make your voice heard.'

A ripple of applause began around the auditorium as the main lights returned and a break for refreshments was announced. But while others moved from the seats, Anthony

257

remained in his. Tears poured from his eyes, ran down his face and seeped through the neckline of his jacket. He felt a gentle tap on his arm. He turned to find a woman in the aisle offering him a packet of paper tissues. He accepted them without shame and dabbed at his eyes.

'Stories like this upset me too,' she began. 'I only wish they were a rarity but they're becoming the norm. And they never get any easier to hear. Is it your first time here?'

Anthony nodded.

'What made you come?'

'Curiosity,' he said vaguely. 'And you?'

'To bring fairness back to our society. For us and our children's sake.'

Anthony thought of Matthew. Did he really want to raise his son in a country where its people would rather die than be pressured into remarrying? Suddenly, Anthony had a pressing urge to feel fresh air against his face. This was all too much; he shouldn't have come. He thanked the woman again for the tissue as he rose from his seat.

She held out her hand to shake his, pressing her palm against his for longer than necessary. 'I hope to see you again, Anthony,' she said. And before he could ask her how she was aware of his name, she ascended the stairs, leaving something in his hand.

48

Roxi

Juices from the cooked chicken hissed and spat like angry fireworks as they sloshed around the tray in Roxi's hands. She walked around the poky kitchen three times before propping open the door to ensure the aroma spread throughout the house before Owen returned.

And, as hoped, the smell was the first thing to reach her husband's nostrils the moment he opened the front door. He made his way into the kitchen, puzzled to find Roxi clad in an apron and loading the dishwasher. This wasn't her natural habitat.

'Oh hi.' She smiled, pretending she hadn't been tracking his car to pinpoint exactly when he'd arrive home. She poured from a bottle of Sauvignon Blanc into two stemmed glasses. 'I've made dinner.'

She watched as he dropped his sports bag and hockey stick on the floor in the corner of the room and regarded the chicken, his wife, and the chicken again.

'Is that . . .'

She nodded and a smile spread across his face. Chicken was his favourite meat and he swore blind he could tell the difference between the real thing and lab-grown food. So using some of her TV appearance earnings, she had located one of only a handful of chicken farms left in the country and ordered a plucked, refrigerated bird to be couriered to her that afternoon.

'I thought I'd treat us,' Roxi continued and kissed his cheek. Anything more passionate might arouse more suspicion than the sight of her cooking. 'Could you pass me the carving knife?' she asked and he removed it from its charger.

'Where are the kids?'

'They're staying over with friends. I thought we could spend some quality time together.'

Roxi clocked the Audite, ensuring that, if it was recording, it was catching her every word. Then she recalled one of the seemingly endless list of quotes it had voiced earlier. '"You can't pay attention to what matters most if you're always in a hurry",' she recounted.

She interpreted Owen's facial response as wondering who the hell this imposter was and what had she done with his wife.

'I've been thinking about what you were saying about finding a common purpose,' Roxi continued. 'Would tonight be a good time to run through a few of my ideas?'

'Um, well, yes, of course,' he said.

Roxi took his jacket and, as she reached the coat hooks, she surreptitiously sniffed the collar, searching for the trace of another woman's scent. She only recognized his cologne.

'Sit, sit,' she encouraged and beckoned him towards a chair in the adjoining dining room. She handed him his wine as an album they'd listened to back in their dating days hummed in the background. 'Dinner shouldn't be long.'

Twice Roxi's phone pinged with message alerts and both times she fought to ignore it.

'Do you want to check that?' Owen asked, reaching for where it lay on the windowsill.

'No, you can turn it off if you like,' Roxi replied breezily. 'How was your day?'

It was okay, he told her, but Roxi knew fine well how his day had been, or at least the early evening. Because he'd spent it with another woman. She was certain of this because she had tracked his car as it travelled from his industrial estate office to the village where Antoinette Cooper lived, the online troll trying to destroy her career and now her marriage. His car had remained there for one hour and nine minutes before he set off for home.

Roxi could not remember the last time she had cried – not during or after the birth of her children, on her wedding day or even at a film. Being shuffled around foster parents did that to a child, she reasoned. It toughened you up. It coated you in Teflon. Nothing stuck to you, no matter how bad it got. Yet as she had waited for his vehicle to leave Cooper's property, something had snagged in her throat. And no matter how many times she'd swallowed, it wouldn't budge.

She glanced at his sports bag in the kitchen, the one Antoinette Cooper had trolled her over. Was his kit unused as she suggested?

'And how was the match tonight?' she asked.

'We were only training.'

'If you pass me your kit, I'll put it in the washing machine.'

'Don't worry, I'll sort it out.'

'It's no trouble.'

'No, you've made dinner,' he insisted. 'I'll do it later.'

The ease of his lies astonished her. But then he'd been

practising for months. After discovering his affair a week earlier, she had scanned the digital family calendar, noting every time he had posted that he'd be working late. It appeared his fling had been going on for almost five months and was a weekly occurrence, mostly Wednesday or Thursday evenings. To her shame, she hadn't even noticed his absence.

Roxi's mind had raced with questions since discovering her husband's double life. How could he have done this to her? Who was Antoinette Cooper and did Owen know she had been trolling his wife? Did they laugh about it behind her back? What would happen to Roxi if he asked for a divorce? What would she be left with if Owen was to leave her? They were already living on top of one another in too small a house. And half the proceeds of any sale meant her next home was likely to be back in Old Northampton and the size of a rabbit hutch while he luxuriated in Cooper's Georgian mansion.

And, most importantly, how would her career fare without the backbone of a marriage? There was a slim chance she might buck the trend by Vlogging as a divorcee, but she doubted it. She could always marry again, but who? It might take years to find a replacement.

Guilt hardened in her chest when she realized she hadn't even considered the kids. Would she get the chance to reconnect with them if they were living separately? If she was being truly honest with herself, there was no 're' about it. To reconnect, you must have had a connection in the first place. And she hadn't allowed that to happen.

Roxi had listed her options: do nothing, put it to the back of her mind and hope their affair fizzled out; confront him and risk further Audite intervention; or remind Owen why he fell in love with her in the first place. So she did what she knew best and returned to an older version of herself, the one so scared of being alone that she diluted her needs for the sake of a partner. Owen was not as progressive as her so she scoured the internet for advice on what men expected from their wives back at the turn of the century when his parents first married. She learned there wasn't the equality in homes that there was now. Back then, couples weren't expected to share all the tasks. Perhaps that was why he was cheating on her with someone older than him? Was she offering a version of a woman that Roxi wasn't? If it could save her marriage, she had little choice but to become a person Owen wanted to return home to, one with a meal on the table and a smile glued to her face.

They continued talking as she carried food dishes into the dining room. She spoke minimally about her own projects and chose to listen to Owen's instead.

'Dinner's delicious, by the way,' he said.

'Thanks, it's your mum's recipe.'

'You kept it?'

'I kept all the ones she emailed shortly before she passed.' Owen appeared touched to hear that. 'She was a good friend. I miss her,' Roxi added, and she meant it.

'So do I,' Owen replied. 'She loved you. She thought you were a little crazy and I was a little square but that you'd round my corners.'

'And have I?'

He laughed. 'A little, yes.'

They reminisced about first dates, clandestine meetings

at work in more roomy disabled toilet cubicles, his marriage proposal on a ferry from Mumbai to Alibaug, how her mother-in-law gave Roxi away at their wedding and his second proposal for their marriage upgrade.

'We had some good times, didn't we?' asked Owen.

Icy fingers grazed her shoulders. 'Had? You make it sound like there won't be any more.'

'I mean with the threat of Level Two hanging over us, you never know what's around the corner.'

'Look, you know that I'm not very good when it comes to talking about this kind of thing, but I want you to know how much I do still love you. I'm not always easy to live with and sometimes I lose sight of what I have when I'm looking for something else. I know I need to find a middle ground.'

'All I ask is that you don't lose sight of us.' Owen reached out to hold her hand. 'And I love you too.'

Without giving it a second thought, Roxi pushed her plate to one side, moved around the table and straddled him on his chair. She slipped her tongue in his mouth and her hand down the front of his chinos. His arousal was immediate. He reciprocated with his own hand, and within moments, she had pushed the rest of the dishes to one side and was lying flat on her back on the dining-room table, while Owen hitched up her skirt and moved his head between her legs.

She purposefully made enough noise to be picked up by the Audite and it wasn't long before Owen was inside her for the first time in as long as she could remember. Sex with him was never an unpleasant experience – but then neither was getting a dental descaling or repainting a wall, yet she wouldn't want to do them every day. But if it kept Owen happy and his attention on her, it was a sacrifice she might have to make more often. She wondered what she used to think about when they had made spontaneous love in the past because, now, she was consumed by how cold the table felt on her exposed bum and whether the dishwasher would need to go on a full or half cycle later. Soon after, she pretended to climax as she knew that her deep moans and groans never failed to tip Owen over the edge. She wondered if his mistress Cooper had learned this trick yet.

'Oh, guess what?' she asked as they slipped their clothes back on. 'We've been offered a few days away on a spa break in the Lake District if you fancy it? As long as you don't mind me filming some content while we're there.'

'Perfect. I could do with a pampering. And just think of the fun we'll have in that hotel room without the kids.' He winked.

'I can't wait,' she said through gritted teeth. 'I'll book it tomorrow. It'll be a midweek treat. Perhaps Wednesday to Saturday?'

'Midweeks aren't great for me at the moment,' he replied and returned to his seat and his dinner.

'Oh, why's that?'

'I've just got . . . a lot on.'

'Can't you take a couple of days off?'

'What about a long weekend, I could take a Friday and a Monday off?'

'But not a Wednesday or a Thursday?'

'I'm sorry, but no.'

Roxi's heart sank and, still semi-naked, she suddenly felt very exposed.

49

Jeffrey

The silence was heavy and stifling as Jeffrey carried three cups of peppermint tea on a tray from the kitchen and into the garden. He felt Noah's eyes burrowing into him as he placed it on a table, took a seat sheltered from the sun by the canopy and turned his tablet on.

He looked to Luca then Noah. Their present demeanour was far removed from when he'd first met them and he'd catch them holding hands or giving each other a reassuring pat on the arm. Luca appeared uneasy, but Noah's expression and body language was tense. He tapped his index finger against his thigh as if waiting for this afternoon's session to begin. But Jeffrey was in no hurry. He was savouring the awkwardness. He took his time as he casually opened a page of notes and pretended to read them, as if reminding himself of what they had discussed yesterday. 'Right,' he said breezily, 'where shall we begin?'

'How about with me being called into my hospital's Human Resources department this morning for an informal "chat" about my marriage?' Noah asked.

'And how did that go?' said Jeffrey.

'Well, let's see. First, my manager told me she'd been informed Luca and I had been Levelled up. Then she asked

266

if there was anything the hospital could do to help. I told her no, it was a misunderstanding that would be sorted out soon.'

'That doesn't sound too bad,' said Luca.

'I haven't got to the best bit yet.' Noah ceased to temper his tone. 'Now imagine a woman old enough to be my grandmother reading from a list and asking me if I'm a "top or a bottom" and whether we've tried "S and M", "watersports" or "rimming" to spice up our sex life? Then imagine her turning the computer monitor around to show me artists' illustrations of suggested sex positions. Does that still not sound "too bad"?'

'Oh my God,' said Luca, covering his face with his hands. Jeffrey couldn't be sure but Luca appeared more amused than annoyed.

'I wanted the ground to open up and swallow me.'

'Why did she do that?'

'Because to remain on the Sanctity of Marriage Act's five hundred Best Businesses list and get more Government funding, the hospital has to be seen to be providing a duty of care to their staff. Divorcees have a negative impact on their reputation and, these days, no one wants to work for a company that can't look after its own, even if it's in the old part of town. It's why they organize those bloody awful mandatory family fun days every summer. If they slip off that list, they'll get even less funding.'

'I am sorry the work we're doing here has had such a negative impact on you,' said Jeffrey, 'but I'm sure that HR is just following protocol.'

'What did you tell her?' Luca asked Noah.

'That it wasn't a conversation I wanted to have, and I

asked to leave. She didn't try and stop me.' Noah looked to Jeffrey, as if daring him to scold him. 'Well?' he asked.

'Well what, Noah?' Jeffrey replied.

'This is usually the part where you accuse me of something . . . Bullying, gaslighting, lying, emasculating . . . they're normally top of your list of criticisms.'

'You were perfectly entitled to respond to your HR department however you saw fit,' Jeffrey said.

'I sense a "but" coming.'

'There's no "but". However . . .'

'"However" is no different to a "but".'

'However, your employers will be asked to submit a report on the support offered and the response received. Your resistance will probably be noted.'

'Babe,' Luca exhaled and moved his hands to his brow. 'Why couldn't you play along?'

'Would you have?'

'Yes! I'd probably have died a little inside but we need to get through this any way we can. If everyone is telling us we have problems then we have to be open to the possibility our marriage might not be as perfect as we thought it was.'

Now it was Jeffrey's turn to suppress a smile.

'No marriage is perfect!' Noah replied. 'I don't *want* a perfect relationship, I don't *want* us to have identical viewpoints, I just want the relationship we used to have before *he* came along.'

'It's not Jeffrey's fault.'

'Before this gets too heated, there's something I need to bring up with you both,' Jeffrey interrupted. 'As you were made aware, Beccy has temporarily withdrawn her offer to be your surrogate. I've also been informed that she has now been placed back upon the Government-approved surrogate list searching for intended parents.'

'She's replacing us?' asked Luca.

'She has been given the option since you've been removed from the process.'

'Removed?' he repeated.

'Were you not aware? I believe an email was sent to Noah yesterday.'

Luca's muscles tensed as he turned to Noah. 'Did you know about this?'

Noah nodded. 'Yes. I read it this morning.'

'And you didn't tell me?'

'We aren't supposed to be talking to one another as per Jeffrey's Positive Disengagement bullshit.'

'You mean you thought it'd sound better coming from him. Or did you keep it quiet to ease your conscience because you know that by fighting this process every step of the way, you're making things worse? You keep blaming Jeffrey but he's trying to save us from ourselves. Only you're too stubborn to see it.'

Noah opened his mouth to respond but thought better of it. Instead, the two men drifted into another stifling silence as Jeffrey's fingers glided lightly across the tablet's screen, pretending to update his notes.

50

Corrine

Days had passed since Corrine and Mitchell had acknow-ledged each other's presence in the house. When one walked into a room, the other exited. Their housekeeper Elena made different meals at different times for them. If Corrine ate in the kitchen-diner, he ate in the den. Their children had the same conversations with them twice over.

'How long is this going on for?' asked Freya. She found her mother in the utility room folding clothes from a tumble dryer. She passed her a bundle.

'Until it's empty,' Corrine deadpanned.

'You know what I mean. You and dad. You've had arguments before but they don't normally drag on as long as this. He looks totally pissed off all the time.'

'That's his default setting. He can't help it.'

Freya raised an eyebrow at her mother, aware she was being palmed off. But Corrine didn't elaborate. For their own individual reasons, neither she nor Mitchell had yet to announce their impending split. But she knew that at some point, their children were likely to discover she had made false claims of domestic violence to accelerate a divorce. It was a terrible example to be setting so she'd tried to offset her conscience with a sizeable donation to a women's domestic abuse charity. It hadn't worked. Her guilt remained intact.

'I don't know why you stay with him,' Freya continued.

'Why would you say that?'

'What does he add to your life? To any of our lives, for that matter?'

'Freya!' Corrine exclaimed. 'Despite his behaviour, he's still your father.'

'No, Mum, he needs to earn that title. He's put no work into being a parent since we were kids.'

Corrine felt an illogical urge to defend Mitchell's inaction. Was she partly responsible? Might she have done more to encourage him to have been a present parent? Or had she hijacked her children at an early age and missed signs he wanted more involvement? Her conscience was already too heavy without the added weight of another burden. So she changed the subject.

'When are you going back to Uni?' she asked.

'Are you trying to get rid of me?'

'Not at all. It's been lovely having you home.' She squeezed her daughter's hand. 'How's student life? Are you making the most of your second year?'

'It's fine. I've got about a million essays to get in by the end of term and a million distractions.'

'Do those distractions include a girl? It's been a few months since you and Brianna went your separate ways.'

'Which is your polite way of saying since I was dumped. It's okay, I'm over it. Besides, who knows, I could be married by the time I graduate.'

'I hope you're kidding.'

'Not if the Uni has anything to do with it. You can barely pass a noticeboard without seeing an ad urging you to sign up to their dating programme to "future-proof your job prospects". Match Your DNA is even sponsoring this year's graduation ceremony.'

'I don't understand why being single might affect your chances of finding work?'

'Apparently along with qualifications and intern experience, the top five hundred employers are now also focusing on recruiting grads who can prove they're in committed relationships with a view to marrying. And did you know a single person can now even be legally sacked if they're caught having an affair with a married colleague? The married one gets away scot-free.'

Corrine ran her fingers through her hair. 'What is this world coming to?'

'So yes, by the time I graduate next year, I might have a wife on my arm.'

'I hope not.'

'Seriously, though, it's something I'll have to think about, Mum. There's the property ladder too. How can I afford to buy somewhere half-decent if mortgages are too high for single people?'

'You don't need to worry about that. Your dad and I will help you out there.'

Freya let out a sharp laugh. 'Dad? He's tighter than Latex gloves.'

'Promise me you won't do anything without talking to me first. The Marriage Act might seem like a solution to a lot of your problems but there are so many components to it that are grossly unfair.'

'Okay, I promise.'

Freya folded the last of her clothes and left her mother alone. Corrine hated that her daughter was already feeling pressured into considering marriage and, once again, she cursed MP Eleanor Harrison, one of the Act's most vocal supporters. As the Minister for Education, she was responsible for driving forward Marriage Act propaganda in schools and colleges. One of her General Election pledges was to ensure curriculums from primary education upwards included lessons on the importance of marriage, how to find a suitable partner, relationship compromises, fidelity and how to maintain a Match. She had also been the first MP to upgrade to a Smart Marriage the day the law was passed. The ceremony had been livestreamed across the Government's own website.

But Corrine knew that Harrison wasn't all she seemed. She had much to hide. First and foremost, she was a sexual predator – and Corrine had the proof.

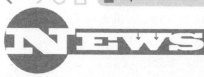

WHO IS HENRY HYDE?

He is the controversial Number 10 presence who has the ear of the Prime Minister.

Yet he is neither a member of parliament nor a civil servant.

Nicknamed Jekyll by colleagues for his split personality and ability to flip from friend to foe with one wrong word, Hyde shuns the limelight in favour of the shadows.

But quite what his special advisory role to PM Benjamin Reece entails remains a mystery. Even those who spot him regularly scuttling around the corridors of Westminster cannot be sure exactly what he does.

We know that he has been involved with the party for at least twenty years. But it was only after the no-confidence vote that ousted Prime Minister Diane Cline when he was first spotted in the company of Reece, then the Secretary of State for Transport. Many believe him to be the architect of Reece's election.

Then, when the Marriage Act was first mooted, his visibility increased, albeit in the background of press conferences or on board election battle buses.

'He's a divisive character,' one insider told us. 'But he's the one the PM listens to. No decisions are made without Hyde's say-so. He's the puppet-master in this game of politics.'

51

Anthony

Henry Hyde was waiting for Anthony at the bandstand in New Northampton's Abington Park by the time he arrived. In the fifteen years since they'd first become acquainted, Anthony couldn't recall one meeting in which Hyde had appeared after him.

His employer was alone and perched on the third step up of the Victorian installation. Dressed typically in his ill-fitting black suit and white shirt, his skin was so pale that if you held his head up close to a bright light, you would likely see straight through to his skull. As always, Anthony found Hyde's inky black eyes impossible to read. He also knew nothing about the man who'd recruited him. He didn't know where he resided, whether he was married or single, had a family or even the true nature of his job or Governmental position. Anthony hadn't asked and Hyde hadn't volunteered the information.

'You look like death,' Hyde began, casting an eye over his protégé.

'I don't sleep much any more,' Anthony replied, choosing to sit on a step below.

'You should try magnesium. One teaspoon in a pot of tea every evening . . . my mother swore by it, God rest her soul.'

Anthony didn't respond.

'But I assume you haven't asked me here for advice on thwarting insomnia.'

Anthony shook his head while Hyde sipped from the contents of a disposable cup and scanned his surroundings and a nearby cafe. He wondered if Hyde had someone stationed in the vicinity to watch them.

'So why have I been summoned to this provincial paradise?' Hyde asked.

'This . . . this project . . . these Young Citizen Camps,' Anthony began cautiously. 'Sending poorly performing kids away from their families because a machine is categorizing them as troublemakers and underachievers . . . It makes me uneasy.'

'Firstly, as I made quite clear in our first meeting, nobody is *sending* anyone away—'

'Like no one is forced to upgrade to a Smart Marriage?' Anthony interrupted. 'Yet those who haven't face discrimination. Isn't the same thing going to happen to parents who don't want to be separated from their kids?'

A vertical crease appeared between Hyde's brows. 'This is an uncharacteristically negative interpretation from you, Anthony. You're usually more . . . complicit. I can assure you our plans are for the greater good.'

'That's what you said about the Act.'

'And I was correct, wasn't I? Upgrading hasn't hurt you or your family, has it? Now you pay only five per cent tax on your earnings and you saved twenty-five thousand pounds in stamp duty when you bought a house double the square footage of your last one. Without those savings, could Jada really have established her design business? Your neighbour-hood has regular police patrols and Matthew's school is the best in its area.'

Anthony didn't know why he was taken aback to hear how much Hyde knew about him; he should have expected it. But he didn't like that it was being used as ammunition.

'You're not old enough to remember how this country's economy suffered for years after the first waves of Covid pandemics,' Hyde continued. 'Trade and investment were disrupted for almost a decade, inflation rocketed, everyone from train drivers to airline staff and even barristers went on strike over pay. Every attempt to reboot the economy or drive growth failed. We wiped through five prime ministers in less than a decade. That was until we realized investing in our people's happiness was key to our economic comeback. Making people understand that they're better off emotion-ally and financially when they're in a committed relationship made them want to work smarter and harder. I appreciate our Young Citizen Camps may be a tougher sell than the Mar-riage Act, but the latter changed our country's direction. Just imagine what else we can do by weeding out the strugglers and giving them purpose?'

'When driverless cars were becoming popular, your pre-decessors chose who might die in the event of an accident based on their importance to society. Now you're deciding upon a person's relevance while they're still a child.'

'Isn't any career better than no career? Do you know how many prisoners we have in the UK right now?' Anthony shook his head. 'There are more than a hundred thousand offenders, including those serving their sentences at home and being re-educated through virtual reality headset training. Do you know how many of them left school with less than three qualifications or were unemployed when they committed a crime?'

'No.'

'Eighty-three per cent. There's a direct correlation between being failed by our education system and criminal behaviour. And we want to redress this. Our camps will help the next generation in subjects and careers the AI believes they're best suited for. We want to educate, not incarcerate.'

'And what will be the long-term emotional impact on kids who are told they're being sent away because they're second best?'

'The offer of a better education away from home is hardly a new concept. The first boarding schools date back to medieval times when boys were sent to monasteries to be educated. Our camps are a revised vision of them.'

'But you're letting Artificial Intelligence pick and choose.'

'AI is helping us reap the rewards of a new industrial revolution.'

'Not all revolutions benefit us.'

Hyde shook his head. 'Another of your alternative facts. AI will *identify* potential candidates. Before parents are approached, tutors and counsellors will also play their part in deciding if a camp is beneficial for a subject.'

'You mean a child,' said Anthony. 'You called them subjects. They're children.'

'Let's not get bogged down by semantics.'

There was an edge to his tone. Anthony suspected his employer was masking his irritation.

'How often will they be allowed to go home to visit their families?'

'Their relatives will be encouraged to make appointments to see them at allocated times. But allowing subj . . . *children* . . . to return home regularly is counterproductive. They need to learn that good behaviour and obedience will earn them rewards.'

'Obedience? You're not training animals.'

'You are increasingly sounding like a member of Freedom for All,' Hyde replied. 'I do hope they didn't radicalize you during your recent attendance at one of their branch meetings?'

Anthony realized he must be under surveillance. He willed himself not to appear rattled. 'Freedom for All is hardly Al-Qaeda, and I'm too old to be brainwashed. At least by the FFA,' he added pointedly.

Hyde rose to his feet and positioned himself in front of Anthony, his hands planted squarely on his hips.

'Where's all this really coming from, Anthony? I don't recall you wrestling with your conscience when it came to using Jem Jones to promote our agenda or questioning my request to silence her.'

Anthony bristled at hearing him use her name.

'In fact,' continued Hyde, 'I believe you still have the weapon you used to shoot her locked away in your desk drawer, rather like a serial killer who keeps a souvenir of their victims.'

Now anger tugged at Anthony. Hyde could only be in possession of this information if his house had been searched or he had access to the cameras Anthony had himself installed. But he wasn't going to be intimidated.

'Do you know what the Nazis did with schoolchildren before and during the Second World War?' Anthony asked.

Hyde shrugged, a little too flippantly to convince Anthony he was ignorant of the answer.

'In the late 1930s, they founded the first Adult Hitler Schools – twelve elite boarding schools scattered around the country and run by the Secret Service. The plan was to indoctrinate students into Nazi ideologies. They released propaganda films to make the schools appear to be the best things in the world and that anyone not invited was missing out.'

'Well, let me stop you there,' Hyde laughed. 'If you're about to make some ridiculous comparison, the purpose of our camps is to educate, not indoctrinate.'

'It was the job of the teachers to ensure their students were loyal to Hitler so the curriculum reflected Nazi philosophies. Academic subjects like maths and English were replaced by fitness and team sports. Parental influence was minimal. Once enrolled, there was no leaving. And as far as I can see, the only difference between what the Nazis were doing more than a hundred years ago and what you expect me to sell to the public is that they chose the best students and you're choosing the most vulnerable. Please jump in and correct me if I'm wrong.'

'Of course you're wrong,' Hyde snapped.

'I had ADHD as a kid and I was disruptive in class because I struggled to focus. If I were of school age now, you'd make sure my aspirations were no higher than car-washer.'

'This is really about your son, isn't it, Anthony? You don't care about the greater good, you just want to ensure that you and yours are taken care of. Well, I can assure you that while you remain on the correct side, you have nothing to fear. In the same way you upgraded your marriage but we will never record your conversations with your wife, Matthew will remain exempt from our camps.'

'And if I don't stay on your side?'

Hyde softened his tone. 'This project will go ahead whether you are involved or not because no one is irreplaceable. But I would suggest that it's in your best interests to get on board. If not for yourself, then for Matthew.'

Anthony's fingers balled, fist-like. He held back from striking Hyde.

'I'm done,' he said.

'This is not a good decision, Anthony. I have high hopes for you, I always have had. Don't let me down.'

'I can't do it.'

'Take some time to mull over the ramifications. How it will affect your family. Especially your lad.'

Anthony's skin prickled, but he would not back down. 'Thank you for the opportunities Henry, but goodbye.'

And, with that, Anthony turned his back on Hyde and made his way out of the park.

52

Jeffrey

It wasn't how Jeffrey had intended to spend his evening, scurrying in and out of shop doorways and hiding behind bus shelters and digital billboards.

But curiosity had got the better of him after accessing Noah's hospital diary. Noah had told Luca that he was covering another junior doctor's shift that night. His calendar said no such thing. He was lying and Jeffrey wanted to know why. Jeffrey had been in two minds about leaving Luca alone in the house and wasting one-to-one time without Noah's interruptions. But the lure of uncovering deceit was too hard to resist.

For an hour, he had followed Noah by car from the grounds of the Old Northampton hospital where he was stationed, to the village of Oadby in the neighbouring county of Leicestershire. Jeffrey parked far away from Noah and hurried by foot to catch him up, while retaining a safe distance. Eventually, Noah turned to enter the grounds of a churchyard and approached an adjoining community centre. Others were making their way along the path too. Jeffrey held back until there was a group large enough to envelop him and made his approach.

He hovered by the doors as Noah went inside, then he

peeked through a crack to observe rows of plastic seating that were gradually filling up with people. He inserted his ear buds and asked his operating system to locate the community centre's online calendar. Tonight's listing was a Freedom for All branch meeting. It was not what he'd expected to hear. Why was Noah seeking the company of a group whose sole objective was to repeal an Act that benefitted millions, including Noah and Luca? Jeffrey slipped inside and hovered about the dark corners of a porch until the meeting began.

For an hour, a variety of speakers discussed a forthcoming rally in London. They voiced their concerns over bias and discrimination and used examples of couples forced apart by Audite's misunderstandings of their relationships. Jeffrey flinched when they described the power Relationship Responders wielded as being 'unethical and unfair'. How dare they criticize him! He had never tried to part a couple who were completely secure in their relationship. Yes, sometimes the line between client and Responder had blurred, but then he never claimed to be perfect.

As tonight's FFA meeting came to a close, he was about to turn and leave when he spotted Noah approaching one of the guest speakers, the group's spokesperson Howie Cosby. Cosby nodded and tapped something into his phone as Noah spoke into his ear. It piqued Jeffrey's curiosity.

Jeffrey hurried back to his vehicle, grabbed his tablet and used his password to access Noah's work account. He scanned his emails and diary again but it contained nothing regarding the FFA or any previous participation in the group. However, his face lit up at the search engine history. Noah had visited dozens of websites relating to divorce. 'How to divorce voluntarily when you've signed The Act', 'Financial penalties for divorcees', and 'How assets are divided'.

This was concrete evidence that Noah had given up on his marriage. He was planning his escape route and a knot of excitement unravelled deep in Jeffrey's gut.

53
Roxi

Roxi inhaled so deeply, it made her lungs burn. She pulled on the ring of an iron knocker. *Hurry up, hurry up,* she whispered, knowing time wasn't on her side. Twenty-three minutes remained before her window of opportunity closed. Eventually she heard footsteps descending what sounded like a wooden staircase before the front door opened.

'Hello,' said Antoinette Cooper, her tone soft and her smile friendly.

Roxi took in her appearance. Her troll must be at least twenty years her senior, but she carried it well. Her eyes were hazel-coloured and above her plump lips there were faint diagonal creases. Roxi's sharp nose for scents recognized Chanel perfume. That, coupled with the fitted cut of her trousers, blouse, matching Tiffany necklace and bracelet all suggested she was someone who appreciated timeless, classic design. To Roxi's relief, she wore no wearable technology. Roxi's line of sight moved over Cooper's shoulder and into the hallway but failed to locate anything recordable.

Cooper's smile began to fade and her brow wrinkled as she awaited a response from the stranger on her doorstep.

'Why . . . why are . . . why . . .' began Roxi, suddenly tongue-tied. This was a huge mistake, she thought. By confronting her husband's mistress, she thought she was controlling the narrative but now she feared it might backfire. It might hasten any plans she and Owen had, and Roxi had yet to find a way to protect her career and her assets.

Since she and Owen's heart-to-heart over dinner, which had culminated in sex on the dining table, Roxi had pulled out all the stops to remind him why he'd first fallen in love with her. Sex, attention, food, family time, more sex . . . she was giving him everything she thought he wanted. Only it wasn't enough to stop those Wednesday night encounters with his lover.

After more sleepless nights and personal insults left by Cooper on social media channels, Roxi reached the end of her tether. Her civil servant contact had revealed to her a little-known glitch in some older models of hardware installed with Audite software. She could trick her wearable tech, which also fed into her carpool vehicle's onboard computer. A specific thirty-seven digit and symbol code inputted into a burner phone followed by her Smart watch's serial number meant all recordings and even her location would be rerouted to the untraceable burner phone and the information not saved or analysed by Audite's software. But it only lasted for a period of twenty-seven minutes. After that, the system would suspect something untoward and report the user to the relevant authorities. This time, Roxi wasn't wearing any cameras to record her confrontation. This was even too personal for her to make public.

'Is everything all right?' Cooper asked, her face marked with concern.

A tightness formed in Roxi's gut. How dare you? How

dare you pretend to care about a stranger after all you've put me through! It snapped her out of her inactivity.

'Why are you trying to ruin everything for me?' Roxi began.

'Do we know each other?' Cooper replied and took a step back.

'I think you're probably more familiar with my husband, Owen.'

Cooper's face tightened as the penny dropped. 'What are you doing here?'

'I know exactly what you are doing with my husband, and it stops now.'

Cooper's eyes shifted to the view behind Roxi.

'What's wrong?' Roxi continued. 'Scared the neighbours will learn what kind of woman you are? Well, you should be; you're old enough to be Owen's mother. You should know better.'

'Would you like to come inside so we can discuss this privately?'

Cooper positioned her back to the door. Roxi hesitated: she hadn't expected an invitation. Tentatively she crossed enemy lines and closed the door behind her.

Roxi took in her surroundings. The hallways smelled like cotton and orchids. A wooden staircase led to a brightly lit landing, a stained-glass window was positioned at the end of the corridor and cornices and plaster mouldings framed an ornate ceiling. This immaculate home was yet another reason to hate Cooper.

'Look at the life you have here. You could have anyone you wanted. Why pick on my husband? Is he your Match?'

'No!'

'Then why does he come to your house?'

'This isn't a conversation I want to have with you.'

'And why are you trolling me?'

Cooper's eyebrows lifted. 'I'm not.'

'There's an account set up in your name and registered to this address.'

'I don't know anything about that.'

'Are you married?'

'Not that it's any of your business but I'm widowed.'

'That makes sense. Look at the size of this place, it must cost a fortune to run. But if you remarry, your bills will be more than halved, won't they? And what about me and the kids? I assume Owen's told you he has children.'

'I am aware of your current marital situation,' said Cooper.

'After today you're never going to see Owen again. Do you hear me?'

Cooper cleared her throat. 'That's not for you to decide, Mrs Sager,' she said with an air of finality. 'That's up to your husband and me. When you return home, I suggest you sit down and talk to Owen and then perhaps we can all have an adult conversation and come to some sort of arrangement of where we go from here. Until then, please leave my house.'

Cooper began to open the door but Roxi folded her leg behind her and kicked it shut.

The last time Roxi had been involved in a physical altercation was with the biological child of foster parents she'd been placed with when she was nine. The girl had deliberately tripped her over then laughed as she'd fallen onto a railway sleeper, cutting her lip and chipping a tooth. Roxi had slapped her so hard that the imprint of her hand across the girl's cheek could be seen late into the night when social services had arrived to take Roxi away. Today, a similar rage tugged at her. And, with all her strength, she shoved Cooper in the chest.

She clearly took her rival by surprise as Cooper had no time to turn and cushion her fall. Instead, she dropped backwards like a felled tree, only stopping when the bones in her neck impacted against the exposed bottom wooden stair and fractured, with a sickening crack.

A moment later and Roxi was left standing over the dead body of her husband's mistress.

54

Corrine

Corrine let out an irritated huff as she closed the window on her web browser. She suppressed the urge to express her frustration aloud as she didn't want her wearable tech to record anything that might later be questioned by Magistrates in her forthcoming divorce hearing.

She had been sitting alone in the summer house for much of the afternoon. And she had been using a Freedom for All approved anonymous server to go online and contact local coach companies to check the availability of fleets to transport local party members to London for the forthcoming anti-Marriage Act rally. It was a more menial role than the one she'd played in the Eleanor Harrison debacle and it crossed her mind that perhaps she had been tasked with this because her colleagues didn't trust her with anything more important. But she refused to give up even though she was struggling to find a firm with enough available vehicles for the 400 campaigners who'd pledged to attend. Corrine had something to prove.

The sight of her children, Spencer and Nora, in the kitchen on the other side of the garden distracted her. They must have just returned from lunch with their father, an event rarer than the appearance of a comet. She closed the lid of her laptop and waved. They didn't reciprocate, but made a beeline for her. Instinct warned her this was not good.

'Is it true?' began Spencer, yanking open the door.

'Is what true?'

'That you're divorcing Dad and lying to the court saying that he hits you?'

Corrine cursed herself for not beating Mitchell to the punch and instigating this conversation before he did. He must have pinned his hopes on their children confronting her and guilt tripping her into changing her mind. But if she admitted her untruths to them, it would be picked up on her Audite and she would lose her case. And Mitchell knew that she would never lie to their faces. She would need to manipulate the conversation.

'Close the door,' she asked, not wanting the pool's maintenance man outside to overhear their conversation. 'It's complicated.'

'What is, that you're divorcing him or making up shit as to why?'

'He'd never lay a finger on you,' said Nora. 'Yes, he's mean and he says nasty things, but he'd never hit you. You have to retract it, Mum. It's not fair.'

'Fair? Do you think it's fair that he tricked me into signing a document to upgrade us to a Smart Marriage making it harder for me to leave him?' Corrine replied. Her children stared at her blankly. 'I assume he didn't mention that part? Apparently we were divorced for a day and then remarried and I didn't have a bloody clue about it. That's the kind of fairness your father believes in.'

Nora and Spencer looked at one another and then back at their mother.

'Look, our divorce has been on the cards for a long, long time,' she continued. 'We were going to tell you when you'd both settled into university, but clearly your father has decided to play by his own rules again.'

'There isn't going to be any university,' said Nora, her voice wavering.

'Of course there is,' said Corrine.

'Not according to Dad. He said all your money is tied up in investments. A divorce means you'll have to split what's left and you'll end up in a higher tax bracket so there won't be enough to cover us or Freya. And we won't be eligible for the married parents student loan discount as you'll be divorced.'

Corrine shook her head. 'You must have misunderstood him. I'm sure that's not the case.'

'That's exactly what he told us,' said Spencer. 'Why would he lie?'

'Because that's what he does! He's desperately trying to find a way to control me and now he's doing it by threatening your futures.'

'Maybe he's doing it because he still loves you?' said Nora.

'Nora, darling, you know that's not true. He doesn't like that I'm not giving in to him any more and that I'm not going to put up with his crap. You *will* be going to university even if it means I have to find a job and work all the hours God sends to get you there. If I back down now, I'll never be free of him.' She rose to her feet and hugged both her children at once. 'It'll be okay, I promise you.'

As they left her alone, fear clouded her face. The increasing desperation in Mitchell's behaviour was a warning. The worst could still be yet to come.

FREEDOM 4 ALL

 Think you're better off married?
You're wrong.
Here's what the Government
doesn't want you to know.

- Unmarried women with no children are **happier** than married mums. Middle-aged married mums suffer more mental and physical conditions than their single, childless counterparts.

- Married women are **more at risk** of heart disease. They frequently internalize stress, which takes its toll on their heart.

- Marriage **weakens** your social ties. You're less likely to visit parents and siblings or spend time with friends and neighbours if you're wed.

- Marital conflict **hurts men** worse than women. Repeated arguments over the same subjects can cause **inflammation** in the body and a **reduced appetite**.

- Married mums are too busy with families to worry about the big society. Single women are **more politically active** than men, helping with fundraisers and rallies.

- Being married can **make you ill**. The stress of worrying if your partner still loves you weakens your T-cells, making it harder to fight off infections.

Statistics provided by independent research

55

Jeffrey

'Appointment: Friday, seven thirty p.m., dinner with Priti and Devon,' began the Audite's synthetic voice.

Luca and Noah looked to one another across the dining-room table. Noah was already shaking his head, second-guessing what was to follow. He drained his gin and tonic in one long gulp.

'Postponed,' both he and the Audite said together.

'Did they leave a reason?' he continued.

'Reason given – stomach upset,' it replied.

Noah rolled his eyes. 'Well, that's a new one. In the space of a few days, we've had a sick grandfather, a broken heating pump and a cat with cancer as excuses for cancelling arrangements.'

'Postponing,' said Luca.

'Don't kid yourself. We're being cancelled left, right and centre. We are toxic.'

'We're not, it's just bad timing.'

'Luca, don't try and placate me. Everyone knows our situation and they're giving us a wide berth because they don't want to catch whatever we have.'

Jeffrey was pleased with himself. Along with introducing himself to some of the neighbours as their Relationship

Responder, he had also contacted not only people listed in the Marital Support Bubble that Noah and Luca had provided when they'd signed their Smart Marriage contract, but everyone else in their contacts list too. 'This is delicious,' he said and used the back of his fork to slice into a vegan meatball in a sticky tomato sauce. 'Where did you learn to cook so well, Luca?'

'My grandparents are Italian.'

'I have Italian blood on my father's side, Sardinia, I think,' Jeffrey said. 'I was raised on food like this.' The truth was he had no clue or desire to know of his family ancestry.

'Oh, are we done now?' asked Noah. 'Conversation over?'

'What else is there to say?' asked Luca. 'If we continue, it'll go the same way all our conversations do. You'll say one thing, I'll disagree, then you'll storm off.'

Noah looked to Jeffrey. 'I've been reading through the contract you so helpfully like to remind us of and it says that people on our support list are supposed to rally round and help when a couple is Levelled up.'

'That's right.'

'Well, where are they?' Noah turned his head to take in the room and held his phone to his ear. 'Because I don't hear the phone ringing or anyone knocking at the door asking us if we're okay.'

'It's a moral contract, not a legal obligation.'

'How convenient.'

Jeffrey was noticing a gradual shift in Noah's attitude. Evidence of confrontation and antagonism remained, like his behaviour now over dinner. But for the most part, there had been a reluctant acceptance that Noah no longer had control over anything outside the hospital where he worked. Past experience with other clients suggested it wouldn't require much more pressure before their relationship collapsed completely.

Noah poured himself another drink, the tonic an afterthought.

'We're not supposed to be drinking while we're in therapy,' said Luca. He looked at Jeffrey who nodded.

'I thought we'd finished for today?' said Noah.

'Do you cook much, Noah?' asked Jeffrey.

'Not since Luca talked us into going vegan. I know what to do with a steak, not so much with an aubergine, unless it's an emoji.'

'You could ask him to teach you. The more you do for one another, the more the other person feels appreciated.'

'Here we go . . .' said Noah and pushed a meatball around his plate, flecks of red sauce splashing his forearm.

Jeffrey blinked away a memory of Tanya's blood doing the same thing when he'd slashed her wrists.

'Can you remember when you last told Luca that he did a great job with dinner or keeping the garden tidy?'

'Why? If I say I don't remember are you going to add that to your notes? Perhaps it can join the list of reasons why I'm an abysmal husband?'

'Stop it,' said Luca.

'Stop what?'

'Behaving like a child.'

'Perhaps that's how I'm treated in this house.'

'Compliments are an important positive affirmation in a relationship,' Jeffrey continued. 'We all like to be praised when we've put effort into something. It's just something to keep in mind.'

Noah mimed pressing an invisible keyboard button with his finger. 'Unsubscribe,' he said and downed the contents of his glass. His focus remained on Jeffrey until he crunched the last remaining ice cube between his teeth.

'Are you . . . are you wearing my clothes?' Noah said. He couldn't hold back his reddening cheeks.

'Of course not,' Jeffrey protested. But the new outfits he'd recently purchased had all been deliberately similar to pieces he'd seen Noah wearing.

'Yes, yes you are!' Noah persisted. 'I have that exact same blue shirt and jean combination. Even our trainers are similar.' He lifted his foot to prove his point. 'Christ, Luca, can't you see what he's doing? He's moved himself into our house and now he's trying to replicate me.'

'I can assure you I'm not,' said Jeffrey.

'Look at yourself!'

The tension was broken by the Audite.

'Email: Friday May third, Message received. From New Northampton Health Partnership. Dear Mr Noah Stanton-Gibbs, We regret to inform you that your scheduled interview has now been cancelled as the position has been filled internally. Your details will be kept on file should any suitable further positions arise. Yours sincerely, Donna Hillyer, Chief Executive.'

Noah placed his fork and spoon on the table, dabbed at his mouth with the napkin and pushed his chair out. He reached for the bottle of gin but left the tonic, and, without saying a word, calmly left the room. Jeffrey noticed Noah had barely eaten his food.

Luca hesitated. He half rose, then half sat again, opened his mouth, closed it, then opened it once more.

'I'm sorry,' he said, standing up. 'I know we're not supposed to be talking away from the sessions. But he really wanted that job. The interview was just a formality.'

'Go and be with him, we can pick up on this tomorrow,' Jeffrey replied.

Once alone, Jeffrey helped himself to more food, roused by the thought of returning home to a meal like this every night once Noah was out of the picture.

56

Anthony

Jada was alone in her office, kneeling on the floor surrounded by matching textured cushions and floor tiles. Behind her, a wall of digital wallpaper alternated, offering changes in patterns and colour. Her eyes were hidden behind virtual reality glasses. The room's decor couldn't be more at odds with Anthony's preference for minimalist styling. Jada had once described it as organized, colourful chaos. He envied her vibrant mind.

She was unaware of him standing beyond the glass doors to the entrance, quietly watching her. Sometimes he recognized traces of Jem Jones in his wife, from the way her nose crinkled when she smiled to the line between her eyebrows that appeared when she frowned. But since Jem's death, the similarities were becoming clearer. Or perhaps he was searching for them more frequently. Because if pieces of Jem were alive in his wife, it might go some way towards minimizing the impact of her death on him.

'Bright summer morning,' Jada spoke. She was giving an instruction to the glasses to visualize a room she was planning. 'Now give me a dark winter afternoon.'

'Hi,' Anthony said and knocked on the wall as he approached her.

'Jesus!' she yelped and removed her eyewear. 'What are you doing here?'

It was a valid question given they'd barely spoken in a fortnight. Anthony tried and failed to remember the last time he had visited her interior design business: another example of his neglect.

'The calendar said you had a meeting in New Birmingham today?' she continued.

Anthony cleared his throat. 'I lied to you, I'm sorry. There was no meeting.'

'Then where were you?'

'At home, emailing my resignation letter to work.'

Jada rose to her feet. 'You did what?'

'I quit my job.'

'Without discussing it with me first?'

Anthony nodded.

'Why?'

'There's a new project I've been asked to work on that in good conscience, I cannot be a part of.'

'Couldn't they move you to something else?'

'It doesn't work like that. We don't question orders.'

Jada bit her lip. Jem did the same when she was perplexed.

'I thought you'd be pleased?' Anthony continued. 'It means I can spend more time with you and Matthew. We don't have to wait before we move to Saint Lucia. We can go whenever we want, this month, this week even. Let's just put the house on the market and book our flights. What's stopping us?'

'Anthony, baby, slow down. I am pleased, I'm just con-fused, that's all. You keep reminding me we only have three more years to wait before you can retire and now you're saying that's it, it's all over.' Jada moved towards her husband and entwined her fingers around his. It felt good to be touched by her again. 'Are you okay? Are you in trouble?'

'No, it's not like that. I've done things in my job that I'm not proud of. And stuff has happened recently that's made me realize that, for too long, I've been fighting for the wrong side. Last week when I said I was going out for a run, I went to a Freedom for All meeting.'

Jada's eyes opened wide. She didn't know the details of what his career entailed, only that he was a Government employee. 'You can't be doing that given who you work for!'

'I had to. And it made me understand something I haven't been ready to admit. The Marriage Act destroys as many lives as it makes. And I've been a part of it.'

Jada held her index finger up to his lips. Her hands were long and slender like Jem's. 'You know you can't be talking about this to me.' She pointed to her watch.

Anthony gently pushed her finger away. 'Aren't you sick of living in fear, Jada? Because I sure as hell would be if I were you.'

'We knew we were going to be monitored when we upgraded. But without the Act and the new business tax breaks, I couldn't have started all this.'

'And is "all this" worth not being able to speak your truth? Of constantly self-editing? Because I don't think it is. It's wrong and I'm sorry for what I've done to you.'

Tears drizzled down his cheeks as they had on hearing Arthur Foley's story at the FFA meeting. They took Jada by surprise: she had never seen him cry, not even at his mother's funeral.

'Babe,' she said and tried to put her arms around his waist. He took a step back.

'I've been such a bad, bad husband to you,' Anthony wept. 'I've lied to you and I haven't allowed you to be who you really are.' He closed his eyes and thought about all the ways he had manipulated Jem too. He couldn't control his chaotic relationship with his mother, but he could dictate the parameters for everyone else in his life.

'The Audite isn't monitoring our conversations, it never has been,' he revealed. 'We are exempt because of who I work for.'

Jada hesitated before her hands fell to her side.

'That isn't funny.'

'I know, but it's true.'

'Are you saying that for three years you've let me believe that in any given moment we could be recorded but, in reality, it was never going to happen?'

'Yes.'

Censoring Jada was up there with some of Anthony's biggest regrets. He had fallen for her the day he'd watched from the audience in the hall as her university debating team argued why bioengineered meat made from animal cells should replace farm meat on campus menus. She was a skilful orator, using wit and wisdom to put forward a case so compelling, he hadn't eaten meat from a slaughtered animal since.

Throughout their marriage he had enjoyed deliberating with her over everything from politics to movies. But when his relationship with Jem had escalated, he'd realized how much her needs were going to overtake his life beyond that office. And he'd feared Jada would not sit silently by as his career took him away from his family. Upgrading their marriage, however, might offer a solution, he'd thought. They could afford a larger home and she could set up the business she had always dreamed of, all under Big Brother's ear. At least that's what he'd led her to believe. Because the sensitive nature of his job meant his home was exempt from being recorded. Jada's name translated to God's gift, which is exactly what she was to him. And now he risked losing her.

'Why would you do that to me?' asked Jada.

'Because I'm not a good person. Because I'm not employed to do good things. Because I thought what I was doing for the country was more important than my own family. Because, when you want to confront me about how I'm failing as a dad and a husband, it's easier to silence you than to admit you're right.' He stopped short at telling her about his relationship with Jem. She wouldn't understand the complexities of their role in each other's lives or how much he missed her.

Jada began to pace the office, shaking her head. 'I have a voice and you didn't want to hear it,' she said. 'My *voice*, Anthony, *my voice*. My husband, the father of my child, decided he did not want to hear what his wife had to say.'

'I know I did wrong, but that's all going to change,' he continued. 'We can be like we used to be, you can say anything now.'

'*Now* you want us to talk? How magnanimous of you to allow me to be heard.'

'Please, Jada, you have to believe me, I'm sorry. I want to make things better between us.'

'Well, maybe I don't because maybe you're not the man I married. Maybe I can't look at you right now without wanting to hit you.'

Jada's attention was suddenly drawn to the office Audite.

'It's not recording us,' said Anthony.

'Then why has a light just flashed around the circle of the rim?'

'I think you're mistaken.'

'Don't you *dare* tell me what I am or am not again,' she growled.

'Then it's probably a software update.'

Anthony's head turned towards it. The light circled the device for a second time and then a third. It definitely hadn't done that before. 'I don't understand,' he muttered and examined it more closely.

'You just told me we weren't being recorded. What the hell, Anthony?'

But before he could respond, Anthony's watch and Jada's phone pinged. They had both received the same Push notification.

'Good evening, Jada and Anthony Alexander,' the voice began. 'After careful consideration, Audite has decided your marriage has reached a stage where it might need assistance. As a result, Level One constant monitoring has now been automatically enabled. Please access your Smart Marriage Guide for further information.'

57

Roxi

'Antoinette,' whispered Roxi. 'Antoinette? Are you okay?'

She knew it was a rhetorical question before the words fell from her mouth. Her husband's mistress was clearly dead. She was lying on the floor, her head bent at an unnatural angle. The nape of her neck rested on the lip of the first step of the staircase, her chin was pressed down, as if in horizontal prayer. The life had drained from the woman's eyes, leaving a glazed, sterile expression in its place.

She placed her fingers on the woman's wrist then neck to search for a pulse and, when that failed, she tried to locate a heartbeat. 'Antoinette?' she asked again, this time more out of desperation than expectation. But there was, predictably, no reply.

The only person Roxi had ever watched die was her friend Phoebe at the hands of her violent husband. That had been a long and drawn-out death, not like this – if Roxi had blinked, she might have missed it. People only died like this in movies. It was why she was struggling to accept Cooper was no longer alive.

Panic beat its drum inside her head. She heard nothing else until the chiming of a grandfather clock distracted her. She turned quickly to look at it: only eight minutes remained before her device would recognize she had illegally bypassed the system and went back online, leaving a digital record of where she was.

She had to act fast, but what to do first? She had no experience to draw from and could hardly search the phrase 'How to leave a murder scene without getting caught' online. Besides, it wasn't murder. She hadn't deliberately hurt Cooper. But who would believe her? Was doing the right thing and calling for help worth losing her career over? Especially when it involved a woman who had been making her life hell? If Cooper hadn't been trolling Roxi and sleeping with Owen – and she had near enough admitted the two were in a relationship – Roxi wouldn't be staring down at her lifeless body now.

Assuring herself their fracas hadn't been recorded by an Audite became her priority. She must ensure she would not be a victim to a system she so frequently championed. Cooper wasn't wearing recordable technology but it didn't mean there wasn't any somewhere in the house. The clock was ticking. So she hurried from room to room, opening each door with the sleeve of her jumper and touching nothing else. She glanced at framed family photographs on the landing walls of a younger Cooper with three children, two boys and a girl, who grew older with each frame she passed. The last was a more recent shot, of her holding the hand of a young girl, likely her granddaughter. A man appeared in some – her late husband, Roxi assumed. There was also a framed Order of Service with the name David Cooper on it dating back two years.

Roxi looked to a digital clock by the side of Cooper's

four-poster bed. Six minutes remained. She ran back downstairs, carefully stepping over the body again and scanning
each room until finally she reached a downstairs office. Roxi
hadn't considered that Cooper might be a professional
woman. This room contained an armchair and a large
chesterfield-style leather sofa backing onto bifold doors and
a lush green cottage-style garden. Its only technology was
a laptop computer and a Smart watch lying next to it. She
suddenly recalled Cooper's admission she was a widow and
realized the woman would not be subject to random recordings if she lived alone.

There were more picture frames in here although they
contained certificates and were in her husband's name. He
had apparently been a university Professor in Sociology.
However, only the last two were made out in Antoinette
Cooper's name. And they were enough to take the wind from
her sails. Roxi clamped her hands over her mouth, parting
them only very slightly to whisper the words, 'Oh fuck.'

She might have got this very, very wrong. She had to
make sure. Cooper's laptop, a basic and outdated model, was
still switched on. Roxi hurried towards it, pressing a key to
disable the screensaver mode. It required a thumbprint recognition. With little choice, she ran with it to Cooper's body
and placed Cooper's still-warm digit on the pad. The screen
opened instantly and amongst the many alphabetized files,
Roxi recognized a name.

She glanced at the grandfather clock again – she had to
leave right now. She took one last look at the body, being
careful to avoid Cooper's eyes, and reassured herself that
this did not resemble a crime scene. Instead it would appear

as what it actually was, an unfortunate, fatal accident. Police would assume Cooper had simply lost her footing and landed badly.

Roxi opened the door and peered outside to find the street empty. She closed it behind her, wiping the knocker with her sleeve, then with her head down, she made her way back to her car and climbed inside before setting it to autonomous mode and programming it to drive itself towards a gym that had recently offered her free membership. She would spend the morning there, just in case an alibi was ever required. The burner phone absorbing her data revealed she had a little over a minute left before she would need to hang up and it reverted to her phone. It would be enough to get her far enough away from Cooper's village.

Finally, Roxi went into the settings of the laptop, which was still turned on, and a similar model to one she once owned. She changed the settings so that the security proto-col no longer requested Cooper's thumbprint and disabled the wifi.

Then she located one of the many files with her husband Owen's name attached to it, and pressed play.

58

Corrine

The interior of Old Northampton's Family Court building was unnervingly silent.

Earlier, Corrine had inputted her name and case number into the automated usher system. Now she was sitting in a corridor waiting for her phone to buzz and inform her she was being called before the magistrates ruling on her case. Mitchell and his lawyer, however, had yet to make an appearance. It unnerved her.

'Where is he?' Corrine asked her lawyer, who was sitting next to her.

'He is most likely playing mind games,' she replied. 'It happens frequently in cases like this. Don't let him get to you.'

Corrine didn't want him to, but it was easier said than done. She tried to pass the time people-watching and trying to decide on sight alone who'd be leaving the court in tears and who would be celebrating. She crossed her fingers and hoped to be one of the jubilant ones.

But once again, her conscience pricked. Claiming a divorce on the grounds of domestic abuse felt as immoral as crying rape. Yet she was persevering with it. And on hearing of his threats to pull their children's university funding, her eldest daughter Freya had even offered to lie before the magistrates on her mother's behalf and back up her claims. Corrine had declined. Her hacker friend had, however, found a way when it came to paying for Spencer and Nora's university fees. They had backdated her children's student loan applications to a date before she had filed for divorce. Nora and Spencer would now receive married parents' discounts for the duration of their studies despite their parents' impending split. Likewise, the interest on Freya's loan for her final year of studies was also discounted. But there was still a chance they might not require the loans if Mitchell's claim their finances were tied up in investments proved bogus. She would learn the answer today.

A message on Corrine's phone warned her they were to appear in court next. She had already messaged her children to see if they had seen or heard from their father but they could only confirm his car wasn't parked in the garage.

'What if he doesn't turn up?' she asked her solicitor.

'Unless he is ill or has a very good reason, the court will take his absence into account when making its ruling and I imagine it'll be in your favour,' she replied.

Corrine quietly hoped Mitchell would remain AWOL so that she wouldn't need to lie on oath. She didn't want to feel her soon-to-be ex-husband's narrow eyes boring deep holes into her as she presented her fabricated evidence. But his non-attendance still did not sit easy with her. Mitchell was a man who acted purposefully. He did everything for a reason.

Moments later, the doors to the lift opened and Mitchell appeared. Corrine wasn't sure whether to feel relieved or disappointed. He was dressed more smartly than in recent memory, discarding his usual casual attire in favour of a crisp white shirt and a tailored, dark-navy suit that she didn't recognize.

'You're cutting it fine,' Corrine said. 'And where's your solicitor? We're in next.'

'He's not coming,' Mitchell replied. 'I'm only here out of courtesy as I have plans this afternoon.'

'Plans?'

'Plans,' he repeated, raising his voice as if speaking to someone with impaired hearing. 'You must know what a plan looks like because you seem to make a lot of them. You're rarely at home these days, are you?'

He gave her a knowing wink as if to tell her he was aware of her Freedom for All activities. Corrine's throat bobbed as she swallowed. No, he couldn't know. She had been too careful. She reassembled her face.

'You were told the hearing would take at least three hours,' she continued. 'You can't just walk out halfway through because you're playing virtual golf.'

'I can if I'm not contesting your bogus claims.'

Corrine looked to her lawyer and then to Mitchell again. 'You're not?'

'No.'

'When did you decide this?'

'Life is too short, Corrine. Sometimes you need to take a step back and stop fighting battles that aren't worth your effort. Today is one of those days. You don't love me and I don't love you. So let's go our separate ways. And if the only way you believe you can do that is to conjure up lies about me, then be my guest.'

'This isn't you, Mitchell. What are you up to?'

'It's a new day and a new me. As we speak, my lawyer is filing a no contest plea, which means you will be divorced by . . .' He looked at his watch, 'Approximately two p.m. Let me know how it goes.'

'Where will you be?'

'I'll be at the Guildhall Register Office applying for my Smart Marriage licence.'

'Your what?'

'You should really think about getting hearing implants. I said I'll be applying for my Smart Marriage licence. Tomorrow afternoon, I'm getting married.'

Corrine laughed. 'Don't be so ridiculous. Who on earth will marry you?'

As if on cue, the lift doors behind him pinged and opened.

'If I'm not mistaken,' he continued without turning, 'this is my bride-to-be.'

Corrine's brows arched at the familiar face. It was Maisy, once her closest friend.

59
Anthony

There was no autonomous vehicle or Government opera-
tive to greet Anthony on his arrival at Euston station's
concourse this time.

Alone, he took the Northern Line tube south to Battersea
Power Station before making the rest of the journey on foot
to the office to which he had been summoned for the inaug-
ural Young Citizen Camp project meeting. There, he scanned
the exterior of the building, searching for a way to announce
his presence. But there was no intercom, buzzer or even a
security camera to flag his appearance. His knocks on the
double doors went unanswered so he peered through the
windows, only for his face to be reflected back at him.

Anthony took a step back and once again ordered his
watch to call Hyde. He had lost count of the number of
times he'd tried contacting him since being informed that
Audite was placing him and Jada on Level One. Each time,
he reached a 'number not recognized' alert. He had also
attempted messaging him through the project's internal
servers, only for his screens to fade and a notification to
appear informing him that he didn't have permission to
enter the system he had been a part of his whole working
life. Hyde had been the only person he had liaised with, was

managed by or answered to. Away from their heavily protected intranet, there was also no way of contacting anyone
on his team. Hyde had ensured he was all Anthony had.

It was why, as a last resort, Anthony caught the Express
train to London to confront him face-to-face. Once more, he
knocked on the doors and waited, then repeated the action
again, and again, and again until his frustration reached boiling point and he pounded them with his fists. Only when
his hands throbbed did he give up, but not before yelling a
string of obscenities into an empty courtyard. His voice rico-
cheted off the other buildings. Where was Hyde?

His eyes turned sharply to his vibrating watch and a voice
note from Jada.

'Someone from the bank has just called me,' she began
without pleasantries. 'Not only do I have to pay back my
start-up business loan within twenty-eight days, but I'm now
paying business tax of thirty-five per cent and our mortgage
is doubling. How can they do this when we're still under the
Marriage Act? We are going to lose everything if you don't
sort this out, and quickly.'

Anthony held his head in his hands. Severing ties with
Hyde and transparency with Jada were supposed to have
given him a fresh start. Instead, they were costing him
dearly. He had to find another way to reach Hyde. Moments
later, he knew where he could go next.

60

Corrine

'Ah, there you are, darling,' Mitchell said, slipping his arm around Maisy's waist and drawing her towards him. They kissed on the lips.

Corrine did a double-take. It was the first time she had clapped eyes on her friend in more than eighteen months. Gone was her alcohol-induced bloat, bloodshot eyes, grey skin and unkempt appearance. This Maisy enjoyed a healthy glow, a flawless complexion and a stomach as flat as an ironing board.

'Hello Corrine,' Maisy began. 'It's been a while. Lovely to see you again.'

'Maisy,' Corrine said, perplexed. 'What the hell's going on?'

'Hasn't Mitchell told you? I'm marrying him tomorrow. Exciting, isn't it?'

'Don't be so ridiculous. Of course you're not.' Corrine wanted to laugh at the absurdity of it despite there being no humour in the moment. She searched Mitchell and Maisy's faces for signs it was a joke. 'Oh my God, you're serious, aren't you?' Her mind raced. 'Why . . . how?'

'I had an epiphany,' Maisy recalled. 'I finally understood I was self-sabotaging my life so I pulled myself together and started again. And once I sobered up, I began reacquainting myself with some old friends. Including Mitchell.'

'But you've never been friends!'

'And look at us now!'

'But after everything I told you about him? You know what kind of man he is.'

'I know what kind of man he was with you, Corrine. But with me, he's different. Sometimes we find our better selves in the company of others.'

'I don't believe this. Are you trying to get back at me? Have I hurt you in some way?'

'No more nor less than anyone else. It's nothing personal, Corrine, I just wanted my old life back. And Mitchell can give me that.' Maisy and Mitchell looked to one another and smiled before kissing again.

'Can you give us a moment?' Mitchell asked Maisy. 'I'll see you in the car.'

'It was lovely catching up with you, Corrine,' Maisy added with a wave. 'Let's do lunch some time and we'll catch up properly. And happy divorce day!'

Corrine waited until she'd disappeared behind the lift doors before she spoke. 'What the actual fuck are you doing, Mitchell?' she growled.

He placed his thumb and index finger on his chin. 'Hmm, well, there's no one-size-fits-all answer so let me explain it to you. First and foremost, I'll be humiliating you in front of our children, your friends and our neighbours. Secondly, I'll be ensuring that you will only be awarded the most minimal amount of my money as possible by the court as I'll be the one in a new relationship and not you. And thirdly, I'll be reminding you that I will not be beaten. I will always be one step ahead of you.'

Corrine closed her eyes. 'I can't even bear to look at you. Your children will never forgive you for doing this to me.'

'They can add it to their other criticisms on my feedback form. But don't worry, I'm sure they'll stand by you after your sentencing.'

'What sentencing?'

Mitchell leaned over to whisper in his wife's ear. And when he'd finished, he kissed her cheek and made his way towards the lift, leaving Corrine unsure if she wanted to chase after and punch him or run to the bathroom and vomit.

He turned as the lift doors opened. 'You have twenty-four hours to decide.' He grinned before he entered the lift and the doors closed again.

61

Anthony

Security was understandably tight at Westminster's Houses of Parliament. Once frisked and his National Identity card verified, Anthony went through facial recognition, a blood analysis, retina and fingerprint scans and was swabbed for biohazard chemical risk before being allowed to make his way towards a reception desk in the heart of the palace, the Central Lobby.

'Can I help you?' asked a young man wearing an earpiece.

'I'd like to see the MP Eleanor Harrison please,' he asked.

'Your name, sir?'

'Anthony Alexander.'

'And will she know what it's relating to?'

'Yes,' he replied, but he couldn't be sure. He watched as the receptionist dialled a number. He had chosen Harrison because as well as being his local MP, she was one of only two people he could identify from the Young Citizen Camp meeting. They had not conversed directly, but she was aware of his identity. And she was his last hope of contacting Hyde.

Anthony took in the historic surroundings while he waited. He had seen this lobby countless times on television but only now could he appreciate the imposing triple aspect windows and the intricate pattern of tiles and Latin words printed on the octagonal floor. He was studying the immense chandelier hanging from the vaulted ceiling when a firm pair of hands grabbed his shoulders. He turned to find two armed, uniformed police officers.

'We need you to leave the building please, sir,' one said.

'Why?' Anthony asked.

'If you don't exit voluntarily, we will arrest you.'

'For what?'

'Under the Counter Terrorism and Sentencing Act. It's in your best interest that you go now.'

A confused Anthony wanted to protest but he knew it would be pointless. Instead, he allowed himself to be escorted out of the building, along the driveway and back to the road outside. Despondent, he made his way across Parliament Square, passing statues of Winston Churchill, David Lloyd George and the most recent controversial addition, Boris Johnson. Cleaners were already jet-washing red paint from the effigy and the paving slabs below it. Finally, he reached St James's Park station and sat on a bench at the far end of the platform waiting for a tube to return him to the Northern line and then Euston.

Like the next train, an idea appeared from a dark tunnel inside his brain. He tried to shake it off but it lingered. Wouldn't the world be a better place if he didn't exist? If he simply stepped in front of the next moving carriage, who would care? Matthew would, of course. And probably Jada, for a while. But they would survive and eventually thrive without him. He had when his mother did the same to him. Her image appeared and he asked himself what might've gone through her mind as she deliberately ploughed her car through the motorway crash barriers and into the bridge? And what had Arthur Foley dreamed of as the exhaust fumes had rendered him unconscious? How might Jem Jones have felt the second her finger released the trigger? Vibrations from the coming train rattled his bench and carried through his body. His hands slipped to his sides and then to the rim of the seat. His fingers curled around the edge as he pushed himself up to his feet.

62
Roxi

Roxi pointed her watch towards the secured metal box of medicines stored inside the kitchen cupboard. When it opened, she scanned the barcode attached to a bottle of paracetamol before her Audite spoke.

'Is this medicine for you, Roxi?' it asked.

'Yes.'

'The most common use of paracetamol is for the treatment of a headache. Are you suffering from a headache, Roxi?'

'Yes, I am,' she replied.

'This is the sixth day in a row you have requested this medicine, Roxi. Would you like me to use your wearable tech to run a full body scan and find the root cause of your pain?'

'No.'

'Would you like me to send a report to your General Practitioner, Roxi?'

'No, I just want the fucking tablets.'

'Have a good day, Roxi.'

The war on prescription drugs, now more critical than illegal street narcotics, meant anything potentially habit-forming was strictly regulated, monitored and recorded before it was dispensed. But Roxi was in no mood to be questioned as to the cause of her recent headaches. She knew the reason. Antoinette Cooper. Roxi swallowed the tablets quickly before the cupboard changed its mind and, with a coffee in her hand, made her way out into the garden.

She didn't register the dampening of her soles following last night's drizzle. She just needed enough fresh air to erase the stench of death that had been clinging to her since her ill-fated visit to Cooper's house.

Roxi had made sure to delete all search history relating to Cooper on each of her devices then erased the hard drives twice. Several times a day, she scanned social media and local news feeds for reports of the woman's demise, but without inputting anything that might register her interest in Cooper specifically. She must leave no digital footprint. Roxi had yet to find anything. She also searched images and studies of the human skeleton to gain an understanding of how Cooper had died so suddenly, and learned hitting the exact spot that could sever a spine was an incredible, unfortunate, fluke.

For the first time in as long as she could remember, Roxi craved the comforting clasp of Owen's arms around her body. Today more than ever, she needed to hear his reassurance that everything was going to be all right, like he had after Phoebe's murder when Roxi had fallen into a deep depression. It was Owen who had pulled her out of it, something she conveniently forgot when her ambition belittled his importance in her life. Instead, she had never felt more alone.

63

Anthony

'You look as if you've had better days,' a woman's voice began.

Anthony turned sharply and saw Eleanor Harrison. He had been too wrapped up in his own world to notice her arriving or taking a seat next to him at the station platform. She wasn't facing him. Instead, her attention was affixed to a digital billboard poster advertising a new autonomous motorbike. A stocky man in a dark-blue suit stood a few feet away from her. Anthony's fingers eased their grip of the bench and he lowered himself back down.

'Your visit to Westminster was naive,' Harrison continued.

'I didn't know where else to go. Hyde is ignoring my calls and you're my only link to him.'

'Lucky old me then,' she replied. 'So what do you want?'

Anthony paused as carriages rattled along the tracks. Commuters entered and exited before it pulled away again.

'Why is Hyde targeting my wife and our marriage?'

'Why do you think?'

'I resigned from my job, not the Act.'

'It doesn't matter. He can do as he wants. And it's not as if anyone will listen if you complain. And you know what, Mr Alexander? I'm afraid I really don't care, as callous as it sounds. Your nearest and dearest will pay for your conscience. But as long as you believe you've done the right thing, then I suppose that's all that matters, isn't it? And I'm sure when he's older, your son will look back fondly at his time spent in a Young Citizen Camp.'

Anthony's blood ran cold. 'The camps they're proposing, they're just wrong, you must know that?'

'Just because I turn a blind eye does not mean I cannot see, Mr Alexander.'

'Then why aren't you doing something to stop them? You have a voice.'

'For the same reason you have always done as you were told. Because you and I have a quality of life that we prefer to maintain. And there is no place in your world or mine for morality.'

'So I have no choice?'

'You have a child, don't you?' she asked.

Anthony nodded.

'We all have choices,' she continued. 'You have to ensure you're making the right ones for him.'

'Once this project is finished will Hyde let me leave?'

Another set of carriages appeared at the station. Harrison rose to her feet and patted out a crease in her skirt. 'I shall inform him that you'll be back at your desk in the morning. In the meantime, go home and tell your wife this has all been a misunderstanding.'

She didn't wait for his response. Instead, flanked by her security detail, Harrison left as she arrived, quickly and without making eye contact.

64

Roxi

'What were your first impressions of Roxi when you met?' the voice asked.

'Spontaneous, quirky, funny, unpredictable,' began Owen. 'We've always been total opposites.'

'Relationships that can handle each other's quirks and idiosyncrasies often thrive,' came the reply.

'She had this aloofness about her too,' Owen continued. 'It was only when I started chipping away at her defences that I realized how much of her bravado was an act. What do they call that? Is there a name for it?'

'Reaction Formation. It's a defence mechanism in which a person goes beyond denial and behaves in the opposite way they actually feel. They protect themselves from further hurt and behave in exaggerated ways.'

'Huh, yep, that's my wife,' Owen continued. 'Even more so since this Influencing business started taking off. I'm sure it all stems back to when she was a kid.'

'Many of our behaviours do. Can you expand?'

'She was neglected so taken away from her parents when she was four, then spent her childhood moving around foster families. She once admitted that it was only as an adult that she understood that those foster parents weren't rejecting her; temporary care was the nature of their job. I naively assumed that once we got married and the kids came along, she'd feel less worthless. But Roxi still needs the approval she never got as a girl, and if she doesn't think she's getting it from me, then she seeks it elsewhere, like social media. Even if the whole world told her she was loved, I still don't think she'd believe it.'

'From what you're describing, her "attention seeking" sounds like an addiction. Have you heard of Dopamine? It's a neurochemical found in the brain and is nicknamed the reward chemical because it releases when people behave in certain ways, like gambling or drug dependency. The need for that chemical becomes addictive in some. Perhaps Roxi finds that release in her job, gaining attention and followers for her posts.'

Roxi heard Owen let out a long, drawn-out breath. 'Why can't it be like it was when we first got together?'

'Often we can look back on those halcyon days with rose-tinted glasses.'

'You think I'm misremembering them?'

'No, I'm suggesting that you are placing more emphasis on how happy you were then, because you're comparing it to your relationship as it stands now.'

'But we *were* happy.'

'Most people marry because they're happy. But today? How would you describe yourself in terms of your marriage?'

Roxi counted twenty-two seconds before Owen replied. 'Lonely,' he said.

She pressed the pause button on Cooper's stolen laptop, removed her ear buds and the sound of chatter from the cafe she was visiting returned. Roxi hadn't heard Owen speak in such depth about her or their relationship before, and especially to a stranger. Only Antoinette Cooper wasn't a stranger to Owen. Neither was she his mistress. Roxi had killed his relationship therapist, a fact that had only come to light when she'd searched Cooper's office and read the framed diplomas on her walls. Unless you were an official Government-sanctioned Relationship Responder, such a job was now illegal. No wonder she hadn't identified herself to Roxi and kept glancing behind her to see if any neighbours were overhearing their confrontation. Cooper hadn't wanted to risk being exposed. But if she'd explained who she was, she would still be alive today. It was her own bloody fault she was dead, not Roxi's.

Antoinette had also more commonly gone by the name of Toni Cooper, which is why Roxi had been unable to find out anything about her online before their altercation.

According to dated files on the laptop, Owen had been seeing her for months, long before their Audite decided they had problems. Owen had foreseen the erosion of their relationship and only now was Roxi realizing that if she had listened when he'd tried to broach the subject, they might not have been Levelled up.

Her phone flashed with the first two lines of an email. It was from Suzanne at Talk Radio. Roxi had yet to return her invitation to appear on the station later in the week. Since Cooper's death, Roxi had gone to ground, refusing to see anyone or update her social media content. She took another long gulp from a second glass of wine a waitress had carried over earlier. It wasn't easing her anxiety as she hoped it might.

The guilt Roxi felt for violating her husband's privacy wasn't enough to stop her from listening. So she reinserted her earbud and picked another random recording, made six weeks earlier according to the date on the file.

'I've done something I'm not proud of,' Owen began.

'Would you like to tell me about it?' Cooper asked.

'I don't know if I do.'

'Why?'

'Because you'll make me explore my reasoning and I don't know if I have the energy to do that today.' He paused and Roxi held her breath. 'I've betrayed my wife.'

Roxi's stomach sank. She didn't know if she wanted to hear any more.

'It's my fault we are on Level One. I've been saying things to the Audite that I shouldn't have.'

'What kind of things?' Roxi asked at the same time as Cooper.

'Stupid things. Like I don't love her any more, that I want a divorce, that I'm not happy . . . stuff like that.'

'And is any of it true?'

'No.'

'Can you explain your reasoning behind it?'

'I hoped I was being recorded and it would force us onto Level One. Maybe then she'd take my marriage concerns seriously. But I don't know if she has. She still doesn't seem to care.'

'Have you considered the effect this might have on Roxi's career if your Levelling up is made public?'

Owen didn't reply but Roxi heard him shuffling on Cooper's leather sofa.

'Can I take from your silence that you have considered it but acted regardless?'

'Yes.'

'So – and without putting words into your mouth – have you tried to sabotage her career to regain the Roxi you fell in love with?'

Owen hesitated again before agreeing.

Of all she had heard that day, this stunned Roxi the most. But she barely had time to process it before the next revelation appeared.

'That's not all,' Owen continued. 'I've been trolling her online, leaving nasty, hurtful comments on everything she posts.'

Roxi clasped her hand over her mouth. 'What?' she said aloud. A man sitting by an adjacent table turned sharply to look at her.

'When did this start?' asked Cooper.

'Soon after she revealed she wanted to be the new Jem Jones. Do you remember me telling you how my son asked me if I could find him a new mummy because Rox never plays with him like his friends' mums do? Before I went home, I sat outside your house, set up a bogus account using your wifi and started trolling my own wife.'

'Why?' asked Cooper.

'Because I want to hurt her like she is hurting our family. Because she doesn't listen. But mostly because I'm a bloody idiot.'

Roxi slammed the lid of the laptop shut, devastated by

Owen's betrayal. Yet amongst the hurt, a part of her understood why. And her anger wasn't only directed at him, but at herself for allowing things to become so bad between them.

Something had to change. And, as far as she could see, it had to be her. But before she could give it any more thought, her watch pinged. And when she read the message, she closed her eyes and fought the urge to hurl her wine glass against the window.

65
Jeffrey

'I'm not doing this today,' announced Noah before their morning session began.

'May I ask why?' asked Jeffrey. He noted the dark rings around Noah's eyes and uncombed hair, and a smile tugged at the corners of his lips.

'These sessions are affecting my sleep, my appetite and how I do my job and I can't afford to put lives at risk if I can't concentrate. For my own mental health, I need a timeout.'

Luca turned to him. 'When did you decide this?' he asked, bewildered.

'Last night.'

'Have you considered that our sessions might be forcing you to confront your issues and that they're manifesting themselves into your insomnia and lack of appetite?' said Jeffrey. 'Perhaps we could explore this further—'

'I studied medicine for six years before I became a junior doctor, Jeffrey; I didn't log in to an online course, get a certificate for turning up and call myself qualified.'

Jeffrey allowed the dig to pass unchallenged.

'So please don't patronize me with a half-baked diagnosis. My work is the one thing I don't have to defend to you. Under the terms of the Marriage Act, ruling three point one, each half of a counselled couple is entitled to up to five mental health recuperation days in any one bulk course of counselling. I am taking all mine together.'

'If you can find a medical professional who signs off on it first.'

'Check your emails, you'll see I had a conference call with a consultant early this morning and she has approved it.'

Someone has done their homework, thought Jeffrey. He refreshed his tablet's emails and located the message, which had arrived as he was preparing for today's session. Noah had timed its arrival to disarm Jeffrey. Cunning recognized cunning.

'Where will you be staying?' Jeffrey asked.

Noah cocked his head.

'Under the terms of the Marriage Act, ruling four point seven six, mental health breaks cannot be taken at the property in which you reside, or you risk a delay to the recovery process. So where will you go?'

'Um, a friend's house.'

'Which friend?' asked Luca.

'I haven't decided.'

'As you've told me yourself, many of your friends view your Level Two status as "toxic". Perhaps you had best start calling around now until you find one who is accepting of your situation?'

Noah's jaw tightened before he left the room and disappeared upstairs, phone in hand. Luca followed, leaving Jeffrey alone. He inserted an ear pod and switched the Audite on.

'It's only for a few days,' Noah said in their bedroom.

'And how's that going to help us?' Luca replied.

'You need to trust me.'

'About what?'

'What I said to you before about Jeffrey.'

Jeffrey's eyes widened. He had missed that conversation.

'While I'm gone, keep your guard up,' Noah continued.

'You're being paranoid.'

'We'll know soon enough, won't we?'

Jeffrey heard no more as both men began to whisper. And by the time Noah closed the front door behind him and Luca returned to the lounge, Jeffrey was trying to mask his frustration by pretending to type notes.

'Are you okay?' he asked.

'I'm fine.'

'I assume Noah's decision has caught you off-guard, but it might be a good thing for you both to have some time apart. It will also allow you to process what we've been discussing. And I'm here to help in any way.'

Luca opened the doors and entered the garden alone. Whatever it was that Noah had whispered was echoing. Now Jeffrey had to remind him that he had his best interests at heart.

'Are you okay with Noah leaving you?' he asked as he followed.

'He hasn't left me,' Luca hit back. 'You heard him. He needs to get his head together.'

'Where will he be staying?'

'With his friend Frank.'

'I recognize the name; isn't he an ex-partner?'

'They dated for a couple of months but that was years ago.'

'Oh, okay. Well, it's great that you have that level of trust in one another. Not every couple I've worked with does.'

'Noah would never cheat on me.'

'I suppose you could argue that by Noah inviting other people into your bedroom as he has done, he's already blurred the boundaries of monogamy and might not define cheating in the same way you do.'

'He wouldn't cheat.'

'Look, you've both reached a transitional stage in your relationship. It could go either way. But it takes both partners to fight to keep it together, not just one. If Noah is already thinking of checking out of the relationship, then there is very little that the other can do to prevent it.'

'Why would you say he was thinking of checking out?'

Jeffrey exaggerated wrestling with his conscience. 'I had planned to discuss this in today's session before Noah left. But now you've told me he's staying with a former boyfriend, I think it's important you're made aware that he's been researching divorce proceedings.'

Luca faltered. 'How do you know that?'

'I have access to his work account and browser. He has clicked or bookmarked twenty-four separate divorce-related pages – including what happens if you have a new partner lined up before you leave a marriage.' Jeffrey turned his tablet around to show a screengrab of Noah's search history. 'He has also been emailing colleagues asking for local divorce lawyer recommendations. I can't confirm how many he has approached yet.'

Luca ran his hands though his hair then pinched the bridge of his nose. 'Could you find somewhere else to stay tonight please, Jeffrey?' he asked.

Jeffrey paled. 'Err, yes, yes, of course, if that's what you want. But I think it might be beneficial if you have someone around to talk to—'

'I don't.'

Luca left the garden and made his way back up the stairs until Jeffrey heard his bedroom door close. Jeffrey remained rooted, replaying their conversation to pinpoint the moment he'd misread Luca so badly. Leaving him alone had not been part of his divide-and-conquer plan.

66

Corrine

Corrine stared through a double set of glass doors leading to a balcony and out towards the River Nene. She glanced at her watch; it was almost 10.30 a.m. Last night's sleep had been fitful. Each time she awoke, she replayed her confrontation with Mitchell and Maisy at the Family Court and his parting shot. Even in the midst of a divorce weighted heavily against him, he had found a way to conquer and control her. He had given her one day to make a decision. And there were a little under four hours left.

She took up a position on one of two adjacent sofas and took in her surroundings. There wasn't time for that the last time she was here. The former Carlsberg Brewery dated back to the 1970s and, in its conversion into apartments, builders had retained its original exposed concrete finish, metal beams and joists. The walls were decorated with brightly coloured abstract canvases. But there were no family photographs, anywhere.

A pair of heels clicking against the metal staircase leading up to the front door caught her attention. She heard a beeping as someone input a code before opening the door. Corrine steeled herself.

Member of Parliament Eleanor Harrison was oblivious to the woman who had broken into her flat. Corrine watched her carefully as she placed an overnight bag on the floor before unstrapping her shoes and lining them up neatly next to it. Only then did Harrison turn, letting out a shrill scream when she spotted her uninvited guest.

'Do you remember me?' asked Corrine calmly.

Harrison didn't wait for an explanation. She turned and ran barefoot towards the front door.

Corrine raised her voice. 'I was here the night you claim you were attacked.'

Harrison stopped.

'I know what really happened.'

'My bracelet has a panic button,' Harrison replied as she turned to face Corrine. Her finger hovered above it. 'The flat will be swarming with police by the time you reach the lobby.'

'Don't let me stop you. I'm sure they'll be interested in the footage I filmed that night.' Corrine removed a burner phone from her pocket and threw it across the room to Harrison. 'Open the media folder. It's the only clip.'

She watched carefully as a narrow-eyed Harrison viewed it in its entirety. Her expression remained stoic.

'This doesn't mean anything,' she responded. 'I'll say it's Deepfake.'

'I have sworn statements from the young man in that clip and others who you also drugged and sexually assaulted.' It wasn't the complete truth but Harrison wasn't to know that. 'It doesn't matter if not everyone believes us because there will be enough people who do to ensure your position in the education department is untenable. By the time the police arrive, you will be viral.'

Corrine's awareness of Harrison's predisposition towards younger men began when two boys in their late teens had confided to friends in different Freedom for All branches that they thought they might have been assaulted by her. They had been waitering at separate business functions attended by Harrison, and she had invited them back to her New Northampton apartment under the guise of participating in an informal think-tank on how the Government could improve its education system. There would be others there too, she told them. Only when they arrived, they were alone with her.

They had accepted the alcoholic drink she'd offered, unaware it was spiked with a combination of drugs that had left them anaesthetized, hallucinating, incapable of fending off her advances, yet physically aroused. Later, they had been too ashamed to report their assaults to the police for fear there was no proof and that they wouldn't be believed.

Corrine's branch was tasked with exposing her. Their youngest member, Nathan, was a slim, dark-haired lad who resembled the two boys Harrison had previously assaulted. He had volunteered to infiltrate the agency used to hire waitering staff for local Government functions. Then, on confirmation of Harrison's planned attendance at one, Corrine had been tasked with recording evidence from a bodycam Nathan wore, as well as ensuring his safe transport to the event and evacuation from Harrison's apartment if required. Once an attempted assault took place, FFA's tech team would upload footage of it to all social media outlets and news sites before Harrison's lawyers could threaten them with injunctions and cease and desist orders.

However, their plan went awry soon after Nathan entered Harrison's home. Corrine, watching, thought he was already behaving oddly. Only later did she assume that Harrison had spiked his drink at the bar earlier and incorrectly measured the doses of the two drugs. Instead of arousing and suppressing him, they'd combined to make him uncharacteristically aggressive.

Having watched in horror as Nathan had begun shouting and screaming at a terrified Harrison, Corrine had raced into the building, letting herself in with the code she'd seen the MP input via Nathan's bodycam. She'd run up three flights of stairs to find Nathan crouching over Harrison's unconscious body, the woman's forehead bloody.

'No!' Corrine had gasped and in shock, Nathan had turned around, face contorted and irises wildly dilated. He'd then punched Corrine in the mouth, sending her spiralling into an armchair. Despite his strength, she'd managed to drag him to the front door where he'd dropped to the floor, his body twisting and his mouth foaming in the first of a series of convulsions. Even now as she recalled it so vividly, it made her queasy.

'Who are you?' asked Harrison now. 'A journalist?'

'No.'

'You don't look like a vigilante so you must represent someone.'

'I am a member of Freedom for All but I'm not here on their behalf.'

'Why are you here?'

'I want your help in return for my silence.'

Harrison looked surprised. 'You're here to blackmail me?'

Corrine hesitated. And as much as she hated herself for it, she nodded.

67
Anthony

Although only separated by the width of a garden table, the distance between husband and wife felt wider than the Grand Canyon. Anthony wanted nothing more than to approach Jada, hold her tightly in his arms and, once again, apologize profusely. But he knew her inside and out, and a hug and yet another 'sorry' wouldn't come close to making up for the hurt he'd caused. Forgiveness was out of the question for now. If at all.

Anthony had waited until their son was asleep before offering selected highlights of his meeting in London a day earlier with Eleanor Harrison and how he had little choice but to return to the career he detested if he wanted to protect his family. If Jada knew the details of why he was so desperate to quit his job, perhaps she might be a little more understanding. But he was bound by contracts that guaranteed his silence. And Jada didn't deserve to be burdened by his knowledge.

'So that's it?' she said when he finished. 'We weren't being recorded, then we were and now we aren't again?' Anthony nodded. 'And why should I believe you? You've been happy to lie to me for the last three years; why should I trust a word that comes out of your mouth?'

'You can say anything you want and there'll be no repercussions.'

'Oh, believe me, there's a lot I'll be getting off my chest about you.'

'How can I make this better? I hate that I've made you so angry.'

'Tell me in your own words why you think I'm angry, Anthony.'

'Because I wasn't honest with you.'

'That's only a part of it. I'm angry because you didn't want to hear me. I am your equal but you didn't see me as that. It's taken decades for women to have their voices heard, to be paid the same as men, to not be sexualized, marginalized, bullied or have their opinions overlooked. And it's been twice as hard for women of colour. Even today, I have to fight for my seat at the table. So the last place I expected to be suppressed was under my own roof. And *you* did that, the man I thought loved me.'

'I didn't mean to do that to you.'

'But you did, Anthony, you admitted as much. It was deliberate.'

'I want to find a way in which we can move past this.'

Jada shrugged. 'I don't know how to because I don't know who I'm married to any more. Your work has turned you into someone I don't recognize. I feel betrayed.'

'Betrayed? I'd never cheat on you.'

He thought of Jem Jones and how he might define their relationship. Some would consider it an emotional affair. But it was more of a form of co-dependency. They'd needed one another. And, without her, he had become untethered.

'Nonsexual betrayals are just as devastating as if you'd slept with someone else,' Jada continued. 'You can be betrayed by someone when they don't put you above all others.'

It wasn't just Jada's frankness that wounded Anthony. It was the way her eyes had become cold and hardened. He could no longer see his reflection in them. And that frightened him the most.

68

Corrine

Eleanor Harrison moved towards a decanter and poured herself a whiskey. She held up a glass as if to offer one to Corrine.

She declined. 'You'll forgive me if I don't trust you when it comes to beverages.'

'How do I know you're not recording this conversation?' Harrison said as she took a seat opposite Corrine.

'This conversation needs to remain private.'

'You mean away from the rest of the FFA fanatics? What do you want from me then? Money, I assume?'

Corrine nodded. 'Yes, although not from you. I want what I am owed *because* of you.'

'What have I done?'

'Your support of the Marriage Act has ruined so many lives. And I don't think you even give a damn.'

Harrison rolled her eyes. 'That old chestnut. Why can't people like you appreciate the bigger picture and how much it has helped the economy—'

'Eleanor, honestly, I don't care what you have to say. My husband and I have a fractious relationship. To cut a long story short, he duped me into signing papers that updated our marriage to a Smart Marriage when we were supposed to be divorcing.'

Harrison gave a closed-lipped smile. 'Oh deary, deary me. So, what, you'd like me to pull a few strings and grant you an annulment? I'm afraid I have no sway in that department.'

'No, it's too late for that. I petitioned for a speedy divorce on the grounds of domestic abuse but he found another way to thwart me.'

'How?'

'He found a copy of that video recording I had hidden in the Cloud.'

Harrison's eyes tapered. 'You didn't hide it very well then.'

Corrine ignored her. 'And now he's blackmailing me. Shortly before our divorce hearing yesterday, he warned if I don't withdraw my application immediately and go back to him within twenty-four hours, he'll make it public. Not only might I face criminal charges for unlawful entry and joint enterprise assault but he'll be the one divorcing me, and on the grounds of criminal activity. Then he'll marry someone he already has lined up. And the law being as biased as it is, I'll barely see a penny from the settlement. But if I do return to our marriage, we can continue as we are.'

'And was he abusive?'

Corrine hesitated. 'No.'

'Interesting. Using the suffering of others for your own benefit.'

'I don't need a morality lecture from you.'

'So you're not yet divorced?'

'No, I put a hold on it.'

'And if you go back to him, what will happen to the new bride-to-be?'

'He'll break it off with her. He's using her as leverage. He admitted as much.'

'Then I don't see you have a choice. Stand your ground and we're both at the centre of a shitstorm or do as he asks and we're free.'

'He doesn't want me and I don't want him. He just wants to control me. You haven't got to where you are today by rolling over and doing what you're told, have you? So why should I?'

'Then I'll ask again, what do you want me to do about it?'

'Our finances are invested in land he's purchased and is selling to the Government for the creation of New Towns. I need you to ask one of your colleagues to put pressure on him to rethink his choices at home or risk his contracts.'

Harrison snapped her head back and laughed. 'And what makes you think I have any level of influence over other departments?'

'You helped to pull the wool over voters' eyes and got them to sign up to the Marriage Act. If you can do that, you can do anything.'

'And if I agree?'

'I'll delete the video.'

'That means nothing when your husband has it too.'

'I'll tell him this morning that I'll go back to him and that I'll play the dutiful housewife. I'll make it my only stipulation that he surrenders that recording. He will do just about anything if it means he thinks he's beaten me.'

'And what do your Freedom for All compatriots have to say about you using me for your own gain?'

Corrine's failure to answer was answer enough.

'They don't know, do they?' Harrison laughed. 'Your ability to be so self-serving would make you a very useful Member of Parliament.'

Corrine looked away like a scolded dog.

'I will help but it's not going to happen overnight.'

'I know that. When, though?'

'When it happens. There's a paper and a pen in that top drawer.' Harrison pointed to a console desk next to the sofa. 'Write down his name and the name of the company.'

Corrine did as she was asked then made her way to the front door.

'You know, you and I are not that dissimilar,' Harrison added. 'We'll both screw over anyone who gets in our way to get what we want.'

'We are nothing alike,' Corrine snapped.

'Keep telling yourself that. And, FYI, you were right not to accept the whiskey.' Harrison poured the contents of her own untouched glass into a plant pot. 'You'll hear from me in due course.'

Corrine wanted to leave her with a wounding, parting shot. But her armoury was exhausted. Instead, she made her way out of the building, disappointed in herself for colluding with one enemy to topple the other.

69

Anthony

Anthony was unsure of why he had been summoned to the Young Citizen Camp project meeting in London. Much of what was being discussed in another disused building he had been driven to had little, if anything, to do with his work. He could only conclude his presence was Hyde's way of reminding him who was in charge.

There had been no direct communication between employer and employee in the fortnight since his return to work. Access to Anthony's computer had returned but he liaised only with the anonymous members of his team. Today was the first time since Anthony's aborted resignation that he and Hyde had shared the same space.

'We have already begun drip-feeding into the public's consciousness that an overhaul to the education system is coming,' one of the faces around the table began. 'The media is reporting on how there has been an upsurge in interest in boarding schools since we announced we are looking at making them accessible to not only the privileged. And we'll follow that up with a study about underperforming students experiencing significant improvements when separated from high-achievers.'

'When do you envisage the latter appearing?' asked Hyde.

'As soon as the press releases are approved. That's when I believe Maddy and her team become involved.'

MP Maddy Cordell, Minister of State and whose remit included the prison service, nodded earnestly. 'We'll begin placing stories about the rising numbers of young offenders who are forced into mainstream prisons due to a lack of space,' she began. Cordell appeared much more enthusiastic at this meeting that Anthony remembered her at their last. 'To emphasise our point, we'll utilize the names of innocent members of the public who've been killed by youngsters released from adult prisons. Then we'll wheel out our experts to warn how our prisons are at bursting point and toss in a few stats about how most convicts will return to crime once released. The lack of investment angle is going to make us look bad for a couple of news cycles. This is when we'll tell everyone we understand their concerns and are discussing massive reforms, which will begin at school level.'

'And Anthony,' said Hyde, finally, 'perhaps you might update us on your department's work?'

Anthony curled his toes. 'We are on target,' he said curtly.

'Excellent. You're certainly earning your seat at the table.'

Anthony struggled to interpret the look Hyde was giving him. Then he recalled he had heard that exact same phrase from Jada's mouth very recently. A coincidental turn of phrase? Perhaps, but unlikely. There were no coincidences where Hyde was concerned. It meant his conversations at home were being monitored, this time to keep Anthony in check and not his marriage.

With the meeting at an end, Anthony was the first to exit the building and was approached by the security operative who had driven him to this East London meeting place. She opened the door to an awaiting vehicle with blacked out windows. Anthony shook his head. 'I'll walk.'

'To Euston?' she asked. 'That's at least five miles.'

'I need the exercise.'

He began by making his way along Bow Road before switching off his phone and removing the battery. Then, as he approached Mile End, he weaved his way across roads and into side streets until he was sure he wasn't being followed. It didn't mean he wasn't being tracked by CCTV though. Anthony didn't know where he was going until he spotted people entering and leaving an off-white, rectangular church with a towering steeple. He hurried up the cobbled path until he reached a door and pushed it open. Noise came from an adjoining room and, as he entered, he scanned the crowd queuing at a food bank. He singled out an elderly man to approach.

'I'm really sorry to bother you,' he asked, 'but my mobile won't charge and I really need to make a call to check on my mum. She's not been well. Do you have a phone I could borrow? I can pay for my call?'

The man looked Anthony up and down and deciding he was legitimate, removed his phone from his pocket. 'Be quick,' he urged.

Then he removed a scrap of paper he had been carrying around with him since the woman he had met at the Freedom for All meeting had pressed it into his palm and dialled the number written on it.

70
Roxi

Roxi took a seat in her dining room where she had fixed her tablet to a stand. She pressed the video camera icon and gave her appearance a final check. She examined her teeth for lipstick stains, set the lightbulb above her to halo mode and closed a curtain to prevent the sunlight from giving her skin a washed-out appearance.

Today, there was no script for her to read aloud or bullet points scrawled on colourful Post-it notes stuck around the device. She would be speaking from the heart. She took one last moment to compose herself before she stared directly into the lens and pressed record.

'I didn't own very much when I was a little girl,' she began. 'And when I say not very much, I'm not exaggerating – a couple of books and a Barbie doll were the sum total of my possessions. Back then, kids like me in the care system travelled lightly because the more you had, the more you were likely to lose when you moved from family to family. The first time I ever had something to call my very own was my husband, Owen. Then, soon after, our daughter Darcy came along and then Josh and, before I knew it, I had what I always wanted. A family.

'They gave me everything I never had. But recently, I've

lost sight of that. Instead, I've focused my attention on wanting what other people have. If I'm being honest, I think my desire for more and better is an addiction. Gradually I'm coming to understand that I don't need free holidays, luxury make-up and exercise equipment to make me whole, nor do I need the validation of strangers.'

Roxi allowed the recording to continue while she hesitated and looked beyond the lens to gather her thoughts. 'So I've made a decision that this will be my last public appearance,' she continued. 'There will be no more Vlogs and no more spots on TV. I've enjoyed being a part of those worlds but it's time to sign off. I know that my opinions have sometimes been controversial and, on occasions, I may have been guilty of getting caught in the moment and playing up to that. But that's come at the expense of the people I care about the most. For everything else, I make no apologies for speaking my truth.

'However, my aspirations are turning me into someone I'm struggling to like.' She hesitated as a pin-sharp memory of the moment Cooper died came into view. 'I've . . . hurt other people,' she continued. 'And I've put my marriage at risk. Not so long ago, Owen and I were informed by our Audite that we were being placed on Level One. He tried his best to get us back on track, but because I was too ignorant to take the threat seriously, it's now too late. This afternoon, we've been informed that we're about to join Level Two. And I don't need to tell you what that means.

'The idea of being under the care of a Relationship Responder, someone who can make decisions that will shape our future, scares me. I had enough decisions made for me when I was a foster child. And now here I am again. Although, this time, I'm to blame. And, to be frank, it's humiliating, especially as I've been so vocal about supporting the use of AI and the Marriage Act. So that's another reason for me to take a step back.

'But before I do, I want to thank all my subscribers and followers for their support. It has meant so much to me. You made my dreams come true until I realized they weren't my dreams any more. And I'll always be grateful for that.'

Roxi smiled and waved to the camera before leaning forwards to press the stop button. And without adding any extra filters and only a new hashtag, #IDidMyBest, she pressed the upload button and allowed her tablet to do the rest.

She sank into her chair, expecting a weight to be lifted from her shoulders. Instead, it felt like a bereavement, as if she had lost a part of herself that she had only recently found. She could shout it from the rooftops until she was blue in the face that Vlogging and Influencing didn't complete her and that her family did, but it wasn't true. At least not yet. But she wanted it to be, and that must count for something, right?

Roxi switched from the present to the past, reliving again the moment of Cooper's death. Last night Owen had gone to his scheduled counselling appointment while she had been hunched over her tablet following the car's route on an App. He had only stayed five minutes before driving home and informing her that hockey practice had been cancelled. They had both been subdued that evening, but only she knew the whole story.

'Are you for real?' began Darcy, entering the dining room. 'Have you really stopped Vlogging?'

Roxi focused on her daughter, glad of the distraction. It wasn't just a cursory glance as she'd been prone to doing, but a focused, all-encompassing stare. The last time she had looked, a child had been standing in front of her. Today it was a young woman. Darcy's teenage years were just around the corner and she was going to need her mother more than she ever had before. Roxi had been forced to charter those waters alone; she did not want the same for her daughter. But quite how she was suddenly going to be the mother her family deserved, she had yet to figure it out. Perhaps it would come naturally.

'Yes, I've quit,' Roxi replied. 'Why?'

'So you're not saying it for attention?'

'Absolutely not. My followers can beg me to change my mind until the cows come home, but it won't make any difference.'

Darcy cocked her head as if searching for a lie.

'I was going to start making lunch soon if you're hungry?' Roxi added.

'We make our own now.'

'Okay, well, perhaps I could make my own too and we could eat together?'

Darcy offered an almost imperceptible nod and Roxi followed her into the kitchen.

She hoped this might be the beginning of a second chance, one that she didn't deserve. And she tried to silence the voice inside that asked her if she really wanted it.

71

Corrine

Corrine used a napkin to dab at the corners of her mouth as the guests seated around her dining-room table ate their desserts. She had long lost her appetite but, for appearances' sake, took a couple of spoonfuls of the dark chocolate truffle panna cotta and vanilla mascarpone. A long sip from a glass of Chardonnay followed.

As the chatter bounced from wall to wall, she took a moment to survey the guests she had once considered friends. Karen had always been shrill but it hadn't bothered Corrine until tonight. Now her voice irritated like the squeaking wheel of a supermarket trolley. Corrine recalled how she, Hayley and Sara had spent many a weekend together being pampered on spa breaks. The thought of being that woman again ran across her skin like a blade. Next to them sat Shanelle and Johnny. Most weeks, she'd joined them for spin or step classes at the gym, then to reward themselves for a job well done, they'd polish off a bottle of Bollinger over a restaurant lunch. There was Jakub, who she had learned to ballroom dance with, and Taylor and Carlos with whom she'd set up a book club. And finally Derek, the man who had divorced her former friend Maisy and married another woman while Maisy was fighting cancer. She loathed this gutless man. Yet she had little choice but to exchange pleas-antries with him and his new wife all night as if nothing had ever happened.

Corrine's cheeks pinched from hours of feigned smiles. And as the soirée dragged on longer and longer, it was becoming harder to continue with the charade. She desper-ately wanted to sneak upstairs, bury herself under the duvet and sleep for the next hundred years. However, the night wasn't over yet. Not until Mitchell said it was.

The get-together had been his idea, announcing the per-fect way to celebrate their marriage upgrade with their closest friends. Corrine protested that she had nothing to celebrate and reiterated how much she had grown apart from their neighbours. But Mitchell wasn't interested. And, as punishment, he gave housekeeper Elena the weekend off and cancelled the private catering company they hired for functions. Instead, Corrine was to prepare the dinner herself, using a menu of his choice. At least Freya had returned from university to assist.

Three long weeks had passed since Corrine had reluctantly withdrawn divorce proceedings and agreed to continue with their Smart Marriage. In that time, she had grown to despise a new facial expression Mitchell had developed – an insidi-ous eyebrow raise that said 'Argue with me about this and I'll use that video to ruin you'. Gone from her life were her Free-dom for All branch meetings and new friends like Yan. They had been replaced with Audites and recordable technology that forced her to consider her words and made her every move trackable like an electronically tagged prisoner. The only saving grace of this marital mockery was that Mitchell was once again paying for his children's further education.

Finally, when Corrine could no longer tune out the incessant dinner-table jabbering, she offered to make coffees and memorized the orders of those who said yes.

'Can I help?' asked Karen.

'No, it's fine, honestly,' she said a little too sharply before faking another smile and making her way into the kitchen alone. As the coffee machine percolated, she poured herself another glass of wine and stood by an open window taking in the cool evening air.

Mitchell's voice appeared from behind her. 'Probably best if that's your last,' he began, pointing to the bottle. 'You can get a little opinionated when you've had too many.'

'Are you asking me or telling me?'

He gave her that eyebrow raise she despised again and it was all she could do to stop herself from hurling the bottle at his head.

'What would you like to monitor next? How much air I inhale?'

'Now, now, Corrine.' He puffed on a cigar and turned his head towards the dining room. 'It's just like old times out there, isn't it?'

She sighed. 'It certainly is.'

'Have you enjoyed any of it?'

'You know my answer to that. It's why you organized it.'

He shrugged. 'Not everything revolves around you. Perhaps this was for me. Maybe I needed it.'

'Why?'

He hesitated as he considered his words. 'To remind me

things weren't always like this between us. That, once upon a time, we were better than what we became. That we worked. And that we might still work again.'

Corrine waited for the punchline but it didn't arrive. It was the closest Mitchell had come to sincerity in as long as she cared to remember. Not so long ago, she would have longed to hear him say something like this: an admission that she hadn't imagined the happiness they had once shared. Once, it might have thawed her. Now, she remained frozen.

'You had plenty of time to repair us,' she said sharply. 'But you didn't. You broke us. And we are beyond repair.'

Mitchell's shoulders slumped ever so slightly before he regained his posture and offered a nod towards a wall-mounted Audite.

'You forgot to take my coffee order,' he added. 'Black. And you might want to hurry it up, our guests are waiting.'

As Mitchell shuffled away, leaving a cloud of smoke in his wake, Corrine cursed Eleanor Harrison for her inaction. In return for deletion of the footage of her attempted sexual assault on a young waiter, she had promised to use her Government contacts to put pressure on Mitchell to allow Corrine a divorce. However, Corrine had heard nothing since. Short of releasing the video clips and potentially incriminating herself, she was at a loss over what to do next.

So she drained the remaining wine in her glass and returned to the dining room with a tray full of coffees and another painted smile.

72

Jeffrey

A night spent sleeping in his car had bruised Jeffrey's ego but it hadn't damaged his resolve.

He yawned and stretched out his legs as far as possible in the limited space. He was parked on a stretch of land in Old Northampton where driverless taxis awaited their next App request. The motors of these electric cars were whisper quiet, but even with his privacy windows switched on, their headlights woke him frequently.

He checked the car's touchscreen dashboard. There were a handful of messages but nothing from Luca. He sighed. But it was early and he was probably still asleep. Between Luca and Noah, Luca was the one who preferred to lie in as long as possible. He and Jeffrey were similar like that. They were similar in many ways.

Jeffrey removed a protein bar from a door pocket and, as he chewed it, he recalled the day three years ago he received the email notification to confirm he'd passed his probationary period and qualified as a Relationship Responder. Within the hour, Jeffrey had carried only what he could fit in his hands from the flat and down to his car, making it his new home. He'd never returned as there were rarely more than a handful of days between posts and new houses to move into. He spent those eating his meals in cafes, showering in electric charging service stations and sleeping in his vehicle.

This life had become his norm until he found himself an actual home. One with Luca. A night apart was all it had taken to cement the depth of his attraction and make him realize how hard and fast he had fallen for him. Noah was too selfish, too blind and too arrogant to see that he had everything he could possibly want in Luca. Now it was up to Jeffrey to ensure Luca recognized his husband's ingratitude.

As if on cue, a message appeared from Luca. Jeffrey's heart fluttered.

'Hi, I'm sorry about yesterday. I needed to get my head together. I'm up and about if you want to come over?'

Jeffrey waited ten minutes before he dictated a voice note reply.

'No problem, we all need a little time out,' he said casually. 'I'll be over after I've run a few errands. Put the coffee on.'

There was no more time to waste. He would need to execute the final part of his plan soon before it was too late.

73

Corrine

Corrine awoke groggy the morning after the party. The prescription sleeping patches and her alcohol consumption had left her with a pounding in her skull. She didn't need to open the App and read her Smart blanket's evaluation of her sleep pattern to know it had been miserable. As she removed one patch and replaced it with another for pain relief, she couldn't decide if the raised but muffled voices were part of the hangover or coming from elsewhere in the house.

Suddenly her bedroom door opened wide. 'What's wrong?' she asked, squinting bleary-eyed at her son Spencer.

'There's something wrong with Dad,' he replied and, for a moment, Corrine hoped Mitchell was lying on the floor in the midst of a major aneurysm. 'He's going, like, proper nuts. He keeps arguing and screaming at people on the phone.'

'That's nothing new. What's he on his soapbox about this time?'

'I don't know. Can you go and talk to him?'

'I don't think I care enough to find out.'

'Please, Mum. This isn't his usual kind of angry. He sounds . . . I dunno . . . a bit scared too?'

'Okay.' Corrine sighed. Resentfully, she climbed out of bed, slipped on her dressing gown and trudged to the end of the landing. The closer she came to Mitchell's office, the more she realized Spencer's description wasn't inaccurate.

A blurred object flew across the room and shattered against the wall as she opened the door.

'Mitchell!' she yelled, startling him. His face was puce, breaths sharp and fast and his eyes wired. He paced around the room with pods in his ears, stepping over remnants of ornaments he had already hurled before she arrived. Spencer was correct. Beneath today's rage, she sensed fear in her husband.

'What the hell is going on?' Corrine asked.

'I've been cancelled,' he said in disbelief.

'What do you mean you've been cancelled?'

'What the hell do you think it means?'

Now it was Corrine's turn to look to the Audite and then back at him.

'Fuck that,' he snapped, and moved towards it, yanking it from the wall and stamping on it with the heel of his trainer until the bamboo casing split. Corrine took a step back. 'Every one of my Government contracts has been revoked with immediate effect,' he continued. 'Even the ones we were in the middle of negotiating have been cancelled.'

'Why?'

'They're claiming there are dozens of safety issues with the Phoenix estate we built in New Swindon . . . poor workmanship, sink hole risks, cracked concrete foundations and weakened steel. They're suing us for breach of contract if we don't rebuild and use a higher percentage of renewable resources like wood. And they're refusing to buy the land they'd agreed in principle to purchase from us if we don't.'

'Can't you do as they ask?'

'No, because their claims are all bullshit! We don't have the means to build an entire estate from scratch.'

'So what does that mean?'

'It means everything we've invested in is now worthless. We're left with thousands of acres of land that no one wants.'

'Are you just being stubborn and don't want to admit there are problems?'

'How can I admit anything when these problems don't exist? They're all fabricated. I've been through every one of them with my team and none of them have any merit.'

'Can you take legal action against them?'

'A counterclaim will take years and I can't afford the legal bills. We'll have to consider liquidation if they don't change their minds. We'll be broke.'

'You mean the business will be?'

'No, us. I've ploughed all our savings into it.'

'Oh my God, Mitchell! How could you have done something so stupid?'

'I don't need a lecture. For years it's been a sure thing. Predict where to buy next, shell out for the land, get the contracts for the developments, build and then sell it to the Government. It's what we did in New Halifax then New Portsmouth and we made millions. Invest, earn, invest, earn and so on. Once we go into liquidation, they'll probably be able to buy the land more cheaply from the liquidator.'

Corrine rubbed at her eyes. 'Well, at least we still have the house.'

Mitchell turned away.

'Mitchell?'

'The business owns the house,' he said quietly.

'Since when?'

'Since we bought it. I told you we could afford it but, at the time, we couldn't. So it became company property and we paid a nominal annual rent. And when the business took off, I didn't see the point in buying it back.'

'There must be something you can do?'

'I've been making calls all morning but no one is budging. It's as if they've targeted me and are deliberately trying to destroy me.'

Eleanor Harrison's face appeared in Corrine's head with such speed it almost knocked her over. She was responsible for this. It was why her request to put pressure on Mitchell had taken so long. She wasn't only going to destroy Mitchell, she was going to take down Corrine with him too.

74
Jeffrey

Five days had passed since Noah had left Luca to stay with a friend. And as far as Jeffrey could ascertain, contact between the couple had been minimal and perfunctory. Jeffrey regularly accessed Noah's private and work emails and scanned his browser history. They yielded little information, only an interest in Freedom for All's forthcoming London protest march. There was certainly no clue as to what he had planned next, if anything at all.

Jeffrey briefly mulled over following Noah again as he had when he discovered his attendance at an FFA meeting. But he chose to take advantage of his alone time with Luca instead. And to his surprise – and delight – it was his client who had asked to continue their counselling sessions, albeit alone. Jeffrey was careful never to directly criticize Noah or their marriage, preferring to ask questions he knew might illicit negative responses. Each one of Luca's tears filled Jeffrey with hope.

As each session ended, they switched effortlessly from Relationship Responder and client to something resembling friends. If they weren't going into battle with headset controllers in the virtual world of computer gaming (which Noah hated), they visited the cinema (large screens gave

Noah migraines), went running (Noah suffered painful shin splints), sang along to pop songs on music playlists (Noah preferred classical music) or Luca cooked for them as an appreciative Jeffrey savoured every mouthful.

Jeffrey had never felt so comfortable in someone's presence as he did with Luca. Earlier that day, they had bumped into each other as they'd loaded the dishwasher and Jeffrey had wrenched his hand away from Luca's chest. And when Luca tried to tame the hair that always stuck up on the crown of Jeffrey's head with product, Jeffrey thought his goosebumps might pop. Now, as they streamed a classic James Bond movie, they were sitting so closely together on the sofa that their legs were touching, as Luca and Noah's often had. Neither Jeffrey nor Luca hurried to separate them.

It had been Jeffrey's suggestion to open a bottle of wine despite it being only late afternoon. He had to make Luca understand that closing one chapter to immediately open a new one wasn't something to be wary of; some opportunities were there to be seized.

Jeffrey's phone vibrated for the third time within the hour. Each call had come from his supervisor Adrian and he had ignored every one of them. Nothing was going to interrupt these important moments with Luca. As he looked up, he noticed Luca's attention had shifted from the movie to the window, as if waiting for someone to appear. Jeffrey poured them both another glass of wine.

'Are you thinking about Noah?' Jeffrey asked hesitantly.

'Not as much as I thought I might, which kind of says something, doesn't it?'

'And what do you think it says?'

Luca turned to him and placed his hand gently on his arm. 'Jeffrey, tonight you're my friend, not my counsellor.'

'Sorry,' he blushed. He couldn't recall the last time anyone had referred to him as a friend, if ever. When his phone vibrated again, he switched it off.

'The first couple of days without him were tough,' Luca continued, 'but now I feel like the dark clouds are in someone else's sky. And I don't know if it's because he and I aren't in the same room constantly discussing the state of our relationship or because I'm accepting that, despite our DNA match, perhaps we don't work in the confines of a marriage. Which should make me sad, but it doesn't. And, honestly, I can't remember the last time I laughed as much as I have with you over the last few days.'

Warmth radiated across Jeffrey's body. 'It's probably best not to mention that to Noah,' he said. 'He really doesn't like me, does he?'

'Not especially, no.'

Jeffrey rehearsed how to say the next line in his head before he said it. 'And how about you? Do you like me?'

'What do you think?'

Luca tilted his head and offered a slightly drunken grin.

It was the confirmation Jeffrey had been so desperately waiting to hear. He hadn't imagined any of this. Luca had fallen for him like he had fallen for Luca. He moved his hands towards Luca's face, allowing them to briefly graze his cheeks.

And before Luca could say anything, Jeffrey punched him hard in the side of the head to disorientate him, then pushed his own body on top of him and wrapped his hands around his throat.

75

Anthony

'What are you doing in here . . . ?' Jada's voice trailed off as she entered the bedroom to find Anthony, alongside four suitcases stacked upright against the wardrobe.

Weeks had passed since the couple had last shared a bed, but now he was perched on the end of it, fingers in a steeple-like position and covering his mouth. 'We need to talk,' her husband began.

Jada sensed his solemnity. Instead of declining his request as she had done so many times of late, she took a seat in the armchair opposite, retaining the space between them.

'I love you more than you will ever know and I have treated you badly,' Anthony continued. 'I'm struggling to forgive myself just as much as you are struggling to forgive me. And I can't see a way forwards for us while we're living under the same roof. So I think it's for the best if we take a timeout.'

'What does that mean?'

'I want us to separate.'

'Separate? Really? Just like that,' Jada said, folding her arms.

Anthony nodded slowly.

'That's your answer to our problems, is it? Out of sight, out of mind.'

'No, not at all. But you know as well as I do that we can't continue like this. It isn't fair on either of us and it's only a matter of time before Matthew realizes there's something wrong.'

'So you're already packed and moving out.'

'No, I want you and Matthew to.'

Jada pushed her head back and laughed. 'Say what?'

'I want you to go and stay with your mum and stepdad at their place in Florida for a while.'

'Oh, this just gets better! So not only do you want your family out of the house, you want us out of the country too? Well, fuck you, Anthony. We're not going anywhere.'

'It's not like that,' Anthony replied calmly. 'I've given this a lot of thought and it's the best possible solution. I've packed yours and Matthew's clothes and toiletries and booked a car to take you to Heathrow Airport. Your flight leaves tonight.'

'I don't believe this! You think you can just click your fingers and you get what you want? A marriage, if that's what you can call this, doesn't work like that. What about my job? What about Matthew's education?'

'You can work and he can study remotely.'

'You've got it all planned out, haven't you? You're the one who's in the wrong but we're the ones being punished?'

Anthony rubbed his eyes with the palms of his hands and rose to his feet. 'Jada, I will always love you but sometimes we have to accept that isn't enough to hold a relationship together.'

'And now you're trying to lecture me on what makes a relationship work? How about not lying to your wife for years about what she can and cannot say?'

Anthony averted his gaze to their Audite, then back at Jada. He had only recently explained the device would not be recording them and now he was trying to tell her he had been wrong. It wasn't their relationship that was being spied upon, it was him. Hyde had been watching him. 'I'm sorry,' he mouthed.

'What?' she replied. Her brows snapped together as if trying to fathom out what her husband wanted to tell her.

'I have a lot of work to do on this new project so I won't have much time for you and Matthew anyway,' Anthony continued. 'So you'll be better off with your family. You've been saying for a while that you want to spend time with them.'

'Please, believe me,' he mouthed again.

'I don't understand,' Jada mouthed back at him.

Husband and wife remained where they were, their eyes fixed on one another, Anthony willing her to grasp all that he wasn't saying.

'The return flights are open ended,' Anthony said, looking back to the Audite. 'So you can come back when you're ready for us to talk.'

Jada went to say something else, but had second thoughts. 'Okay,' she said slowly instead, her eyes glistening. As she made her way towards the suitcases, Anthony placed his hand on her shoulder.

'I love you,' he mouthed. And hesitantly, she did the same. And an hour later, he was standing on the porch waving his tearful family off in a taxi.

76
Roxi

Roxi's blank stare travelled beyond the figure sitting in the armchair and drifted into her hallway. Next to the front door sat a neatly positioned briefcase and a matching pair of slip-on loafers. She detested them and the faint aroma of cheddar they emitted even from this distance. Their presence had become such a regular occurrence in her home that they felt like a part of the furniture. However, she would not see them or their owner again after this morning. Her and Owen's four weeks under the eye of a Relationship Responder were finally coming to an end.

Once she had figured out what Adrian, their appointed counsellor, and Owen had wanted to hear from her, their sessions hadn't been as awful as she'd feared. But they hadn't been a box of delights either. Always in the back of her mind was a warning to herself that she must toe the line or face the consequences. She had slipped up early on and been caught out. Adrian had access to her online search history and discovered she had been looking for 'what Relationship Responders want to hear' and 'how to pass Level Two'. She had found no answers, learning that, by law, service providers faced steep fines by regulators for hosting such sites in the UK. The only saving grace was that Adrian had not asked to move into their home like some Responders did with their clients.

Week one was the most surreal. He'd advised the family that while he was observing their behavioural dynamic, to pretend as if he wasn't there. It was no mean feat given he must tip the scales at more than twenty stone. 'He's the proverbial elephant in the room,' Roxi had joked to Owen.

'Body shaming is a hate crime,' he'd reminded her.

Adrian was there monitoring everything, from the humdrum day-to-day routines of meals, family activities and school runs to how present they were for their children's distance-learning days. His continual presence meant she'd picked up on and amplified his irritating habits, like the tap-tap-tapping of his fingernails as he made notes on his tablet or how he whistled from his nostrils when he exhaled.

Often, when Owen was at work, it was just him and Roxi orbiting the same tiny universe, her always aware of his hawk-like eyes while she read a book, did laundry or binge-streamed a TV series. There was a lot more time to fill now that she had no social media to prepare content for.

The hard work began in week two. Intense Therapy, Adrian had branded it. And it soon became apparent that he was prone to siding with Owen, not her. After one particularly frustrating session in which she was blamed for everything that was wrong in their marriage, Roxi had given serious consideration to calling Adrian out on his bias. But later, when she'd calmed, she'd been glad she hadn't. Protestations would make her appear hostile and would be as pointless as a footballer arguing with an AI referee's decision. And it might even prolong the process if she wasn't seen to be taking constructive criticism on the chin. She had given up so much of herself already, she wouldn't miss another piece.

Roxi had been expected to open up to Adrian about her entire life, from the baggage she carried from foster care to motherhood and even her sex life, past and present. She played along but the only subject on which she remained tight-lipped was the accidental killing of Antoinette Cooper. Likewise, Owen was also expected to bring honesty to the table. Yet he failed to mention his therapy sessions with Cooper. She knew that confronting him with it would open a can of worms best left sealed and might drag out this process further. However, she was pleased not to be the only one holding back from the absolute truth.

Roxi grew accustomed to Adrian's presence, like she would an elusive mouse scurrying about her loft. She revealed just enough tiny increments of herself and her thoughts to convince Adrian she was taking the process seriously.

'Have you heard of the kurinji plant?' Adrian had asked her out of the blue.

Do I look like bloody Wikipedia? she had wanted to say. She'd shaken her head instead.

'They're found in the blue mountains in South India; beautiful little plants that only blossom once every twelve years. You're like one of those. You can't be hurried but, once you're ready to bloom, it's worth the wait.'

He had laughed and Owen had joined in and she had wanted to take the spade leaning against the shed in the garden and batter them both to death with it.

She was a better actress than she gave herself credit for,

though, as, within a few short weeks, he announced their work was complete, and well ahead of schedule.

'How do you think your communication has changed since you joined Level Two?' asked Adrian.

'I used to find myself resenting Roxi when she asked me to do something when she could've done it herself but she was too engrossed in social media,' said Owen. 'But now I know when she asks for something it's because she needs my help as her partner and not as an employee.'

Inwardly, Roxi rolled her eyes.

'Excellent,' said Adrian. 'And how does it make you feel to hear that, Roxi?'

'Like I'm contributing to my husband's emotional needs,' she replied. She fought the urge to finish with something dripping in sarcasm.

'That's great,' said Adrian and tap-tap-tapped something else into his tablet. 'Always remember that a request for help is a way of reminding you how capable and worthy you are of completing that task.'

Roxi and Owen nodded their acceptance of yet another one of Adrian's pearls of wisdom. There had been enough of them to string together to make a necklace that stretched to hell and back.

'Okay, folks, well, that pretty much wraps things up for us all. I'm going to head back to the office and leave you to enjoy one another.' Adrian closed his tablet's case and let out a final nostril whistle. He explained that, later in the day, he would file his report and a myriad of algorithms would decide if Roxi and Owen's marriage should continue or if it should go before Family Court magistrates to rule upon. But he assured them that was unlikely.

'I'll leave this thought with you,' he added. 'So much of our lives are spent trying to solve problems, that we forget marriage is a relationship and not one handicap after another. Keep this in mind and you won't be seeing the likes of me again.'

All three laughed – again, Roxi's was contrived – as Adrian rose slowly from his seat, slipped on his cheesy loafers and Owen closed the door behind him.

'Has he gone?' came a voice from upstairs on the landing. Darcy was peering out from her bedroom door.

'Yes,' Owen replied.

'Are you still married?'

'I think so.' Owen grinned and looked to his wife.

'Very much so,' Roxi replied and entwined her fingers around his.

Her well-rehearsed smile had got them through the last few weeks. Now it had to get her through the rest of their lives together.

77

Anthony

Anthony placed the electronic device inside the palm of his hand and worked his way around his office, swiping and waving it in front of each section of wall until it began to emit a low beep. He had found it.

He'd installed security cameras both inside and outside the house, but not like this one. He took a closer look at the near-translucent circle, no bigger than a centimetre, positioned just below the coving. It was an optical fibre camera used to record every word and every movement in his office. It was how Hyde knew that he kept the weapon used to kill Jem Jones in his bottom drawer. He had likely been monitored around the clock long before his attempted resignation. He ripped the circle from the wall and stamped on it.

Back in the office, Anthony unlocked the bottom drawer of his desk and removed the gun. For a moment he thought he saw traces of Jem's blood on the barrel. It was impossible; his mind was playing tricks on him. Next, he opened a carton of bullets, then the gun's chamber and placed each one inside until it was full. He stretched out his arms and aimed the weapon at the screens on the wall in front of him.

Then he pretended to fire the weapon, one imaginary shot after another.

Finally, Anthony turned himself towards the translucent lens, staring directly at it. He placed the barrel to the right side of his head – the exact same place as Jem Jones' entry wound – and, ever so gently, began to squeeze the trigger. Only when all six screens in his office turned on remotely did he release the pressure.

They contained the same image. Hyde was glaring at him from inside the rear of a moving vehicle. It was the first time Anthony had ever witnessed an uneasiness in his employer.

'Don't,' Hyde said sharply.

'Why not?'

'Because things will take an unpleasant turn for Matthew and Jada if you do.'

'Then just let me go.'

'I can't do that.'

'You told me yourself that none of us are irreplaceable.'

'I have invested too much time and effort in you to let you fuck up your future.'

'Stop recording me. Turn off the cameras in my house,' Anthony replied. 'Don't monitor me. Let me get on with my job.'

Hyde hesitated. 'You attended a Freedom for All meeting. You disappeared from surveillance after our last meeting in London. I cannot trust you.'

'Likewise. But I'm doing as I'm told. I've sent my family away so that I don't lose focus. When the next stage of this project is over, I want out. And I want a guarantee there will be no repercussions.'

When Hyde didn't answer immediately, Anthony's finger again squeezed the tigger. It was enough to secure an answer.

'Okay,' said Hyde. Anthony lowered his weapon, the screens turned themselves off as quickly as they had switched on.

78

Jeffrey

Jeffrey's head turned sharply as the front door swung open, hitting the wall with a thud. He knew who was there before their eyes met.

Noah was breathless, his cheeks a dark crimson colour. He stopped at the entrance to the lounge when he caught sight of Jeffrey sitting on the sofa. Jeffrey wore only his underwear.

'So you got my video?' Jeffrey asked. 'I wasn't sure because you didn't reply.'

The clip had lasted a minute. It was of Luca lying face down on his and Noah's bed and Jeffrey on top of him, smiling to the camera as he rocked back and forth.

'Why?' asked Noah.

'You gave up on your marriage. Did you expect Luca to wait around?'

'I needed space.'

'And look where that got you. But based on everything I've seen and heard over our time together, your marriage was over long before I arrived or you walked out. Luca was never going to be enough for someone like you and he knew it. So he wasn't going to waste any more of his life.'

'We are DNA Matched. We belong together.'

'So why have you been looking for a divorce lawyer? I've seen the search history on your work computer.'

'Because we were happier before we got married! If we get divorced then we can start again; go back to the way things were.'

'Well, as you can see, it's too late for that. You've lost him. He and I are together now.'

Noah's eyes narrowed. 'Is that what you told the others, Jeffrey?'

'What others?'

'The other couples you've sabotaged and picked apart and forced to split up even though they wanted to stay together? And what about the others who didn't survive your intrusion? Those who ended up dead like Harry and Tanya Knox? Or disappeared like Mickey Richards or the Armitages?'

Jeffrey's body tensed. How could he know their names? Then he recalled catching a glimpse of Noah talking to someone at the Freedom for All meeting. Could they have been colluding?

'Freedom for All has built a substantial case against you,' Noah continued, confirming Jeffrey's suspicions. 'Every couple you split up, each client you were supposed to counsel but instead created conflict for, the ones who rejected you and you ruined . . . we've all made official complaints against you.'

Jeffrey cleared his throat. 'Sour grapes. Even if any of that is true, who'll believe you? My employers know I choose more challenging cases than other Relationship Responders. Amongst the successes of course there'll be failures and bitterness.'

'You don't "choose more challenging cases"; you pick on the vulnerable and, bit by bit, you chip away at them.'

'And if you're strong enough and meant to be together, you survive.'

'What about Rosie Morrison? Or your brother Bobby? Were they meant to be together?'

Their names packed a punch. Sixteen years after this all began, someone had slotted the pieces together. Rage began to build up inside Jeffrey.

'Has your supervisor been in touch yet?' Noah continued. 'He seemed very interested when a group of us went to meet him this afternoon.'

Jeffrey flinched when he remembered the many calls from Adrian he'd ignored.

'And, while I remember, you should install better security measures on your tablet,' added Noah. 'Because before I left the house last week, I cloned everything on it. The friend I was staying with works in tech and helped me sift through every report you've ever written, drafts that contradict one another and blatant lies you've told. I even know you've made voice recordings of Luca and me having sex when you said the Audite was turned off. And, on the way here, I forwarded Adrian the video you sent me tonight. That in itself is enough to get you fired.'

'Do or say what you want,' Jeffrey replied. His anxiousness belittled the bravado of his response. 'I have what I want now. I have Luca.'

'And does Luca have any say in this?' asked Noah. 'Is he still upstairs?'

'He doesn't want to see you,' said Jeffrey, quickly.

'You don't get to be the judge of that.'

Before Jeffrey could stop him, Noah ran up the stairs and disappeared out of sight. By the time he reached the bedroom, Noah was already halfway inside. Noah had stopped to take in his husband, lying face down in his bed, his head resting on his forearm, his naked back, buttocks and legs exposed.

'Wake up,' Noah began sternly but Luca didn't budge. He raised his voice. 'Luca, I said wake up.'

'He's drunk,' Jeffrey said quickly. 'He passed out.'

Noah inched forward. 'When Luca's drunk, he vomits. He doesn't pass out.'

'You need to leave.'

'It's my house.'

'I'll tell him you came by.'

'Luca,' Noah repeated but still no answer came. He turned to glare at Jeffrey, his face paling. 'What have you done to him?'

Noah moved towards Luca but Jeffrey grabbed his shoulder and spun him around. With all his might, Noah shoved Jeffrey in the chest, but he was no match for Jeffrey's strength. Jeffrey grabbed him by his right arm and, before Noah could release himself, it was twisted behind his back and his face slammed against the wall.

'I don't want to hurt you, Noah,' threatened Jeffrey. 'But I will.'

'I'm not going anywhere,' said Noah. He continued to shout Luca's name as he struggled to loosen himself from Jeffrey's grip. But his efforts to kick, elbow and headbutt

Jeffrey were in vain. His opponent was well-schooled in all manoeuvres.

'This is your last chance,' snarled Jeffrey. 'Get out.'

'Not without my husband,' protested Noah.

My husband. It only took those two words to trigger Jeffrey. He was not going to allow Noah to ruin everything. He yanked Noah's head backwards then pushed it with all his force against the wall. It was powerful enough to stun his victim because the man's body perceptibly weakened. Jeffrey took advantage of his debilitated state and repeated the manoeuvre, again and again until he heard a crunching sound inside Noah's head. Only when he glanced at the wall did he see smears of blood that had seeped from a gaping wound above Noah's eye. Two more blows against the wall and he dropped the man's body to the floor.

Noah was dead.

The strength required to kill a man with his bare hands had left Jeffrey's arms weak and his lungs breathless. Noah hadn't been the first person to take on Jeffrey, but he hoped he would be the last.

Now wasn't the time for reflection, though. He must gather himself fast and clear up his mess.

79

Corrine

Corrine had been waiting on a bench by the River Nene outside Eleanor Harrison's apartment for much of the day. On her arrival she had tried the passcode to the door but, as she suspected, it had been changed after her last visit.

Corrine's hacker contact had searched the MP's online diary and found a gap in her schedule but Corrine couldn't be sure when she would be returning home until Harrison's vehicle entered the gated community and the underground parking. Corrine only just squeezed through the closing gates before hurrying down a steep slope until she reached Harrison's car.

She was an arm's-length away from the driver's door when it opened, but she was taken by surprise when a burly man in a dark suit exited first. He launched himself at her, grabbing her by the shoulders and turning her around, then pushing her face first against the rear passenger window. Corrine howled in pain when her collarbone jarred as if ready to jump out of its socket.

'Get off me!' she yelled as Harrison left the car and glared at her from the safety of the other side.

'What do you want?' Harrison asked sharply.

'You know why I'm here. Tell him to let me go.'

'I repeat, what do you want?'

'You bankrupted my husband and you've left my family with nothing.'

'Search her,' she told her bodyguard. Keeping a firm grip on Corrine, the man scanned her body with a metal object and removed a phone from her trouser pocket. There was a second, a burner phone, tucked into a jacket pocket. 'Ensure they're not recording.'

The man examined them closely then shook his head. Then he grabbed Corrine's wrist and checked her watch. 'Rec-tech,' he said in a gruff Eastern European accent.

'Use the signal jammer.' He removed something from his pocket and held it against the watch. 'Now give us a moment please.'

The man moved a few metres away but kept both women in his line of sight.

'You'll have to forgive Andrei but I'm sure you understand that I need to protect myself after my last brutal attack.' She gave Corrine a sly grin.

'You've taken everything away from us,' Corrine complained. 'Every single penny.'

'I didn't think terrorists cared about money, only equality? Regardless, I did as you asked. Well, you didn't quite ask, did you? You blackmailed.'

'I didn't ask you to destroy my whole family.'

'You told me to get my colleagues to "put pressure" on your husband to make him "rethink his choices". So that's what I did. It's not my fault that by putting all his eggs in one basket he's left you with nothing.'

'You must know that now I've got nothing to lose, I'm

going to use that video against you. To hell with how it might damage me.'

'Funny, you're not the first person to make that threat against me today. Your husband contacted me earlier this morning saying the very same thing. He told me he had the video and that he'd make it public if I didn't help him.'

'Mitchell?'

'Uhuh. And I'll tell you what I told him. Check your Cloud.'

Corrine grabbed both devices from the roof of the car but there was something different about the screen of her regular phone. The screensaver photograph of her children had vanished. Inside, her contacts and call list were empty and there were no Apps. The phone had been returned to its factory settings. So had the burner. Corrine glared at Andrei. He must have erased their contents with his scanner.

'You can delete as many devices as you like, but you can't delete the Cloud,' Corrine argued.

'You're right, but under the Domestic Counter Terrorism Act, we can force a service provider to allow us access into any account we believe might be a danger to the public. And as my assault has been categorized by the police as an Act of Terror, everything on your computer, every device in your household and each and every person listed in your contacts have had their Clouds scanned and searched and that video removed.'

Corrine paled. 'You can't do that.'

'I can and I have. As I said in my speech after my assault, I will not kowtow to anyone. Especially not bullies, blackmailers or misguided members of Freedom for All. Now, is there anything else?'

But Harrison didn't allow her to respond. She nodded to Andrei who frogmarched Corrine out of the car park, through the gates and back out into the street.

80
Jeffrey

Jeffrey's eyes darted in all directions like startled birds as he made a priority list. On the bed lay Luca, and, on the floor, the crumpled body of Noah. The latter's blood and strands of hair were smeared across the wall.

He was wracked with guilt over what he had done to Luca but not Noah – Noah only had himself to blame. He was supposed to process what had happened between Jeffrey and Luca, declare his marriage over then leave. But when he'd lashed out, Jeffrey had had no choice but to suppress him. And, in doing so, Noah had created an extra layer of complication. Eventually he decided on dragging Noah's body downstairs to store in the boot of his car until he could find somewhere to dump it permanently. Then he would come back and handle Luca.

Jeffrey made his way into the guest bedroom, slipped on the rest of his clothes and turned on his watch to check the time. He had missed a further eleven calls, alongside voicemails and voice notes from his supervisor Adrian. He didn't need to listen to or read the messages to appreciate the mess Noah had left him in.

On his return to the other bedroom, a first glimpse of a lifeless Noah created an unexpected tidal wave of memories that hit him with great force. Suddenly, he was his fifteen-year-old self again, the night he'd killed Rosie Morrison. He was on his knees, straddling her body and glaring at her as if waiting for her to suddenly awaken. However, before he had time to understand his actions, the bedroom door opened and his brother Bobby appeared, reeking of last night's booze.

Jeffrey scrambled to his feet as a bewildered Bobby glared at his naked brother, then his motionless girlfriend, and back to Jeffrey again.

'It was an accident,' Jeffrey blurted out, tears rolling down his cheeks and onto his bare chest.

'What did you do?' Bobby gasped and approached Rosie.

'I begged her to stop shouting but I . . .' His voice trailed off.

He watched as Bobby slipped his arm under Rosie and scooped her upright, his other hand patting her cheeks as if to rouse her from a deep slumber. When that failed, he laid her back on the bed and tried resuscitating her. It was too late.

Jeffrey was too hindered by shock and grief to avoid Bobby's first punch. It caught him clean on the jaw and sent him sprawling to the floor. 'You killed her!' he screamed as the second blow reached Jeffrey's eye socket with a crack. Next he felt Bobby's hands on either side of his head, lifting it up before smacking it down against the floorboards with great force. Twice more it happened, dazing Jeffrey. But it wasn't disorientating enough to make him drop an empty vodka bottle he'd grabbed from the floor. He slammed it against the side of Bobby's head, stunning him. And with just a jagged piece of bottle left in his hand, he plunged into the back of Bobby's neck, fracturing the bone connecting his spine to his skull.

Bobby fell to his side as Jeffrey scrambled to his feet. He steadied himself against the wall and watched helplessly as a haemorrhage sent his brother's eyes spinning in the back of their sockets before the final breath left his lungs.

Jeffrey stumbled backwards into the corner of the room, trying to understand how he had just killed two people he loved. Despite his own fractured eye socket, blurred vision and a pulsing head, he slipped on his clothes and used a wet towel to wipe his fingerprints from outside and inside Rosie's body. And before he called the emergency services, he made sure Bobby's palm and fingerprints were spread across the pillow.

In his police statement, Jeffrey claimed he had woken to hear Rosie's muffled screams and witnessed his drunken brother smothering her. Bobby had been too robust to be dragged away from her and had lashed out at Jeffrey, knocking him to the floor and causing him to black out.

When he came to, a frenzied Bobby was trying to kill him too and Jeffrey had only struck him in self-defence. Thanks to Bobby's criminal convictions for actual bodily harm against a former girlfriend a year earlier, Jeffrey's claims were accepted and no case was brought against him.

Now another message on Jeffrey's watch flattened the tidal wave and returned him to Luca's bedroom. Adrian was clearly desperate to speak to Jeffrey but he would not be returning his call. Instead, he approached Noah. The man's face was barely recognizable under a sheen of crimson, matted hair. He could just about make out a golf ball-sized concave dent in his forehead. He placed his hands under Noah's lukewarm armpits and began to drag him towards the door.

A groggy voice stopped him in his tracks.

'What happened?' asked Luca.

81

Anthony

Anthony closed his eyes and took a moment to listen. Aside from a faint tinnitus ringing in his ears – a hangover from a childhood punch by one of his mother's violent exes – the only sounds in his office were his breaths and the tap of a stylus against the surface of his desk.

On purchasing their home three years earlier, a team of security experts had been sent by Hyde to soundproof Anthony's office, install steel doors with biometric locks alongside reinforced glass windows and thick metal shutters. Then, Anthony thought transforming that room into a modern-day Faraday cage was an exaggerated and unnecessary measure, but now he was grateful. Because hidden inside it, he was protected from the interference of the outside world.

The silence engulfing the rest of the house was a different matter. It was uncomfortable. As he made his way out into the kitchen, he missed the excited squawks coming from the playroom as Matthew participated in virtual reality games with his friends in their 3D metaverse. He longed to hear the sizzle of oils in pans as Jada brought recipes from around the world into their kitchen. He craved the laughter of friends and family around the garden dining table on balmy summer nights. An absence of sound created by those he loved most rendered the house soulless.

He opened the fridge to remove a cold bottle of beer and finished it with the door still ajar. He did the same with a second. But no amount of alcohol could smooth out the rough edges. Anthony missed his family more than he ever thought possible.

A notification appeared on the wall-mounted digital calendar. There was apparently a takeaway delivery waiting outside on the doormat. Suspicious because he hadn't ordered it, a quick check of the family organizer revealed Jada, still in Florida, was responsible for arranging it. A full monthly shop was to arrive tomorrow. She must have been remotely monitoring the contents of the fridge and cupboards through their sensors and saw that he was eating poorly. After all he had put her through, she was still caring for him, even halfway across the world.

On the doorstep, he unattached the food box from the drone's pincers and pressed the recall button to return it to the Thai restaurant. Back in the kitchen, he habitually removed three sets of knives and forks from the drawer before realizing his mistake and replacing two of them. Then he returned to his office to eat alone.

Many times, he had clutched his phone ready to videocall his family, only to hold back. By seeing their faces, and hearing their voices, he might lose his focus and that would only prolong his work on the Young Citizen Camp project and being reunited with his loved ones. His plan was to condense three months of work into one. The sooner this was over, the sooner he could leave his job and put the camps and Hyde behind him. So he and Jada only communicated by concise, matter-of-fact emails. He hoped the emotional distance between them was not as wide as the oceans separating them.

Back in his locked office, Anthony ate as he scanned the screens on the wall and the volume of work he and his team had accomplished in such a short space of time.

By the morning, he had completed his workload for that week and logged out of the system. And, for a moment, he surrendered to his irrational but niggling fear that Hyde's people had somehow snuck into his hideout and planted new listening devices while he was elsewhere in the house. He swept the room again until he was sure he was safe. Then he removed an outmoded laptop from under his desk and switched it on. He had already detached its wifi, Bluetooth, 7G internet and tracking capabilities, making it impossible for anyone to know that he was using an unmonitored, non-approved device. Then he plugged in a digital memory stick to continue working on a side project of his own. One that Hyde and his team were oblivious to.

82

Jeffrey

Jeffrey's chest tightened at the sound of Luca's voice.

Luca remained on the bed, his eyelids only partially open, and his irises straining to regain focus. He fanned out his fingers and bent them at the knuckles, trying to pull his way up towards the pillow. He was too weak to continue.

'What happened?' Luca slurred again. 'My head is killing me.'

Jeffrey froze. 'You're not well,' he said. 'Stay where you are.'

But, before Jeffrey could move Noah any further from view, Luca tilted his head in the direction of his husband, face down and spread out across the floor.

'Noah?' he asked slowly. 'Is that you?' He turned to Jeffrey. 'What's wrong with him?'

'There's . . . there's been an accident. He fell and hurt himself.'

'Is he bleeding?'

'Yes.'

'Oh, Jesus, have you called an ambulance?'

'Not yet. I was about to.'

'You need to help him.'

'It's too late, Luca. I'm sorry.'

'I don't understand.'

'He's dead, Luca. Noah is dead.'

The blood drained from Luca's face as he processed Jeffrey's words. He tried again to move, slowly inching himself across the bed and towards Noah. The closer he came, the more his arms weakened and he lost his balance, falling off the bed and onto the floor. A reanimated Jeffrey dropped Noah and helped to prop Luca up against the side of a wardrobe. He watched carefully as Luca attempted to pair what Jeffrey was telling him with his husband's bloody body.

This wasn't how Jeffrey had envisaged his evening to end. Earlier, Luca hadn't needed to verbalize his feelings for Jeffrey to understand how he felt. His body language and non-verbal communication had revealed an unequivocal romantic interest. Jeffrey had no choice but to act quickly and seize the moment. That meant rendering Luca immobile so that he could bring about a swift end to his client's marriage. *Short-term pain for a long-term gain,* he'd told himself.

'Noah, wake up,' Luca pleaded. 'Please, babe. Tell Jeffrey he's wrong.'

'It was an accident,' Jeffrey continued. 'But it will be okay. I promise to make sure you don't get the blame.'

'Why? What did I do?'

'He came home and you got into an argument, you were fighting and you both fell,' Jeffrey said. 'Noah hit his head and stopped breathing.'

'I hurt him?' Luca asked, horrified. Jeffrey nodded. He watched as Luca's eyes welled up as he racked his brains, trying to recall the events of the night. 'No, that can't be right. Why don't I remember?'

'We'd been drinking. But I'm going to help you.'

'If it was an accident then you can tell the police what you saw.'

'I can't. I was downstairs when it happened. You said he was strangling you and you were trying to protect yourself. It's going to be your word against a man with a fatal head wound. Let me take care of it. I'll move Noah somewhere until we can decide what to do.'

'Noah wouldn't lay a finger on me,' Luca wept. 'He can't be dead.'

'I won't let you throw your life away for someone who doesn't deserve it. He wasn't in love with you any more, Luca; he came into the house and told you he was going to divorce you because he'd found someone else.'

'No, no, I'm sure that didn't happen. We love each other, he's my world.'

Jeffrey tried to ignore Luca's declaration. 'It's when you began to argue . . . it became violent. Look at your neck, Luca. There are red marks from where he was trying to strangle you.

Luca shook his head and pressed his flesh, wincing at the spot where Jeffrey had had him gripped in a chokehold. Jeffrey had deliberately compressed the arteries delivering blood to his brain, which knocked him out in seconds. Luca had begun to stir again by the time Jeffrey had dragged him to the top of the stairs and Jeffrey had known that it was too much of a risk if he asphyxiated him too many times or for too long. So he'd swapped strangulation for an electroshock weapon he had last used on Harry before stabbing him with a screwdriver. It fired two sharp darts into Luca's neck so that its current disrupted his muscle control. By holding the trigger for long enough, a disorientated Luca had slipped into unconsciousness again. Jeffrey had had little choice but to repeat the action each time Luca had begun to rouse. The final attack had come when Jeffrey had spotted Noah's car pulling up on the drive.

Now, Jeffrey held Luca's face in his hands and brought it so close to his own that he could feel the warmth emitted by Luca's tears.

'Your marriage wasn't destined to survive,' Jeffrey continued gently. 'You couldn't see how unhappy you were until I showed you how much better things could be without Noah. Earlier today you told me that you haven't laughed like we have in ages. There's no reason why that can't continue, is there? Let me take care of you. Let me love you like Noah couldn't. I'll be your Babe and you can be my Ziggy.'

He had finally said it. Jeffrey had admitted he loved Luca. His heart jackhammered.

'What did you say?' Luca asked.

Jeffrey swallowed hard. 'I asked you to let me love you. If you give us a chance, then something positive can come of this mess. We both want the same things out of life – a relationship, marriage, a family – Noah was rejecting all of that. You and me . . . there's a connection there, I know you feel it like I do . . . together, you and I can have all of it and more.'

Luca shook his head. 'No, no, we need to get Noah help.'

He went to move his arms, but Jeffrey held him back. Luca was too weak to make it a challenge.

'Please let me go,' he begged.

'I can't, not until you accept that I have your best interests at heart.'

'I don't love you, Jeffrey,' Luca wept. 'I love Noah.'

'For now, maybe, but it won't always be like that. You can grow to love me. We don't even have to touch; we can be intimate in other ways. If you want others to join us, I don't even have to take part, I can just watch. I'm used to it.'

'No, no, you don't understand . . . we only spent time together because we were lonely. I thought you knew that.'

Jeffrey shifted his body away from Luca's. His words wounded as deeply as when he'd heard them from the mouths of others. Had he really got this so wrong, or was Luca confused?

'Luca, you're upset, you're not thinking straight,' he said in desperation.

Luca suddenly caught his reflection in a mirror and, for the first time, realized he was naked. He tried to pull the duvet from the bed to hide his modesty. 'Why am I . . .?' he began, but, as he looked up to Jeffrey, he registered Noah's blood on the wall behind him.

Jeffrey's hope began to deflate as Luca slotted the pieces of the puzzle together. And Jeffrey saw their future together slipping through his fingers.

'You . . . you hurt Noah, didn't you?' Luca asked. 'And me . . . I remember . . . you had your hands around my neck . . .'

Gradually, Luca began pushing himself up against the wardrobe. But he was still weak and kept sliding back down to the carpet.

Meanwhile, Jeffrey caught sight of an email icon flashing

on his watch. Assuming it to be another message from Adrian, he was about to dismiss it until the sender's name caught his eye. It was from the Match Your DNA domain name. And the three words in the subject title knocked him for six.

'You've been Matched!'

83

Corrine

Days had passed since Corrine had last seen her husband. The last she had heard from Mitchell was the morning he and key members of his finance team were to meet with lawyers to discuss the next step after his Government contracts were cancelled, leaving him insolvent. It was to be followed by a series of appointments across the country to discuss various incomplete projects and the appointment of liquidators.

Corrine was torn over how she should feel. Eleanor Harrison had double-crossed her, leaving the family penniless. But Corrine was savvy enough to realize that, by erasing from the Cloud the incriminating video of the altercation that left Harrison injured, it had brought to an end the hold Mitchell had over her. Corrine was no longer forced to remain in a loveless marriage. The timing left a lot to be desired but she had nevertheless filed for divorce again, this time citing irreconcilable differences and not domestic abuse. She had heard through her lawyer that Mitchell had agreed not to contest it, allowing a faster expedition. Harrison had inadvertently given Corrine her freedom.

There was much Corrine and Mitchell hadn't discussed with their children in recent weeks – the sudden halt to their first separation, why Corrine had returned to him and now a second attempt at divorce. And now they had another secret to hide. They were not going to tell the children what had happened to the family finances until alternative accommodations had been decided upon and Mitchell had been informed of the personal items the insolvency practitioner would allow them to keep.

There were seven weeks and four days left inside the house she had just pulled up outside of. In all likelihood, she would soon be swapping New Northampton for the Old part of town. But it was a change she was going to embrace, not shy away from.

Corrine's only regret was that Harrison was going to escape punishment for her sexual assaults. Even if Corrine persuaded the two victims she knew of to make police statements, along with her and Nathan, with no video footage or DNA evidence, a criminal case was unlikely, especially once Harrison's legal team became involved. Now the MP knew she was being watched, she was likely taking extra precautions. Corrine could only hope that, one day, Harrison would make an error in judgement and assault the wrong person who had the means to expose her.

Corrine left her car – another possession likely to be handed over to creditors soon – and began to make her way inside to start the online hunt for rental properties and jobs. Before the front door opened, she heard a vehicle's tyres on the road behind her, followed by a familiar voice calling her name.

'Yan!' Corrine exclaimed as she turned.

'I'm sorry to turn up unannounced,' her friend began

as she exited her vehicle. 'I know your text said that you couldn't be a part of FFA any more but . . .'

Corrine wrapped her arms around her and drew her in tightly. 'It's so good to see you,' she said. 'I'm sorry I left you all so abruptly but I had no choice. Please come in and let me explain.'

Yan smiled. 'I've brought someone to see you.'

She waved at her car and, as the window unwound and the passenger came into view, Corrine clamped her hands over her mouth.

84
Jeffrey

Without warning, everything and everyone in Noah and Luca's bedroom fell away into nothing. There was only Jeffrey and the email that had told him he'd been DNA Matched.

He re-read the subject title again to ensure he wasn't imagining it. Someone out there had been Matched to him. Just him. Only him. And, all at once, the possibilities became endless. He might find a love he had never felt before, a genuine one, not an unrequited obsession. There would be no need for any more lies, manipulation or misdirecting to get what he wanted. He would no longer have to grasp for affection as and when it appeared. No more being rebuffed, rejected, refused, shunned, scorned or pitied.

Only loved.

A thousand small explosions ignited throughout his body at just the notion of it. His eyes darted towards Luca, only now with fresh perspective. Perhaps Luca was right. He might never love Jeffrey because Noah was his Match. Could Jeffrey really live the rest of his life being second best? Just moments ago he'd assumed he could, but this email had the power to change his perception of everything he thought he knew.

Luca appeared to sense a shift in the room. Again, he pushed his back against the wardrobe, although this time with more urgency, and tried to lever himself up. Jeffrey watched him, only this time, he didn't try to stop him or talk him around.

'Luca, I'm sorry,' Jeffrey whispered instead, before inching towards him. His eyes brimmed as, for the second time that night, he wrapped his hands around Luca's neck. But now it wouldn't be enough to only render Luca unconscious. Now, he must go further.

Luca, still operating at half speed, tried in vain to fight back, grabbing at Jeffrey's arms and hands and trying to prise them off him. Like Noah, Luca was no match for Jeffrey's strength.

'I really mean it,' Jeffrey wept, and pushed himself up close to Luca's head, burying his face in his hair and inhaling him one last time. He barely registered Luca thumping his fists against Jeffrey's head. 'You were right. We wouldn't have worked. I see that now. Thank you. I hope you can forgive me.'

Jeffrey stared into Luca's eyes as small blood vessels in the whites burst, leaving fine red ribbons. And as Luca's punches and slaps weakened, Jeffrey began to imagine how his life would truly begin the moment he walked out of that house, each room behind him burning in white hot flames. He could already feel a slipstream of excitement in starting a new chapter.

85

Corrine

Corrine wheeled three decrepit office chairs across the con-crete floor of the warehouse. This last remaining undemolished building in New Northampton's Brackmills Industrial Estate was empty. Through a broken window, she could see where workers had begun constructing a wall to separate the Old part of town from where another estate of houses was to be built for Smart married couples.

Corrine leaned forward and placed a hand on the shoulder of the young man sitting between her and Yan who had driven them there.

'It's good to see you, Nathan,' Corrine said. 'I've been so worried about you. The hospital wouldn't tell me anything.'

'It's okay, thanks for thinking of me.'

'Were you questioned about what happened to you?'

'Two blokes came to talk to me a couple times when I regained consciousness but I said I didn't remember anything.'

'The police?' asked Yan.

'They spoke like coppers but they avoided answering the question when I asked them. I kept telling them the last thing I recalled was leaving a function I was waitering at before everything started spinning. I assume they believed me because I didn't see them again.'

'I'm so sorry for everything that happened,' said Corrine. 'I only wish I could have reached Harrison's flat sooner.'

'It's not your fault. I think she micro-dosed me when she bought me a beer at the bar because I was already feeling a bit out of it when we reached her flat. If I was thinking straight, I wouldn't have accepted the second drink. It wasn't long after that I was fully out of it.'

'And how are you now? Have there been any lasting effects?'

Nathan shook his head. 'No. What about Harrison? I saw pictures of her injuries and what I did to her. I'm so ashamed.'

'Trust me, you have nothing to be ashamed of. She lied about most of them for public sympathy.'

'Really?' Nathan closed his eyes and offered a long, relieved breath. 'Can I see the video? Yan says Freedom for All won't be using it.'

Corrine hesitated as her conscience reared its head. She could lie and say she had deleted it. But they deserved her honesty, no matter how bad a picture the truth might paint of her. Only when she'd finished filling them in did she lift her eyes from the floor and dare to look to Yan and Nathan for their reaction. 'I'm sorry,' she added. 'I was desperate and it was selfish and now I've ruined any leverage we had over her.'

'I'd have done the same,' Yan admitted. 'But I can't say everyone else at the FFA will agree with us.'

'What if I go on the record and tell the media what she did to me?' asked Nathan.

'As much as I would like to believe the truth will out, we

live in morally bankrupt times. It's her word over yours. And who are people going to believe? A respected MP or a teenager? Plus you'd be contradicting FFA as it claimed we had no involvement in it. No one is going to come out of this smelling of roses.'

'So there's nothing to stop her from doing this again to others?'

Corrine shook her head slowly. 'No. There's not.'

A hush fell across the warehouse until a voice came from the doorway.

'There might be another way for you to expose her,' it began. All three turned quickly to face their uninvited guest. 'And, if it works, it'll destroy her.'

86
Roxi

'**Do you miss posting on social media?**' asked Owen suddenly. He picked at a plate of blackberries and blueberries as Roxi placed the tablet she was surfing face up on the sofa. Never hold a conversation with the world in your hands, their Relationship Responder Adrian had advised them. As much as she wanted to forget about the whole experience, some of his advice stuck to her like burned pasta at the bottom of a pan.

'No, I don't really miss it,' she lied. 'It was fun while it lasted.'

'Not even a little bit?'

'That part of my life is over.'

'But it meant so much to you.'

'Not as much as my family does.'

Owen's gratified expression told her it had been the right thing to say and he returned to watching his football match on the television.

Roxi didn't mention that while she had placed blocks on her phone and tablet preventing her from accessing her former accounts, she had only suspended them and not closed them completely. She was not yet ready to take that final step. Her former career was now a ghost roaming the

410

halls of the internet, waiting for her to return or to act as an exorcist and hit the delete button.

'I still keep getting invitations to be a talking head,' she added. 'I turned down another request for a podcast interview this morning.'

'Really?' said Owen, surprised. 'I assumed interest in you would've faded by now.'

'I guess I made more of a lasting impression than I thought.'

'I'm sure they'll forget about you soon enough.'

He hadn't said it unkindly, but it still smarted.

'I'm going to put those away,' she said, pointing to a basket of freshly laundered clothing in the corner of the room. All this time to fill meant a t-shirt barely graced the bottom of the wash bin before it ended up in a spin cycle. The swap from Influencer to housewife made her weep if she thought too much about it.

What she actually wanted was a few moments of respite from her husband, even if it was while they were still under the same roof. Since Adrian had left and they were Unlevelled, Owen had stuck to her like a limpet on the hull of the *Titanic*. His reasoning was that to remain close emotionally, they had to remain close physically. He had even condensed his working week from five to four days so that he could spend long weekends with his family. If it were up to Roxi, she'd have asked his employers to increase them to include Saturdays and Sundays. Upstairs, she placed a balled-up pair of freshly laundered trainer socks into her mouth, covered her face with a towel and screamed until her throat was hoarse.

Roxi had naively assumed that, with no online distractions, she could become the wife and mother everyone in that house wanted her to be. But that role and her family's love didn't fulfil her. To her shame, it didn't even come close. She yearned for her old life so much that sometimes it made her nauseous. Some nights she found herself padding silently down the staircase and into the garage to sit inside Owen's car. She had perfected sobbing so silently that her tears couldn't be picked up by her recordable tech.

She frequently asked herself why she couldn't be like other women. Why couldn't she live in the moment instead of always wanting more? Millions of single people would kill for a husband and children like hers. She had even killed at the thought of losing them. Now, this perpetual suppression and claustrophobia was suffocating her. And she couldn't find a way past it.

When Darcy had turned thirteen a fortnight earlier, she'd asked for her mum's help in creating new social media platforms. It was like inviting a recently sober alcoholic on a pub crawl. It was intoxicating helping her with content creation, editing, lighting, promotion and watching her subscriber numbers steadily rise. Mother and daughter finally had something to bond over. The notification sounds returned her to a time when she had been at her happiest. Antoinette Cooper had been right when she'd suggested to Owen that Roxi's need for social media was an addiction. But going cold turkey hadn't ended the cravings. She briefly considered that it might be just about enough to live vicariously through Darcy. However, she knew she'd be fooling herself.

The front door sensors beeped, alerting her to company,

and she suddenly became self-conscious of the footwear in her mouth.

'Can you answer that?' she yelled to Owen as she removed them. 'It'll be the courier picking up the products that were sent last week.' She hadn't bothered to open the boxes; it would hurt too much knowing there was nothing she could do with whatever gems were inside.

A moment later Owen called back, urging her to join him downstairs. His tone unnerved her and she hoped to God that Adrian hadn't returned. It was only when she saw the figures huddled by the front door that she understood Owen's edginess. Half a dozen men and women, some uni-formed and others without, had her in their eyeline. For a split second, she treasured the attention. And then, from the window directly above the door, she noticed three marked vehicles lined up along the road outside.

'It's the police,' Owen said, his voice taut. 'They have a warrant to search the house.'

87

Corrine

Corrine had last visited Oxford's Magdalen College early in the year to drop her daughter Freya off for the start of a new semester. Today, mother and daughter were making their way through the historic university grounds for a very different reason.

Corrine's eyes fell upon a yoga group making the most of the lush green lawns and a late summer afternoon. Elsewhere others sat under shady trees chatting or with their heads buried in textbooks. If only her life was this uncomplicated, she thought.

It was Freya who'd appeared out of the blue in the warehouse where her mother, Yan and Nathan were catching up. Corrine later discovered it followed weeks of suspicion on Freya's behalf, convinced that her increasingly preoccupied mother was keeping something important from her. She'd approached Corrine on several occasions, concerned about her well-being. Each time, she received a contrived smile and reassurances that all was well. On a whim, she had followed Corrine after spotting her climbing into a vehicle with a woman she didn't recognize. And, at the warehouse door, she had listened to their conversation and suddenly her mother's secrets made sense. She was both astonished and proud of Corrine's double life. And, most of all, she wanted to help.

'It's through here,' Freya said, leading the way under a brick archway and through a set of double doors. A brass plate on a wall read Longwall Library. 'Lizzy says she saw him in here an hour ago.'

Corrine followed her daughter up a staircase until they reached an arched window and a desk piled high with reference books and a laptop. She immediately recognized the young man sitting there.

'Will,' Freya began.

Eleanor Harrison's son looked up from his work and smiled. 'Oh, hey, Freya, how are things?'

'Probably like you, drowning in essays, but it's all good. This is my mum Corrine.'

'Hi Will,' Corrine said as a swarm of butterflies gathered in her stomach. He shared the same prominent cheekbones as his mother and her smile. She hoped that was the end of their similarities.

'Listen, I'm sorry to bother you,' Freya continued, 'but have you got a few minutes?'

'Sure, what's up?'

Freya glanced around the room, checking they weren't being overheard. 'I need to talk to you about something sensitive. It's regarding your mum.'

Will's body language altered immediately. He moved back in his seat and folded his arms. 'If you want me to ask her to lobby for you, I'm afraid you'll have to go through official channels. I have no influence on her . . .'

'No, it's nothing like that. It's more of a . . . personal . . . nature. Do you mind if we sit?'

Will nodded.

'I need your help with something.'

'Again, I can't help. She and I are busy people so we don't see each other very often. You know how it is.'

Corrine lowered her voice. 'I understand, Will, but I think there's more to your estrangement than that. I watched you in that interview she gave after claiming she'd been attacked. You knew she wasn't telling the truth.'

'I don't know what you mean.'

'I think you do. And I think you've discovered certain . . . behaviours . . . that have upset and disturbed you. And that's why the two of you no longer have a relationship.' Corrine had no evidence to suggest whether her theory might be factually accurate, or if she just wanted it to be.

Will opened his mouth as if to argue, then stopped himself. And Corrine knew her hunch was correct. But now came the difficult part.

88
Anthony

The two vehicles parked side by side in Anthony's garage had not been used in weeks. Anthony had barely left the house. There had been no more project meetings in London, no unauthorized visits to Freedom for All gatherings nor runs to clear his head.

But, today, there was somewhere Anthony needed to be. His estrangement from Jada and Matthew was coming to an end once their flight from Orlando landed later that afternoon. And nothing was going to stop him from greeting them as the doors to arrivals opened. The idea of it flooded him with joy until he caught his reflection in the car's wing mirror. He turned away before he could completely take in this shadow of his former self. God only knew what Jada would think when she saw his hollow cheeks, red eyes and flashes of cobweb greys that seemed to have appeared in his hair overnight.

As the gullwing door to his vehicle opened, he climbed inside, pushing the ignition button in the centre of the steering wheel. A red battery sign illuminated on the dashboard warning that it had run out of charge. He cursed himself for forgetting to switch on the charging pads embedded in the garage floor. Anthony entered Jada's vehicle instead, a more modern autonomous car than his own. Vehicles like this came without steering wheels or an option for manual driver control, which always made him nervous. He'd not forgotten the terrorist attack on British vehicles years earlier in which hundreds were taken over remotely. But there was too much to be done today to await a taxi.

Anthony dictated the airport's address into the satnav, and then removed a scrap of paper from his pocket containing a second address, which he also read aloud. An animated map appeared on his screen as he slipped his hand into his jacket and wrapped his fingers around an object to reassure himself it was still in his charge.

His head felt simultaneously alert yet foggy as the car made its way through the streets of New Northampton. Weeks of working twenty-hour days on two separate projects – one for Hyde and the other for himself – was culminating in his near exhaustion. He had pushed himself harder and further than he ever had before and would ever do again. Today he was running on caffeine and adrenaline.

But the light at the end of the tunnel was finally in sight. As long as Jada was on board with the next part of his plan, they'd be driving through France by nightfall. Switzerland would follow before they caught a flight from Milan to Saint Lucia. The profit made from the forthcoming sale of the house would be deposited straight into an offshore and near-undetectable Seychelles account his brother-in-law had opened. It would offer them breathing space before they'd need to seek employment again.

Anthony relaxed into his seat and allowed himself to daydream of years to come spent on balmy beaches, with endless pale-blue skies above them, silver shimmering oceans as far as the eye can see and as little technology as he could get away with using. And, as the autonomous car drove itself, his eyelids began to droop as he envisaged a new family dynamic, one in which he was a key player and no longer a spectator. He was going to prove to Jada and Matthew that he was worthy of them.

And he would also leave behind him the memory of Jem Jones. To move forward, he had to forget about her. Only now could he admit to himself that he had loved her, despite the absurdity of it. He'd built her up into something she wasn't and never could be. Too much time had been wasted obsessing over a person who never loved him back.

'Good afternoon, Anthony.'

'Fuck!' he yelled as he jumped, his eyes saucer wide. How long had he been asleep? The voice was so crystal clear he turned quickly to see if it was coming from behind him. The rear seats were empty.

'Did I wake you up?' it came again. It was Hyde's voice coming through the speakers. 'I didn't mean to scare you,' he continued, but Anthony knew that he did. 'How are you?'

'Okay, thank you,' he replied coolly, trying to mask his unease.

'I thought it might be a convenient time for a catch-up as we haven't spoken properly for some time. Not since our misunderstanding.'

'It's not a good time.'

'Why? What has you so preoccupied?'

'I'm picking up my family from the airport.'

'Ah yes, a little bird told me they were returning today. But isn't that later this afternoon?'

Anthony didn't reply.

'So where are you travelling to now that requires your undivided attention?'

'Errands. Food shopping . . . and things like that.'

'Hmm . . . I wonder . . . does meeting with Howie Cosby from Freedom for All fall under the "things like that" category?'

Anthony's chest tightened. *He knows*, thought Anthony. Jada's satnav had given away the address he and Cosby were to meet at. And if Hyde had access to his vehicle's operating system, he was also likely reading the signals his watch was transmitting to the central console indicating his rising blood pressure and stress levels. There was little point in denying his destination.

'My part in your project is over,' he said. 'I delivered everything last night ahead of schedule so I no longer work for you. You agreed to that. I've held up my side of the bargain so now I'm free to meet whoever I want to meet.'

'I am justifiably concerned if you're affiliating yourself with an organization in direct conflict with Government policy.'

'I have no intention of telling anyone anything I shouldn't,' Anthony said. 'I've signed enough non-disclosure agreements and official secrets acts to know I'll spend years locked up and away from my family if I do.'

'Then tell me about the digital memory stick in your pocket.'

Anthony froze. How could Hyde know that?

'The vehicles of all employees and their families are fitted with scanners for prohibited electronic devices and gadgets,'

Hyde continued. 'As per your contract, you are not permitted anything resembling that stick in your possession for any purpose, business or pleasure. Since we've been enjoying our catch-up, your car has downloaded everything on that contraband hardware and sent it to us. One can only assume you were planning to share this with your new-found ally Mr Cosby?'

Anthony's heart pounded so rapidly that a 'danger to health' warning appeared on the console.

'Why haven't you had me arrested then?' he asked.

'I prefer a more direct approach. And, to be honest, I've been side-tracked with more pressing matters. You might like to take a look at your screen.'

Footage began to play of Jada and Matthew inside Orlando International Airport as they arrived at an airline check-in desk. Audio recorded them being informed the flight before theirs was delayed but it contained empty seats and, if they wanted to catch it, they'd receive free First-Class upgrades. A grateful Jada agreed.

Before Anthony could ask Hyde what was happening, he was then shown clips of his family disembarking nine hours later in London and making their way through customs channels. Finally, and as they were about to exit with their luggage, border force staff and armed uniformed police officers ushered them into a side room where their suitcases were searched. Jada's contained a handful of canisters that, when opened, revealed dozens of transparent bags of pills.

'Some contain amphetamines, others were stuffed with opiates and the rest Oxycodone,' Hyde explained before Anthony had the opportunity to ask. 'Total street value, approximately a hundred and twenty thousand. And you know how seriously our Government takes the smuggling of prescription medication, much more so than street drugs. Prison sentences are mandatory.'

'No!' yelled Anthony. 'This is bullshit. Why are you doing this to them? Where are they now?'

'Well, your wife is still being interviewed by police. But I'm afraid poor Matthew didn't react well to being separated from his mother. He was clearly agitated, so, for his own safety, he was taken to the psychiatric ward of a private medical facility where he's currently being monitored.'

The next image to appear on-screen was that of Matthew lying on a bed in a room, alone. His eyes were shut and arms and legs secured with restraints attached to the metal sidings.

'My son . . .' choked Anthony.

'I know, tragic, isn't it? Apparently, the only way to calm him down was to sedate him. Ironic, considering your dislike of medicating children.'

'Henry, you don't need to do this,' Anthony begged. 'Let them go and I'll give you what you want. I'll stay on this project or any other one for as long as you want me.'

'But that's the problem, I don't want you. Not any more.'

'No, it's not too late . . .'

'You like to think of yourself as a history buff, don't you, Anthony? Do you know much about the Soviet Union in the nineteen-thirties?'

'Henry . . .'

'Apparently during Stalin's purges, it wasn't just traitors who were arrested, but their families too. It was commonplace for them to be convicted and executed on the flimsiest of evidence. They paid the ultimate price for the wrongdoings of their loved ones. We should be grateful that we don't live in such unfair times.'

'Please, don't hurt them. They don't deserve this.' Anthony couldn't take his eyes off Matthew. He would do anything to free him. 'Just take the memory stick. Have me arrested; I don't care how long I get.'

'The stick is now inconsequential. It's already been remotely erased.'

'Then why are you doing this?'

He paused between each word. 'Because. I. Can.'

Matthew's image faded and a map reappeared, with an alternate destination to the one Anthony had programmed. He looked from the windscreen, only now realizing he was no longer travelling along New Northampton's roads but the M1 motorway. He pressed the cancel route icon but the map remained unchanged. He jabbed at the rest of the screen and then at the ignition button but the car failed to respond. Instead, it accelerated. It was no longer under his control. As a last resort he yanked at the handles but they wouldn't open. And the standard toughened safety glass of the windows were impervious to his fists and feet.

'Where are you taking me?' he asked as his car both overtook and undertook other vehicles with frightening proximity. Both hands clutched the side of his seat as he willed the car to slow down.

'You're not going anywhere,' Hyde replied calmly.

'You've taken over my car so you must be sending me somewhere?'

Anthony glanced at the speedometer. It was approaching the 110mph mark. Other autonomous vehicles were moving their occupants swiftly into different lanes to avoid an accident.

'Henry!' he shouted.

'You're a traitor, Anthony,' Hyde said. If Anthony didn't know him better, he might have sensed a touch of melancholy in his tone. 'To yourself, to your family, to your country and, most importantly, to me. For fifteen years I had your best interests at heart. I was more of a parent to you than your absent father or insane mother ever were. I told myself your crisis of confidence was a blip, an error in judgement, that you'd see sense in the end. And I gave you a second chance, which is not something I make a habit of doing. But I was wrong and you let me down. And I take that very personally. So now it's Matthew and Jada who will pay for your mistakes.'

'We can work this out!' he yelled but Hyde didn't reply. Anthony repeated his name over and over again, only to be greeted by silence. He was alone.

Thoughts raced through his head of his mother's short life, how much of his own life he had wasted, the time he should have spent with his family and how, given another opportunity, he would change so much. He could picture so clearly the palm tree-lined beaches of Saint Lucia he'd left behind a lifetime ago and how tantalizingly close they were to being within his grasp.

Instead, Anthony was helpless as the car swerved from the fourth lane into the third, then the second and the first. And, in a flash, he knew where the car was taking him and what Hyde had planned.

Within view was the spot where his mother had finally given in to her psychosis and ended her life. As Anthony's vehicle ploughed through a crash barrier, his seatbelt remotely ejected.

The next handful of seconds passed too quickly for him to process. He didn't feel pain as the car collided with the bridge and began to crumple, he felt nothing when he was hurled head-first through the windscreen with a burst of glass confetti. He didn't feel his shoulder blades and vertebrae shatter as they hit the bonnet. And there was no pain when his head took the brunt of the concrete pillar. By the time his body came to rest on the grass verge, he was already dead.

ACT 3

DAILY **STUFF**

LIVE – Major towns and cities see protests against the Sanctity of Marriage Act.

Live reporting
13:47pm
Updated 3 mins ago

More than 1.25 million people are estimated to have taken part in today's anti-Sanctity of Marriage Act march in London, with hundreds of thousands more participating in Manchester, Birmingham, Southampton and Cambridge.

Meanwhile, 125,000 protesters are currently converging in London's Kennington Park to hear demonstrators speak out against the Government. Organizers are promising bombshell revelations.

Updates as they happen

89

Corrine

Corrine lifted her uniform from a bowl of warm soapy water, wrung it out and placed it on the plastic hanger in the boiler cupboard to dry overnight. Her shifts in the restaurant kitchen had been increased to six this week but her employers only provided two uniforms cut from a material that trapped every odour of the food she re-heated. Every day, she hand-washed and rotated them so that she could turn up for work not smelling of burgers.

The hours were long and the pay was a little over minimum wage, but it was honest, genuine work and paid the rent for her Old Northampton flat. In her spare time, Corrine was rekindling her love of painting and pottery and, each month, she put a little money aside for the use of a small studio in a nearby village. She'd even plucked up the courage to enter some pieces into an exhibition of amateur artists curated by one of her favourites, Elijah Beckworth. He had responded personally and favourably and they were to meet via video later in the week.

Corrine had often used Mitchell's discouragement as a reason for no longer pursuing her creative side. He made it feel whimsical and apropos of nothing. It was only recently that she'd realized it was unfair to blame him. He had only ridden roughshod over her interests because she had allowed it to happen. He had not been in charge of their marriage. It was one of many aspects of her former life she had picked apart since the divorce. In the end, it didn't matter, because she couldn't rewrite the past. She could only ensure she didn't repeat her mistakes.

Weeks had passed since she had last spoken to Mitchell. After their initial separation, there had been limited contact through lawyers. And that was primarily to discuss the division of their remaining joint possessions following their house falling into the hands of creditors. The night before he'd remarried, she had, however, received an email from him apologizing for the way he had treated her.

'I'm sorry I wasn't the man you deserved,' he'd written. 'Everything that happened is on me.'

She had felt strangely relieved by the admission, as if a tiny part of her still feared that she had made him that way.

'Learn from your errors,' she had replied. 'Or it will have all been for nothing.'

According to their children, their new stepmother Chantelle was the pushy sort, a widow and mother of two, who kept Mitchell in check. Corrine wondered if the leopard had really changed his spots and for how long he could play second fiddle to a much wealthier spouse. She and Corrine had yet to come face to face, but Corrine was grateful to her for paying for the children's university fees.

Now and again Corrine found herself thinking about Maisy and how she had been dispatched from Mitchell's life as quickly as she had reappeared. The last she heard, her former friend was moving to Germany to be with her own

DNA Match. Corrine hoped that, despite the pain Maisy had tried to cause her, she had found happiness.

Corrine, too, had found someone she enjoyed spending time with, although as far as they knew, it was not through biological or chemical interference. Gregory was a handful of years younger than her and everything Mitchell wasn't – good-humoured, spontaneous and kind-hearted. Being in the presence of someone with shared philosophies was refreshing. He was also a member of Freedom for All in the neighbouring county of Bedfordshire and they had met through their campaign work, culminating in today's rally. Corrine had briefly considered trying to locate her soulmate through her DNA but ultimately decided against it. She had spent too long with Mitchell determining her future to have her genes making decisions for her. Her destiny was going to be her own making.

'Mum, are you ready?' came Freya's voice from the spare room. 'We should get going.'

Corrine looked at her watch: it was time. 'I've never been readier,' she replied, and she meant every word of it.

90
Jeffrey

Jeffrey shook his head as he turned off the television. It was making him irritable and he couldn't watch any longer. For much of the morning, the twenty-four-hour BBC news channel had given voices to political pundits discussing Freedom for All rallies about to take place across the country later that day. Back and forth they bickered, and, even though the channel was supposed to remain impartial following its privatization, there was an obvious anti-Act bias in its reporting. He would defend the Act to the death, regardless of public opinion.

Jeffrey struggled to comprehend how the tide had turned so quickly against such an effective concept. Many blamed him for a sharp downturn in the numbers of new couples signing up for it. The man charged with saving relationships had actually been killing to serve his own needs. The FFA had capitalized on his story, scaremongering the public into believing that if their marriages reached Level Two, they could be placed in the care of someone just like him. They should be so lucky. Yes, he'd made mistakes and sometimes he had behaved inappropriately. But no one was more passionate about relationships than he was.

And to prove it, today, another couple were about to put

their faith in the Act – Jeffrey and his bride-to-be. His heart swelled with pride at the thought of that morning's ceremony in which he'd once again come face to face with his DNA Match. She had changed everything for him.

American-born Kendra Martinez was twenty-three years his senior and a grandmother living in San Antonio, Texas. Jeffrey was on remand and awaiting his first court appearance when he'd sent her an introductory email. He'd cursed the bad timing and was honest about his circumstances, at least his current residence. The rest, he'd venomously denied, laying the blame at the feet of Freedom for All campaigners who were targeting him because of his success rate in exposing and separating those couples who married only for financial benefits; he was paying the price for his determination.

To his surprise, he must have convinced her of his innocence because, two days later, she'd responded, sparking a long-distance relationship. The first time she'd ever left her hometown was to take a flight to Los Angeles then a connection to London's Heathrow Airport, using a ticket paid for by a man she had never met. And as they'd finally seen each other in person on either side of a Perspex window in the prison visitors' room, Jeffrey had felt the instant rush of blood to the head he'd only ever read about. It had been an immediate, emotional, biological and chemical attraction; an all-consuming desire for someone that he might never be able to touch. But a physical and sexual connection had never been his priority. A Match meant that, even behind bars, he would never be alone again.

Prior to his arrest, his outgoings had been minimal so

he'd amassed much in his savings account. So before his expedited trial, he'd paid for three more of Kendra's return flights and accommodation at the Hilton Hotel. Then he'd forked out for a short-term rental apartment near London's Old Bailey courts so that she could attend his four-week court case each day.

Kendra had accepted Jeffrey's marriage proposal despite the jury's unanimous guilty verdict on eleven charges, including four murders, along with a life sentence. They might never consummate their Smart Marriage, honeymoon or cohabit, but her commitment was all Jeffrey required. And today, in a little over an hour, they would be face to face in the chapel, reciting their vows to one another.

Jeffrey smartened a crease in a crisp white shirt Kendra had purchased for him and he shined his shoes with spit and toilet paper. A firm knock on the thick metal cell door was followed by the opening of a hatch. He had been pre-warned it was to be a nine a.m. ceremony to avoid public or press intrusion, and that, for its duration, he'd be clad in wrist and ankle cuffs. It wasn't ideal but as long as Kendra was still prepared to devote her life to him, it didn't matter. He turned his back to the door while officers clamped on the restraints.

The corridors of his segregated unit were unusually quiet as he made his way towards the rear of the building, flanked by three guards. Jeffrey was desperate to see Kendra again. In long, lonely stints in his cell, he tolerated their separation by creating an imaginary world where he and his wife owned a beautiful house in a village near San Antonio and spent their days working on a horse ranch and taking long mountain hikes with their children, two sons. Jeffrey gave them the childhood he had been robbed of. Sometimes his fantasy was so vivid that, when he snapped back to the present, his confined surroundings confused him and it took him a moment to adjust to reality.

Kendra had shown him photographs of the Camden chapel where they were to tie the knot. The location mattered more to her than to him. Her first wedding had been in a Las Vegas drive-through. This second union would be perfect, despite her disapproving family's refusal to join them.

Jeffrey and his escorts approached a large, square van with open rear doors in the loading bay. It was familiar to him, having spent his trial commuting to and from court each day inside a similar vehicle. He took a seat as one of the guards affixed his hand and ankle cuffs to a metal pole in front of him. But, instead of sitting with him, the guard exited the van, closed the doors and left him alone. That went against procedure and a wave of unease struck Jeffrey. There was something amiss about this sequence of events.

But, before he could decipher what it was, the doors opened again and, this time, an unfamiliar uniformed guard appeared and took a seat opposite him. He held a tablet in front of him, its screen facing Jeffrey. It flickered before it came to life. A thin man with pale skin and dressed in a dark suit was seated and staring at him.

'Who are you?' Jeffrey asked after a short, uncomfortable silence.

'Me?' the pale man replied. 'I am the one person in the world you shouldn't have come to the attention of.'

Jeffrey stared hard at him; he was sure they had never met. Was he related to one of Jeffrey's former clients? 'What

435

do you think I did to you?' he asked, nerves catching in his throat.

'I spent a very long time planting the seeds of change in the public's collective consciousness. I fired up their imaginations and I offered them something they didn't know they needed. From behind the scenes, I organized, planned, promoted and executed what was required to get this country back on its feet. I made people work, I made relationships work, I made the country work. I thought of all eventualities – apart from the arrival of someone like you. Even I couldn't predict all it would take was one psychopath with a God complex to destroy public confidence in all my efforts.'

'I don't understand?'

'The Sanctity of Marriage Act was my child. Smart Marriages, Smart towns, Smart lives, Smart jobs, Smart fucking everything . . . all ideas conceived and brought into this world by me.'

'I . . . I didn't mean—'

'What you did or didn't mean to do is irrelevant,' the man interrupted, his voice raised. 'What's done is done and now we must play the cards we've been dealt. And God knows which direction that will take us after today's rally.'

'You can't blame that on me.'

'No, you're right, not all of it, no. Hairline cracks appeared before you turned up at the shitshow. But, by the time you'd finished, those cracks were so wide you could push a fist inside them. You gave the enemy what they needed – the face of a monster.'

An image of Kendra appeared in Jeffrey's mind. He

urgently wanted to see her again. She was the first person he had ever felt safe with. Here in this van, he was unprotected. 'What do you want me to do?' he asked. 'I can make a public apology, tell everyone I'm sorry and that they should still support the Act despite what I did.'

The pale man laughed. 'Let me tell you something, Jeffrey. Throughout each industrial revolution, we have created technologies that have changed the pattern of how we live. And we've taken advantage of technology to help us evolve. These upheavals used to take centuries but we are moving at such a rapid speed with AI and robotics that now they can evolve in a heartbeat. Smart Marriages were leading us into our fifth industrial revolution, one that was of *my* making, of *my* planning, of *my* execution. And then you, one solitary cancerous tumour, appeared from nowhere, your cells dividing and eating away at the trust of the public that I have spent such a large proportion of my career cultivating. So, no, Jeffrey; your apology will mean nothing. Your day of public reckoning has long since expired. And the next time your name appears in the media will be when the public is learning of your suicide.'

The prison guard placed the tablet on the seat next to him so the screen remained facing Jeffrey. And before Jeffrey could defend himself, the guard threw himself across the prison van, wrapped a cord around Jeffrey's neck and attached it to a hook in the van's roof. He used it to yank Jeffrey forward, forcing him to his knees. Helpless, Jeffrey hurled his body around to try and free himself but he was stymied by his handcuffed wrists and ankles and the other man's strength. He began to choke.

'For the rest of her life, your darling Kendra will believe the note I have left in your cell which says you'd rather be dead than married to her, your DNA Match,' the pale man continued, his face up close to the lens. 'How do you think that'll make her feel? Her brothers, sisters, mother, grandparents, children and grandchildren have already disowned her for being with you. And without her beloved Jeffrey, she will have absolutely no one. It wouldn't surprise me if she followed in your footsteps. And if she doesn't, then perhaps my colleague and I can pay her a visit and encourage her to do the right thing.'

'No,' gasped Jeffrey, 'Please, no.'

The thought of leaving her alone was heartbreaking, but the thought of her being hurt because of him was unbearable. 'I beg you,' he whispered.

'Chalk her up as another casualty to add to your tally.'

Two of Jeffrey's fingers slipped under the cord, allowing him to gasp the tiniest amount of air. 'I'll . . . do . . . anything.'

'That's if she was actually real at all.'

'W . . . what?'

'Perhaps it was someone from my department who intercepted your emails and communicated with you. Maybe the Kendra you met was one of my team. Who knows? You certainly won't.'

Even in his desperate heightened state, Jeffrey could read the pale man's expression. He was here for revenge and to punish, and not to negotiate.

And in a few short moments, when Jeffrey allowed his fingers to slip from under the cord, the pale man got what he wanted.

91
Roxi

Roxi checked the monitor behind the window and spotted two familiar faces. Breakfast news presenters Esther Green and Stuart James had interviewed her several times when she was Influencing and she felt comfortable around them. And, because they were unlikely to grill her to the degree other hardened hacks might, she had agreed to appear on their programme. They wouldn't be letting her off the hook, but she wasn't concerned.

Because throughout the week, media training experts had been rehearsing with her all potential lines of questioning and the most advantageous ways to respond to them. She was as prepared as she could be.

'What do you think, hun?' asked her friend, Tracy. 'This look all right?'

In the Perspex mirror, Roxi checked the reflection of her hair from all angles. She loved her honey-blonde extensions.

'It looks perfect,' Roxi replied, 'thank you.' She ran her tongue over her newly re-plumped lips then opened and closed her eyes and tried but failed to frown. Her facial muscles were satisfactorily paralysed. The natural Jem Jones-look no longer interested her, not now she had access to Harley Street cosmetologists. If this was going to be her Second

439

Coming, her physical reinvention might as well be as much of a talking point as what she was about to reveal.

'Good luck,' said Tracy and blew her an air kiss. 'We'll all be watching.'

Roxi was alone for the first time in weeks. It was normally a situation she actively sought to avoid, because silence gave the voices in her head space to breathe and to remind her of those she had trampled over to get to where she was today. However, for the time being, they were mute.

A few minutes passed before she heard her name spoken in her earpiece.

'Roxi Sager, you are no stranger to controversy, but surely this offer must have taken even you by surprise?' began Esther. 'On the day protesters are preparing to march against the Sanctity of Marriage Act, the Government has just made you the brand new face of it.'

'It did take me by surprise as I'm sure it will a lot of people,' Roxi replied, staring into the camera above the monitor. 'But who better to argue the case for it than someone who will do anything to protect their marriage?'

'Even kill?'

'Even kill,' Roxi repeated, a firmness to her tone.

Cheers echoed along the corridor and into the recreation room of the women's prison Roxi now called home. And a fire she once thought extinguished suddenly lit up inside her.

*

The offer to become the spokesperson for anything, let alone a national Government campaign, came out of the blue. It began with a guard leading Roxi to the prison visitors' room. Waiting for her in the empty space was a thin, pale-faced man with eyes as dark as his hair. He was sitting upright, drumming his fingers on the table, but not out of impatience. He stretched out his hand to shake hers. She responded cautiously. His bony fingers were ice-cold. She racked her brains for how their paths might have crossed but she was stumped.

'I've watched you so often in the media that it feels as if we're already friends,' he began.

'And you are?'

He ignored her question and rested each fingertip on his chin. 'I have a proposition for you, Roxi.'

'If you're a journalist, I'm sorry but I'm not doing any interviews . . .'

The man looked around the room. 'If I were here to interview you, do you think the Governor would've cleared the room for me?'

Roxi shook her head.

'I represent His Majesty's Government. We have followed your story with interest. You're unique, aren't you?'

'I'm not the only woman to have made a mistake.'

'"A mistake"?' he repeated. 'Let's call a spade a spade, shall we? You killed someone.'

'You're wasting your time if you're here to make me feel any more guilty than I do already. I've tortured myself enough without your help.' She pushed her chair out and prepared to leave.

'Sit down, Roxi,' he said. The narrowing of his eyes suggested it would be in her best interests to comply.

'In describing you as unique, I was referring to how people on both sides of the Marriage Act are using you for their own agendas. The pros believe you're an example of someone who'll do anything to protect the basic principles of the Act, while their counterparts believe you're the victim of an oppressive regime.'

Roxi couldn't deny the level of support had taken her by surprise, particularly after admitting to the charge of manslaughter. She'd no choice. Technology had her bang to rights.

Before Roxi had listened to Owen's recordings on Cooper's laptop, she had turned off the wifi first, making it untraceable. What she hadn't considered was that Cooper's devices had been registered to analyse her online biometric behaviours. They knew all her operational habits, from the speed she used a trackpad, to how quickly she moved her mouse and navigation patterns. Hundreds of hours of insights had created a unique profile, like a digital version of a fingerprint and near impossible to duplicate. And, like millions of others, Roxi had a profile of her own online biometric behaviour. Each time she'd accessed Cooper's laptop to play Owen's sessions, the computer had registered it was not Cooper using it and identified Roxi from her own stored records. But, by briefly connecting to a cafe's wifi, the device had reported the unregistered user and Roxi's match to a cyber security team.

And when Cooper's family had told police her laptop was missing, they hadn't had far to look. The search team had found the device wrapped in refuse sacks and hidden in a box inside Roxi's wardrobe. 'I didn't mean to kill her,' Roxi had blurted out to the surprise of officers who appeared at her door. 'It was an accident.' She'd been arrested in her kitchen and charged the following day.

'It's like she wanted to get caught,' she'd overheard one of the officers say later. 'She couldn't wait to get out of that house.'

As the news cycle was beginning to move on from Jeffrey Beech's guilty verdict, the media was obsessed with former Influencer Roxi's story. She'd become rejuvenated by the attention and public debate. The joy she had once gained from Vlogging and Influencing was returning.

Roxi had pleaded guilty to Cooper's manslaughter and, in mitigation, her barrister had explained to the court how concern over her husband's infidelity had pushed her to breaking point. 'Mrs Sager lives for her family and fear of its disintegration pushed her into confronting the "other woman",' her legal counsel had said. 'And when Mrs Cooper had refused to explain the nature of their relationship, a brief physical altercation ensued, in which Mrs Cooper lost her footing and fell.'

Roxi's team had warned her to expect a prison sentence of around four to six years, so it came as a surprise to everyone when she was sentenced to just twenty months in a minimum-security facility. It had divided public opinion and only added to the demand for her.

'We want to strike while the iron is hot and capitalize on your currency,' Roxi's prison visitor continued. 'Following the awful, awful death of Jem Jones, there is now a place for someone else to be the spokesperson for the Sanctity of Marriage Act. And, with a general election predicted within the next few months, we would like to offer you that position.'

'Me?' Roxi laughed and glanced around the empty room. 'How on earth can I be the spokesperson for anything when I'm in here?'

'You gave up a successful career as a Vlogger soon after Mrs Cooper's death. Why?'

'Because I thought I needed my family more,' she said.

'The word "thought" suggests you no longer believe that to be the case.'

Roxi hesitated and was pricked by an image of the last time she saw Owen, Darcy and Josh together. She had spotted them in the public gallery following her sentence and moments before she was led out of the court's dock. But her maternal urge to want to comfort them was less than her desire to show gratitude to the vocal strangers cheering her name from the gallery. She waved to them and made a heart symbol with her fingers. Once again, the interest of people she didn't know became more important to her than her own flesh and blood. By the time her attention returned to her family, they had left.

'You miss the attention, don't you?' the man continued. 'The approval of strangers fills a hole inside you that, with the best will in the world, your family cannot.'

Roxi slowly nodded her head. It was the first time she had admitted it to anyone but herself. A cold, arrogant smile crept across her visitor's face. In their brief time together, he made her uncomfortable yet he knew her better than her own family did.

'What if I told you that you can have it all back?' he continued. 'That I can ensure you're more famous than your court case has made you? That people worldwide will want to hear what you have to say? Because I can make you the first Influencer who Vlogs from behind bars. I can give you a platform to talk about anything you want to discuss, to connect and interact with the public through live chats and to show what prison is like from the other side of the bars.'

'And what do you want in return?' she asked.

'That you also throw your weight behind the Sanctity of Marriage Act, talk about how important it is, and how, if the opposition is elected, it will be revoked and that will cause cata-strophic damage to the country. You are just about old enough to remember Brexit. That will be a walk in the park compared to what will happen if we're forced to return to the dark ages where people only marry out of choice. We also have other plans to radicalize the education sector, and, as a mother, I'm sure you can become involved in that too. But we can discuss that further down the line when we are re-elected.'

Roxi was torn. 'I promised my family that I'd turned my back on a media career. I haven't done any interviews because I didn't want to bring any more attention to my kids than I already have. They're bullied at school, my husband has been forced out of his job . . .'

'All trivialities that can be taken care of. We can ensure Owen doesn't need to work again to support his family and that Darcy and Josh are enrolled in the best private schools. You'll be doing this as much for them as you are for your country.' His eyes darkened as he smiled. 'And perhaps a little bit for yourself. Play your part in making that happen and you have a wonderful career ahead of you.'

'You're asking me to choose between fame and my family. What if you're not re-elected? I'll have lost everything.'

445

'Life is a gamble, is it not? I'm offering you the opportunity to win big.'

The man gave Roxi two days to consider it. By the time he stood up, she had already made her decision.

Trying to convince Owen of her intentions the next day had not been as straightforward.

'You can't do this,' he warned.

Roxi moved her chair forwards, its legs scraping against the floor.

'Why not? This is the perfect solution. You and the kids are taken care of financially and I get to resume my career.'

'No.' Owen shook his head. 'No, no. Just keep your head down and serve your time and, when you get out of here, we can carry on as we were.'

Roxi flinched. It didn't go unnoticed by her husband.

'What's wrong with that?'

'I don't want to carry on as we were,' she said quietly. 'And I don't want to be with you any longer.'

Owen's face dropped.

'I'm so, so sorry but I've tried being that woman and it's just not me. You and the kids . . . it breaks my heart to admit it but you're not enough. And please believe me, it's not your fault; this is completely on me. The fact is I am what I am, and, first and foremost, it's not a wife or a mother.'

Roxi closed her eyes and didn't open them again until she heard the door to the visitors' room slam.

Three weeks had passed since she'd last spoken to either Owen or her children. She considered recording a video to send to Darcy and Josh, assuring them they were blameless, but decided against it. She had also denied Darcy's request to visit her, partly because of its potential for awkwardness and also because it coincided with a sponsor's appointment to walk her through a collection of Vlog-friendly prison outfits.

Meanwhile Roxi's lawyer had informed her that Owen's divorce proceedings had been thwarted by Family Court magistrates at the first hearing. She could only assume her pale-faced ally had exerted his influence.

Roxi pushed her familial guilt to one side and diverted all her focus towards her reanimated career. She worked with a team of script writers on discussion points and assembled a team of fellow inmates she nicknamed the Glam Squad, all with experience in hair and make-up. Others were chosen to participate in a crash course in filming, lighting, sound and editing, and tutored by television industry professionals.

Within hours of her first Vlog going live, the news that Roxi Sager, Influencer, mother, wife and protector of Smart Marriages everywhere had returned to social media from behind bars went viral. Her numbers escalated at a rate she had never experienced before.

She had never felt as free as she was right now.

*

'This is the first time the Government has used a convicted killer to promote anything,' continued presenter Esther Green, 'which is something that has riled your critics.'

'Obviously I'd rather it had happened under different circumstances, but what's done is done and now I have to make the best of it,' Roxi replied.

'Do you regret Antoinette Cooper's death?' co-presenter Stuart James asked.

'Absolutely, and if I could take that awful day back, then of course I would. But I'd like to reiterate, it wasn't a deliberate act. I've never been one to shy away from responsibility, which is why I pleaded guilty to manslaughter. I hold my hands up and admit that, because of my mistake, two families have lost mothers.' She blinked Darcy and Josh's faces away.

'You're slipping into shoes last worn by Jem Jones,' said Esther. 'And we all know how tragically that story ended.'

'What happened to Jem was a terrible thing, but I'd like to think that I am a stronger woman than she was. Given the way I was raised in the care system, I've had to be. And I intend to show the world who I really am with my new series of prison Vlogs, while reminding people how important it is to support the Sanctity of Marriage Act, especially with a general election on the horizon.'

'But the altercation between you and Mrs Cooper was because of the Act, wasn't it? You were scared your husband's "affair" might lead you to divorce, and not only might you lose him, but your lifestyle too?'

'I will never blame the Act for anything,' Roxi replied. 'Our confrontation was my fault. Act or no Act, I wanted to save my marriage and keep my husband. What happened that day was a tragic misunderstanding. But as many have argued, had Mrs Cooper not broken the law herself by working illegally as a couple's therapist, our paths would never have crossed and this whole mess could've been avoidable.'

'Of course, yours was not the only court case to receive media attention,' Esther continued. 'What are your thoughts on Jeffrey Beech, who, according to reports, was found hanging in his cell earlier this morning?'

That was news to Roxi, a line of questioning she hadn't prepared for. But she didn't let it faze her. 'Like everyone else, I'm horrified by how he took advantage of couples with marital difficulties. He deliberately hurt people whereas I did not. My actions aren't comparable to his crimes so good riddance to him. I want to help others to learn from my mistakes and remind people they're better off married than alone. That's all any of us can do, isn't it? Love and learn to be better?'

'And what happens if the anti-Government groundswell continues to rise? If they fail to win the next election, are you out of a job?'

'We'll have to see,' she replied with a rehearsed smile. 'So let's hope not!'

'Then what would you do?'

For a moment, Roxi stared blankly at the camera. It was a good question. What would she do? There was nothing and no one out there waiting for her beyond her career. Plan B was not an option because it did not exist.

'I'm a survivor, Esther. Don't worry about me.'

Roxi gave the camera a final smile and, for a moment, she almost believed she had nothing to fear. But if the lens ever stopped focusing on her again, she knew that she would cease to exist. She had been that person once before and hated it. She would always find a way to continue being burned by the flames of fame and not extinguished as a nobody.

92

Corrine

Corrine held the hands of the two young men standing either side of her as they accompanied one another across the stage in a show of unity. Their limbs trembled every bit as much as hers until they reached the podium. Two more followed behind them, equally as nervous.

It was halfway through the afternoon before they took to the stage and it was impossible not to feel intimidated by the vast audience of London's Kennington Park. News reports suggested that of the million-plus people who had descended upon the capital that day to protest against the Sanctity of Marriage Act, more than 100,000 people were now standing in front of her. Many of the audience wore t-shirts with Freedom for All's logo emblazoned across the chest, others held brightly coloured banners aloft. Giant screens had been erected in parks to broadcast the speeches of keynote speakers, of which she was one.

Corrine and her guests waited in a line until the audience's applause tapered off before she drew the microphone to her mouth. She had expected to be terrified by the daunting task ahead. Instead, a sudden burst of adrenaline offered her a new-found confidence.

'Good afternoon, everyone,' she began. 'My name is

Corrine Nelson and I am part of the Northampton chapter of the FFA. Several months ago, my colleague Nathan Deakin and I became tasked with investigating allegations against education minister Eleanor Harrison, my local Member of Parliament. These brave young men on my left and right came forward to warn us that she had a history of intoxicating and sexually abusing young men. They knew this because they are survivors of her attacks.'

She waited for the gasps to die down before going into further detail of what happened to them along with the FFA's failed sting operation, of Nathan's reaction to the drugs Harrison had plied him with and her fabricated injuries.

'The FFA distanced itself from the events in Eleanor Harrison's apartment as it feared that, in the aftermath of Jem Jones' suicide, pro-Act supporters would capitalize and expand upon the anti-FFA feeling already playing out in the media. But it has since acknowledged that was the wrong decision and, in the spirit of full-transparency, it has given us its blessing to speak here today for the first time.'

Despite the size of the audience in front of her, she recognized Freya's voice yelling from somewhere, 'Proud of you, Mum!' Corrine smiled. 'That's my daughter,' she explained. 'And I love you too.' The audience responded with cheers.

'I am sure, that right now, Ms Harrison's somewhat stunned lawyers are already planning their rebuttal along with accusations of slander, demands for apologies and evidence. Unfortunately, due to circumstances beyond our control, we no longer have the footage that was shot that night.'

She handed the microphone to Nathan.

'I've been warned of how much I'm risking my future career opportunities by going public,' he explained. 'I know Harrison's people will victim shame us all. They'll tell you not to believe us and that we approached her and that she turned us down. They'll say we tried to extort money out of her or that we were trying to become famous by rubbishing her. They will say anything to make Freedom for All look like we're the bad guys. It's for those reasons that Corrine and I have brought someone else with us who is more qualified to explain what Harrison is capable of.'

Nathan passed the microphone to the fifth figure on the stage. Corrine gave him a reassuring nod that said *You can do this.*

'I'm William Harrison and Eleanor is my mother,' he began, his voice tight. 'I believe what these guys have told you about her behaviour is true because she has twice done this to former friends of mine.' Will took a deep breath and recalled to the crowd how Harrison had been an absent parent, and on the occasions she was at home, often disappeared into the private sanctuary of her home office to work for days at a time.

'Six years ago, I was curious as to what kept taking her attention away from her children so I took a look at her unattended laptop. On it, I found page after page of pornography, of young guys having sex with much older women. She caught me and tried to laugh it off, telling me it was research for an anti-porn legislation project she was working on. But I knew she was lying. However, I didn't mention it again because I assumed she was embarrassed. After that day, she never left a device alone in a room again.

'Fast forward to my first year of sixth form college, and a friend was staying with us while his parents were holidaying abroad. Mum made him feel very welcome and, as they were both nightbirds, they'd stay up late watching classic movies from the early 2000s when the rest of us went to bed. But, midway through the week, he packed his stuff and disappeared without saying goodbye. When I finally got hold of him, he said he was staying with his grandparents instead. And when we returned to college, he went out of his way to avoid me. I couldn't understand what I'd done wrong.

'Something similar happened in my first year at Uni. Mum asked me if I wanted to invite some of my political student friends for a tour of Westminster. We took a train to London, attended a political debate and, at the end of the night, one of our group became deeply engrossed in a conversation with her. We left them to it and crashed at the hotel. The next day, my friend caught an earlier train home than us, and even changed one of his Uni courses so we didn't share lectures. He went on to slip out of our friendship group completely. It was history repeating itself and my mum was the common denominator. They'd both been left alone with her.

'This time, I approached the Uni friend and practically bullied him into telling me what the problem was. He admitted something had happened sexually between him and Mum but he couldn't be sure what. All he knew was that he hadn't instigated it and had no control over it. My former sixth form friend was harder to trace, but when I found him, and he eventually agreed to meet me, he told me the same story.'

Corrine took a moment to scan the crowd's faces for their reaction. They shared her same sense of shock and disbelief that she had when Will had tearfully regaled her with the same story in their first meeting at the university library.

'Why would I believe those people over my own mother?' Will continued. 'If you knew Eleanor Harrison, if you saw how detached and cold she can be, how secretive she is, how determined she is to get her own way no matter who it might hurt, you'd know she isn't like other mums.'

Will turned to the left of the stage and raised his hand. On cue, an image appeared on a screen behind him of typed notes on headed private hospital digital notepaper. Corrine's hacker friend had once again proved useful. 'These official medical notes disprove her assault claims,' explained Will. 'She had a bruise to the head and slight swelling but no other injuries. Her missing tooth was a temporary plate she was waiting to get fixed.'

A second image was of the MP on the steps outside her apartment with her family by her side.

'You might remember this photograph, me still standing by my mum as she lied to you all,' said Will. 'I have even benefitted from her crimes. When I confronted her with what I knew she'd done to my friends, she denied it. Yet she offered to pay my student loan fees, accommodation and living expenses in return for me not bringing up "such awful accusations" again and making an occasional public appearance. I was selfish to have agreed. My silence made me complicit. Today I am no longer standing by the side of my mother, but by the side of Nathan and the two friends I have so badly let down. I apologize unreservedly for taking so long to be the person they needed me to be. I hope this afternoon might go some way towards finding the justice they have a right to expect. It's the very least I owe them.'

Will handed the microphone back to Corrine as the audience applauded.

'The Marriage Act is as corrupt as the people who stand behind it,' Corrine concluded. 'No couple in a Smart Marriage should be treated any better than a couple who have chosen not to upgrade or a person who wants to remain single. And a democratically elected Government should not turn its people against one another even if it believes it's for the greater good. Love is one of the last remaining things in this world that is free. Please, let's stop putting a monetary value on it. Thank you.'

By the time Corrine and the others reached the back of the stage, all they could hear was the sound of 100,000 people chanting, 'Love is free.'

93

Luca

From his position in the wings of the stage, Luca stared at an ocean of people as far back as the eye could see.

His anxious stomach churned so he made his excuses and hurried to the portable toilets behind the stage for the fourth time in an hour. He yanked his jeans down but there was nothing left inside him but nerves. He washed his hands regardless and returned backstage, trying to centre himself as his therapist had advised.

Today was always going to be stressful and that was before news of Jeffrey Beech's death had begun to filter through to the news network and then his phone in a flurry of texts, emails and news alerts. He felt relief, anger and hope that the nightmares that plagued his sleep and sometimes paralysed his days might now come to an end. But this wasn't the day to try and process his emotions. He would have to push them to one side and deal with the matter at hand first. 'One thing at a time,' he whispered to himself.

'Hi Luca.' A young woman with sparkling blue eyes distracted him. 'Here's your mic and we've uploaded your speech onto the autocue positioned directly in front of you.'

'Okay,' said Luca, his throat dusty.

'Can I get you a drink?'

'Water would be great, thanks.'

He briefly considered how, while she was gone, this would be the perfect opportunity for him to run. He could leave the mic on a table, exit past the security guards and return home, never having to think about that awful night again. Noah's lifeless body, Jeffrey's desperate attempts to convince him they belonged together and then his hands around Luca's throat . . .

He shook his head. No, he told himself. He must stay. He had a duty to all Jeffrey's victims, living and dead, to tell his story.

'Good luck,' said the stagehand and passed him a water bottle. Luca took a long drink as Freedom for All's spokesperson, Howie Cosby, took centre stage.

'Many of you will recognize our next speaker from the court case that gripped the country,' Cosby began. 'He and his husband Noah were the last victims of Relationship Responder and convicted killer Jeffrey Beech. Today, I'd like to welcome to the stage, Luca Stanton-Gibbs.'

Luca's legs were leaden as a cheer rang out and he made his way to a black X taped to the floor. The last time he'd stood before an audience was at Jeffrey's trial. The evidence he'd given was widely reported upon and had been damning, refuting the defence's claims that Luca had led Jeffrey on and was a co-conspirator in a plan to kill Noah. It took a jury only four hours to side with Luca and the prosecutor's many others witnesses. Luca had since declined all media requests for interviews to concentrate on his own mental health recovery. But when event organizers had approached him, he knew that he must participate.

He grasped one side of the lectern, focused on the autocue and cleared his throat.

'Many of you will know parts of my story, but not all of it,' he began. 'So I'm here today to fill in the gaps.'

After explaining how he and Noah had met and married, he recalled how a flawed Audite system had Levelled them up and brought Jeffrey into their lives.

'Noah warned me about him several times,' Luca continued. 'He was convinced that there was something disingenuous about him. But, despite being let down by the technology that was supposed to help us, I still had faith in the Act. I believed a human being and not a machine would realize it had been a huge mistake and overrule the decision. I was sure Jeffrey was on our side. I was open to his suggestions, I listened to his advice. And I have never been more wrong about anything in my life.'

The audience maintained a respectful silence as Luca described Jeffrey's divide-and-conquer techniques, of slowly but surely chipping away at their confidence in each another until their marriage was genuinely in crisis.

'That last night, when Jeffrey strangled and kept electrocuting me . . .' Luca's voice cracked and he paused, taking a sip from his bottle, 'the only reason I'm alive today is because, when Noah returned home on receiving Jeffrey's video, the fob that Jeffrey used to control the Audite must have fallen from his pocket and landed on the stairs. Noah picked it up and switched it back on to record their forthcoming confrontation as he ran up the stairs to find me. For once, it worked in our favour as key words triggered the system to alert emergency services. The police arrived as he was trying to kill me and arrested him.'

To rapturous applause, the woman who had given Luca his mic and bottle appeared, pushing a wheelchair containing Noah. Luca leaned over to kiss his husband before holding his hand.

'The damage Jeffrey wreaked on both of us was psychological and physical, and it continues to this day,' Luca continued. 'I have been diagnosed with PTSD, which makes me relive that night over and over again. But Noah has suffered much more. He was dead when the paramedics arrived and only their persistence resuscitated him. The attack and lack of oxygen has left him with a brain injury, which led to a series of strokes. He has difficulty with his short-term memory and the right side of his body is partially immobile. The stress on his windpipe makes communication difficult. He has been forced to leave the career he loved. But he is still very much alive, and that is what matters.'

More applause followed and Luca waited until it subsided. 'In the aftermath of what happened to us,' he continued, 'we were granted special dispensation for a voluntary divorce, but we are still very much together. Noah's health aside, we have everything we could ever want. We have left our home in New Northampton and we're renting a flat in London close to the hospital where Noah is an outpatient. Our surrogate Beccy has taken herself off the Government's approved list and, once Noah is ready, we will restart our plans for a family. And we have donated half of the compensation money we were awarded by the Government to the Freedom for All party. The rest we will use for Noah's medical bills.

'We want no part in what a Smart Marriage has become. The Marriage Act has taken love out of the equation and has made us focus on wanting better cars to park outside better homes and to live in better towns. A marriage shouldn't be monitored by anyone, especially Artificial Intelligence. It shouldn't create societal division. It shouldn't matter if we marry or not. Being single, cohabiting or widowed are not dirty words. But marriage is one, unless you do something about it.'

The crowd's cheers only grew louder when, with Luca's assistance, Noah rose from his wheelchair and walked five steps unaided to the lectern. Holding on tightly to Luca's hand, he opened his mouth to speak, taking time to pronounce each word.

'We do not need money to be happy,' he said slowly. 'We managed it before the Act was introduced and we can do it once it is repealed. If enough of you here or watching at home agree with us, fight to make your voices heard as I am now. If enough of us vote with our hearts, then perhaps we can have the equal society we are owed.'

Noah's speech received the largest cheer of the day as he made his way back into his wheelchair. Luca kissed him again before they waved farewell to the crowd and they left the stage to continue with their brand new but familiar lives.

94

Jada

The view of the stage from the rear of the park might not have been clear, but it suited Jada. She could have watched today's event on television from her sister's home where she and Matthew had been staying since Ally and Marley had bought her house. But she had a duty to finish what Anthony had died for, and that didn't involve hiding away. And she wasn't going to miss for the world the public's reaction to what was to come.

She checked the passport App on Ally's phone once again. If all went according to plan, she would meet her sister and brother-in-law in Paris later that night when her Eurostar pulled in. They had already travelled there yesterday with Matthew. Ally had used Jada's passport and their strikingly similar appearances meant no suspicions of officials had been aroused. After this afternoon, Jada was sure her own travel document would be flagged and she would be arrested. She would be using Ally's passport instead.

Jada had been advised by rally organizers that her contribution would mark the end of the day's events. Nevertheless, she had been there at the start of the rally to march through the streets and later when protesters converged in the

461

grounds of Kennington Park to listen to each speaker, celebrity guest and musician.

The trauma her former clients Luca and Noah had suffered with their Relationship Responder unsettled her the most. She wanted to meet or at least write to them to express her apologies on Anthony's behalf. But she had held back. Perhaps after today it might be easier to explain.

Anthony's death had hit her as hard as the sudden loss of any loved one. Her grief arrived in waves and when it wasn't threatening to drown her, it filled her with rage. She had long accepted there was a sizable part of his working life that he could not discuss, but she had never considered how damaging his projects were to others. As much as she loved him, she was ashamed of his legacy. And it was something both she and Matthew would have to learn to live with.

Her anger was also directed towards Anthony's employers for what they had done to her. Mother and son had been separated for two days following her arrest on drug smuggling charges at Heathrow Airport. She had been kept in a holding cell until, without explanation, she was suddenly released and reunited with a traumatized Matthew. But before they were allowed to leave, a tall, skinny man, whose dark eyes she couldn't read, had informed them Anthony had been killed in a car accident a day earlier. Instinctively she knew it was not a chance collision. On her return home, Anthony's office had already been stripped of every gadget and electronic device.

Later, she refused to believe a police report confirming there was no fault with the vehicle's operating system and which ruled the accident was driver-led. And an inquest suggested the fact that Anthony's car collided with the same bridge pillar that killed his mother indicated he had likely intended to take his own life. But Jada knew her husband and the effect his mother's suicide had on him. He would never put Jada and Matthew through it. She was convinced his job had killed him. Finding someone, anyone, who could verify this or help her appeal against the inquest ruling proved impossible. She was completely alone.

A voice booming from speakers scattered about the park caught her attention. She had grown to know Howie Cosby personally from their many recent meetings.

'Thank you so much for your attendance today,' he began. 'If the numbers here are indicative of support against the Act then I have little doubt that we will overcome it. Our final guest speaker is unable to be here in person, but what you are about to hear might be the most important video you watch all day.'

As he exited the stage, Jada clenched her fists and looked to the sky. *This is for you, babe,* she said to herself, *There's no going back from here.*

Kennington Park fell silent as the screens faded to black before a stationary image appeared.

It was of Jem Jones.

It wasn't the woman that fans had grown used to watching in the last few months of her life. This wasn't the browbeaten Jem, the desperate Jem, the Jem drained of fight and fury. This was the fresh-faced Jem of old, the girl the public had fallen in love with long before she'd nailed her colours to the mast of the Marriage Act.

'Good afternoon, Kennington Park. My name is Jem Jones,'

she beamed. 'I bet you weren't expecting to see me.' She hesitated, as ripples of confusion spread through the crowd. 'What the hell?' asked a woman in front of Jada. 'When was this recorded?' Others began to chant 'Lock her up' and 'Stay in hell'.

'I have no doubt that most of you recognize me,' Jem continued. 'Some of you have followed me from the start of my Vlogs while others might only have heard of me after my death. But whether you loved me or loathed me, you all have one thing in common. None of you ever really knew me.

'Today it's time I set the record straight. The first thing you need to know is that Jem Jones isn't a real person, I've been playing a character. I'm the result of a Government initiative to create someone the British public could fall in love with, and more importantly, trust. Research into what you liked and didn't like about celebrities and Influencers began long before we ever met. Hundreds of existing Vloggers and Influencers were studied to decide what made you accept and listen to them. Their every intricate detail was recorded to decipher how often I should smile, the sound of my voice, the colour of my eyes and even how much they should sparkle. Teams were put together to decide how my make-up and hair styles should alternate over the years, along with my wardrobe, the locations where I recorded my videos, the pitch of my laugh and, of course, the subjects I should Vlog about. All of this was done to get you, the public, to trust Jem Jones, the product.'

Small sections of the crowd began to boo and jeer but the majority were now maintaining a fascinated hush.

'The second thing you need to know is that I am not dead,'

she continued. 'I didn't put a gun to my head and I didn't pull the trigger.'

The camera Jem was staring into moved closer to her face. 'None of that happened. I didn't end my life because I don't exist. I have never existed.'

She paused as the lens drew so close that only her eyes were in view. 'I am a Deepfake and I'm designed by this man.'

Jem shut her eyes and, as they reopened, her irises were no longer blue, but green. Jada's stomach somersaulted as the camera slowly panned out and Anthony's face filled the screen.

More breathing space followed to allow a disbelieving crowd to make sense of what they were witnessing.

'My name is Anthony Alexander and I created Jem Jones,' he began. 'As Jem said, she is a Deepfake. Over the last decade or so, much of the world has banned the creation of these videos for malicious intent or as weapons of fraud and political propaganda. This hasn't stopped our own Government's intelligence from using them to fool enemies into believing they are talking to real people. However, Jem was the first time a Deepfake has been used to hoodwink its own people.

'I'm a designer and programmer and the basis of Jem's face and body belongs to a handful of actresses hired in the early stages of her creation. Days' worth of footage was recorded of their every movement and facial expression, from the expansion of her irises in bright lights to how her hair shifts when she moves suddenly. Then, based on research into the kind of faces people trust – even elements of my wife's appearance, mannerisms and personality – I designed how Jem should appear. And we used actresses to scan these motions for every post and appearance Jem made. She became the closest thing to reality a computer has ever created. Yet everything about her was false. The interior of her home, her friends, her pets, her relationships . . . it's why she was never interviewed live, or seen out in public, why her family and friends – who you also never met – didn't reveal the country in which she died or where she was buried. Because there was no family or friends, no death to register, no body to transport home and no daughter to bury. Even the house where fans left flowers is owned by a company managing the Government's portfolio of state-owned private properties. The money Jem made in sponsorship and product placement was ploughed into the destruction of Old Towns and creation of New ones. The only genuine thing about Jem was how much she was adored, for a time, by you.

'For a long time, I expected the truth to come out and for this to blow up in our faces, but it didn't. Perhaps if our print journalism hadn't been decimated by social media then we might still have paid investigative reporters who would've asked more questions about who she really was and where she came from. Instead, the life and death of Jem Jones was accepted at face value by you all.

'When it became apparent the tide was turning against the Marriage Act, my employers made the decision to kill Jem and make it appear as if she had been driven to death by people like you: those opposed to the Act. First, my team and I created thousands of fake accounts to troll her. Then, months later, we would end her life as it had begun, on social media. I lived with Jem for so long that I felt I owed it to her to be the one to kill her. So we filmed my hand holding the gun and pulling the trigger before mapping hers onto it. I Deepfaked a Deepfake.

'And it worked, at least for a while. But what my employers didn't count on was you FFA members fighting back, refusing to be bullied into retreating. Instead, you came out fighting. And some of you died for your cause, for which I will never forgive myself.

'Many of you might be asking why you should believe me. Am I even real? Well, I've met with Howie Cosby and he can vouch for the fact that, when I recorded this video, I was very much a human being and not a computer-generated image. But if I'm not with you in person today explaining all this, then it's most likely that I'm dead. Why? Because not only was I planning to expose the Government for defrauding you with Jem but also for what is next on their agenda and how it will affect your children if you vote for them in the next election.'

Jada stood silently, absorbing the escalating animosity as her late husband revealed the Government's plans to send poorer performing pupils away from their families to Young Citizen Camps. And he explained how it was his team's role to bring to life a Deepfake cast for a TV show to sell the concept to a manipulated public, old and young. Graphics appeared on screen containing designs he and his team had been working on. There were images of buildings and children's faces, some close to completion, others containing only outlines. A handful featured moving mouths and blinking eyes. There were designs for uniforms and sketches of dormitories, his copious notes scattered about the borders suggesting where improvements should be made. He played clips of actors rehearsing scenes filmed against greenscreen backdrops while Anthony and his largest team yet supervised the layering of digital images on top of their faces.

Even now, it was every bit as shocking to Jada as when she had first discovered the hidden memory stick containing this recording soon after his death. It had been a chance discovery when her Audite had begun offering uninvited inspirational Push notifications to 'help her through this difficult time'. No matter how many times Jada had asked, ordered and pleaded it to stop, it had persisted. And when it had caught her on a particularly bad day and suggested she 'make the pain a positive and turn that frown upside down', she'd grabbed the device, hurling it across the room. It had shattered against the tiled floor. It was only when she'd scooped up the broken pieces later that she'd spotted the memory stick hidden inside. It had been years since she'd last seen one, so she'd driven to her sister's house and slipped it into Ally's old laptop and watched, paralysed, as her late husband filled the screen with his confession. Jada could only assume that Anthony had hoped the Audite – the architect of so much recent misery in their relationship – would at some point bear the brunt of her further frustration.

There had been no question in her mind what she must do with it, or that it had to be done covertly, as she couldn't be sure if she was being watched or bugged. If his employers could murder Anthony and sedate a child in a psychiatric unit, she'd known that they were capable of anything.

Her sister had organized the meeting with Howie Cosby on her behalf where Jada had played him the recording and showed him the documentation. Once legitimized,

Anthony's film had been kept under wraps from almost everyone including event organizers until today.

'Don't be like me,' Anthony concluded. 'Don't do as you're told when you know something is morally wrong. Have the strength to stand up for what you believe in. Don't be afraid to confront your enemy or they will continue to rise in the most unexpected ways.

'When all is said and done, I didn't do much in my thirty-five years to improve people's lives. But I hope that, in my death, I might accomplish a lot more. We all live to learn but some of us die to teach.'

Jada's tears fell faster than she could catch them.

'You did just that, babe,' she whispered as the screen faded to black and she made her way through the chanting crowds and towards the exit. She kissed Anthony's mother's St Christopher pendant, which was hanging around her neck, and looked up to the sky. 'Now it's up to the people to decide where we go from here.'

 **NOW news** | **MORE STORIES**

Notification Centre

LONDON, ENGLAND   04:55

PRIME MINISTER CONCEDES ELECTION DEFEAT AFTER LANDSLIDE WIN FOR OPPOSITION

398-seat win gives Freedom for All the largest majority in election history.

LONDON, ENGLAND   07:01

FREEDOM FOR ALL PRESS STATEMENT PROMISES SANCTITY OF MARRIAGE ACT REPEAL BY END OF THE YEAR.

WASHINGTON, USA   08:07

BRITISH PM'S EX POLITICAL STRATEGIST APPOINTED AS SPECIAL ADVISOR TO US PRESIDENT STANLEY

Henry Hyde to oversee country-wide rollout of new schools targeting underachievers. Stanley claims new education camps will give 'every child a chance'.

ACKNOWLEDGEMENTS

This is the first book I've written that wasn't based on an idea of my own. I actually have my husband (also called John, just to confuse you all) to thank for it. It began on a dog walk as we were discussing two married friends of ours who announced they were to separate. They had been what we'd described as a Forever Couple – two people who would last the course come what may. But it wasn't to be. It started other John thinking – what would relationships be like if we were all being recorded by our home-tech? If our Alexas and HomePods picked up on our everyday conversations and sent us Push notifications if its AI believed that we might benefit from a recalibration of sorts? Could AI ever really understand the intricacies of a human relationship? Or could it pull us apart? For hours, other John and I discussed this concept and he suggested it might make the basis of a novel. It got my brain whirring and before I knew it, *The Marriage Act* was born and the warped world in which it was to be set began to develop.

The Marriage Act is, of course, a work of fiction. But a surprising number of parts have been inspired, some loosely and some more closely, by facts, studies and statistics. For example, a study by a London business school suggests that soon, in-home listening devices will be able to interpret a couple's arguments and come up with solutions to relationship problems. Elsewhere, an American-based church is dispatching real-life Relationship First Responders to step in and help couples whose marriages are at risk. Meanwhile, Deepfake online content is growing at a breathtaking rate and experts warn that they will be indistinguishable from real images before long. In my research, I also found websites already offering interactive AI avatars and recreations of your loved ones who you can talk to after they've died. Here in the UK, studies are being carried out to see if virtual reality headsets for convicted criminals tagged on house arrest could be used to retrain or educate them. And when it comes to self-driving vehicles, it's no longer, 'if it happens' but 'how soon?'

There are many people I'd like to thank in helping to get this book from mine and other John's heads and into your hands (or your ears if you're listening to the audiobook). In no particular order, thanks to other John for the idea, for designing the original graphics in the first few drafts of the book, overseeing the AI stuff my brain is too small to comprehend and being my first reader. Next, I want to thank our little boy Elliot for putting up with all the hours Daddy Chops spent in the office living in his imagination while he wanted to watch YouTube videos of tractors being unboxed on my computer. Huge gratitude goes to my editor Gillian Green for her unwavering support. This is our fourth book together and, once again, I've so enjoyed working with you. Thanks to my mum Pamela for her encouragement and to my early readers for offering me their opinions on what worked and what didn't. Also my gratitude goes to the Pan Macmillan team plus Jon Cassir at CAA.

Online book clubs have always been a huge support to me, including Tracy Fenton and all at Facebook's THE Book Club, along with Emma Louise Bunting and Wendy Clarke at The Fiction Café Book Club and everyone at Lost In A Good Book.

Immersing myself in the world of failing relationships involved a lot of research and reading self-help books. Particularly inspiring to me were *The Seven Principles For Making Marriage Work* by John M Gottman; *Your Other Half* by Sophie Personne and *5 Love Languages* by Gary Chapman. They, however, offer much more positivity than the characters in my story received!

I'm no futurologist so I like to read up about the technology we'll all be eventually reliant upon. I'd wholeheartedly recommend the annual *The Wired World* magazine, which is a fantastic resource for predicting what will be the norm very soon and decades from now. And please check out Richard Godwin's article in *The Observer* entitled 'Houses of Tomorrow' to see where we will be living. In a speech my character Anthony hears at a FFA meeting, the reference to AI admitting it is unable to appreciate art or a sense of humour is based upon a study by writer and programmer Gwern Branwen. For more of his essays and studies, check out www.gwern.net.

Finally, thank you to all my readers. This is my tenth book and whether this is your first or you've been with me all the way on my journey so far, you have my gratitude.

NORTHAMPTON BOROUGH MAP
POST SOMA IMPLEMENTATION

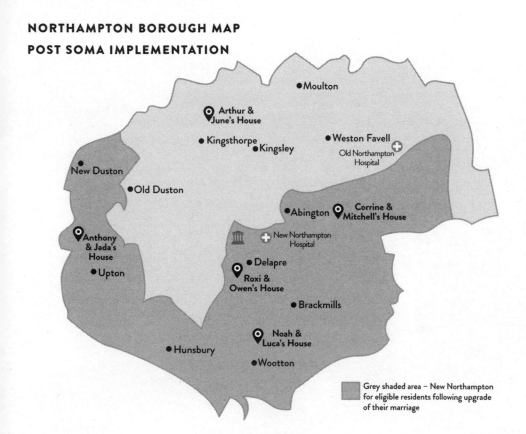

Grey shaded area – New Northampton for eligible residents following upgrade of their marriage

Reading Group Guide

1. Like John Marrs' previous speculative novels, *The One*, *The Passengers* and *The Minders*, *The Marriage Act* is set 'five minutes in the future'. What are the main differences in the world of the book to our reality?

2. If Smart Marriages were a real thing, would you sign up for one? What are the benefits and the pitfalls of such a system?

3. Audites are loosely based on existing technology – how does that make you feel about devices we already allow into our homes?

4. How believable is it that the government would use devices like Audites to record and monitor intimate relationships?

5. Which was your favourite storyline/couple in the book and why?

6. Did your opinions of characters change as the book progressed?

7. Have you read any other books by John Marrs? How would you compare them to *The Marriage Act*?

8. Which books might you compare *The Marriage Act* to?

9. If you could ask John Marrs anything, what would it be?

10. John's previous novel, *The One*, is now a Netflix show. If *The Marriage Act* was turned into a TV show or movie, who would you cast in the lead roles?